DANCE WITH THE DEVIL

A CRIMSON SHADOW NOVEL

NATHAN SQUIERS

Published by
Tiger Dynasty Publishing, LLC

Copyright © 2020 by Nathan Squiers
Cover Design by Bewitching Book Covers

ACKNOWLEDGMENTS

Holy hopping hell! Was writing this book ever a crazy train dragged by a disturbed bat straight outta the abyss!

Between the constant mood swings, bouts of mania, enraged struggles, and a fair share of a fat man crying over a fictional animal, I have to pretty much unload an entire semi-truck's worth of "thank you"s to my lovely fiancé and fellow author, Megan J. Parker. Without this lovely lady's (insert chosen generosity: assistance, kindness, patience, diligence, persistence, silence/refusal to be silent, suggestions, enforcement, motivation, presence, etc...) I can pretty much guarantee that these words wouldn't exist—be it in this gnarly order or otherwise. Many of the more romantic dialogues are based off of things I've either said, wanted to say, or have every intention of saying —SURPRISE, BABY!—to my wife.

I'd like to also thank my cat, Trent—yes, I'm one of *those* guys —for somehow knowing *exactly* when I needed a little pair of eyes to add some extra pressure to the manuscript as well as always being a blank, unresponsive face when I need to bounce dialogue off of somebody. Like the more romantic bits with Megan, I owe Trent a great deal of the emotional motivation behind the exchanges between Xander Stryker and his own fuzzy (not so) little buddy.

A special thanks also goes out Jacob Marrapese, who inadvertently co-created the "fire flies" scene in this book.

I'd also like to thank all the head-shrinkers who kept me breathing, but never quite fixed me (I don't believe a totally sane mind could have done some of the things I've done in this book).

As always, loving mentions go out to those of my family and friends and everyone else in the rag-tag group of gnarlies who have stuck by my side through all of this nut-fuckery known as life.

I love you guys!

Finally, as always, a very special thanks to The Legion of readers who keep me rocking my role as The Literary Dark Emperor, and (last but by no means least) you, the current reader of these words and, by that token, a very special member of The Legion, indeed.

Much love & stay gnarly,
    Nathan Squiers
    (The Literary Dark Emperor)

Dedicated to all those who have been touched by a bit of their own **madness.**

MYTHOS SPEC SHEET

LIVING DEAD: *(Any entity that comes into being AFTER the death of the body (very rarely with the same consciousness as when the body passed). The process involves the body becoming possessed by a new aura after the original has left OR a magical means of attracting new auras into the body to provide strength to the original.)*

- **Ghoul:** Corpses that have been reanimated by wayward auric energies. These new creatures are stronger and faster but, like possessed humans, need to remain hydrated at all times. The longevity of a ghoul varies depending on external stimuli (ranging anywhere from several months to a few years in optimal conditions), but eventually the auric energies (like a body rejecting a transplanted organ) will begin to refuse the foreign aura and the body will begin to destroy itself (both physically and mentally). The ability for a ghoul to blend in to society rapidly dwindles when this occurs, not only because of its physical abnormalities but because of its increasing insanity. A driving need for fresh organic matter during this stage compels the ghouls to try to feed on living things.

- **Zombie/Golem:** These are not individually-sentient mythos so much as they are the result of magical influence (be it through advanced witchcraft or magically-derived mythos activity). These entities are minions called upon to do their master's bidding by the creation of (a) temporary/"fake" aura(s). This manifested life-energy can be inserted into a specially-made body (which, if done right, can be made of any solid material) or, more often, a corpse. Once animated, these beings are nearly impossible to stop without completely destroying them. Despite their enhanced abilities, their strength and speed are only as great as the strength of their master/creator.

- **Leiche:** These creatures are very much like ghouls in that they are dead and decomposing bodies kept alive by an aura; the only difference being that the aura is the body's original. Leiches are the result of a very powerful practicer of magic who, through either strong spells or a combination of magic and technology, was able to keep their auras inside their bodies after their natural death by bringing additional auras (either real or, like zombie/golem creators, fabricated) to "pick up the slack" of the original.

LIFE FEEDERS/VAMPIRES: (*Any being that, through biological or habitual needs, must take biological energy from others. This energy can range from physical [blood & organic/"life-filled" fluids] to psychic/bio-electrical [auric/psychic energy]. Over time, adaptations have separated life feeders to different sub-species, each with unique abilities to optimize their ability to hunt/obtain energy.*)

- **Auric:** Life feeders that have fused with their auras

(their bio-energy becoming an internal extension of themselves that can be controlled). This heightened awareness and control allows for both manipulation of tangible objects (lifting and moving items that otherwise appear to be floating) as well as feeding/draining psychic energy from others. The ability to give/feed energy into others is possible, as well, and both of these powers are amplified through touch (an auric can draw energy from a living thing with their natural writing hand and give it with the opposite hand). Auric vampirism is hereditary and CAN NOT be made outside of reproductive means. While there's no natural/physical reason, aurics (like all life feeders) feel an aversion to sunlight.

- **Sangsuiga ("sang"):** Life feeders that have adapted to feed on blood. Though they have no/limited control on their auras (and, therefore, nearly no natural magic ability) they can move faster than the human eye can register (what's known to some as "overdrive") for a limited amount of time as well as using their vastly superior strength and reflexes to catch their prey. As an evolutionary perk, sangs have a combination of neurotoxins (that paralyze their prey during feeding) and naturally-occurring healing accelerants to "trap" the mutagens (as well as concealing the wound). These mutagens, present in the glands of the sang (either located in the hollowed fangs of pure-borns or in the saliva of "mades"), attack the victim's organs and begin the metamorphosis after the body's death (unlike undead mythos, the aura remains intact and sentient during this process). Because the cellular structure of a sang is designed to detect trace heat signatures to alert them of potential prey, their bodies are overloaded from UV rays and, when in sunlight, are incredibly agitated and, over time, can contract severe skin irritations (eventually becoming irreversible). There are three different types of sangsuiga:

- **Pure:** Born vampires—at least one sang parent. These types are slightly stronger, faster, and more resilient to injury. Their fangs are hollowed and filled with the necessary substances for feeding. Because of this, they are the only type of sang that can turn a human into a made-sang through a bite.
- **Made:** Those turned from the bite from a pure-blood. Their fangs are not hollow and the delivery of their toxins & mutagens is solely through the saliva and, as a result, they CANNOT create new vampires (their victims, if left to go through the change, become "freaks"). Some strength is compromised in comparison to pure-bloods, but nothing substantial.
- **"Freak":** Created from a "made" vampire bite and are, as their title may imply, flawed both physically and mentally. Uncontrollable, insatiable, incoherent, and (for most) unstoppable.
- **Perfect:** A vampire that is more closely tied to what is believed to be the "original" state of vampires. Perfects can use the strengths of both sangs and aurics.
- **Varcol:** One of the (if not the) most powerful of the mythos creatures. Able to move faster than a sansuisuga and have an ability to manipulate their auras on a scale that puts them on the level with multiple well-trained auric vampires. Varcol can not only physically and aurally feed from their victims but can also separate themselves from their body and feed in an astral form (though most are too obsessed with themselves and confident in their physical prowess to

rely on this method). On top of their seemingly bottomless strength, speed, and intelligence is the ability to transform their bodies to fit their needs. Their enhanced auric control also allows them to make slight changes in the weather and can call upon dense cloud coverage to avoid the sun and hunt during the day. Varcol are also incredibly difficult to destroy due to a pair of hearts that operate independently and must BOTH be destroyed to kill them. They are believed to be extinct.

MAGICAL: *(While not exactly mythos, these beings [be it through natural birth, rites of passage, or extensive training] have risen to superhuman levels because of their advanced understanding of energy and spell-casting.)*

- **Astral:** Humans who, through intense training, are able to separate themselves from their physical bodies and travel the world in an astral form. This leaves them extremely vulnerable and, if their mortal body is destroyed while they're outside of it, they are unable to sustain themselves without trying to occupy a new body (typically resulting in haphazard and confused ghouls). The ability, however, is ideal for finding others and collecting information as a "supernatural spy."
- **Taroe:** Magical & tribal humans. Keeping themselves and their practices hidden from the rest of the human world, the taroe, at an early age are given intricate tattoos all over their bodies with a magically-enchanted ink that allows them to harness and focus their magical energies. These tattoos will glow when the energy is being used and the abilities, if the taroe is well skilled enough, are nearly limitless.

- **Tirwech:** Humans can psychically/emotionally communicate with animals and often form close bonds with one or more animals (this is what created the popular myth that witches have animal familiars). Other, more "extreme" tirwechs have been known to make the ultimate sacrifice and transform into an animal of their choosing (a process that is irreversible, painful, and life-threatening & takes anywhere from several weeks-to-several months of prolonged suffering as their bodies shift).
- **Witches/warlocks/wizards/"practicers"/etc:** Humans who either have a predisposition towards the magical "arts" or have trained over time to gain the skills. A lot of the time witches/warlocks/ "practicers"/etc are either in league with mythos or have come to hunt them (either way, they are subconsciously attracted to the supernatural world).

NATURE-BASED: *(Mythos with appearances, tendencies, and abilities that make them more animal-like.)*

- **Alv:** The alv are what most would consider "elves" (if they ever had the chance to see one and walk away from the encounter with their lives). The alv have snow-white skin and pitch-black eyes. Their teeth razor-sharp and lined up in rows like a shark's (usually 2-3). The alv are malicious to everything but their own kind, usually taking up arms against other mythos as supernatural hunters. This tendency does not make them soft around humans, however, who the alv view as play-things for amusement if not a quick meal.
- **Anapriek:** Tall, beautiful creatures with pointed ears. The anapriek, though wingless, are what many would

view as "fairies;" appropriately elusive, they rarely venture into the human world—usually traveling and settling in tribes. Anaprieks can also commune with nature and have an advanced knowledge of plants and they're medicinal uses. Unfortunately for them, anaprieks are also extremely appetizing to meat-eating mythos (including sangs, who can become addicted to their blood), making them susceptible to attack. It is this constant threat that makes their nimbleness and speed so useful; often times leaping and moving with such swiftness and grace that many would claim they were flying.

- **Gerlin:** Often called the "gargoyles" of the mythos world. These beings have bat-like wings that are hidden under their human-like arms. Their wings are attached to their hand by a "hinged" pinky finger that can snap open to stretch the fleshy wings open for brief glides.
- **Nejin:** A bipedal, cat-like species who are believed to originate from Asia. Unable to change their shape, these highly elusive mythos, when out-and-about, are NOT capable of changing their shape and thusly tend to dress in layers to hide their appearance from humans.
- **Tergoj:** Large creatures (usually 9-12ft tall, 5-7ft from shoulder to shoulder) who are almost ogre-like in appearance; they have no eyes, however, completely relying on its sense of smell and hearing to guide it. Tergoj spend most of their lifetime asleep and will "nest" by burrowing into the ground and then excreting a muddy substance from its pores to "fuse" itself with the earth. Once it is a part of the ground, it hibernates (often for periods spanning from months to years). This prolonged period of sleep causes the

surrounding landscape/vegetation to grow around/on the creature's body. When it finally emerges, the creature will often be covered with portions of earth and grass/plant/vegetation (often rooted so deep as to have penetrated the skin and taken hold in the muscles).

- **Theriomorph ("therions"):** The "origin" of every werewolf, werecat, werebear, and so-on-and-so-forth legend, these creatures can change their shape at will from that of a human to one of a monstrous beast. Unlike the legends, however, their bestial forms are just as diverse as their human forms; ranging in height, bulk, shape, etc...

- **Watsuke:** The watsuke are an aquatic mythos, preferring salt-water but able to live in fresh, as well. Unlike mermaids, instead of a lower half looking like that of a fish, watsuke have very large webbed feet and hands. Though they rarely go onto land, they are capable of it but must take care to cover not only their feet and hands but also their gills to avoid being noticed by humans. Like other deep-sea species, the watsuke have the ability to generate electric fields while in the water and, while on land, generate strong internal energy waves, making them enticing to auric vampires.

- **Ykali:** Ferocious lizard-like creatures once thought extinct who are nearly unstoppable when the potential for food is involved. Normally these creatures move about in packs, intelligent enough to hide themselves from human detection with thick layers of clothing and able to, most of the time, avoid hunting/feeding in the public eye.

PROLOGUE
GET THEE BEHIND ME

The cabby raised his eyebrow as the man entered his taxi. Though it was late and the air was still dank from that evening's rain storm, the man's approach seemed to bring an electric hum to the air, and the otherwise sleepy moment came alive with it; not far off, a jet took off and the roar momentarily drowned out the din of the airport. The windshield wipers squeaked slightly against the drying windshield, leaving a greasy streak across the glass; the sound pulling the cabby's attention away from his new fare long enough to feed the parched glass a dose of washing fluid. As the man took his seat, he let out a relaxed sigh and the door shut behind him.

The cabby frowned and swiveled his head to see if somebody was standing outside the cab.

Had the door just closed on its own?

Sighing and shaking his head, he snatched the nearly empty can of Rip It from the cup holder—wishing again for possibly the hundredth time that night he'd had the money for something better—and took a sip, hoping that the dose of caffeine would clear his hazing mind. Holding back a retch at the stale, lukewarm beverage, he forced himself to nearly empty the can and gulp the contents.

Though the man didn't appear any different than any other fare he had an unsettling air about him. He carried with him only a single, small overnight bag—looking foreign and expensive—which he set beside him before laying a meticulously carved wooden walking stick across his lap. The driver eyed him through the crud-covered rearview mirror, tilting his head irregularly in an effort to get a decent look before finally sighing and turning in his seat so he could face him.

The man was dressed in a long black coat that wrapped around his body with such intimate tailoring that it seemed as though it were a part of him; the crisp collar hugging his neck and birthing the tanned, flawless skin of his throat. As the driver took him in a smile stretched across his chiseled features—a smile that forgot to carry over to his serious and eerily penetrating blue eyes—and he ran a gloved hand through his blond hair; tucking the bulk of his loose bangs into the black of his collar. The cabby frowned; though the strange man had been standing in the rain for some time before finally getting picked up neither his clothes nor his hair seemed to have suffered a single blemishing drop. Sniffing nervously, he took this all in with a single passing glance and wetted his lips.

"Where to, buddy?"

The man tapped his thumb three times against his walking stick as he thought; his smile never fading and his gaze never softening. For a moment he seemed lost in his own mind before his smile grew even broader and his eyes became even fiercer.

"I think I'd like to visit the West Ridge high school."

The cabby frowned at this and blinked in confusion, "The school?"

The man gave a single nod.

"At this hour?" he pressed on.

The man's smile remained as his eyes narrowed, "Is that a problem? You *are*, after all, being paid, are you not?"

Wetting his lips again, the cabby shrugged and put the taxi into gear, "True enough. You're the boss."

"I'm certainly one of them," the man's face relaxed and he leaned back, letting out another relieved sigh that ended with a sharp, audible inhale. After an uncomfortably silent moment he chuckled and leaned forward, "I must apologize, it's been a very long day of traveling and my behavior must be unnerving, to say the least."

The cabby shrugged, "No worries here, pal. I've seen all types in this cab."

"I'm sure you have," the man nodded. "But none like me."

"Pardon?"

The cabby could feel the man's smirk growing behind him, as though the air in the car chilled with every curve of his thin lips. "You've seen many types, but you've never seen any like me, have you?" he asked.

"I'm not sure what you—"

"You know what I mean, and my question is sincere. Have you—or have you not—encountered another like me? Or have any of your colleagues recounted any like me in their recent dealings?"

"Listen, man, I only thought it was weird that you wanted visit the high school in the middle of the night. I ain't calling you a freak or nothing, and I definitely don't know what you mean by others like you. You're just another fare after all, y'know."

The man nodded, "Yes. Another fare," he looked out the window. "A teacher."

The cabby looked back at the mirror, "What's that?"

"You were curious about the school; I used to be a teacher there."

"You don't say," the cabby peeked over his shoulder to check for oncoming traffic before signaling and turning to the neighboring lane. He was surprised to find that getting out of the airport was easier than usual; the customary line of cars inching impatiently forward and honking at one another seeming to have taken a break at that very moment and giving him a clear path through. Settled by this, he eased back in his seat before peeking back at the man in the backseat, "So why'd you stop... bein' a teacher, I mean?"

The man didn't seem to hear him at first as he peered out through the window at the rain-slicked city. The awkward silence stretched for some time before he finally parted his lips, "Family."

"Oh yeah?" the cabby smiled politely for effect, "I got a sister in Paris." He shook his head with a scoff, "She visited there a few years back and decided to marry this wine-maker she met. The folks complained about her moving out of the country, but— y'know how it is—what're y'gonna do?"

The man acknowledged this with a soft hum and a single nod, still keeping his gaze aimed out the window.

The cabby frowned, feeling the discomfort creep up his spine like icy spider's legs.

As though the fare could sense this, he turned his head to face the rearview mirror and the cabby's eyes reflected therein. "Is she happy?" he asked in a low, even tone.

"Huh?" The cabby suppressed the shudder he felt in his shoulders.

"Your sister," the man clarified. "Is she happy in Paris with the wine-maker?"

"Oh, yeah. Yeah, she is. She whines about not being able to see us as often as she used to, but we always got Christmas."

"Yes. There's always that," the man's eyes shifted back towards the window and his face dragged after.

"So who were you visiting?" The cabby pressed, not wanting to face the silence for too long.

The man blinked, but didn't look away from the window, "I'm sorry?"

The cabby gulped, "You said you were visiting family..."

The man shook his head, "No I didn't. I said I stopped teaching because of family."

"But..." The cabby thought for a moment, "wouldn't you have been visiting if you left your teaching job?"

"Not at all," the man's tone remained calm and polite. "My family is not the type one willingly visits. I was running from them."

The cabby furrowed his brow, "Running? Why on Earth would you—"

"Some families aren't as loving as others," the man interrupted, "Sometimes it's safer *not* to be around them."

"So—what?—you owe them money or something?"

The man scoffed, "If only it were that simple." He shook his head. "No. Money I've got; more than I or any beneficiaries will ever need, in fact. No, the people I'm running from are after much more than that."

"Jesus-H-Chri—are they dangerous?" the cabby asked, remembering the man's questions about others like him. As the pieces came together, he felt himself getting more and more nervous. Maybe this fare was a member of the mafia... or worse! He bit his lip and pulled a dry piece of skin free, almost instantly tasting blood.

Had he just put his own life in danger by picking up this man?

"Very dangerous," the man nodded, "but you have nothing to worry about."

"But you just said—"

The man turned his gaze towards him, "*Nothing* to worry about."

The cabby's eyes closed tightly for a moment as a sudden pain gripped his temples. His body slackened, his foot lifting from the accelerator briefly. The taxi swerved slightly in the lane as it passed a Sheriff's patrol car, but then straightened as the wheel righted on its own and the cabby was distantly aware that his taxi was driving itself.

"What in the…"

"Relax and take the wheel," the man's voice was calm and steady, "You're about to be pulled over."

"What did you—"

The dark, rain-slicked road went alive with flashes of red and blue as the wail of a siren sounded behind them.

"Oh shit!" the cabby cursed.

"It's fine," the man assured him, "Just relax. You have nothing to worry about."

"Why do you keep—"

"*Nothing* to worry about."

The cabby felt his mind flutter again, but as his body fell slack behind the wheel a second time the cab seemed prepared and maintained its speed and course without him.

In the neighboring lane, a blood-red sports car honked its horn as it rocketed past the pursuing cop car; a beer bottle flying from the window and smashing against the Sherriff's windshield.

"What in the world…?" the cabby watched as the sports car gunned its engine and rocketed by them.

Sure enough, the Sherriff steered into the open lane, shifting his focus on the other car and driving by the taxi.

The cabby stared for a moment and tilted his head to see the man in his mirror. How had he…?

He shook his head as another wave of pain hit him. Bad migraine; probably one of his worst yet. Lucky he had medicine in the glove box.

The cabby was halfway through reaching across the seat to retrieve his pain killers before he suddenly remembered he'd never suffered a migraine before and that there was *nothing* in the glove—

As his fingers triggered the latch on the compartment and dropped it open, he saw the prescription bottle.

"What the hell?"

"*Nothing* to worry about," the man repeated.

Another wave of dizziness.

The cabby nodded and popped a few of the pills and washed it down with the nearly full can of Nos in the cup holder. As the sweet, ice-cold beverage carried the capsules down his throat, he smiled.

The man was right; he had no reason to worry.

"So how was your—" the cabby paused. What had they been talking about again?

In the distance, the high school came into view and he let out a relieved sigh. Something about this fare was creeping him out and he would be more than-glad to be rid of him. Pulling up to the empty building, he shifted into "park" and forced himself to face the man.

"Here we are. You want me to keep the meter running?"

"No need. I can walk the rest of the way," the man took his bag in his free hand and moved to get out. "What do I owe you?"

"Thirty-two forty-five," the cabby announced after a quick look at the meter.

The man looked over, sounding—but not looking—surprised, "That much?"

The cabby shrugged, "Times've changed, buddy."

"That is far truer than you know," the man sighed as he straightened himself. Quickly and methodically he worked his way around the back of the cab and stopped at the driver's side window, reaching into his pocket. The driver, not happy about having to open his window in the rain, reluctantly pressed the switch and recoiled as the cold, wet air swept in through the opening. "Thanks again for the chat," the man said as he held out his hand and pressed a folded bill into the cabby's own, "Keep the change."

The cabby smiled and opened his palm to make sure he hadn't just been handed a twenty. As the hundred-dollar bill came into view, his eyes lit up.

"Whoa! You sure?" he asked.

The man smiled and nodded, "I am always sure."

"Hey, thanks!" the cabby smiled, feeling bad for ever having thought poorly of the man. Quickly, he tucked the bill away.

"It's no problem," the man assured him, "No problem at all."

Still beaming, the cabby nodded and rolled up his window as he pulled away from the school.

THE MAN STOOD in the rain for a moment as he watched the taxi grow more and more distant until it turned off onto a new street. When he was sure that the driver was out of his range, he lifted the hold he'd had on his mind. It hadn't been too difficult to ease the driver's panic—no more than it had been convincing him that the crumpled dollar bill was something of far greater value. Of course, by the time the poor cabby realized that he'd been tricked he'd be long gone.

Sighing, he turned away from the street to face the school and allowed the wave of nostalgia to crash over him. It had been a very long time since he'd last seen it, and he suddenly realized that he'd missed it a great deal more than he'd ever thought he would. For a long time, he stood and stared, letting the life he'd abandoned flash in tiny bursts within his mind. He knew that any normal human being would have been hindered by the rain and cold, but the truth was he didn't feel the biting sting; hadn't felt it in so long that he'd forgotten what *true* cold was.

He wasn't sure, in the long run, why he'd had the cabby bring him there. After all, he hadn't come all this way just to be reminded of the past. In many ways, he supposed he was delaying what needed to happen. Stalling what he'd come back for in the first place. Unfortunately, time was against him, and as the rain picked up and the wind kicked up his coattails he turned away from the school and started up the street.

"I'm coming, Xander," he whispered to himself, "And so are they..."

1

(NOT SO) HAPPY BIRTHDAY, XANDER!

*T*repis was dying.

And there was nothing Xander could do to stop it. As the vampire slowly ran his hand along the tiger's heaving side, he forced a smile for his old friend's benefit. Behind him, visible within his mind's eye, he "saw" Estella standing in the doorway, looking in at the scene with a locked jaw and shimmering, tear-filled eyes. Her lip trembled slightly as her dark-orange aura sagged, giving away her own wavering emotions.

"You don't have to stay," Xander looked up at his lover for a long moment, once again forcing himself to smile for the sake of another's comfort. "He knows you care, and neither of us want to see you in pain."

She attempted to return a smile, only to have a sob trickle out from her throat. Clapping her hand over her mouth, she turned and hurried out of the room, her steps resounding down the hall and dimming with her growing distance.

Xander bit his lip and shook his head at the whole situation. His tiger-friend hadn't been given much longer to live—a couple of days, maybe a week or two at the most—and, though he wanted to have something to blame the truth was that the animal was simply getting old. Sickness could be cured, but nothing—or at least nothing Xander could find—could stop nature's course.

Even then, the tiger had lived well beyond what was expected of his species, though this fact didn't help to appease Xander or any of those who'd come to know Trepis.

He'd thought, for a brief time, that perhaps he could find a pure-blooded sangsuiga to bite Trepis and change him into a vampire; hoped that he might save him by turning him into one of their kind. Unfortunately, along with the realization that the mutagens responsible for the transformation only worked on human DNA, there was the moral dilemma concerning whether or not Trepis would *want* to be turned.

Dwelling on this, Xander wondered which he resented more: the biology or the ethics.

Neither had been his strongest subjects as a human…

Trepis took in another heavy and labored breath that was followed by a long exhale and Xander shook his head.

"I know it's boring, buddy," he gave Trepis a gentle scratch behind his left ear. The tiger let out a whimper and struggled to raise his head to face Xander. The earthy shades that made up the tiger's aura swirled about like smoke caught in a ceiling fan, and as Xander saw this he suddenly had a craving for a cigarette. Scoffing at the notion of becoming an addict all over again, he passed it off as an emotional response and rose to his feet. "You get some rest," he said, keeping his voice low and noticing Trepis' ear twitch as he did.

With that he stepped out of the room and started in the direction that Estella had run off, navigating the halls as he let his mind wander.

The mansion had, several years back, been the headquarters of the Odin Clan; a clan that Xander's own father, Joseph Stryker, and a powerful auric vampire named Depok had teamed up to create. The duo's aspirations for peace and unity earned them many enemies, and those enemies had, over the course of nearly two decades, seen an end to not only Xander's father and Depok, but the entire Odin Clan itself. It had been then, following Xander's initiation—as he'd lain deep beneath the ground undergoing the change from human to vampire— that the radical naysayers had stormed the mansion and destroyed the once proud clan from the inside-out. Even then, after all the changes that had come to pass, the memory of navigating those very halls before the chaos choked up the already emotional vampire. Fighting against the wave of depressing nostalgia, he sucked in a deep breath and swallowed away the lump in his throat as he turned a bend and started up the stairs that would take him to the ground level.

Memories of the Odin Clan were frequent for Xander. Though his time with them had been cut painfully brief, the mansion *had* been their headquarters and they *had* been the closest thing he'd had to a real family. It was for this reason—as well as the determination to send a message that what had been lost had *not* been forgotten—that he'd reclaimed the old mansion and erected the newly-formed Trepis Clan in its place. Those with the mythos government known as The Council who'd worked directly with Xander's father had been delighted when the still-young vampire had approached them with the proposal to rebuild his father's legacy and further his own, and with their support the renovations had taken no time at all.

In the end—though he'd seen it coming all along—he'd had to accept the role of clan leader during a *far* too elaborate ceremony filled with *far* too many mythos who were all *far* too excited.

He sighed and shook his head over the whole ordeal… *again.*

Exactly two years after he'd first been introduced to this building *and* to the world of vampires and other mythos, and now it was under new management.

His management…

He'd almost felt guilty for praying that the ceremony might be struck by a rogue attack.

Almost.

Like it or not, though, he *was* a clan leader now—blessed-and-burdened all at once with all the duties the title carried—and, as such, he held great power.

But what did all of that matter when he could do *nothing* for his dying friend?

"Happy birthday to me..." he mumbled to himself.

As he reached the top of the stairs, he started towards the larger set that led to the upper levels.

But something stopped him in mid-step.

Turning around, he pointed his gaze towards the hallway that led to the front entrance. He'd spent so much of that night in the underground level with Trepis that he hadn't realized that it had started raining. This, however, was a minor detail—a momentary and neutral discovery—and, ultimately, not what caught his attention or what drew him towards the door.

There was something else...

Something *in* the rain.

Something cold.

Something dark.

Something familiar...

Xander didn't bother calling for somebody to investigate, though he knew that that was the proper protocol for such a situation.

If there ever *had* been such a situation before.

The mansion, perched atop a tall hill that overlooked the city, was neighbored by nothing but forests and wildlife. Separated from the public streets by several miles of winding, unwelcoming pavement canopied by dense trees, the unfriendly path was shadowy and foreboding even on the brightest of days. Even those who were terribly lost seemed to know better than to follow blind hope to the mansion's gates, and, were an unwelcome wanderer ever to stumble upon the grounds, the large concrete wall that encompassed the mansion was certain to deter them. However, in the event that the too-long, too-dark, too-perilous, and far too-unfriendly wall weren't enough to stop an uninvited guest—in the event that somebody *that* devoid of common sense didn't get the hint or, more likely, some of Xander's or the once-proud Odin Clan's enemies showed up—they had a very aggressive and very lethal set of enchanted security precautions in place. This decision had been put into action soon after a few of the bolder rogues who had not approved of Xander's efforts had been caught trying to stop it on their own. Since then, any intruders that *weren't* cleared to enter were soon after ripped apart by some particularly nasty protection spells—the "bug zapper" enchantments—that Estella had put in place.

Simply put, if Xander Stryker didn't formally invite a visitor in, they weren't getting in.

Period.

End of story.

No negotiations.

But there, in the rain, was an exception.

An unprecedented exception.

An exception that demanded the proper response.

As the leader of the clan Xander more than understood the rules; he had made them, after all. In the event of any potential attack—whether or not the enchanted defenses had been successfully breached—the first person to detect it was to make the call for an armed response. After seeing what an attack had done to the Odin Clan, Xander wasn't willing to take chances.

There were to be *no* exceptions to that rule; an unwelcome intrusion was to be met with a fully armed team of mythos warriors.

But it *was* already the night of exceptions...

And Xander knew that nobody—neither one nor a hundred

of the warriors with the Trepis Clan—could fight what was coming.

Nor, Xander smirked, would he order them to.

Ignoring his own rule, he started towards the door.

"Xander?" Estella's voice was still shaky as she called to him from the stairs that led to the second level. "Are you alright?"

Pausing a few paces from the door, Xander let his aura linger a moment on the other side. The visitor was waiting just outside the door.

He frowned, *Waiting for what?*

"I—I was just..." Xander clucked his tongue and dragged his eyes away from the door and locked them onto Estella's. He wetted his lips, waiting to see if their guest would act before he'd have a chance to speak. When nothing threatened to interrupt him, he said, "We have a—"

A shadow slipped past; an oily specter that moved with slick and rapid intent.

Xander smirked.

Not slick or rapid enough, however.

The intruder was inside—already in the room with them—without the benefit of a door. Were it any other sort of visitor, Xander would've thought it was impossible, but impossible was *exactly* what their visitor specialized in. Any sort of barrier—walls, gates, enchantments, *anything*—didn't mean a thing when this one was involved.

And, unsurprisingly, the intruder wanted to test them; to see what Xander and Estella were capable of.

"MOVE!" Xander called out to his lover as he caught sight of the shadow flying across the wall and over the railing towards Estella.

Estella's eyes widened with awareness, and, chanting something under her breath, she vaulted over the railing just as the intruder materialized behind her, a set of inky-black limbs swinging in a desperate attempt to grab her. The magic that she'd called upon went off like a flare, bathing the staircase in a blinding light that radiated from the carpet. The visitor's shadowy form tremored—a high-pitched hiss rolling from its depths—and it drew back, a pair of bright blue eyes breaking through the solid black haze.

"Couldn't be bothered to call first?" Xander scoffed as he leapt towards the figure. Calling upon his aura, Xander cast the red-and-black energy mass and ensnared the visitor.

Seeing the blue eyes widen in surprise at his swiftness, Xander dropped down on his opponent.

The intruder tried to jump back, but Xander's aura held.

An inky fist flew for Xander's left temple, he rolled under it and drove his elbow forward, pushing his aura through the impact.

The visitor made no sounds as it pitched back. Rather, it rolled like a wad of oil along a rain-slicked street, moving backwards up the stairs. Xander followed, shaking his head.

The visitor wasn't retreating.

He was leading them to the second level.

"Do I pass, professor?" he quipped, keeping pace after his opponent as he swiped out again and again with his aura at the living shadow and stumbling as it jumped over the attack. "Estella!"

"On it!" Estella's voice called from the first floor.

Then, in the blink of an eye, she was on the second floor with the two of them, once again chanting a new spell. As the magic ensnared their opponent—Xander seeing her orange aura following her chants and binding the visitor—a few of the clan's members began to poke their curious gazes out; intrigued as to what their leader and his lover were struggling against.

"You know," Xander sighed and shook his head at their intruder, "you *could've* just asked for an invite."

Estella's chants faltered at that, "Xander, do you *know* this... this *thing*?"

Chuckling, Xander nodded and wrapped his own aura around the intruder, beginning to strip away the layers of auric residue. "We both do, baby," he said as the shadowy form melted away like wax dripping from a candle until it revealed the smiling face of Xander and Estella's high school guidance counselor, Stan Ferno.

Long before his birth, Stan had been a simple human who, with a little help from Joseph Stryker and Depok, had unlocked the means to call upon great power from otherworldly forces. Despite wielding abilities that Xander's late vampire mentor had compared to "a devil on Earth," Stan had pursued a life as a teacher and, years later, had honored his late friend's legacy by keeping a super-powered eye on his son. Before leaving to travel the world shortly after Xander's reawakening, however, Stan had worked with him to release his full auric potential and reunite him with the lingering spectral traces of the father he'd never had a chance to meet.

"Hey," Stan smirked, "am I too late to wish you a happy birthday?"

Xander nodded, "Yeah, about two hours too late, actually."

Stan faked a pout, "Aww… missed the cake and—"

Estella squealed excitedly as she jumped towards their visitor and wrapped her arms around him. "Oh my… Stan, it's been *forever!*"

Stan laughed at that and nodded, rubbing his left shoulder. "Forever, huh? Not sure about that—about two years by my count—but it's certainly been long enough. Just *look* at you! The timid bookworm, Estella Edash, finally out of her cocoon of shyness and taking to the streets as a truly beautiful vampire warrior!" He shook his head in disbelief, "I couldn't be more proud."

Estella beamed at the compliment as she stepped back to let Xander offer his greetings to their friend.

Xander, still a bit taken aback by the sudden arrival of the man—if he could still go by such a simple title—who had kept him alive in a time when he wanted exactly the opposite; the man who had proven over and over to be so much more and, as such, helped him become so much more. It was as if he'd never left. He looked no different than he had the day Xander had watched him vanish in the rearview mirror of a stolen sports car on the road to vengeance. He still had the same young-yet-infinitely wise face wearing the same bright-yet-mysterious blue eyes and adorned with the short-yet-messy crown of blond hair. He could've been any other human on any other day.

But he was the exact opposite.

Nothing ordinary; nothing simple.

"I see the rumors haven't been exaggerated," Stan offered, smirking at Xander, "though your mind still wanders quite a bit, I see."

Ignoring the taunt, Xander cocked an eyebrow at his old friend, "The rumors?"

Still smirking, Stan shifted his focus to Estella and nodded back towards Xander. "Is he always so modest, or is he still just as stubborn as ever?" he asked

Estella giggled, "Well, he's certainly not modest."

"Thought so," Stan mused, chuckling to himself as he shook his head and looked back at Xander. "So much has changed, and yet so little, eh?"

Xander looked past his friend to Estella, "Not modest? *Really*? Whose side are you on?"

"Well you're not," Estella flashed him a grin.

He couldn't bring himself to argue. Instead, he looked back to Stan and, shrugging, tried again: "What are the rumors?"

Stan rolled his eyes, "If you're not astute enough to pick up on them yourself, then I'm not going to spoil the hunt." He moved to scratch his temple and paused as his pointer and middle finger met his still-wet and travel-worn face, "Dear lord! I must look like absolute hell! Pardon me a moment," he held up his left hand for silence and ran his right hand through his soaking-wet hair. His fingers were met with no resistance as they passed through the gnarled and knotted strands, and when he'd finished his blond hair fell into place atop his dry and pristine head. Xander and Estella stared at him, startled that such a simple gesture would make it look as though he'd just stepped out of a salon. He smiled at their reactions as he made a similar pass over his face from forehead to chin, the act offering a similar outcome for his once exhausted features and the start of stubble along his jaw. Then, clean-shaven, rejuvenated, and otherwise immaculate, he offered a slight bow. "There," he smiled and flexed his jaw—staring off into the distance for an uncomfortable moment as though admiring his reflection in a non-existent mirror—before turning to Xander, "isn't that better?"

"Please tell me you didn't come here to perform cheap parlor tricks for my clan," Xander gave his old friend a punch in the shoulder.

He didn't hold back.

He knew he didn't need to.

As the two shared a laugh one of the clan's warriors appeared several feet away.

"Is everything alright here?" the sangsuiga asked, looking at Stan—sizing him up in the event that Xander actually give the order to kill him—and running his hand along the grip of the sword at his side. A flick of his thumb brought an inch of the blade from the scabbard while the rest of him stood patiently— ramrod straight and motionless—to await Xander's orders.

Xander smirked and nodded. "Everything's fine," he assured the warrior, "Go tell the others not to worry."

The vampire gave a single nod and let his sword fall back into place before disappearing once again into overdrive, leaving the three alone in the front hall.

"Loyal," Stan smiled, nodding his approval.

Xander rolled his eyes, not overlooking Stan's condescending tone. "They all are," he said in a low, flat voice. "And for the record, I wouldn't have needed an entire clan to take you out. I was about this close"—he held out his fingers in a mock-pinch—"to killing your ass while you were still standing out in the rain! If I hadn't taken the time to read your aura..." he trailed off to let his reputation finish for him.

"Then you'd have been even more embarrassed when I wiped the floor with you and then followed it with yet another lesson in flexing your inquisitive nature over your brash instincts, wouldn't you?" Stan quipped, snapping his fingers for effect. As the sound resonated, the long black coat—which still looked unnaturally inky with rainwater—rippled like a distorted reflection. When the shimmering haze finally calmed, Stan stood before them in a finely tailored sports jacket over an AC/DC shirt and a pair of khakis. Lowering his right hand, Xander and Estella watched as a length of wood began to emerge from the floor, rising up to meet his hand.

Estella clapped at the display as he gave the floor several taps with the wooden cane to finalize the act.

Xander sighed at Estella, "Don't encourage the man."

"Oh hush!" Estella nudged him, "That was incredible! How did you—"

"—do it?" Stan shook his head, "A true master never gives away his secrets, but I *will* tell you it wasn't much different than my next trick."

Xander groaned, "Your next—"

Stan's left hand shot out, stopping only a few inches from Xander's face. As Xander and Estella both blinked at the sudden movement and the looming threat of the gesture, the empty hand suddenly opened up and—

PLOP!

The two jumped back as a small travel bag fell out of nowhere and into Stan's outstretched hand.

"Thank you. Thank you! I'll be here all week," Stan smirked and gave a bow. "Be sure to try the veal and don't forget to tip your waitress."

Xander frowned and took a step towards Stan, opening up a private psychic connection. He didn't need Estella worrying. Not yet, at least...

What is this really about? Xander demanded. *You disappear for all this time and then show up to spar and do some cheesy magic show? You could've taken this entire building apart and walked onto the grounds and reassembled it around you—could've put everyone in this building, myself and Estella included, to sleep while you did it, too—but you choose to make the most public entrance possible?*

Stan frowned and looked over at him, *I'd heard you were doing well and wanted to check in.*

Then where were you when I needed you, huh? Where were you when I was being hunted down by Depok's vengeful son; y'know, the guy that butchered *the Odin Clan—your* friends!—*and my father? Where were you when Marcus was getting his head lopped off? Or how about when Estella was kidnapped and her parents were ripped apart in front of her? Was it not worth checking in then? Don't you think a flashy entrance and a few well-placed magic tricks would've been nice for* any *of those moments? You know that I died, right? You catch that little detail in the rumors? Yeah, I died! Dead; like fucking GONE, Stan! And Estella nearly killed herself as well working to bring me back! How easy would that have been for you?* Xander narrowed his eyes at him. *You're not a bad man, Stan, so I know you weren't missing all that for* **nothing***. You were doing* something *out there for all this time, I know, and I understand, but you're here now—now over any of those other times, and it certainly ain't for our sake—and I want to know* why?

Estella cleared her throat and crossed her arms, "Do you two think I'm so clueless as to actually believe that you're *just* staring at one another? You *do* realize that *both* of your faces are still emoting with whatever it is you're thought-talking, right?"

Xander frowned and looked down, "Damn…"

Stan laughed, "Don't be too surprised. She always was a smart one, Xander." He turned towards Estella, offering a nod, "Xander was just expressing some understandable skepticism towards the situation." He glanced back at Xander and nodded again, "And I'm sorry to say they're not misplaced skepticisms…" Clearing his throat, he turned and started up the stairs. "I'd rather not discuss this in clear view of your clanmates, however," he explained, "so I'll be waiting in your office."

Xander let his eyes fall closed and sighed, nodding, "Third floor; it was—"

"Depok's old office, I know," Stan called back with a chuckle. "And, speaking of which, we still need to work on that psychic shield of yours."

THERE WAS no talking Estella out of joining them to hear Stan's news. To make matters worse, she was already nervous. Despite all his strength and powers, Xander's sudden entrance into his office still made Stan flinch.

"You ready to tell me what this is really all about?" Xander glared, slamming the door behind him and Estella and noticing his old friend flinch for a second time.

Stan frowned and looked over, "I want to start by apologizing for not being here to help when things got bad. It broke my heart when I got word of what Lenix was putting you all through, but…"

Estella visibly shuddered at the mention of the murderous vampire who had turned her, and Xander reached over to give her hand a gentle squeeze.

Though Estella had finally found her niche as a vampire, the memory of the rogue that had turned her was still one that gave her nightmares. Not that Xander could blame her, though. Lenix had been nothing short of a lunatic—and Xander had encountered his fair share of crazies to gauge from—who had left a horrific stain of memories within his mind, as well. The bitter and vengeful son of Depok had been enraged with his father for dedicating his efforts with the Odin Clan in the States when, unbeknownst to him, his wife had died in Finland. Choosing to overlook his own direct involvement in his mother's death, Lenix had placed all blame on his father and the American warrior who'd driven him to stray in the first place, Joseph Stryker. Eager to see every shred of legacy that had been built destroyed, Lenix had proudly boasted the murder of *both* the late Odin Clan's creators as well as the ringleader behind the entire massacre. He'd been so intent on ruining Xander's already sketchy image that, after going through great lengths to stir up trouble and literally throw Xander's name all over it, he'd gone after Estella. Though Xander had succeeded in killing him, it was not before he'd taken the life of his mentor and transformed the girl he loved.

All things considered, even Xander had to admit that he still got a shiver at the memory.

Seeing their reactions, Stan bit his lip and offered her an apologetic nod.

Estella smiled weakly, "I can't say that I'm happy with what happened, but it *has* allowed me and Xander to have this life together, and I wouldn't trade that for the world."

Xander growled and shook his head, "Though it *would* have been nice if you'd *told* me about that psychopath in the first place."

Stan shook his head, "I *am* sorry about what happened, Xander, but the less you knew at that time, the better."

"How do you figure that?" Xander glared, "People *died* because of that son-of-a-bitch!"

Stan looked down at that and sighed.

"Xander," Estella looked over, "please… I know it hurts, but you can't blame him."

"No, Estella," Stan nodded, "I might not have been able to tell Xander everything before I'd left, but that didn't mean you all deserved to be left without any warning. I was preoccupied with my own concerns and I was careless, and for that I am sorry." He looked over at Xander, shaking his head, "Believe me, I wish I could change how I'd done things, but I can't regret what I did. No fault I accept can change the truth."

"What truth?" Xander demanded.

"That you would've leapt at the chance to avenge your father," Stan offered, narrowing his eyes at Xander. "It's the same reason I don't tell you any number of things right now; you're not ready to hear them. You're still impatient and arrogant and, despite everything, morbidly self-destructive! With the wrong truths in your mind, you'd act too quickly, and you would die. Be truthful with yourself, Xander; you were barely ready to take on Lenix!"

Xander scowled and shook his head, not wanting to acknowledge what his old friend said as the truth.

Stan nodded, seeing that Xander understood. "You've progressed as you were meant to. Any other path would've been catastrophic. With any luck, you might actually see what's coming through with your head still on your shoulders."

Xander frowned, "What? You can see the future now or something?"

"Oh no, nothing like that," Stan assured him. "I just…" He sighed, "I know that there are still struggles for you to face when the time is right."

"All hocus-pocus bullshit put to rest, Stan," Xander bit his lip, unable to keep a tear from falling across his cheek, "You could've been here!"

Xander struggled to hold himself together, not wanting to have yet another emotional collapse in front of Estella. Furthermore, while Stan—even before Xander had been turned—had seen the young man at some terrible lows and, on many occasions, even helped to drag him out of them, there was a reluctance to let the pain he was feeling show to his old guidance counselor. He knew that, like always, Stan's words held not only great wisdom, but great truth, as well. He'd always been one to leap before he looked—often opting out of looking for the sole purpose of having an excuse to come out of it wearing the wounds he felt he'd deserved—and, if he'd known that the likes of Lenix and who-knew-who-else were out there, just waiting to cause him trouble at some point or another, he'd go out of his way—strong enough or not—to get them first.

Even with that truth burning too bright to ignore, however, he still couldn't bring himself to forgive Stan for being gone all that time…

A whimper slipped from Xander's throat. There was so much he wanted to say—so many sentiments he wanted to express—and, despite all his growing and everything he'd learned, he couldn't bring himself to know how to say them. Stan had, more times than Xander wanted to admit to even himself, saved his life and continued to instill him with a fighter's spirit. Even when nobody, not even himself, had faith in him, Stan had been there to remind Xander that there *was* reason to get up each morning. It had even been Stan that had gotten him reunited with Estella. Stan had been at every pivotal moment, pushing and motivating and cheering and encouraging. The truth was he'd been the closest thing Xander had ever had to a father.

And now, facing him after all that time, Xander had to come to grips with the fact that he'd felt abandoned, and that it was *that* pain that he resented Stan for the most.

"I missed you too, Xander," Stan nodded, "And I *am* sorry that I had to leave you like that. You deserved more of an explanation."

Xander bit his lip as more tears spilled from his eyes. Though he didn't take his eyes from Stan, he felt Estella's arms wrap around his left arm and the threat of a smile tugged at his lip as she whispered that it was alright.

It didn't feel alright.

"The explanation"—he fought against the lump in his throat and his voice's threats to crack like a sheet of ice and drop him into the frigid depths of silence—"can I hear it now?"

Stan sighed and nodded, "It's only fair, I suppose." His aura writhed in slow, tight spirals of torment and regret as he leaned forward like he always had when he had a story to tell. "What I am—what I can do and the abilities I possess—is not something that is exclusively mine. They are, when all is said and done, a *gift* that I was able to request access to from powerful forces beyond this realm. That's all…" he chortled at his own thoughts, "I'm just a very powerful asker; an exceptional prayer, I suppose you'd say. What makes *me* special over all others, though, is that my prayers were delivered in person to… well, whatever you'd like to call the Other Side, while others have their voices lost in the near infinity existing between us and There. But I'm not the only one who can reach that far. There were those before me who could do it, and there are those who will come after me who can do it."

Xander frowned, "So what does that have to do with why you left?"

Stan rubbed at the back of his neck, "Because sometimes the ones that can do it aren't good people, Xander, and when somebody awful gets that kind of power… the first thing they do is target anybody else with that power—the only ones strong enough to *stop* them—and make sure that they aren't around to interfere with what they plan to do next."

"There was another one like you?" Xander shook his head, "So why leave? Why not just wait for them to show up and then take them apart?"

"You've seen what I can do, Xander," Stan rolled his eyes, "Now imagine what I could do if I didn't care about *anything* but destroying somebody else like me; didn't care who I hurt or how much damage I caused. Now, I've gotten quite advanced in my travels—I'll admit—and what I can do doesn't necessarily represent what anybody who's been gifted with that power can do, but even a novice can turn this city into ash within only a few days. As soon as I knew that there was another one like me —one who was hell-bent on finding me and destroying me—I knew I had to lead them away from here. For a while it was touch-and-go; sometimes I'd lose them and have to double around to make sure that they didn't just start running amok wherever they'd landed themselves, and other times I had to take extreme measures to go into hiding just to keep them moving—keep them using their powers to find me so that I could get a lock on them—just so I could start all over again. A few times we'd wind up coming toe-to-toe, and it was always a total mess that I'd typically have to duck out of just to avoid having untold destruction on my conscience. About half-a-year ago, however, I was getting hopeful that I'd be able to lead them somewhere vast and desolate where I could finally dispatch them easily without the threat of lost lives or property, and I made my way for Australia."

Estella looked over, "Why Australia?"

"Vast deserts and very little media coverage. Trust me, the first isn't that hard to find, but the latter…" Stan shrugged, "Seemed like a decent enough option to lure this guy in and deal with him quick and clean."

Xander clucked his tongue; he knew a giant "but" setup when he heard it coming. "So what went wrong?" he asked, cutting to the chase.

Stan looked over at him, "He showed up with others."

"Others?" Estella frowned, "You mean others like you?"

"Like *us*," Stan corrected her. "Remember: I am not unique;

not by a long shot now. But"—he nodded—"yes, they are all just as empowered as he is."

Xander shook his head, "What do you mean? How many more? I get that you're not the only one who can do this, but—god damn!—just how many *can* if this guy has help?"

Stan sighed, "That's the thing, Xander, the others didn't *earn* The Power; though that's really giving the other guy a great deal more credit than he deserves."

"Well if they didn't earn their powers," Estella chewed her lip for a moment, "then how *did* they—"

"The other one *gave* them The Power," Stan finished, shaking his head. "See, this other guy might be shifty as a bag of snakes, but he's not stupid. He's made an entire life out of being a destructive, power-hungry sociopath, so when I lured him into a massive plain of *nothing* he caught wind of what I was plotting and decided to show up with reinforcements—three others, to be precise—and the four of them came at me with all they had."

Xander sneered, "Cowards!"

"What'd you do?" Estella pressed.

Stan shrugged, "What I'd gone there to do: I fought... for nearly thirteen goddam straight weeks!"

"God..." Xander shook his head, "How is that even possible?"

Stan smirked, "You'd be surprised what those like us are capable of, Xander. I can only pray you never have to experience it for yourself."

Xander nodded and smirked, "So you kicked their asses, right? I mean, you're here now, so you must've finally put all of them down in that desert for the ultimate dirt nap, right?"

Stan's face lost its color then and his eyes sank to the floor.

Estella's eyes widened.

Xander's eyes narrowed. "You *did* kill them, didn't you, Stan?"

"You have to understand, Xander," Stan held up a hand, "I'd

never been up against *one* other person like me before, let alone *four!*"

Xander took a step towards him, "Stan?"

"I put them in the center of the earth, Xander! I mean, we fought and fought and fought and I was certain I had the upper hand! I figured trapping them in Earth's core would do the trick! At the very least they'd be stuck there for the rest of time!"

Xander's fangs started to unsheathe. "Then they're..."

Stan nodded slowly, "I felt their life forces swell back into existence just before I landed. I was so certain that it was finally over; I thought it was safe to come home."

Estella shivered, "Then they're coming *here?*"

Stan closed his eyes, "I can't be sure. I was afraid that they might have already beaten me here, but, if they haven't, there might still be a chance that they won't."

Xander frowned, "What's that supposed to mean?"

"Did you not hear me? I left them in the *center of the* **earth**, Xander," Stan gave him an exasperated look. "That's not exactly the kind of prison that *anybody* just breaks out of. I'd hoped they were *dead*, but it would appear that they've got a strong enough hold on their powers to keep their physical bodies intact under some rather... *strenuous* conditions."

"That supposed to make me feel better, smartass?" Xander sneered.

Stan shrugged, "I suppose not. The fact that they didn't show up here an hour before me and incinerate the place should, though."

Estella gasped.

Xander glared.

Stan sighed, "Look, this guy *knows* where I am, but that's it right now. He doesn't know why, and he doesn't know who I'm here to see; *that* sort of information he'd have to be near enough to me to siphon. And, once again, they're in the center of the friggin' planet! So—no!—I didn't just show up to reminisce and crash at your groovy new pad, you caught me there! It had *started* that way, sure, but shit went down. I'm sure you know all about that," he motioned up at the two of them, "*both* of you!" He rolled his eyes and leaned back, "The moment I thought there was a chance he could be here, I made a point of coming in with every possible defense in my favor. But they're *not* here; not anywhere in this entire city! So it's still a very fair guess that they're still—say it with me, kids—in the center of the friggin' planet! And there is a very strong possibility that they'll *never* get out of there! Ever!"

2

ARRIVAL

*T*he roar of the flames greedily swallowed little Gwen's screams as she buried herself deeper into her mother's chest, smearing a tear-soaked face into her yellow blouse. Hugging her daughter against her, Joanne struggled to find a path out of the inferno that had, in so very little time, come to consume every visible corner.

Everywhere she looked, there was only more fire…

A short time earlier, it had been like any other evening.

A short time earlier, Joanne had been walking through the door with her briefcase in one hand and her mail—mostly bills —in the other.

A short time earlier, life had been, though unappreciated at that time, just fine.

Tiffany, Gwen's babysitter, had stuck around a few extra minutes to help Gwen's mother put away the groceries and take out the garbage—a gesture that had earned the babysitter an extra five dollars—while the excited four year old chattered on about her day of finger painting and her struggles with the letter "Q". After Tiffany had left, Joanne had put a pot of water on the stove to boil, smiling at the excited chants from little

Gwen for boxed macaroni and cheese and broccoli florets, while she made a quick phone call to her boss concerning a troublesome account.

She'd been several steps away from her bedroom door when the blood-curdling shriek—the first of many—from her daughter had drawn her back.

"I'm sorry, sir, I'm going to have to call you back," she'd mumbled robotically into her cell as she rounded the corner, ready to kill whatever bug had reared its ugly head to frighten Gwen.

Instead of a spider, however, she was greeted by a wall of fire.

A half-second was dedicated to staring in awe at the spectacle; the entire wall—neither near nor neighboring the stovetop but, rather, on the opposite side of the kitchen entirely—had somehow combusted in the short time she'd been in the other room. Each of the four corners, though neither the side walls nor the ceiling or floor, and the entire surface existing between them had seemingly been replaced by a fiery mimic of its prior, less menacing form. While the dumbstruck moment of gaping had been brief—a second or two at most—it had been enough for Joanne to see, but still not believe, what appeared to be four silhouettes emerging from the flames; as though the surface had ceased to be a wall and had, instead, become a wide, hellish doorway.

But that had only been an absurd thought; nothing but a fear-induced hallucination!

Still enough, however, to get Joanne moving.

Breaking her hypnotic stupor, she'd hurried into the room to pull Gwen away from the imminent danger and flee from the room.

"What happened?"

"I dunno!" Gwen answered, shaking in fright, "The w-wall jus' sudd'nly was fire, Mommy!"

"Doesn't make sense… That doesn't make any sense," Joanne chanted over and over, shaking her head in confusion as she hurried down the hall towards the door.

The smoke alarm roared to life like an angry creature and howled after them.

"Mommy!" Gwen sobbed at the sound.

"It's okay… it's okay… it's okay…"

No point in wasting time. No point in trying to argue the laws of physics or logic to an apartment that would still insist on engulfing her and her daughter in the flames.

Oh god… she'd had such plans!

No! No, you're not *dead yet, Joanne, and you won't be! Just MOVE!* she pushed herself, guarding her and Gwen's faces as the television—mirroring her movements in its dark, dead screen; were there really other faces cast in the reflection… No! No, she couldn't believe that now! Move! Just move!—burst into flames and spit shards of the screen into her shoulder and arm.

Don't cry! she pressed on, still hiding Gwen's face from the hell that their home had exploded into, *Don't cry… and don't stop! Gwen's counting on you! Gwen's—*

Joanne's momentum tumbled her into the short, narrow hall that led to the front door; her bloody, numbing shoulder slamming into the coat rack and finally earning a pained cry from her.

"Mommy?" Gwen's voice rattled with terror.

"Mommy's okay," Joanne assured her daughter. "Just a bump, that's all. We'll be okay, hun; we'll be okay, and we'll go see Grandma. Does that sound good? Would you like to see—AHH! SHIT! NO! NO!"

The smell of burning flesh filled Joanne's nostrils and she hissed in pain, glaring down at the scorching doorknob.

Stupid! she growled to herself, doing her best to ignore the mangled hunk of rare meat the old brass handle had turned her hand into. *Not checking first? Even Gwen would know better than to—*

"Mommy!"

"Don't worry, baby," Joanne reassured her little girl through clenched teeth, moving to pat her daughter's hair but stopping short when she realized that the flesh of her free hand was blistered and bleeding.

Think, Joanne... think!

With the entire living room consumed in flame there was no way of making it to the fire escape at the far end of the room, and that was the only other exit she could think of. Again she stared at the door to the outside hall. Maybe—just maybe—she could break through it without touching the knob again...

Stupid! No! There was a reason the knob was so hot!

She shuttered to imagine what sort of inferno was waiting on the other side of the door.

How was that possible?

Hadn't the fire started in their kitchen?

When could it have reached the...?

"Doesn't make sense! None of it makes any—" Joanne chewed her lip.

Fear and concern were growing into a painful lump in her guts, and the rising heat was cooking it!

"Mommy! I'm scared!"

The alarm continued to fill her ears with the crass reminder that they were all going to die.

"N-no... No! That's not true!" she shrieked back before suddenly wondering who she was responding to.

She could've sworn she'd heard...

She shook her head and turned back. Fire or not, the hall was her only option! There was an extinguisher and a fire escape just on the other side!

Pulling back and kicking the door again and again...

Again!

Again...

She kicked on, screaming obscenities in a driving effort to conjure some sort of strength from the rage. Her daughter's panicked cries grew, and her body tensed as she saw something over Joanne's shoulder.

"MOMMY!"

"It's gonna be okay, Gwen!" she assured her, refusing to look. She didn't need to look to know it was there; didn't need to look to *feel* that, whatever it was, it would have been too much. If she looked, there would be no hope for either of them!

Do you want to get through, my pet?

"Yes... yes... God in Heaven, please yes!"

*I'm afraid that **HE'S** not here with us, but as a sign of* wretched *faith...*

The door squealed happily as its latch released on its own and let the tortured door swing open. Joanne's tear-filled eyes shimmered with joy at the sight of her and Gwen's salvation; opening before them like a miracle...

"Thank you... thank you!"

"*No 'thanks' necessary, my pet,*" a dry, icy breath ran over her left shoulder and into her ear—a frigid mockery of Gwen's tear-laced, burning own in her right—and made Joanne's breath stop in her lungs. "*Just leave the girl and we'll call it even.*"

Joanne's eyes widened with panic and she pushed herself to run. "NO! STAY AWAY FROM US!" she demanded, passing through the threshold of the door frame and charging right...

Back into her apartment...

"Doesn't make sense! None of it makes any sense!"

"Marx, keep everyone clear of that window—yes, that one, idiot!—and watch out for a backdraft! The last thing these people need is glass in their burns!"

"Jesus-H-Christ! It's like the fire's actually *thinking*!"

"Shut up, rookie!" Fire Chief Andrews shot his icy blue stare at the stammering newbie, "That's the sort of cheap praise a blaze like this thrives on! Stupid firefighters breed smart fires! Now do your god-damned job!"

"Y-yes, sir."

Andrews turned away as the newbie threw himself back into his duties with renewed dedication. He refrained from nodding his approval; knowing there'd be plenty of time to praise the kid when the chaos was over. Before that, however, he had a job to do.

"Is everyone out?" he gave a few sharp pats to Breinski's layer-padded shoulder.

"We think so! It's hard to—"

"You *think*? God dammit, Breins, that's not good enough! I need to *know* if anyone's left in there!"

"Sir, it's not that simple! Nobody's sure how many were in there in the first place. We've made a run of the lower levels, but we can't get to the upper floors; the stairs won't hold, and the elevator shafts might as well be tunnels to Hell. Until we get some eyes in the sky, I can't give you a better answer than 'think,' I'm afraid."

"Then you get on the horn again and tell them I need that air-unit *yesterday*, is that clear?" Andrews turned to stare at the burning building for a moment, pinching the bridge of his nose. If his time in 'Nam had taught him nothing else, it was what a losing battle looked like from ground-zero. "God dammit…"

It was horrifying to say the least.

Horrifying… and perplexing.

NONE of the building's tenants—none of the burnt and terrified many huddled in quivering masses in the street waiting for more medical treatment than could ever arrive—could give a straight answer for what had caused the fire. No matter who was asked the story, with the occasional accusatory or guilt-soaked interjection laced in, was the same: one moment all was well and calm and the next there was nothing but the all-consuming flames. Minds filled with unanswerable questions; they all simply stood and stared as the firefighters waged a futile war against the inferno.

Nobody seemed to care or even notice as the three strangers stepped unscathed from the depths of the flames and casually made their way down the steps. Though their exit was a marvelous display of calm in a scene of total strife, none of the residents or firefighters—no one!—seemed to be looking at the right place at the right time to notice their serpentine stroll between them. They simply meandered about the scene, musing at the bewildered stares that aimed everywhere *except* where they stood. Then, moving on to enjoy the spectacle from yet another angle, the onlooker's gazes would move back—certain that *somebody* had been standing there—only to have just missed them.

Nobody thought to question them.

Nobody thought to arrest them.

Nobody even *saw* them!

Not a single soul was able to take in the eerie view of the three as they slipped towards a disheveled teenage girl and, spotting her connection to the morsels their master was playing with within the inferno, they moved in. Stepping behind her, they passed their palms a hair's distance from her frail form—relishing in the nervous chill they won from her in the process—and breathed in her terror. Then, after letting the morbid breaths hold in their lungs for a long moment, they finally let it ooze past their lips with a collective recollection that awoke a fresh batch of panic in her.

They'd done their part.

It was Devin's time.

~

"OH GOD! Joanne? Gwen? Oh god... no! No! JOANNE! GWEN!"

Fire Chief Andrews eyes went wide, and he spun on his heels to face the disheveled girl. At first glance he figured she couldn't have been older than fifteen—sixteen at the most—though her sweat-matted blonde hair and sooty face could've been adding a few years. Her tear-filled and panicked eyes grew wider and wider as they darted around the crowded street in desperation; her lower lip trembling. It wasn't a pretty sight, and if her words were any indicator it wasn't a pretty story, either, but at least somebody was finally saying something that amounted to more than "I think" or "I don't know;" finally he had *something* he could work with.

He pushed his way through the crowd, closing the distance. "Who are Joanne and Gwen?" he demanded, "Are they still inside?"

The teenager shook her head as she began to sob, "She's... oh God! Oh shit!" Her eyes darted back and forth again before locking on the chief's and she took in a deep breath to steady herself. "Gwen... she's this little girl I babysit on weekdays. I... I don't see her or her mother anywhere!"

Allowing himself a brief glance back towards the fire, Fire Chief Andrews felt a twinge of suspicion. Then, with the same abrupt impact of its arrival, it vanished and left him feeling suddenly helpless to so much more than just the inferno. Finally, rubbing several beads of sweat from his graying mustache, he turned away.

"Are you sure they were in the building before?" he asked, trying to hide the shakiness in his voice.

A quick nod confirmed his fears. "I just left their apartment, like, a half-hour before all this started!" she cried.

"What floor?" he demanded.

"Uh... the f-fourth? No, the fifth! The fifth floor!" she stammered, trying to work her frantic mind, "In five-G!"

SOMETHING OUTSIDE JOANNE'S bedroom door snapped and collapsed, causing her to jump and awakening a fresh batch of whimpers from her daughter. Running out of reassurances to offer—her own faith having fizzled away into nothing with the incessant taunts in her own mind—Joanne could do nothing more than absently run her burned hand over her daughter's already stained chestnut hair; the charred skin flaking and exposing the severity of the wound with each pass. With her mouth still gaping open, the little girl jabbed her thumb inside and went back to whimpering.

"God, please..." Joanne continued to beg, though the words had already lost the meaning; the prayers nothing more than an idle practice to keep her voice occupied.

The framed pictures on the near wall opposite the kitchen— the other side of the wall that had first caught fire—had begun to warp from the heat on the other side. Every other room was nothing more than a forest of fire. After the miracle of the open door had exposed itself as nothing more than a cruel cosmic hoax that planted Joanne right back inside her front hall, a path had wormed itself ahead of her; beckoning her to continue the fight for survival. Scrambling along the fire-free trail—no longer questioning how such a thing were possible—she'd found herself in her bedroom; a curious scene of controlled flames that seemed to exist solely to keep her from the windows and appliances.

And, even then, the air was breathable and the temperature, though stifling, was not enough to cause any further harm.

The mother and daughter were enslaved by their own safety…

But, for the time being, they were still alive.

"God in Heaven, please… don't kill us. Don't let us burn like this. Please, God… Please."

One of the warped pictures fell from the wall and crashed to the floor, sending another panicked jolt through Joanne and driving her prayers to spill past her lips that much faster.

"Please… Please, God. I beg of you…"

A crack formed in the center of the door and began to spider web in either direction.

"Oh God no!"

The sweat that ran down her face felt like boiling oil and her drenched bangs slipped from behind her ears and fell into her vision. Through the curtain-like veil of her own hair she watched as the door burst in from the other side. A gust of air swelled as the vacuum seal between the two rooms was broken and a fresh swell of oxygenated air from the bedroom mated with the flames in the hall and a ball of fire burst into the room and raked the ceiling.

"NO!" Joanne wailed.

"Mommy!" Gwen shrieked.

Like a malicious creature, the sweltering heat lurched into the room in search of fresh nourishment. Like the mother and daughter, the fire didn't want to die; it needed fuel to survive, and with so much of the building already turning to ash it was growing desperate and angry. A lamp on a nearby counter suddenly burst, ridding the room of artificial light and usurping the role as light bringer. Squinting her eyes at the inferno that spread through the open doorway, Joanne thought she saw movement.

"HELP!" She cried out. "PLEASE HELP US!"

"*Help?*" the voice crackled and sparked and set the moistened hairs on the back of Joanne's neck on end, "Where's the fun in that?"

The figure emerged then, taking shape amongst the flames like a hellish phoenix. He stepped past the threshold, his bare feet coming down softly. Joanne's eyes widened as the man stood before her. He stared at her a moment, his bright blue eyes—shimmering like the base of flame—lighting up with excitement and his long, blond hair swirling about his head.

"Oh god..." she gasped.

The strange man smirked at that. "Oh? So you've heard of me?" he asked.

As his words sizzled in Joanne's ears, he stepped forward again, running his hand against the wall and leaving a fiery trail in its wake. His steps brought him closer, each movement of his long, thin limbs reminding Joanne of a coiling snake's. Behind him, as though it had been patiently waiting its turn, the fire slithered into the bedroom and began to consume everything around him.

"My dear, sweet, naïve lambs," he crouched down before them, spreading his arms and letting the fire swell proudly behind him. "Don't you know you're all just meat for the fire?"

OUTSIDE, THE FIREFIGHTERS' efforts had begun to pay off; the blaze beginning to die down. Though all eyes were firmly glued to the building, none of the spectators or emergency crew seemed to see the single figure as he—like his sired three before him—emerged from the blaze and stepped casually into the street.

Devin smiled to himself as he weaved through the crowd unnoticed. The blaze, though an impressive sight on its own, was far more than just a simple act of destruction. The doorway he'd created needed energy to exist, and though he'd been able to borrow the raw force he'd needed—a cosmic loan of sorts—it wasn't the sort of investment that the laws of physics took lightly. He'd needed to be cunning to ensure a return.

Destruction. Fear. Pain. Desperation. Blood.

Like anything else in business, it was all about location, location, location.

And his investment had been returned.

"Who said crime doesn't pay?" he mused to himself as the raw destructive energy he'd set into motion flowed back into the balance. With the doorway no longer open, the only remaining source for stability within the tormented structure faded.

The building began to crumble under the magical force.

"Oh my, gentleman," Devin spoke to the fire crew as he continued to walk unseen around them, "I don't think it's going to hold much longer. You may want to think about clearing these streets."

No reactions.

Just as none of the people in the streets could see him, none could hear him either.

Just as he wanted it.

"Suit yourselves," he offered a salute to Fire Chief Andrews, who gaped up at the fifth floor, where he'd been certain he'd heard screams a moment earlier. "Don't say I didn't warn you."

Beside him an elderly woman shivered and, immediately after, wondered why.

Turning away from the burning building and all the people brought together under that single tragedy, he started towards the alley on the other side of the street.

"Come," he called out. "Our wayward brother is near, and I'm eager for our reunion."

Barely a moment passed before three of the onlookers—

smirks still plastered upon their faces—turned away from the others and joined him, walking casually away from the chaos.

The moment the four slipped into the shadow of the alley, the building gave way and began its foretold collapse. As the cracks and fissures in the concrete and glass gaped further—pouring more oxygen into the dying inferno and churning the dying embers—the fire was reawakened. A roaring bellow issued as the roof caved in, the pressure forcing the collapsing rubble to spill outward and begin a fiery mockery of a landslide that began to crash down on the helpless onlookers.

Devin smirked as a fresh wave of chaos and death seeped into him, and he playfully shook his head. "I told you so," then, offering one last mocking salute, "Farewell, Fire Chief Andrews."

Bianca, the youngest and only female amongst the four, slowly wetted her full lips as she brushed a short, jet-black strand back into place with the rest of her moist, slicked-back hair. With her sharp, catlike swagger drawing her nearer to their leader, Devin glanced over his shoulder at the petite black beauty; her skin contrasting against her totally white ensemble —a too-tight button-up dress shirt and a pair of pressed dress pants—as her slender feet propelled her silently after him.

"So what's the plan now?" she asked in a soft purr; her sea-blue eyes swimming over him.

Smirking at the question, Devin moved his burning gaze forward as he led them deeper into the darkness of the alley, "Same as it's always been, my dear. We take him."

"He hasn't been making that easy," Lars said with a hard sigh as his dusty, grayish-blue eyes floated to Devin. "And why would he come here of all places?" he demanded before he turned his head to blow a speck of ash from the shoulder of his duster; the pale, well-oiled leather of the knee-length coat matching his complexion in more ways than one.

There was a gravelly, course sound from the rear of the

group as Gerard wound up inhaling the wayward ash and coughed on it before working it out and clearing his throat. Unlike Bianca and Lars—who were sleek and elegant and healthy-looking—he was large and bulky with dry, cracked skin. Even his eyes—cold and gray like a frozen stone—lacked any sort of shine. Though his movements were slow and casual, it was still an intimidating gesture as he raised his hand to scratch the top of his bald head.

"Do you think he'll start running again?" he asked, his voice hollow and seeming to echo in his own throat.

Devin shook his head, his smile growing wider. "No. I can sense his reluctance," he chuckled as he cracked his knuckles one-by-one with his thumb. "Something—or, rather, some*one*—appears to be keeping him here."

"Why would he stay for anybody when we've killed every ally he's ever tried to collect?" Bianca spat.

Lars hissed, "Same old tricks?"

"Or maybe he thinks he'll be able to bury us again," Gerard let out a hard laugh.

"No," Devin shook his head, narrowing his eyes as he let their brother's exposed history pass before his gaze, "this one *is* different."

Lars raised an eyebrow towards him. "Another like us," he asked, "is he recruiting now too?"

"Doubt it," Gerard scoffed, "Pretty-boy's too down-to-Earth to play at Devin's level."

Devin chortled at that, "Quite right, my friend; he's *not* quite so desperate. Still…"

"What then?" Bianca pressed.

"A vampire; a young, brash, *angry* vampire," Devin mused.

The other three shared a laugh at that.

Devin seethed and spun on his heels to address them:

"Now you listen to me, fools! There is little of this world that we cannot control, but should you allow yourselves to lose control of your minds in exchange for wasted confidence then you're of no more use to me than any of the gawking idiots back there!" he thrust a finger back towards the collapsed building and the dead bodies it had claimed. "So should any of you feel a reluctance to commit at this time, I'll gladly replace any or all of you with one of *them* and put you in their place!" He snarled and turned away, the fiery rage sparking some of the loose trash around them and forcing the three to hurry after in fear of being caught in a reluctant inferno. "This vampire, if our brother saw fit to seek him out, may very well represent a hindrance. Our brother is mine, but when we encounter him, I want him and everything associated with him destroyed!"

3

"SOMETHING SPECIAL"

The Next Day

The sun was about to rise, and though Xander's vampire instincts to fall into unconsciousness nagged at him he could not bring himself to settle his thoughts. Estella, lying beside him with a mystery novel, occasionally let her eyes drift from the book's pages to his side of the bed. Though he'd said nothing—given no hint to his thoughts—there was no doubt between them that something needed to be said

She just wasn't about to break the silence.

Not yet, at least.

Xander didn't need to read her thoughts or analyze her aura to know what she was thinking. She'd seen him upset plenty of times in the course of his life.

When they'd been young and human they'd been the best of friends, and even then Xander's emotions had been every bit the open book to her as the mystery novel before her at that moment. It had never been hard for Estella to see the pain and misery in his eyes; pain and misery that stemmed from his abusive life at home. In many ways she had been the only one that *could* see it, or, more likely, the only one who cared enough to look. And though he never told anybody, not even his only friend, about the horrors that he faced on a daily basis from his stepfather, it had always been evident that he was never happy.

Except when he was around her.

For Xander, there had never been a time when Estella hadn't soothed out the ripples of torment in his mind. When the day finally came that the abuse in Xander's home had turned to murder and Xander had lost his mother, the pain of witnessing her death became the only thing he knew, and the threat of losing that was too much to bear. Misery and bitterness grew, festering, and Xander, in a desperate attempt to cling to the torment that had come to define his life, convinced himself that Estella thought the worst of him and turned her away. From that day on, self-loathing and the constant hope of escape turned into his only companions.

Nevertheless, despite all of his hatred and anger, Estella had never stopped caring for him.

So when Xander's eighteenth birthday brought with it his sudden disappearance—his home burned to the ground and his grandmother found murdered—she'd been crushed by the news. Everybody else in their school had seemed intent on letting the freaky goth kid who had made everyone nervous become barely a memory within the halls, but Estella had refused to let her old friend's memory go so easily. Eager for answers, she'd gone to Stan, the school's guidance counselor and one of the only other people Estella knew to care for the young man, and finally worked a bit of truth from him. But that bit of truth had been more than enough. Xander *wasn't* dead—not in body, anyhow. Then, on Stan's word—his ever-insightful guidance—Xander had gone to her. Only after becoming a vampire had he begun to see the error in his ways and, in doing so, rekindled his long-lost friendship with Estella.

A friendship that had since then become so much more.

It was an unnerving fact, then, that there was no hiding his emotions from his lover. This being the case, the only question that hung in the air was "why".

At that moment his body abandoned him, and a heavy sigh forced its way from his lungs.

Estella could ignore it no longer.

"What's the matter?" she asked, setting her book aside and turning to face him.

Xander's thoughts swam in his head, and though he'd heard her he didn't answer.

How could he? What could he say?

Estella frowned, "Xander?"

He turned his head to face her and forced a smile, "What makes you think something's the matter?"

The urge to slap himself in the head flared up and he fought not to grimace at himself. *Stupid!* he thought to himself, *Like she'd ever fall for that! She's not an idiot, you dumbass!*

Since when had his inner-self-started sounding like Marcus?

She gave him a sharp look. "Don't treat me like an idiot."

Told you, dipshit!

Xander sighed and shook his head, chewing his lip softly enough that his fangs didn't rip through as they had so many times before. "It's… it's just…" He sighed again and hung his head, "It's just… *everything*. It's this clan and this new life and all these new expectations; it's Trepis"—he felt his voice nearly choke on a sob just saying the dying tiger's name—"and it's Stan…"

Estella's stern look melted away to concern and confusion, "You're upset about him coming back then?"

"Not that part… well, not so much at least," Xander coughed on the lump growing in his throat. "There's just… just so much happening. Some incredibly good, mind you—incredibly over-whelming, but I can't complain about them, you know?—but... but then there's..." He stopped to clear his throat and look away, cursing the way Estella's eyes could just make truths he wasn't ready to admit spill out like that. "Trepis is one of my best friends, Estella," he looked over, biting his lip—failing to be careful that time and trying to ignore the trail of blood that seeped down his chin—"and I know that's pathetic and stupid— a man being *that* attached to an animal—but he really is. And... and now he's..." His voice finally gave out and he dropped his head as the first sob betrayed him.

"Oh, Xander..." Estella reached for a handkerchief from the nightstand that she kept there for just that reason. As she began to blot the blood from his face, she hooked her index finger around his chin and gently moved his face to bring his shim-mering gaze to her own. "There's nothing to be ashamed of. I never even got to know that beautiful animal *half* as well as you did, and then there are all the attachments he has to the Odin Clan and Marcus and... hell, Xander, even your father! Nobody can see this and think any less of you for being torn up about it, least of all me. I've always known you were a gentle soul, sweetie, and this just proves it."

Xander's tears came easier then as he nodded, "I love that fuzzy bastard so much, Estella. And he looks so... I just wish there was something I could do!"

Estella wrapped her arm over his shoulders and kissed his cheek, "You just need to be there for him now; to show him that he's meant something to you. Which is exactly what you've been doing."

Xander nodded, letting out a deep breath and reigning in the pain as he stared outward; thinking. "I wish I could just focus on him right now, too, but..." he shook his head.

"What?" Estella leaned towards him, "What is it?"

"What Stan said, about these four that are tracking him

down," he shook his head and looked over at her, "I've seen what Stan can do, Estella—seen it firsthand—and not just those cheesy parlor tricks, either. There's magic and then there's *that*," he groaned and shook his head again. "*Four* of these things—these *gods!*—is just... it's not good. What if they do make it out?"

STAN HAD, by his own request, been given the room directly across from Xander and Estella's. Conveniently enough, this was the room that they left available for special guests, though that *usually* consisted of prospective new members, those from other clans, or the occasional visit from somebody on The Council. This, however, was the first time it had been used to house a personal friend.

Luckily enough, there were no other visitors with the Trepis Clan, so Stan's request could be facilitated without any awkwardness or threat of incident.

Despite the large, comfortable bed, Stan "sat" cross-legged several inches above the floor, bathed, despite no natural source, in pale luminescence. It had been a long time since he'd had a chance to relax, and when the opportunity had finally presented itself he had wasted no time in taking it.

Across the hall, he could sense Xander's tension, and while he didn't blame his old friend for being concerned, he resisted the urge to offer any further explanation. Whatever happened next was up to fate to decide, and he could offer neither condolences nor comfort with any sense of honesty before then. Devin and his sired gang were a dangerous and insane lot, but they, like himself, were far from immortal, and they'd yet to arrive. He mused on that thought a moment, asking himself if there might be a chance to flee once again before they found a way back from their prison in the earth's core.

There could still be a chance of not dragging Xander and Estella into—

The optimistic thought barely had time to register in his skull before the first ripple of chaos struck.

A shiver of raw agony crept slowly up his spine to the base of his neck before turning back and returning to the tip of his tailbone. In that time he "saw" the fire, feeling the flames lick at his skin as though he were right there with them as they consumed the inhabitants of a local apartment building. He was distantly aware of tears forming in his fluttering eyes, but his body—his human body, which had been left behind in his forced out-of-body journey—meant little to him at that moment. Realizing that he'd already been found and that the four had already arrived, he turned back and guided his astral form back to the mansion.

Maybe he had time to get away before any more damage could be done.

Where are you running off to so fast? Even without hearing the actual voice, Stan could detect the malice in Devin's psychic message. *Why don't you linger here a bit longer? There's a lovely peach I've just plucked that I'd like you to meet. Her name's Gwen. Come on, brother, won't you enjoy the show?*

The sound of a little girl's shrieks waned in-and-out of focus as Stan struggled to sever the psychic connection that Devin held between them.

There's nothing enjoyable about what you do! Stan stalled, trying to get back to his body. *And I'm not your brother!*

He knew that, while in his astral form, he was more susceptible to an attack; both physical *and* psychic.

If he allowed Devin to keep him from returning to his body, then they could trace him down and have access to everything—both his physical form *and* everyone at the clan—and Stan would be helpless against it. Letting Devin's hold linger a moment longer, Stan situated himself on the fading plane of reality—he'd already been separated from himself too long; the astral form wasn't equipped to maintain focus on such mundane concepts as direction and location—and fought to keep his goal in mind. Soon there would be nothing but sweet, eternal blackness and the ethereal truths therein.

Temping; very, very tempting.

But nirvana would have to wait for another day.

Sorry, Cobain, he thought to himself, *some other time.*

Devin's psychic assault continued, ***What are you babbling about, brother?***

It's a beauty thing, Devin, you wouldn't understand. Stan took hold of the psychic strand connecting them and directed his focus. *And I'm **not** your goddam brother!*

With that, he severed the hold and felt his astral body careen back towards the mansion.

Even before he had fully returned, he was aware of banging at the door, and, as he slipped back into himself and regained consciousness, he felt Xander's aura as it began to creep under the door in an attempt to spy on him. He frowned at the intrusion and, using his own aura, pushed the invading tendril away.

"What is it?" he demanded, still winded from his endeavor.

Before Xander's aura disappeared, it wrapped around the latch and unlocked the door, allowing him to open it from the other side. Frowning at this, Stan tried to get to his feet, only to find that after his astral form had left his body he'd stopped levitating and, in the awkward position he'd been left in, his legs had fallen asleep during his "journey." Still working to push himself up on shaky limbs, Stan looked up as Xander stormed in.

"Just what the hell's going on?" Xander growled, closing the distance between the two of them. Though he was wearing a faded pair of blue jeans, Stan could tell from his bare torso that he'd obviously just jumped out of bed.

"Xander! Wait!" Estella stood at the door in her nightgown, refusing to cross the threshold.

Xander growled and turned to face his lover. "What is it?"

Estella blushed, "We shouldn't just barge in…"

"Bullshit!" Xander turned back to Stan, shaking his head, "We've got the *king* of 'barge in' right in front of us! He barged in *here*, and I just felt his 'friends' barge in across town. I'm sure you can't feel it, Estella, but something *major* just went down—lots of lost lives and lots and *lots* of stolen energy—and it all feels *really* goddam familiar! And I'm willing to bet I know where those assholes are planning to barge in next…" Xander narrowed his eyes at Stan, "So how's about you start telling me everything I need to know before your four friends come knocking at my gate."

Stan shook his head, already beginning to gather his things to leave. "Xander, you need to trust me when I say you want no part in what's coming. I'd hoped I could enjoy a reunion with you, but I've made a grave error coming here."

Xander frowned, suddenly feeling a strange tickle in the back of his mind. Something *was* wrong; very, very wrong.

"So what happened to 'a very strong possibility that they'll *never* get out'?" Xander growled, noticing how scared his old friend looked. This, more than the threatening sensation in the back of his mind, unsettled him. He tried his best to ignore both and narrowed his eyes at Stan, "What's really going on?"

Stan opened his mouth for a moment, his dark aura flaring around him and giving away his protest before it'd been spoken. "The truth is I'm *scared*, Xander!" his voice came out distorted and inhuman, the confession dragging something dark to the surface with it.

Both Xander and Estella stared at their friend, dumbstruck.

"Scared?" Xander shook his head, "No. No, that can't be right. You're *Stan*—a goddam devil on Earth—an invulnerable and—"

"I am a *man*, Xander Stryker," Stan's hands slammed down on the bedspread and the two vampires watched as the furniture shifted and warped like a Salvador Dali painting before returning to normal once again. Stan groaned, "That didn't help…"

"Alright," Xander said in a low, steady voice, "say I'm willing to accept the idea that you're scared of these guys, why come back here? Why come to me?"

Stan sighed and shook his head. "I'm not sure," he admitted, sitting on the edge of the bed, "by all logical reasoning I *shouldn't* have. You're still young—still brash and irrational—but you're also a Stryker." Shrugging, Stan offered the slightest smile as he stared off at nothing, "And, a long time ago, when I was barely even a man, a Stryker saved me when I was lost and scared and helped show me a world where I could be more—where I *did* become more—and I've been trying to make it up to him ever since. I can't say *why* I came back here, Xander—I certainly wasn't expecting to find your father"—he bit his lip at that and shook his head again—"but I guess fear can make a man do dumb things. These four are after me to kill me and take my powers. More than likely when the ringleader of this whole mess is finished he'll just kill the other three, as well; he's rather adamant about being the only one. You wouldn't understand and you won't be able to deal with this, so I'm sorry that I put you at risk in the first place."

Estella finally stepped in, crossing her arms over her chest. "So you knew they'd be coming all along?" she asked.

Stan stared at her for a moment before offering a solemn nod.

Though Xander knew that his lover was a strong and capable fighter it still caught him off guard to see her abilities in action. She'd successfully replicated his combat skills and knowledge with a spell, and, while this had represented a quick and simple means to get her up to speed at the time, she had since that time surprised Xander with her dedication to furthering her training.

At that moment, however, it was Stan's turn to be surprised.

The ability to move faster than a human eye could follow was one of the sang vampires' greatest assets. It meant that the blood-drinking predators could close the distance between them and their prey and get their fangs into them before any recourse could be taken. It was, however, *also* a sang's greatest means of defense *and* offense, allowing them to evade almost all attacks and counterstrike just as swiftly.

In less time that it took to blink, Estella had crossed the room in overdrive—vanishing from her place near the door and reappearing right in front of Stan—and brought a heavy and furious hand down across his face.

The air hung heavy with tension as Xander's lover held her attack hand in their guest's face, an accusatory finger jutting towards him.

For a long moment, nobody said a word.

Estella, her orange aura seething and spiking out towards Stan, was the first to break the silence: "How *dare* you, Stanley!"

Xander started towards her, "'Stell…"

"No!" Estella's hand shot back, a gust of magic staying Xander in his tracks, as her enraged gaze remained locked on Stan, "No, Xander, this needs to be said."

Xander bit his lip but didn't make a move or protest to stop his lover.

Stan, looking back at his once timid student, raised a hand to his aching cheek.

Estella shook her head, "You talk to Xander like he's nothing more than a child, but I don't think you have any real appreciation for just how wrong you are. Even *as* a child that marvelous man held on in ways even he didn't understand. Before he was even a *teenager,* he'd known fear and helplessness that no person should *ever* have to face!" Clenching her teeth, Estella shook the finger in Stan's face for emphasis, "And it only got worse! Until the nightmare of a nightly *suicide* ritual became his only means of relief. Now you and I can sit around and play with the notion that we had some minute hand in keeping him alive, but the truth of the matter is that *he* had the power to end it all in the blink of an eye. But he dealt with it; he dealt with his fear and, through it all he didn't place that burden on a single other person. It was selfish and it was stupid, I know—believe me when I say I've given him a piece of my mind about keeping all that locked up—but there's something to be said for a *man* who doesn't use his fear as a weapon to punish others!" She took a step towards Stan and, in an astonishing display of power, Stan stepped back, "You're right to say that you didn't find Xander's father in coming here, because Xander's father is *dead*; *murdered* by the vampire who showed up only a short year after his reawakening to bring more terror and hellish brutality down on Xander than, *again*, most have *ever* had to face! And do you know what he did, Stan? *Do you?*"

Stan took in a jagged breath before opening his mouth, "He…"

Estella advanced on him again, "He *dealt* with it, Stan! Alone and hurt and *scared*, Xander Stryker *dealt* with it! *That's* the legacy that he's created for himself in only *two* years of being a *vampire*, Stan." She scoffed, her eyes traveling over his body, "You've had the powers of a god for *how long*, Stan? And what's your legacy? Hmm? The *man* who achieved the impossible and did *nothing* with it? The *man* who ran from those who loved him in the face of a struggle? Or the *man* who came running back when everything else failed?" Estella sneered and shook her head at him, starting a slow, calculated walk around him, "That's the man I love that you're talking down to, and if you think you can come into our home after so long and speak ill of the bravest, strongest soul I've ever known then I'd like to give him a breather and kick your ass myself. So before you try lying to *us* again, Stanley, I suggest you try lying to yourself a little better, because I can't even read your mind and I can tell you why you came back:" she leaned in and hissed, "Because you knew that Xander was a man who could handle fear—a man who could handle *anything*—better than you!"

Finishing her slow prowl around Stan, Estella shook her head and walked away from him—the power and strength showing with each step she put between them—and paused in front of Xander long enough to kiss his cheek and offer him a smile that melted all the tension from his shoulders.

"I'll be in bed when you're done with him," she offered.

Xander stared at her for a long moment, every response he could muster paling in comparison to what he'd just witnessed. Finally, he went with what was tried and true: "I... I love you." Then, feeling it was only right, "Thank you."

Estella shook her head, "You needed to hear that truth just as much as he did, Xander." She looked back at Stan and narrowed her eyes, "I just hope *neither* of you is ever too scared to forget that."

With that, she walked out the door, using her magic to slam it shut behind her.

Stan stared after her for a long moment, disbelief swallowing any sign of anger or resentment. Finally, he let his hand drop from his cheek and, immediately after it, let his gaze drop to the floor. "I didn't mean it like that, you know," he offered.

Xander shrugged and crossed his arms in front of his chest, "Yes you did. Let's not pretend you're a saint, Stan; you don't wear it well. I can't say that I was expecting all of... well, *that*—she doesn't usually get pissed off like that, and if she *does*..." he shook his head and started towards his old friend. "You've always been a rather 'holier than thou,' condescending shit—albeit a justified 'holier than thou,' condescending shit—and I can't much say I'm surprised by any of this. What *does* surprise me is how quick you are to think that I—that *we*—wouldn't be able to help. After all, you *did* train me; you awakened in me all the strength and power of the one *you* talk so highly of. So what good is channeling my father's auric skills if you're not going to trust me to use them?"

Stan looked up at that and looked at Xander with a renewed appreciation, "Did you *really* die out there? Like, for real *dead*?"

Xander nodded, "Can't say for how long, but yeah; for real *dead*."

"And Estella brought you back?"

Xander nodded again.

"All on her own?"

Another nod. "Wasn't much else around to bring me back but a gawking hodgepodge of brave mythos."

It was Stan's turn to nod. "You know that girl is something special, right?"

Xander smirked, "Why do you think I fought so damn hard to get her?"

"So when are you going to propose?" Stan asked, smirking at him.

Xander blushed but fought to keep his composure, "Is now really the time to ask me that?"

"That's a tough-guy way of saying you haven't worked up the guts yet." Stan looked towards the door and sighed, "Did I ever tell you about the time I had to send Estella to the principal's office?"

Xander raised an eyebrow and looked over. "The principal's office? Estella?" He shook his head, "I'm sorry, but I'm just not seeing that. She's always been so…"

"Peaceful?" Stan smirked, rubbing his cheek again, "Yeah, I think we've seen where that line is drawn." Nodding, he turned back to face Xander, "It was like any other day, I suppose; you were moping around and talking to Trepis"—Xander bit his lip at the mention of the name, not just for the memory of the dying tiger several floors below him, but also for the memory of the voice in his head that he'd grown up with; a voice that he'd later learned was the auric remains of his late father—"and Estella was buried in a book. Like I said, just like any other day. So the day wears on, and I'm heading back to my office from lunch, right? Then I hear this ruckus starting up around the bend. Now I've heard my fair share of schoolyard fights—life of a public school guidance counselor in a nutshell—but this one was... well, it was different. See, I've always known there was something special about you for obvious reasons, and the fact that Estella, even as a little girl, could look past all the judgments and unsettlement that surrounded you, made me realize there was something special about her, too. So I'd already come to recognize both of your energies by that point, and the fact that one of the energies in this particular fight—the only energy standing up against *five* others—was Estella's got my attention. So I hurry around the corner and, sure enough, there's Estella screaming like a banshee and telling these five older girls that she'll curse them all for what they were saying. Naturally I had to break up the fight—the five skanks, I can say that about them now, claiming that Estella jumped them for no reason and just went crazy—and, without any proof against them outside of what I could see in my own head, which, obviously, I couldn't use in that case, I had to take her into the principal's office on her own. Along the way, I get to talking to her—asking what the whole thing was about—and she tells me that the five girls were talking about you; saying awful things, from the sounds of it. Even then that girl's line was drawn and defined; nobody messed with Xander Stryker."

"Especially not Xander Stryker," Xander laughed, blushing at the story. He'd gotten his own fair share of Estella's wrath when he said or did anything that she deemed another self-destructive act, so, while it was the first time he'd ever heard Stan's story, he couldn't bring himself to not believe it.

"Like I said: something special," Stan smirked. "You know that you're something special too, right?"

Xander stopped at that and looked off. "We'll just have to see about that, I guess."

"No need," Stan shook his head, "I can already see it. I don't know what happened when you died, but what Estella brought back is leagues and legends ahead of the Xander I knew."

"It just put things into perspective," Xander shrugged.

"Sometimes that's all it takes." Stan narrowed his eyes and glanced over his shoulder. Trying not to call attention to the gesture—and failing—he changed the subject: "I heard about the Night Striker situation earlier this month. You realize The Council had been after her for a *long* time, right?" He shook his head and smirked, "And *you* took her down. Just"—he clapped his fists together and made a show of "blowing" them apart—"ended her reign of terror. Just like that."

Xander nodded, "Yeah. Just like that."

Stan looked at him, "Weren't you scared? I mean, that crazy chick had taken out so many good, strong warriors. Shouldn't going toe-to-toe with her have scared you out of your wits? How did you do it?"

"I did it *because* I was scared, Stan," Xander shrugged and let his aura sweep the mansion's perimeter, checking for any sign of whatever could be making Stan so twitchy. When the scan showed no sign of anything out of the ordinary, he glanced over his own shoulder in the direction of his room and Estella. "The Night Striker—McKayla—she was dangerous and insane, and I knew that my fears were validated when I saw what she could do. And I couldn't let something like that go on scaring others." He unfolded his arms and scratched behind his ear, "So I killed her... because it was what needed to be done."

Stan nodded slowly, smirking at Xander's words, "You really are something special, Xander Stryker."

Xander chuckled and turned away, shaking his head. "Yeah, so I've been told."

THE HIGH-NOON SUN was just beginning to dip into the early afternoon when Xander shot upright in bed like he'd been shot out of his dreams from a cannon. Every nerve was on end and alive with raw energy; his entire body tingling and every synapse in his brain firing an array of responses ranging from excitement to hunger to raw, unbridled panic.

Something was here.

Something big.

Something…

Throwing himself off the bed, Xander started for his bedroom door—his aura whipping out to retrieve his pants and Yang, his eight-chambered, ivory-white revolver—and charging through Stan's door.

He could already sense it was unlocked.

Keeping Yang gripped in his aura, he slipped into his pants and scanned the room for Stan, spotting him standing in the open doorway to his balcony. Starting towards his friend, he let Yang fall from his aura—taking the red-and-black tendrils of bio-energy back into himself—and caught it in his right hand before checking to be sure the cylinder had all eight chambers occupied by an enchanted round.

"What is that?" he asked, feeling his fangs already beginning to unsheathe in response to the energy waves.

Stan looked back. "It woke you—" he shook his head and turned back to the balcony, "What does it feel like for you?"

Xander frowned, "It *feels* like goddam Christmas, Stan; there's something down there that I can't yet identify, and my body is lighting up like a decorated pine tree with excitement and panic for what it's going to find. Would you care to shed some clarity on this before I'm forced to guess that Santa's about to roundhouse me in the face?"

"It's them," Stan said simply, as though that answered everything.

Unfortunately, it did...

Xander, feeling his lover's nervous aura approach from behind, looked back at Estella.

"Get out of here," he commanded. "Get your tonfas and a few of the warriors and run. Now!"

Estella's hands tensed around a tightly wrapped leather bundle. Still approaching, her eyes looked past the two of them and out towards the source of the energy. She shook her head. "I'm not leaving you."

"Dammit, Estella, this isn't about being a team or watching my back!" Xander roared at her, "I don't know what's coming and I'm not about to find out with your life on the line!" Feeling another swell of panic in his chest, his eyes turned desperate, "Please... I can't face them with everything I've got if I have to worry about you and the others. You're the strongest warrior we've got; this clan and everyone in it will be doomed if we both die."

Estella's focus finally fell on him and she clenched her jaw, "I'll fall back to give you your focus, Xander," she shook her head at him, "but if I feel for even one second that you're about to die, I'm coming back!"

"Please..." Xander couldn't bring himself to plead any further with her.

"You come back to me or I'm coming after you! That's the condition," she said flatly before tossing the bundle on the bed in front of Xander. "And I'm sending help. It'll take a bit to get the warriors collected and suited-up, but don't be surprised when they arrive."

Xander looked up to protest, but she was already gone.

"Dammit! Are all women so stubborn?" he cursed, grabbing

the bundle that she'd left for him. The freshly oiled red leather of his jacket filled his nostrils as it unraveled around his boots, Yin and Yang's second generation "cousins"—a pair of black and white nine millimeter pistols that had been created to replicate the dynamic of the Stryker family's world renowned revolvers —and his holsters.

"Wouldn't know," Stan admitted, sighing and shaking his head. "You know, you *don't* have to get involved in this. I know it was unfair to show up like this, but I really don't want to see you get—"

"Fuck that to Hell and back! This is *my* home!" Xander scoffed.

"Be that as it may—"

Xander snarled. "My *home!*" he shook his head, his hands balling up into fists and his aura flaring up, "Save your breath. I'm not going anywhere!"

Stan nodded slowly, stepping back and slamming the balcony doors closed in a clearly futile effort to keep out the approaching darkness that dwelled just beyond it. "Suit yourself."

Satisfied that Stan was seeing things his way, Xander jammed his feet into his boots and pulled his jacket on over the holsters. No matter how many times he'd been forced to go shirtless onto a battlefield, he'd never gotten used to the feeling of his guns slapping against his naked chest.

Stan looked over at him and cocked an eyebrow. "That's not the same jacket that Marcus gave you."

Xander sighed and shook his head, "No. I lost that one when I was fighting Lenix."

"Pity," Stan said, giving Xander a once-over. "I liked that jacket."

"Well, I guess Estella did too, 'cause she bought me this one to replace it," Xander made a note of tugging the collar for emphasis.

Stan chuckled and shook his head, "You truly are the Crimson Shadow."

Xander frowned at that. The old nickname had been something that had flashed in his mind shortly after he'd first woken up as a vampire, and Stan had been there to "see" the thought. After telling Marcus about it, Xander's vampire mentor—in what had turned into a sort of rehearsed squabble between them—made a note of using the unwanted nickname as a means of taunting Xander whenever possible.

Hearing it again made Xander's heart swell.

Still, there was a tradition to uphold, and he wasn't about to let it die with him.

"Don't call me that," he countered.

4

BRUTALITY

*I*t started with a crack.

Like an angry, ever-inflating balloon of dark power, the abysmal vacuum of energy on the other side of the windows grew and pressed harder and harder against the glass. With each swell of energy the darkness became denser—more ominous—and the pressure began to take its toll. The crack started small, emerging like a scar in the middle of the window and beginning to spider-web to the bottom-left corner. Watching the damage spread, Xander's eyes flashed with an animalistic fury, his aura swirling about him like a crimson electric storm.

The growing energy within the room served to balance out the onslaught from the other side of the window, and the crack's progress halted for a moment.

Then the moment passed...

The encroaching force swelled once more, slamming inward with even more pressure and the crack finally robbed the glass of its strength and it exploded inward. The other windows were quick to follow, and the two were forced to guard their eyes as shards rocketed at them like crystal shrapnel. Before the tiny jagged missiles could make contact, however, they slowed and finally stopped in midair. Xander glanced over at Stan, realizing that his friend's power had flared up then and spared them from any pre-battle lacerations. Though he knew that a few cuts weren't about to stop either of them—hell, his own injuries would have healed over in just a few seconds!—he knew that going into a fight with *any* sort of lag was never a sound option.

Plus, healing from such a thing *did* take energy, and, from what he was feeling of their visitors, he'd need all the energy he had.

The glass fragments hovered a moment longer, bobbing up-and-down before Stan held out his right hand and formed a fist. Tightening his grip, the pieces of glass began to break down further and further until nothing but a few flakes of shiny dust remained.

Only several seconds had passed between the formation of the crack and the molecular disintegration of the shattered glass, but in that time Xander had watched the day practically vanish. And still the darkness came; swallowing the light of the late afternoon sun and creating a twisted mockery of night over the mansion.

Then, like oily fingers slipping over the shattered window frames, the darkness began to creep inside.

"What the hell is it?" Xander's voice instinctively fell into a hushed murmur. He wasn't sure if the toxic-looking blackness could actually *hear* them, but he wasn't willing to test it at that moment.

Stan didn't answer.

"What's the matter, Ferno?" a gravelly voice echoed from the darkness, accompanied by a burning-hot and unnatural wind. "Don't you want to introduce us to your *friend*?"

"I was hoping I wouldn't have to!" Stan sneered, glaring into the darkness.

Xander frowned, knowing that his old friend could see

something in the growing abyss that he could not, and that made him all the more nervous.

"Well that's not very polite," the voice taunted, "you're going to make us look bad, and inside his own pretty home, no less."

Stan let out a heavy, shaking breath, "Then at least I'd have that going for me!"

"My, my! Just as morose as ever, aren't we?" the owner of the voice, still mostly hidden within the dense darkness, began to take shape. Behind him, three other figures stood, equally as shadowed.

"Who are you?" Xander growled. "What do you want?"

The figure's head shook back and forth, and though there was a slow, mechanical drive behind the movement Xander was startled as the vision grew hazy and his head appeared to jerk and twist. "Stanley, Stanley, Stanley... you appall me! You accept this young vampire's generosity and show none in return?" A maniacal chuckle issued, and the room became unbearably hot, "You should have at least warned him."

"You could come with us, you know." Another deep and rumbling voice emerged.

"It'd make all of this go by so much more smoothly," another voice chimed.

There was the distinct sound of a woman's giggle, "Yes, Stanley, and so much easier on the boy."

Stan seized up, his muscles tensing as his eyes narrowed and his jaw worked slightly. Xander frowned, turning his head to face him fully.

"You're not actually considering this, are you?" he growled.

Stan didn't take his eyes away from the intruders, "I'm sorry, Xander."

Rolling his eyes, Xander turned away from his old friend. "Apologize later," he muttered, pulling out Yang, "*After* we've dealt with these assholes!"

"After you've 'dealt' with us?" The first voice scoffed, "Stanley, he really has no idea who we are, does he?"

"What? Another batch of giggling god-wannabes?" Xander shook his head and leveled the revolver towards the intruders, thumbing back the hammer, "Ask me if I give a shit! I kicked his ass for coming in uninvited and now I'll kick all your asses too!"

Xander roared, sprinting at them.

"Xander, NO!" Stan called out.

The black void pulled back suddenly and the four figures— previously hidden therein— emerged. Xander's eyes scanned over the four as he closed the distance; three men and a woman. The man in the lead—a lanky blond with a psychotic glimmer in his eye—stood calmly with his hands stuffed inside the pockets of a long, black jacket. Behind him on his left was the female of the group. Though younger-looking than the others, Xander saw something malicious and dangerous in her grey-blue eyes that made her seem older. On the other side were the remaining two, a man who looked like a professional bodybuilder with a severe skin condition and another who, despite an awkward, mismatched appearance, swayed on his feet with a rhythmic confidence.

All of them had the same inhumanly blue eyes as Stan.

Xander aimed himself at the blond man, guessing he was the one in charge, and squeezed four rounds out around him—two towards the bodybuilder and one towards each of the others— before jamming the revolver back into its holster and jumping into overdrive. The process of moving into the next stage of vampiric movement was always a jolt; the sensation of watching the world freeze around making him feel detached from reality. Along with this was the exhilarating rush from the energy boost and, with the shift in his vision to allow for him to follow his own movements, a renewed sense of perspective. In overdrive, most creatures—aside from those capable of achieving the same speed—were totally helpless.

The four intruders stood, frozen in time as he drew closer. The bullets he'd just fired hung in midair, pointing towards their intended targets, and made promise of a bloody scene when he returned to normal time. The leader, however, he left open. While the others had the magic-infused bullets to worry about, he wanted to personally rip the arrogant punk's heads off before he even realized that he'd left Stan's side.

This was *his* home, and he had worse things to worry about than all of this—

There was a slight movement in his intended victim's face; almost too subtle to notice.

Had his eyes *really* just moved?

Was he looking at him?

But that was...

Impossible? The voice roared inside Xander's mind along with an echoing laugh and a little girl's scream.

The enchanted bullets—infused with a powerful magic that behaved like an exploding round when it came in contact with mythos blood—began to vibrate on either side of Xander as he started to pass between them. His eyes widened as he caught sight of this, realizing what he was seeing was the slow-motion view of the magic being triggered early.

Oh shit...

Indeed, the voice chortled in his mind. *We'll continue this outside.*

And then they were gone.

Xander faltered in overdrive, the world shimmering around him as time began to catch up with him, and he worked to turn away from the bullets before they could explode in his face. Stan stood where he'd left him behind, staring with a partially time-frozen gaze as his friend noticeably fought to catch up to the heightened perception.

Stan... Xander pushed to move faster, to keep the magically propelled explosions from going off with him at ground-zero.

Xxxaah—Stan's psychic voice was sluggish in his head; the call still being lagged between the two different time-frequencies that separated them. The casing of the bullet closest to him began to crack, the shimmering start to the explosion glowing from behind the time-slowed tearing metal. Xander pushed harder to sprint back towards his friend, still not yet sure what he had planned.

—aande—

That's it, Xander thought, seeing that Stan was catching up. Maybe if he could spot the bullets. *Come on, Stan! Push! I can meet you halfway, but I can't stop this on my—*

Auric shield! Rear window! Don't stop until we're in the air! Stan's orders rang clear as a bell in Xander's mind.

The first bullet burst, and the wave of enchantment rippled through the room, moving freely through the time-frozen world as a concussive force of magic programmed *specifically* for just that purpose. Should any of those rounds ever go off around a vampire slipping in or out of overdrive, the blast would see to it that they were grounded long enough for Xander to act.

Going off in midair *while* in overdrive, though…

Xander grabbed Stan by the arm and leapt for the window in front of them, letting the laws of physics catch him as his feet left the ground.

The sound of four enchanted exploding bullets was almost as jarring as the blasts themselves.

Almost!

With the momentum from overdrive still propelling the two through the already broken window, Xander felt the force slam into his back and their bodies pitched, threatening to fold their spines in half as the impact caught them at their tailbones.

Xander fought to hold himself partially in overdrive, hoping that seeing the world in slow motion would give him some extra time to collect some obviously much needed information on what he was up against.

Alright, he kept the psychic hold with Stan open as their airborne bodies began to get dragged towards the ground, *that was stupid of me...*

Stan's auric connection with him went red with rage, *YOU THINK?*

Not much time to clue me in here, Stan, Xander shot back.

A tickle over Xander's right ear echoed like a sigh in his mind. Nevertheless, Stan explained what he could, *They'll be waiting for us. Gerard's dumb as a bag of rocks*—Xander "saw" the body builder in his head as Stan fed him the details—*he follows a strict rule of crushing something a lot until its dead, so don't give him the chance.* Xander suddenly "saw" the shifty one, *Lars likes to talk* —a lot!—*he'll try to distract and deter you to earn an opening; keep your feet under you at all times. Bianca is sinister and cunning*—the vision of the black girl in the tight white outfit replaced Lars —*she will figure out your weaknesses and she will work to exploit them. Best advice I can give you is to accept that it's going to happen and be ready to face it head-on.* Finally, the blond man's face appeared in Xander's mind, drawing a shiver in his core, *Devin prefers scare tactics and deception, never believe that he's behind you; he'll be in front of you the entire time and waiting to burn you alive.*

How are they doing these things? Xander asked, already seeing the shimmers of the four materializing on the ground beneath them.

They're like me, Stan explained, *they can bend and twist the rules to their hearts' content, but they* cannot *break them. Transference, matter manipulation, constructs... all the old toys of the trade, but they're nearly limitless in their control. More than anything, though, is their affinity for illusions; they paint fake realities in your head to make you* think *they're doing the impossible, but it's* still *just magic! They were* never *in the room with us in the first place! They were just projecting themselves in our minds! Be sure to keep your shields up; do whatever you can to keep them out of your head!*

Just magic... Xander nodded as he let himself fall completely out of overdrive and they fell the rest of the distance, landing on their feet. "Got it!"

"No more stupid mistakes," Stan glared at him.

"Silly little man," Bianca cackled and lunged at them. "*All* mistakes are *stupid* mistakes!"

"And you just made one!" Xander hissed, baring his fangs as he swung out at her face with Yang.

Her head rippled like a ball of water, letting Xander's hand pass through harmlessly.

Xander's eyes widened, "What the he—"

"You were saying, doll?" Bianca's face leered inches from his own—no sign of liquid-like ripples or distortion left—before she head-butted him, sending him toppling backwards.

Even crashing and tumbling as though he'd been hit by a truck, Xander could feel Devin's burning gaze following his ragdoll form.

"Teach the vampire a lesson in respect," he ordered as Xander's body came to rest nearly a hundred feet away, "our brother and I need to have a little chat."

"Just magic," Xander groaned to himself, pushing to remember everything he knew about the arts. Misdirection and confusion, *that* was the real weapon here. His hand hadn't even *touched* the girl's head—she'd probably ducked under it or never even occupied that space as he'd seen it—but, by getting into Xander's head and creating the illusion that she'd suddenly become a liquid she'd caught him off guard. Thinking back of the one time he'd seen Stan in a fight, Xander suddenly realized that the greatest feat he'd achieved had not been what he and their enemies had seen, but what Stan had *convinced* them they'd seen. Everything else that had happened from that moment on had been a product of panic and an amazing control of magic. "It's *just* magic…"

"That may be, chap," the one called Lars called from behind Xander as the other two came at him from the front, "but magic isn't much of a laughing matter, is it? It can mean the difference between your reality and *our* fantasy, *boy!*"

Xander felt his insides seize as he felt himself begin to fall. Looking down, he was startled to see that, though he was still standing, he was growing ever-nearer to the ground; his pants and jacket growing around him as the holstered guns at his chest grew heavier and heavier.

"What the hell are you—" his eyes widened as the sound of his own voice emerged in an alien pitch.

Like a child's voice…

Teetering under gravity as his body continued to shrivel, and, as he toppled, he threw his hands out to catch himself. The hands that filled his vision were not his own. Gaping, he pushed himself to his knees and gawked at the small, childish digits, testing the fingers and crying out—the high-pitched voice once again spilling out—as the tiny fingers wiggled under his command.

"Not real…" he reminded himself. "It's not real. It's just a trick."

Lars chuckled, "Is it? Can you be certain? Doesn't our friend seem a great deal larger than you remember?"

Xander looked over his shoulder as the shadow of Gerard drew nearer to him. Though he could recall the initial size of the behemoth being intimidating under normal circumstances, he couldn't deny that the proportions were all wrong. Moreover, the rising terror he felt seemed wrong; he felt helpless and consumed by the forced vulnerability. All of his training—all the time he'd spent honing his combat skills and all the abilities and prowess that he'd gained as a vampire—were suddenly gone; he couldn't *feel* his aura let alone control it. Even the simplest movements seemed a struggle for his body to adjust to.

Stand, dammit, he willed himself, begging his body to push the illusion aside.

"Wouldn't be the first time I've crushed a baby's skull," Gerard's chest heaved with laughter and he raised his arms over his head.

Xander's eyes squinted against the few rays of sunlight that fought through the minute cracks in the darkness the four had brought with them, and he whimpered as the gigantic fists raised over him—eclipsing the light—and began to merge together.

"N-no," Xander shook his head, forcing himself to look away in the hopes of fighting the illusion by removing it from his vision. "It's all just a trick! Stan! Stan, where are—"

"Already dead, I'm afraid," Lars' voice perked up again, suddenly standing over Xander. Though not as large as Gerard, he couldn't deny that he, too, was larger, and he cried out as the sandy-haired man stooped over to scoop up Xander; cinching the guns' harnesses in his hands and lifting Xander...

Just like a child!

Xander struggled, kicking his legs and flailing to get a grip on something; *anything.*

"Aw! He's so adorable like this!" Bianca's voice was shrill in Xander's ears as he pitched his head around towards the source. Catching sight of her, he instantly regretted looking. The woman's face had twisted and warped to leer over him as something far worse; her eyes occupying nearly half of her face and widening in morbid excitement to expose a pair of bright, toxic-looking yellow irises. As the eyes took him in, her mouth broadened—Xander flinching as her jaw visibly popped and dislocated over and over to accommodate for the hideous, unnatural grin's growth—and her teeth shimmered like jagged metal shards. "You just want to EAT... *HIM...* **UP!**"

Xander thrashed, trying to figure out how to free himself from whatever manipulation he was caught in. The terror of being so small and powerless among these three pseudo-gods was too much. Any reality *except* the one he was trapped within was inconceivable. The lingering thought of the clan and Estella and Stan—could he really have been so easily killed?—shadowed his mind like a wonderful dream that he'd just been startled awake from. Even if it was all just deception, he couldn't fight like them if he couldn't bring himself to face them; couldn't conceive of a world where he *could* fight.

"Too... too afraid to fight?" he struggled to stifle the whimper that wanted to seep from his mouth and, instead, forced the words that he felt his dream-self would have said...

No! he clenched his eyes and balled his fists. *It wasn't a dream! It wasn't a—*

Dream or not, you little shit, the voice in his mind felt like sandpaper on a slab of granite, *you don't want to see what a **real** fight with me looks like!*

Xander cried out as he felt his skull crumble into pebbles. Reaching up to hold his head together, he felt the worms his fingers had become slither between the gaps and slip behind the rotting orbs of his eyes.

"No!" he cried out, struggling to hold himself together. Though his vision was gone, he was somehow aware of his legs as they walked away without him and left him—

"It's too much for him already, boys," Bianca's voice giggled over him.

Xander blinked. The grass beneath him shivered under a mild breeze, letting him know that he'd gotten his sight back—had he ever really lost it?—and, feeling as though the weight and fit of his body was once again his own, he dragged his hands to confirm that he was, in fact, himself again. With his mind once again his own, the energy signatures from everyone around him flooded back into his awareness and he let out a deep sigh of relief as he sensed Stan in the distance.

"Sick motherfuckers..." he panted, spitting a wad of panic and the lingering illusion of the dirt-and-worm taste in his mouth. "When I figure out which one of you was responsible for that worm trick I'm going to—OOMPH!"

Xander barely had time to register the phenomenon of the ground opening up directly in front of him before one of Gerard's fists came through and drove into his jaw. The world went red and hazy and more and more distant in Xander's eyes as he shot upward. He'd taken his fair share of hits in the past—more than he was willing to admit even to himself—but never had an impact been enough to—

Above him, Lars' already familiar aura appeared in a powerful swell of energy. Xander fought to focus, but the more he tried to rope in the swimming fragments of his jumbled mind the more they escaped him.

Oh good, they can fly now... Xander felt his gut churn at the realization.

"You wanted a fight?" the pseudo-god's seething voice hissed in his ear as he was caught in mid-flight and dangled by his jacket. Swaying once more from Lars' grip, Xander let his eyes come to focus on the battlefield the mansion's lawn had become below him. Near the side-wall of the mansion's perimeter he spotted Stan, surrounded in a dark, mist-like haze, as he ducked and weaved around Devin's blurred attacks; a fiery trail burning the grass and leaving a charred map of every move he'd made. Then, shifting his focus, he saw Gerard and Bianca soaring towards him. Lars chuckled above him and dangled him like a piece of bait, "Well, here comes your fight, Crimson Shadow!"

Xander was beyond the point of witty retorts. He'd underestimated the sheer malice of his super-powered opponents and he'd be feeling the aches for his misjudgment for days to come, he was certain. Pulling Yang from the holster under his arm, he jammed the barrel to Lars' throat and pulled the trigger. A startled and gurgled cry issued just above him—a hefty spurt of blood splashing across the left side of his face and the shoulder of his jacket—and the grip that held him slipped. Somewhere far above him, the magic of the bullet went off and he felt Lars' aura stammer with pain and rage as he was propelled towards the ground. Out of the corner of his eye, he spotted the sandy-haired pseudo-god clutching the front of his neck—a spurting trail of blood decorating the air behind him—and he realized that the shot had been a clean in-and-out, and, though the sight of one of the four struggling to breathe around a gaping hole in his windpipe was a rewarding one, Xander cursed that he hadn't taken the extra moment to secure a headshot and actually *kill* the man.

Spotting Gerard and Bianca still shooting towards him, however, Xander realized he had better things to concern himself with.

Releasing Yang and letting the revolver corkscrew beside him in freefall, he crossed his arms under his jacket and took the twin pistols into his hands. The two pseudo-gods were nearly ten yards below him when he started firing down at them, and it came as little surprise when their bodies shimmered in-and-out of focus as they began darting around the bullets.

Xander smirked at this. While he'd been uncertain if they'd be able to achieve such speeds while in flight, he'd been *hoping* for it.

Not sure your boss appreciates your swiftness, chumps! he let the psychic message linger between them as they came to an abrupt halt in midair to look back.

Gravity continued to carry Xander down, and as he fell past the two he enjoyed he panicked looks on their faces as they saw Devin glaring back up at them; a series of smoldering craters surrounding him where the enchanted rounds had peppered the ground around him, forcing him to sacrifice his attacks on Stan to avoid being incinerated.

Then he took flight…

How hard can it be to kill one little vampire, you fools?

Xander barely had enough time to holster the two pistols before Devin reached him; Yang, still spiraling through the air, jolted within the vampire's aura as he reached out to it...

Only to have its retrieval interrupted.

The impact of the pseudo-gods' leader spearing into his midsection was like nothing he'd ever experienced. Gravity's pull was rendered nothing more than a cruel memory as the only true force of nature controlling Xander's body was handed over to the roaring psychopath. Every cognitive notion of up, down, or a world where breathing was a luxury vanished as Xander lost count of how many of his ribs had been broken.

Do you think you know pain, you fanged turd? Devin's psychic message felt like acid sloshing in Xander's head, and though he wanted nothing more than to cry out in pain—to let the pressure of agony find some escape—he was distantly aware that he no longer had a mouth or nose to breathe through; no air to even fuel the screams. The cold-burning depths of Devin's eyes leered in Xander's own as they careened through the air, *Just because some little mind-feeder used to beat you and your dead, ravaged mommy, you feel you're somehow versed in the intimate nature of suffering? Let me show you pain! Let me offer you a crash course in MY beautiful world of brutality! That will be my gift to you before you die!*

5

SPELLBOUND

*X*ander fought to stay awake as he felt every inch of his skin and every fiber of his insides sear with an unbearable heat. Whatever Devin was doing to him it seemed to be burning him from the inside-out, and he wasn't certain how much more of the torture his body would be able to take. Fighting against the sheer force of Devin's spiraling path as they rocketed through the air—soaring so high that he could make out the curvature of the planet and so low that the whipping blades of grass felt like razorblades against his face and then back again—Xander finally succeeded in retrieving a weapon. Though his right arm was pinned to his side by Devin's relentless grip, there was a moment of hopeful celebration as his left hand slipped under his jacket and into the holster beneath his right arm...

Only to find that the grip of the white pistol—what he'd been calling "Yang-Two"—was burning-hot to the touch. At that moment, feeling the superheated metal scorch his hand, he guessed that the heat he was feeling wasn't just another illusion; that what Stan had warned about Devin burning him alive hadn't just been a cryptic warning.

So, Devin's acidic psychic taunt drove Xander to miss his ability to scream more and more, *hoping to shoot me like you did Lars, hmm? Not that it did much to him; not in the long run, at least. Though I must say that it was quite a sight seeing him fall out of the sky like that*—Xander felt a cold, slimy shiver inside the back of his head that he realized was Devin's internal laughter —*I have to give you this much: you did put a smile on my face with that stunt.*

More and more sweat began to streak across Xander's face, its burning moisture boiling against his skin and pelting into his wind-whipped vision. Not that his eyes were of any use to him at that moment; though there was no way to guess just how fast Devin was moving with him it was enough to send the world around them into a blur.

A blur of speed...

Xander would've smirked if the force against his face would allow it.

He jumped into overdrive.

So his body was caught in the pseudo-god's grip?

So he wasn't able to move a muscle under the force?

At least he'd be able to *see*!

Perception shifted, the blurs around him beginning to take shape and become trees and clouds and Stan standing over a giant, gray mass of dirt and grass.

What the hell... Xander lingered on the sight a moment longer before Devin's path eclipsed the view behind the mansion.

He was just moving in a circle!

A wide, constant circle!

Another would-be smirk moment passed.

Don't want to be too far from Stan when you've finished microwaving me, huh? he thought to himself.

The shift in perspective gave him a greater sense of what was happening to his body. From his ankles to his ears he could feel blisters beginning to form from the heat. Shifting his gaze, he could see that the leather of his new jacket was already beginning to melt, the time-frozen bubbles and drops of lique-fied material starting to drag across the surface. The heat was beginning to take its toll on more than just his body, it appeared.

Then he remembered his burning-hot gun...

One of two pistols strapped *directly* to his bare, burning flesh...

Two pistols with enchanted explosive rounds in the magazines...

Shit!

The time to fight his immobility was upon him. The fact that the superheated metal of the guns' grips hadn't acted as an oven for the rounds inside of them was nothing short of a miracle at that point. Xander struggled, fighting harder and harder within Devin's grip; trying to mentally calculate how many shots he'd already fired from the pair of pistols. He'd personally seen what just *one* of those rounds was capable of after he'd placed one inside the body of any number or species of mythos—vampire, therion, alv; it didn't matter—and watched with no shortage of satisfaction as all of their bodies bloated around the releasing force of the magic a fraction of a second before they erupted into a fiery, gory mess. All from a single bullet; just *one* of those explosive rounds! Xander felt himself shiver as he fought to keep his melting mind focused.

Fuck...

Xander shuddered and doubled his efforts to tear free of Devin's grip; the thought of the two super-heated pistols with all those remaining explosive rounds inside of them just waiting to go off motivating a greater effort. Just *one* of those bullets would be enough to rip Xander apart and fertilize the entire mansion's lawn in a single pass of one of the hyper-charged cycles the psychotic pseudo-god was taking around the grounds...

He'd already had four rounds destroy an entire room of the mansion.

Creating a circle of explosive magic around the building was condemning it to untold levels of damage.

Not to mention the warriors inside…

Estella, Osehr, Timothy, Sawyer, Trepis…

All of them!

He couldn't let that happen!

Accepting that the speed and force was too much on his body, he sacrificed his physical struggle and closed his eyes, forcing his mind to focus inward. As his limbs and muscles went slack within Devin's grip, he sensed the pseudo-god's rising confusion just on the other side of his eyelids. He felt his aura writhe inside of him—suffering from the heat in much the same ways his body was—and he willed it to save them from their fiery fate.

Doesn't need to be fancy, he told himself. *It just needs to* WORK!

What are you doing in that little head of yours, vampire? Devin's acid-speak returned inside Xander's head. *What sort of nonsense are you concocting?*

Xander clenched his teeth against all the pain and agony he was experiencing and pushed his aura to act. *It's a fireworks show, asshole!* he offered back, finally feeling his aura spark and thrash forward; emerging from his throat and slamming into Devin's leering face. *And it's gonna blow your mind!*

The force of the auric strike knocked Devin back—his body cartwheeling through the air—and released Xander from his grip. Feeling his body begin to fall, Xander struggled to ignore the draining exhaustion and stifling fatigue so he could stay in overdrive. It was better that he be able to think and move faster than the impending explosions literally strapped to his chest. Whipping off his melting jacket and tossing it back, he struggled to pull the guns free, only to find that the heat had fused them to the holsters. Left with no other option, he shifted his focus to the network of straps that harnessed the weapons to his body. Fighting with the clasps, he used his sweat-drenched hands and panicked aura and, in one desperate moment, even his chattering teeth to tear through the nylon and plastic. Through his aura's contact with the guns, he could "see" several of the rounds that had already begun to rupture; the magical energy beginning to spread outward. He fought harder to rid himself of the holsters. If he let his hold on overdrive slip even enough to let a moment of real-time take control, he'd already be swallowed in the explosion...

One of the thicker straps snapped and opened up the network to be yanked off in one desperate pull. Then, mustering every bit of strength his aching, tortured muscles could manage, he hurled the waiting bomb away from himself and the mansion.

Finally, cursing under his labored breath, Xander Stryker dropped out of overdrive...

~Several seconds later~

STAN HADN'T BEEN able to follow Devin's movements for long after he'd snatched Xander right out of his impressive, bullet rain spewing moment in freefall. One moment Stan had been locked in a struggle with the fire-throwing murderer and the next he was off the ground and flying after the source of the thirteen smoldering holes that had nearly ripped him apart. A short distance behind him, Lars—clutching a bloodied wound at his neck—crashed to the ground, falling halfway between the grass of the lawn and the classic, cobblestone walkway that led towards the mansion. Stan had a moment of morbid enjoyment when he saw that the left side of Lars' face had been the first to make contact with the unforgiving stone, and that he was clearly having some difficulty willing the whistling hole in his throat to heal with half of his face caved in. Knowing that neither of those injuries would hold him back for very long, Stan swept Lars off the ground in a magic vortex of dark energy and pinned him to the walkway; sealing his mouth and eyes so he could neither call out to nor see his comrades.

Bianca and Gerard, seeing that their leader had taken the incentive with Xander, turned their attentions on him. Gerard, in a classic display of his crush-happy approach to combat, simply let his body drop out of the sky; aiming his hulking form at Stan. Bianca, however, was more tactical—just as she'd always been in their past encounters—and whipped her body around in a wide arc to strike at Stan from the side. Letting his mind linger on Xander's wellbeing a moment longer, he'd decided that he was no use to anybody if he let Gerard crush him or Bianca rip him to pieces.

Calling upon the molecules around him, he conjured a mass of spongy earth from massive craters around him—packing soil and sod and turf into a giant pocket—and let it billow into a solid form over his head. Gerard's startled cries sounded on the other side of the earthy pillow as he sank harmlessly into its center, and the distended form of his struggling body passed several feet over Stan's head. Shifting his stance to face Bianca then, Stan extended his shadowy essence into the ground below him and cast a shadow-copy of himself as he let the ground swallow him.

The copy stood—a perfect decoy in the exact spot he'd been standing—beneath the still-hovering mass of grass and dirt and decayed plant matter that held Gerard captive, and, as Bianca closed in to take the bait, Stan let his trap snap shut.

All at once the shadow-copy vanished, forcing Bianca to stall in mid-flight to avoid driving herself face-first into the unforgiving ground, only to have Gerard's spongy prison drop down on top of her. Stan emerged from the ground a short distance away, casting out his dark magic and dragging Lars into the solidifying mass of earth as he dragged the air and water particles from the solidifying tomb. The futile cries of Bianca—a panic-prone claustrophobic—were swallowed up as he superheated the mass and let the three struggle in the baking clay.

Stan barely had a moment to appreciate his handiwork before he felt a sudden swell of energy and spotted Devin hurtling through the sky. Then, just as suddenly, the shadowed horizon went alive with an explosion that spread across the sky and Stan watched in shock as Xander was rocketed back with enough force to propel his body though one of the upper levels of the mansion.

"XANDER!" Stan felt his own feet leave the ground.

It had been some time since he'd last flown, and even then he'd spaced out the event as much as possible. A fear of heights, among other things, robbed the act of much of the luxury and splendor he imagined it held for the others. Despite this, however, seeing Xander so violently thrown through the side of a building was more than enough to make him forget about phobias and reservations, and it wasn't long before he was passing through the hole Xander's body had made and crouching over his old friend.

Though he was bruised and bloodied, Stan was relieved to find that the resilient vampire had survived the ordeal.

But, if he didn't do something about Devin and the others, that could easily change.

After casting a shadow spell over Xander's body and hiding it from sight Stan turned away and returned to the hole in the wall. Back on the ground, Devin was hard at work freeing the other three from the makeshift prison Stan had encased them in. Though he couldn't be sure how long it would take for his malicious counterpart to break his flunkies free, Stan wasn't too interested in using that moment as a learning experience.

Jumping through the hole and letting his body drop like a stone, Stan directed his focus on the ground below him. The grass rippled and swayed beneath him, and as he continued to fall the surface of the ground moved like water in a gentle breeze before he slipped underground as though he'd jumped into a pond. The momentum of his fall carried him as he directed his path and slipped free just behind Devin. The spike in energy didn't go unnoticed, and as Devin turned to face him he saw the psychotic blond's hair flare up.

"It's time for you to leave!" Stan informed him, resting his hand on Devin's chest and narrowing his eyes as he pushed a wave of energy into his opponent.

Devin's eyes went cold and dizzy as the magic in him was neutralized. Not wanting to see how long the effects would last, Stan moved his free hand to the giant slab of cooked earth that held the other three and focused his powers on lifting both it and Devin from the ground. Letting his powers replicate the unique patterns of each of the murderous four, Stan began to construct a barricade around the interior of the mansion's gates and cast a spell to hold his enemies out. Such a spell wouldn't last long, he knew, but it was the best he could do for the time being. Finishing the barrier, he tossed Devin and the clay-like prison into the air and let the magic take hold of the four and launch them into the distance.

Where they'd come to land, though a lingering concern, was hardly the most pressing matter for Stan at that moment, and he turned away from them once he was certain they were off the property to return to Xander.

6

TAINTED

"Well," Xander sighed, staring into the untouched cup of diner coffee in front of him, "*that* was, I'd say, about a twelve-point-five out of *ten* on my scale of monumental failures. What about you?"

After a painful visit to the clan's med-center to have his burns and broken bones treated, it had taken Xander nearly two thermoses of synth-blood to feel up to going out. Even then, as he'd taken back Yang from Stan, who'd retrieved it from the burnt grass after he'd dropped it, Xander had felt a powerful ache in his pride.

Stan shrugged, gulping down the last of his third cup of coffee and motioning to their waitress that he needed another refill. Sliding the empty mug to the edge of the table, he set his sights on Xander. "At least you're still alive."

Xander rolled his eyes. "Barely!" he rebutted, "I mean—shit, Stan!—do you realize those assholes nearly killed me about a half-dozen fucking times in a span of *about* five minutes? Five minutes, Stan! *Five!* That averages to about one near-death experience every *minute*! And that's another thing!" he jabbed an accusatory finger at his flustered friend, "You *do* realize that, technically speaking, I'm a high school dropout, right? Do you know one of the leading motivators in my decision to become a vampire and *not* just refuse the call and waltz back into Hell High the next day? *Not* having to dick around with math, Stan!" An angry fist was slammed down on the table to punctuate his point, but Xander only served to startle and irritate some gawking Bible salesman the next table over. Catching wind of their irritated stares, Xander shot them one of his own, making sure they caught sight of his blood-red right eye, "Something I can do for you gentlemen?" he asked, curling his lip in disgust.

The two quickly shook their heads.

"Thought so," Xander nodded towards the bowls of steaming soup in front of them, "Now get back to your chowders before I make you wear them."

The two murmured between themselves for a moment before shaking their heads and averting their gazes.

Stan pinched the bridge of his nose, "Still just as cheery and social as ever, I see."

"Eat shit, Stan," Xander spat before looking back down at his untouched cup of coffee. Finally, unable to stomach the thought —much less the sight—of the sludge, he pushed the cup away. After Stan had chased the pseudo-gods away from the mansion and had woken him up, it had taken a full thermos of enchanted synth-blood to get his injuries healing. While this had seemed abnormally excessive for a few broken bones, lacerations, and burns, Stan had explained that Devin's fire magic was a slow-acting burn that continued to eat away at an object long after the flames had gone out. After hearing this, Xander had downed a second thermos of the foul blood substitute just to be certain. After that much of the horrible tasting vampire cure-all, however, the diner's coffee seemed even more vulgar than usual. It was at that moment that the waitress arrived with the carbon-crusted coffee pot and topped off Stan's emptied mug before turning to leave again. He rolled his eyes again, "Speaking of which…"

"Still not a coffee drinker, huh?" Stan asked, going about the process of dumping two tiny plastic containers' worth of creamer and five packets' worth of sugar into his cup.

"You're joking, right?" Xander stared at him.

Stan laughed, "Ah yes, the brooding vampire refusing the working-man's lifeblood; how apropos." He hung his hand from a limp wrist and mimicked Bela Lugosi's classic tone, "I never drink… coffee."

"Stan," Xander leaned forward, crossing his arms on the wobbly table, "I just got the shit kicked out of me… on my own clan's turf, no less! I've got a dying tiger who's been looking out for me longer than I've even known about him—since before I was even *born*—back at the clan's mansion; a clan, I should add, that I'm now expected to be the leader of when just last year I could barely handle my own problems! I spent *half* of my twentieth birthday crying into a heaving tiger's mane and the other half ripping through a dozen reinforced sandbags in the gym! I am being dragged into the pits of madness by an unforgiving universe and you… *you* want to bust my balls over a goddam cup of shitty diner coffee?" Xander sneered and knocked Stan's cup over with the back of his hand, not batting an eye or breaking his rock-solid gaze as the contents spilled across and over the edge of the table.

Stan looked down at the mess, taking in the sight of the coffee's flow as it slowed to a steady trickle over the edge of the off-white surface. Then, begrudgingly looking up at Xander with tired-looking eyes, he said, "I'm sorry."

The apology hung in the air a moment as the waitress started towards them.

"Oh my," the well-aged woman cooed, "had ourselves a bit of spill, huh? Let me just get that cleaned up for you before I get'cha a refill." She began to work a stained rag she'd retrieved from the back of her immaculate apron over the tabletop. Xander frowned, watching as the woman worked more to mop the mess over the edge of the table and all over the floor than to actually soak up the mess, and he made no effort to hide his actions as he drew his feet away from the growing puddle on the floor. "Are you ready to order anything, or is it just going to be coffee for now?"

Stan's apology echoed in his eyes a moment longer before he nodded to the woman, his gaze shifting to her own and her body going ramrod straight as it did. "I'll have the 'bac-on-and-on-and-on' omelet—extra bacon—and a side of lightly toasted rye with extra butter, please. Oh, and if I bat my eyelashes real nice-like would you ask the chef to add some jalapenos to that omelet?"

The waitress stared for a moment, seeming to have a hard time with something. "S-sure… let me just… just finish with this spill…"

Stan raised an eyebrow, "What spill, miss?"

"Why *this* spill of cou—" the waitress looked down at the table, her shrill voice cutting short as she saw that the table was completely spotless save for a small ring of coffee several inches from Stan's upright and still-filled mug. Stepping back, the woman gaped at the immaculate floor and stood, blinking, for a long moment. "I… I could've sworn…"

"Long shift, huh, Lorraine?" Stan offered.

The woman's eyes—wide and nervous—rocketed to his. "H-how do you know my name?" she demanded.

Stan blinked at her as he took a sip of his coffee. Setting the cup down with a steady hand, he nodded once towards the waitress' chest, "It's on your name tag."

The woman—Lorraine—looked down, a healthy blush beginning to spread across her jowls, as she let out a forced chuckle. "Oh… oh yes, of course," she shook her head. "Yes, I guess it *has* been a long shift."

Stan smiled and nodded, "I'll tell you what, Lorraine, why don't you put another coffee on the bill and treat yourself to a cup on me, alright?"

"Oh… why thank you, sir! Thank you so much!" the waitress' eyes lit up at that and she smiled, looking over at Xander. "And what can I get for you, young man?"

Xander looked up at her and tried not to laugh as she flinched at the sight of his previously hidden right eye. Before he could open his mouth, however, Stan spoke up once again:

"He'll have a plate of those beautiful pancakes I keep seeing floating around. I gotta say, it really says something about this place's pancakes to be moving so many stacks even in the afternoon," he lingered a moment before pretending to suddenly notice Xander's eye. "Oh, I'm sorry; that must seem like an awful fright out of context. My nephew here is an up-and-coming actor and he's recently landed a role as a vampire warrior-type thing—pretty dreadful stuff, I know, but a job's a job, right?—and that contact lens is just such a bother to keep taking out that he's taken to just keeping it in between shoots."

"O-oh…" the waitress stared a moment longer before offering a complimentary smile. "Well isn't that just the bee's knees at a hundred degrees? An actor! How exciting!" She jotted down the order in her pad, giving another "thank you" to Stan, and then hurrying off to drown her apparent insanity in cheap, burnt caffeine.

Staring in disbelief at Stan, Xander felt his head begin to shake. "Tell me you aren't drinking that coffee after it's been on the floor," he stifled a gag.

"What? You think I can't filter out any of the unwanted stuff?" Stan rolled his eyes and made a note of taking a longer sip, "It's *magic*, Xander! This ain't just picking up dropped food off the—"

"Whatever, man," Xander looked away. "You can enjoy your boot-brew without telling me about it."

Stan sighed and shook his head, "Look, I'm sorry about everything that's happening, okay? I really didn't know, least of all about Trepis…"

Xander looked down at the mention of his tiger friend.

"Any idea how much longer he has?" Stan asked.

Xander shrugged. "We're surprised he's held on this long, honestly. I've been trying to find a way to replicate the process that Sensei used to keep him young for as long as he did, but nobody can figure it out."

"Sensei *was* something special, Xander," Stan nodded, "I mean, he was one of the oldest vampires I'd ever met, and he…"

Xander rubbed his eye and moved to rest his head against his palm, "And he looked like a preteen, I know. He obviously had some sort of, I don't know, auric trick or something; some kind of healing touch that kept the two of them from aging, but…" he choked on the beginnings of a sob and hid it by clearing his throat, "But since he's died the time must've started catching up on the big, furry bastard."

Stan offered a sympathetic smile, "It's tough, I know, but you're handling it a lot better than you would've only a few short years ago."

Xander scoffed, "What? When I was a suicidal little shit?" He rolled his eyes, "Yeah, *there's* a proud source point to gauge from."

"Actually, Xander, it *is*," Stan smirked. "You realize that a lot of people that find themselves at that point can't boast any sort of growth for obvious reasons."

"So—what?—I should be fine that the world's taking a steaming shit on me just because I'm not presently food for the worms?" Xander grumbled.

Stan shrugged, "I'd say being shit on is better than being worm shit, wouldn't you? I understand that it's a stressful time, and I certainly haven't showed up with the gladdest tidings on your birthday—not unless you want to view those four superhuman psychopaths as some sort of demented present—but it says something that you have a friend like Trepis who's meant *this* much to you, or that you've proven yourself strong and capable enough to be trusted by The Council to carry on your father's legacy to this extent. You *do* realize that less than one percent of the mythos population gets to boast the sort of role you've earned in only *two* years, Xander? There are vampires out there who are *hundreds* of years old who are still serving as *warriors*; they're answering to their own clan leaders while you— you, Xander Stryker—*are* a clan leader! Everyone has their moments in their own pit of madness, believe me on that, but your pit is on a goddam *mountain* that you've built from the ground-up from *less* than nothing! Just look what you've turned that mansion into after half-a-year! Place looks better than it ever did!"

Xander smirked and shook his head, "All this time and you're *still* acting like my guidance counselor?"

"I'll stop when your ass stops needing guidance *and* counseling," Stan smirked and took another sip of his coffee. "Damn that's tasty," he added, winking, "must be the boot."

Xander rolled his eyes, "I'm in no mood for your guidance *or* your counseling. I want to know who those four are and how I can kick their asses."

Stan frowned and shook his head, "No, Xander, this is not your fight to concern yourself with. One way or the other I need to deal with this on my—"

"I'm going to stop you right there," Xander held up a hand. "Whether you want to call it a mistake or fate or just you being a dumb bastard, those guys showed up on *my* property and beat the crap out of me—nearly blew my ass up with my own damn guns!—and I'm not just going to consider that a lesson learned and walk away from it."

Stan rolled his eyes, "No. I suppose you wouldn't, would you?"

"Watch it," Xander narrowed his eyes. "You've got some sarcasm showing."

"I'd hope so. I layered it on extra thick just for you," Stan shook his head and offered another fake smile as the waitress came with their food. "Lorraine! How was the coffee break?"

"Haven't had a chance to appreciate it yet, doll. I wanted to get these plates out to you while they were still piping hot. Another coffee for yourself?"

"Oh yes, please," Stan beamed, holding out his cup.

The waitress set down the omelet in front of Stan before filling his mug again. Then, turning back to her tray, she pulled a plate of pancakes and made an exaggerated note of putting them in front of Xander.

"And for the big, famous actor!"

Stan smiled, "Wow! Just look at those, kiddo!"

Xander glared at him, "Call me 'kiddo' and I'll stab you in the balls with my fork."

Lorraine gasped.

Stan laughed and shook his head, "You'll have to excuse him, Lorraine. He's one of them method actors and he really immersed himself in this whole bad-boy routine. I assure you he's a total sweetheart of a man when the makeup and prosthetics come off."

"Yeah…" the waitress turned away and scooped up the tray and stand. "Right."

Seeing the plate of pancakes in front of him, Xander shot Stan a look. "How am I supposed to eat these?"

"What? No True Blood to pour on those?" Stan offered a coy grin after shoveling a steaming bite of omelet in his mouth, "Oh well, guess you're going to have to settle for maple syrup!"

Xander sighed and, abandoning his own reluctance, drowned the plate in front of him in syrup before taking a bite. "So who are those guys?"

Stan shook his head, realizing that Xander wasn't about to

drop his pursuit. "Devin was the first of them. He was a total monster even before he got it, but once he *did* get them he decided that they'd be best used to create total havoc across the globe. Problem is, for whatever reason—whether it's because he sees me as somebody who could stop him or maybe just as somebody who could compete with him—he decided that he needed to kill me first; to claim the title as the only one like us."

Xander frowned, "But he travels with *three* others just like him?"

Stan shook his head, "Near as I can tell they're just manufactured lackeys. The Power that exists in them doesn't originate from the same source as mine or Devin's, so I'm pretty sure he just gave them their power by sectioning off a bit of his own, which is saying something since his powers were improperly obtained in the first place."

Xander took another bite, unable to take his eyes off Stan. "Improperly obtained? How's that?"

"Well, I received The Power as a gift. The Source extended them in their entirety. Devin's, on the other hand, were taken, and the quality of The Power is lost when you treat it that way. Kind of like if you're given a glass trophy; mine was offered to me on a satin pillow where his was yanked from a cracked-open vault. It's chipped and jagged and..." Stan shrugged, "Well, it's *wrong.*"

"So he's weaker then?" Xander asked, "And his lackeys are even weaker than that, right?"

"Well, kind of... but no. Not really," Stan sighed and set down his fork. "It's more complicated than that."

Xander shook his head, "Bullshit, man! You said it yourself: Devin's powers are 'wrong' and those others got their powers from *him.* That means they aren't as powerful as you!"

"It's not that cut-and-dry, Xander," Stan argued. "Just because God is stronger than the devil doesn't mean that the devil isn't more powerful."

"And what the hell is that supposed to mean?"

Stan shook his head. "It doesn't matter. You wouldn't understand."

"Now *that's* just rude," Xander glared. "I get your example—a righteous god can't be as powerful as a malicious devil if there's certain lines that the god can't cross; heard it before!—but what does that have to do with *you*, Stan? You're not some do-good god; you have every bit the capability to be an asshole as that psycho, so I say the playing field's pretty level. So what's the deal?"

"It doesn't matter," Stan repeated.

"It matters to me!" Xander growled at him.

"Xander, you have to understand, these were evil people when they were still human! There are boundaries I can't cross that they won't hesitate to, and that gives them the upper hand."

Frowning at that, Xander leaned forward. "What kind of boundaries are we talking about?"

"Human life, for one," Stan shook his head. "As long as I'm a sympathizer who won't stoop so low as to burn down an entire building and kill hundreds, they have a weapon against me. And unless you've decided to stop giving a crap about others— which, pardon the assumption, I don't think is very fucking likely—then I'd say it's a weapon against you, too. Past that, there's a matter of raw numbers, Xander; no matter how you look at it it's four of them against me."

"So let's focus on the worst-case scenario here," Xander kept his voice low, but the irritation in it still managed to make Stan shiver, "in this pussy-world you've built around yourself, what happens after Devin's killed you? You think that he's suddenly going to grow a righteous bone like you and *not* make as many people as inhumanly possible suffer? Isn't it worth it to be willing to let a few hundred suffer rather than giving him the freedom to massacre thousands or even millions?"

Stan shrugged and let out a heavy sigh, "At that point it wouldn't really matter."

"Why? Cuz you'll already be dead? Nice plan! 'It's too tough to be the good guy when you're breathing, so how 'bout I take the easy way out,' right? Let yourself get snuffed out of the picture so you can't be remembered for *not* being the good guy, but still fuck the rest of us in the process! Great plan, ass-wipe! So tell me, just what kind of destruction will these bastards be capable of once you're not around to distract them?"

Stan's eyes sank down to his partially eaten omelet.

Xander sneered, "You selfish son of a bitch! And you've got the balls to call me on at least *trying*."

Stan rubbed his temples, "You've got to believe me when I say I didn't mean for them to come here!"

"Then you were selfish *and* stupid!" Xander snapped, pointing his fork in Stan's direction. "You've got all this fucking power and you use it to turn off your brain when some real bad shit comes your way? These motherfuckers have the same powers as you *and* they're willing to use them to kill people in some fucked up pursuit to be seen as *gods* and your first thought is 'I should run around like a chicken with my head cut off until they finally fry my ass, at which point it'll all be okay 'cause I won't have to see all the feathers fly'? Seriously, Stan, what the fuck is wrong with you?"

"Xander," Stan's voice was desperate and pleading, "there's *nothing* that can be done!"

"Oh, please!" Xander rolled his eyes, "That's just the lie you've convinced yourself of so that you can keep up feeling sorry for yourself since *nothing* is what you've dedicated your-self to doing! Grow a damn pair, already! I've watched you do the impossible before, so don't sit there and tell me that you've got nothing."

Stan stared at him for a moment. "Wow... you really have matured."

Xander shook his head and pulled himself from the booth, yanking his wallet out of the inner pocket of his jacket and tossing a fifty-dollar bill on the table. "I guess one of us had to."

THE OLD BRASS bell on the diner's door rattled violently as Xander slammed his way through it and stepped out into the sunny afternoon. Almost instantly, his vampire body began reacting to the waves of UV assaulting his radiation-sensitive skin. While having skin that could detect a source of heat was normally a convenience while hunting and, on several occasions, had offered him a bit of an advantage in battle, it ultimately represented an example of evolution taking one happy step forward and two aggressive steps back; effectively rendering the ability—and the vampire wearing the skin—almost entirely useless during the day. While it wasn't quite as dramatic or permanent as the explosive reaction Hollywood had cashed in on, it was definitely an inconvenience and, if one was stupid enough to ignore the burning *and* the growing irritation for long enough, still very fatal. The burning itch that plagued every exposed inch of flesh reminded him of the still-lingering agony of Devin's magic and he growled at both the sensation and the memory. For the time being, however, Xander figured having a little extra anger in his voice would prove useful.

Pulling out his phone, he opened his contacts and selected Sawyer's cell number.

The head of the Trepis Clan's warrior task force answered on the third ring.

"It's still sunny out," the groggy voice complained.

"I know," Xander growled, "I'm standing in the middle of it."

"Well," Sawyer's voice perked up quick, "I suppose that

would explain why you sound like you're ready to drop-kick a newborn."

"Like a game-winning field goal punt, I assure you," Xander added, glancing over his shoulder and seeing Stan offering his pleasantries to their waitress as he started to leave.

"So to what do I owe the honor?" Sawyer pressed.

Xander cleared his throat, "I'm guessing you've already heard about the mansion's 'guests' earlier today, right?"

"I stayed awake long enough to make sure you were still breathing and got a look at the half-assed file that was written up." Sawyer sighed, "I'm guessing that last part was your handiwork?"

Xander flipped his middle finger at the receiver of the phone. "Yeah, I'm a real fucking slacker. Especially after I get mind-fucked back into diapers and blasted through a wall."

There was a long pause, then, "Oh god, that hole was made *by* you? I mean, I figured you'd made it *somehow*, but you actually went *through* the wall."

"Still think that file was half-assed?" Xander growled.

"No way, man! Not now that I know that the other half of your ass must be hanging off the side of the damn building!" Sawyer laughed.

Xander stayed quiet.

Sawyer's laughter dried up soon after. Xander heard the warrior clear his throat, "So what's up?"

Xander rolled his eyes and silently asked himself when he'd start being taken seriously. "I need security and surveillance doubled on the grounds ASAP. My friend—our newest guest—created some sort of force field that *should* keep those other four out, but they're still a major threat to the rest of the city and I don't need them rousing up any other crazies around here."

"Definitely got plenty of crazies around here to stir up, too," Sawyer agreed. "Now you said that force field 'should' keep them out. I hope you don't take this the wrong way, boss, but that sounds pretty uncertain, and when we're talking about the sort of guys that can throw you through the side of our building I begin to cringe at uncertainty."

"I can't much blame you for that," Xander sighed, sitting on a bench beside a concrete ashtray with a beaten sign that read **BUTT OUT** in faded letters. Glaring at the sign for a moment, the increasingly irritated vampire tore it from the concrete and crushed it in his palm. Tossing the crumpled metal into the over-mulched garden lining the front of the diner, he focused back on the call: "My friend said that the magic should work to keep them out for the next few days, but he made it real clear that these guys aren't pussies. If they want to get in, they'll get in."

"What's the best guess on that shield then?" Sawyer asked.

Xander laughed at the absurdity of the answer he was forced to recite, "A few days—tops."

The bell over the diner's door chimed and Xander felt Stan's auric signature draw nearer from behind him.

Sawyer shared in the laugh, "Lovely."

"Ain't it though," Xander nodded. "So I'm hoping we can track the fuckers down first. If we can get a handle on them, we can go at them with everything we've got and make them nothing more than a bad memory and a worse stain."

"I like the way you think, boss-man," Xander could tell from Sawyer's voice that he was already getting ready to put the plan into action. "I'll put the call out for the added manpower around the mansion and redirect our warriors before they head out tonight."

"Thanks, Sawyer. And tell Estella I shouldn't be out too much longer if you see her before I do."

"Can and will do. Over and out," the head warrior killed the line before Xander could taunt him over his typical closing.

"There's nothing that they can do," Stan called out as Xander put away his phone. "Even if you're warriors got lucky and tracked them down, there's no way they'd survive against them."

Xander didn't bother turning away as he eyeballed the ratty ashtray of spent butts with envy. Though his body was incapable of being addicted to nicotine—or any other human drug for that matter—he was suddenly aching for a cigarette. "At least one of us is doing something."

Stan stood over him, blocking the sun's rays. "Even if that something means sending your clan's members to be slaughtered?"

"Why should that matter?" Xander shrugged and stood, jamming his hands into his pockets. "After you're done letting them kill you it won't be your problem who dies, remember?"

Pushing past his friend, Xander started for the black and red 1980 Firebird they'd taken to get there, eager to be behind the wheel and, even more pressing on his mind, behind the tinted, UV-blocking windows. Stan followed after, climbing into the passenger seat and looking over at Xander as he started the car.

"Xander, I'm serious," Stan pressed on, "these guys are *dangerous*! Your warriors—no matter how many or how strong they are—*will not* be able to handle them. You're ordering them into a suicide run if you do this."

Xander frowned and looked over, scowling, "You want me to call off the order then?"

Stan nodded.

"I do this," Xander pulled out his phone once again and held it up to emphasize his point, "and you find your balls. I mean it, Stan, they can't be allowed to run rampant and you can't be allowed to wuss-out like this. I call off my warriors, and you'd better work with me on figuring out a way to take those assholes down. Got it?"

Stan bit his lip, but, after a long pause, nodded. "Deal."

7

RISING TENSION

*X*ander found Estella in the lower level with Trepis. Lingering in the doorway, he watched with a heavy heart as his lover ran her small palm over the tiger's black-and-white fur. On any other day—when Trepis had been in his prime—the sight of Estella's delicate hand on the powerful creature's side would've elicited a tender and awe-inspiring vision of power and beauty. At that moment, however—with Trepis so clearly weak and exhausted in his condition and Estella's vampiric rigidity making her look like every bit the mythos warrior she'd become—the impact of the sight was inverted and sullied with the lingering tragedy of what was coming.

Fighting the growing lump in his throat, Xander stepped through the doorway and took a knee beside Estella, letting his hand move to Trepis' head.

A silent moment passed between them as the tiger's blue eyes opened and shifted to see whose hand it was feeling. Though he was weak in his advanced aging, Trepis' blue-green aura spiked with excitement at the sight of Xander, and his heavy tail shook for a moment before achieving a single, futile

wag and then thudding back to the cushioned surface they'd
laid out below him.

"Take it easy, buddy," Xander offered a weak smile and
continued to pat his friend's head.

Estella looked up at him, her own eyes already shimmering
with tears. She made a note of wiping the moisture away before
she asked, "Is everything okay?"

"Aside from the obvious?" Xander shrugged and, immediately after, sighed. "Sorry..." he looked down at the tiger,
admiring the pattern of his stripes as he thought about how to
structure his words to keep from worrying Estella. "I'm... I'm
going to help Stan fight those guys; those wannabe gods."

Estella frowned. "Sawyer said that something was going on
with that. He told me that you'd ordered a full-scale search and
then, right after, called off the order altogether?" Looking up at
Xander, her orange aura shifted with concern—bubbling and
collapsing like Trepis' labored breaths—"Just what's going on,
Xander?"

"They're just..." Xander shrugged, "Those guys are more
than the warriors can handle. It's not a normal job and I
shouldn't have put them on the front line like I did." He looked
up at her, "This is the sort of job that a clan leader needs to
handle."

Estella sighed, "You'd better be careful."

Xander forced a smirk, "Come on, look who you're talking
to."

Estella shot him a look, "Why do you think I said it?"

Xander chewed his lip and shrugged a shoulder, "Good
point."

"Still no change?" Stan's voice chimed in from the doorway,
and both Xander and Estella looked back, startled.

"Son of a—" Xander shook his head. "How is it that you can
sneak up on us like that?"

Stan shrugged, stepping in. "Heart rate can be slowed with

meditation—same with breathing—and my aura only shows when I want it to and only to those I want it to show to."

Xander gave him a look, "Oh yeah? And what about your footsteps, Mister Wizard? Care to explain how you magically hide your footsteps? What, do you float? Or maybe you disrupt the sound waves before they reach our ears, is that it? Or is it some unfathomable enchantment that I'd never even consider?"

Stan raised an eyebrow, "I don't stomp my feet and I buy comfortable shoes."

Xander stared up at him and shook his head, "You're a dick, Stan."

"Guess that makes the both of us," Stan countered as he kneeled down in front of Trepis. "Long time, old friend," his voice was gentle and slow as he ran the pad of his thumb over the tiger's muzzle, "still a fighter, I see. Have you not lived a long and satisfying enough life? What are you holding on for?"

Estella bit her lip, "Can he understand you?"

Stan nodded, "He can. Not the words so much—those I just say for my own benefit and for anybody around—but the message carries through the mind. Anything alive can recognize another's condition, it's just a matter of knowing how to inquire and, after that, how to listen."

Xander sighed, "So you can't empathize with another human being for shit, but you can have an in-depth, existential conversation with a big cat?"

"People bore me," Stan shrugged. "They're simple and savage and, even *with* the benefit of speech, they're stupid. I'd sooner converse with something noble."

"Good idea," Xander glared. "Maybe you'll *learn* something!"

Stan looked down at Trepis as the tiger let out a heavy sigh and curled its left paw against Xander's knee. Pursing his lips and rubbing his left eye, he stood and nodded, "Maybe I will."

Xander stared up at Stan, dumbfounded. "What?" he asked, "Did Trepis actually answer?"

Stan nodded, "He did."

Estella looked up at that. "What did he say?"

Stan cleared his throat and scratched the back of his head. "He said…"—another pause to clear his throat—"He said that he's not ready to leave Xander."

The room went silent as the three lingered on that.

Xander shook his head, glaring down at Trepis. "Me? You're letting yourself suffer like this because of *me*?" he growled and gave the tiger's side a gentle shove. "Wh-why would…" He shook his head, "Stupid fucking cat! You never did know what was best for you!"

"Xander…" Estella's voice was like the twist of a knife between his ribs, and he was on his feet and through the door before her raised hand could touch down on his shoulder.

THREE CYCLES around the mansion did little to calm Xander's nerves, though it did help to dry up the well of tears that had threatened to spill down his face. Embarrassment and pride kept him from going back to Estella and Trepis to apologize, and a lingering sense of respect kept him from going back to Stan and punching him in the face. Though he'd been eager to know what—if anything—had been keeping Trepis hanging on despite all the discomfort, he could've gone the rest of his extended lifetime and a dozen more like it without feeling guilt like that.

Trepis was staying for *him*?

The idea hurt him more every time he repeated it to himself.

He'd been struggling to find a way to relieve the tiger's suffering, and all the while it had been struggling on his behalf; forcing itself to hold on for his sake.

How could he fix something like that?

It was too much to take…

Too goddam much!

"What the hell am I going to do?" Xander sighed.

"Talking to yourself again, boss-man?" Sawyer's voice echoed down the hall as the warrior started towards him.

Xander let out a breath and fought the last of his lingering emotions into submission, not wanting one of the clan's strongest warriors to see him in such disarray. Even when he'd first met him in the previous December, the sang was, in almost every possible way, Xander's opposite. Rigid and perpetually immaculate—his finely tailored fashion sense and finishing school posture making him come off almost like the clan's butler; an ongoing joke that he hated—he was the sort of fighter who strove to make as few moves as possible and to have what moves he did make go farther than any other option. This ongoing effort to strive for perfection in all things had been something of an abrasive counter to Xander's "keep moving and don't stop until they're dead"-approach that had the two at one another's throats from the moment they'd met. However, when Sawyer's clan had been destroyed and he'd been left, like Xander the previous year, without a home or a comrade, they'd discovered their potential as colleagues. With Estella and a ragtag group of homeless mythos by their side, they'd tracked down the ones responsible for Sawyer's loss. When the dust had settled and Xander had been brought back from death, the decision to rebuild the late Odin Clan was made and Sawyer, having more than proven himself fitting of the role, was brought on as one of their best fighters.

"Sawyer," Xander felt his throat tighten and he coughed before going on, "I hope you've got some good news for me."

Sawyer shrugged, "I don't have any *bad* news, if that's what you're asking."

"Good. I'm not sure I could handle anymore bullshit," Xander forced a laugh, but it came out nervous.

"Speaking of 'bullshit'…" Sawyer scowled.

Xander frowned, worried that Sawyer could see past his efforts to hide his pain. "Yes...?"

"Well, I hope you'll pardon me for saying so," Sawyer paused and cleared his own throat, "but the other warriors and I have been wondering why you called off the orders to hunt down the intruders from the other night."

Xander felt his face go hot under the pressing issue and he wet his suddenly dried lips. "It's... it's complicated, Sawyer; *really* complicated."

Sawyer's face was like a marble statue as he stared at the clan leader, "Try me."

Xander looked away, unable to maintain eye contact. "Look: the intruder from the other night... he's... well, he's dangerous. And it's not just him; there are others."

"Yeah, I know; I read the file, remember?" Sawyer shook his head, "But I can't help but feel that this *deserves* our attention, and I think that the decision to call it off has something to do with that strange friend of yours."

Xander couldn't help but laugh at that. "Well, you're not wrong. But the decision stands for the time being. Until I know more there's nothing we can do just yet, and I don't want to send a bunch of our warriors into the street on a potential suicide mission."

Sawyer scowled at that. "That's not true! We could be out there looking for them! We could be learning what they're capable of! So you don't want us to engage them? Fine! We'll just collect intel, but we've got to at least be doing *something*!"

Xander sighed and nodded, "And nothing would make me happier than to feel comfortable seeking that intel, but these aren't the kind of guys you just sneak up on. They *will* know they're being watched; they *will* figure out who's watching them, and they *will* take great pleasure in killing them, all the time *knowing* that they'd be driving us to throw more potential casualties at them. The truth is that they're far more powerful than anything you or the others have ever faced—I've personally seen what their capable of, and you'll notice how *not* eager I am to see it again—and until we know for sure how to fight them I don't want to risk lives. Besides, we have something they want, so it won't be long before they've smashed through that enchantment at the gates and we'll have our chance; whether we want it or not."

Sawyer narrowed his eyes, "Then—what?—we just sit around and do nothing until they crash through our walls *again?*"

Xander sighed, "Hopefully we'll know how to deal with them before that time comes."

Sawyer scoffed, "The leader of one of the most powerful mythos organizations in the world is running on *hope!*" He shook his head and turned away, "I'm sure your father would've done something!"

Xander snarled and lunged. Though Sawyer was skilled, Xander hadn't earned his title by missing his marks, and as the clan's head warrior spun to evade Xander's attack he was caught under the jaw with Xander's forearm as the clan's leader pinned him against the wall; using his free hand to hold Sawyer's right arm while his aura anchored his other limbs. The two vampires hissed in each other's faces and Xander felt his fangs begin to extend from the challenge.

"And *what*, pray tell," Xander kept his voice low and steady despite the rage flooding through him, "do you think that my father would do?"

"How should I know? He wasn't my old man; I didn't know him!" Sawyer spat, his voice forced around Xander's forearm, "But I do know he wouldn't have pussy-footed around it."

Xander stared at him for a long moment before finally letting him go and turning away, shaking his head. "Well I didn't know him either..." he sighed and leaned against the opposite wall, looking over. "So what would you do?"

Rubbing at his neck, Sawyer frowned at the question. "*If* it were up to me, I'd have the entire clan out there hunting these fucks down and putting the fear back into them."

Xander nodded slowly. "I like the idea, but the execution..." he sighed and let his head fall back against the wall. "Just what are *gods* afraid of?"

Sawyer mirrored Xander's sigh. "I guess that's the *real* problem to solve, isn't it?"

8
GAME OVER

"Xander! So good to see you, bro! It's been too... Hey! What the fuck, man? Where are you going?" The Gamer wheezed and shambled after Xander after he'd shouldered through the back door of the videogame shop. "Hello? Talk to me, man! What's this about? You're not bitter that I'm not moving into the mansion, are you?"

The Gamer lived a double life; triple if one counted his compulsive video gaming. During the day he ran the self-proclaimed "greatest" gaming shop in the area, a simple-yet-bold statement considering it was also one of the *only* in the area. At night, however, he traded in his consoles and twelve-sided dice for a real set of spell books, enough advanced weaponry and enchanted ammunition to take out an army, and a bulk case of Hot Pockets.

At that moment, however, sporting some ratty sweatpants over a new-looking pair of lime-green Crocs and a "WHO FARTED" tee-shirt and clutching a Monster Java in his hand, The Gamer looked neither like a video game geek nor like a powerful, weapons-dealing wizard...

"You look ridiculous," Xander shook his head and started

down the steps towards The Gamer's workshop in the basement.

"I look… are you fucking kidding me? Scab-chewing little shit!" he cursed under his breath—already labored with the task of trying to keep up with Xander—and started down the stairs. "Do you think I was expecting company tonight?"

"You work with mythos, dude," Xander looked over his shoulder. "I have a feeling it's *that* business that keeps that nerd hatchery in the front open. By the way, I hear they're opening a Game Stop a few blocks from here."

"What?" The Gamer growled, "Those turf-hopping drama dealers! Don't they have enough with their little lend-lease pro—"

"Much as I love watching you work yourself up into a frothy lather, can you hold back the heart attack for a little bit?" Xander sighed as he reached the bottom of the steps and looked up after him, "There's some shit going down."

The Gamer, as he usually did when Xander proved that the need to get straight to business was at hand, stopped himself in mid-rant and got down to business. "What kind of shit?"

Xander smiled, appreciating the man's work ethic. "Stan's back and—"

"Stan? Wait… when did he get here? How's he—"

Xander rolled his eyes; so much for straight to business. "There's others—like him—out to get him."

The Gamer stared in disbelief "Others…?"

"Like him," Xander nodded.

"I thought he was the only one," The Gamer mused, descending the remaining stairs. "I never would've imagined…"

"Well start imagining it, big boy," Xander rolled his eyes, "Because they're real and there's four of them and they're here to take him!"

The Gamer shrugged, "Fair enough. So what do you want from me?"

Xander paused, considering what he was about to ask and did a quick sweep of the room; dread and uncertainty beginning to set in. "Don't suppose you've got anything that can take them out?"

The Gamer laughed, "Take out something like Stan? Yeah right! You ever met anyone who made boxing gloves to punch out God?"

"I didn't come here to joke around!" Xander growled, "And if that's what you're in the mood for I got a *great* one about a fat bastard that got rolled up and down Main Street by a pissed off vampire."

"You think I'm joking, Xander?" The Gamer waved his hands around the room, "Look around you! I make magical weapons; fan-*fucking*-tastic ones! But there is nothing—fucking *nothing*!—in my arsenal or *any* arsenal *anywhere* that could put a dent in somebody like Stan; let alone *four* somebodies like him!"

Xander sighed, "Look, I didn't want to tell you this, but one of them—the leader—blew your pistols up."

For a long moment The Gamer just stood and stared, mouthing the words "my pistols" over and over before his eyes widened, "Oh my... the Yin and Yang tributes? Oh no..." He bit his lip sadly, "Those were... well, they *were* obsolete, but still... they were—"

"Obsolete?" Xander glared at him, "What the hell is that supposed to mean?"

The Gamer scoffed and shook his head, plopping himself down on his workbench. "You think I'm as good as I am because I took excessive pride in the first weapons I made and never strove to do better? Shit, Xander, do you know how many pieces I've made based on your daddy's revolvers since the day they were first brought in to me?"

Xander bared his fangs at him. "And when were you planning to tell me about this?"

The Gamer shrugged, "I figured you'd show up needing new firepower and—"

"I'm here *now* asking for firepower!" Xander snarled, grabbing The Gamer by the shirt.

With a wave of his hand, Xander's grip was forced open as the muscles in his arms went numb and The Gamer pushed him back. "Fuck you, fang-face! Don't lay another hand on me or I'll melt your pecker from between your knees, you hear me? You came in here asking for something that could *kill* somebody like Stan, and I'm telling you that *that* ain't a request for firepower; that's coming to me for a *miracle!*"

Xander frowned down at his still-numb hands and shook his arms to return the sensation to them. "Okay... so what would you call magic if not a miracle?"

"I call it advanced science, Xander," The Gamer sat back again, crossing his arms in front of his chest, "and you're asking me to use some very good advanced science against an enemy who is *defined* by exponentially greater advanced science! A magnifying glass can cook an anthill and all the ants will believe it's the most destructive magic they've ever seen. But try holding that exact same magnifying glass up to a gorilla and see what they think of it."

"So what are we supposed to do?"

"Shit if I know! Can't Stan do something about it?"

Xander groaned and shook his head, "He's goddam useless with this. He actually tried to feed me some shit about how they're stronger than him even though he *also* told me that they're weaker."

"Whoa! Weaker?" The Gamer leaned forward in his chair, "So they're not *exactly* like Stan then? What aren't you telling me exactly?"

Xander shrugged. "Stan says that the ringleader of the group didn't do something right in getting his power. Except this guy's, like, totally batshit insane, so he wound up doing something wrong and came out of it even *more* batshit insane. So he's some sort of warped copy of Stan, and since he's the one giving the other three their own powers, they're pretty much starting out the gate imperfect."

"So why go after Stan?" The Gamer asked, "They got The Power and all, why waste their time chasing him?"

"Stan told me that they were after him to take his powers. I guess the leader of these psychos is hell-bent on being the only one," Xander explained.

The Gamer smirked and nodded, "I get it. Like the Highlander."

"The what?" Xander frowned.

The Gamer rolled his eyes and mumbled "goddam kids" before sighing and shaking his head. "Whatever. So this one guy jacks up a bunch of losers to give him the fighting edge to take on Stan so he can take his powers for himself. So why did he come to you?"

"He told me he was afraid—go figure; *the* Stan... *afraid!*—and that he came to the mansion because it was the one place he felt safe the last time he was afraid," Xander sighed and looked over, "Hard to swallow, isn't it?"

The Gamer seemed lost in thought as he nodded, "When he first met your father and Depok... yeah, I remember that story."

"Right..." Xander spotted a loose bullet casing on the table nearby and picked it up to fidget with it; rolling it between his fingers as he went on. "But I'm not sure what he expects me to do for him at this point. These guys are out of our league—I mean, shit, they're practically out of *his* league!—and he just showed up at our doorstep like we'd suddenly have all the answers."

The Gamer shrugged and turned around in his chair, thumbing through a few notebooks as he spoke, "He probably figured that, after all your success stories, you'd be able to figure something out." He scoffed and paused to look over his shoulder, "Though, no offense, I personally wouldn't give you *that* much credit."

"Thanks for the vote of confidence, asshole," Xander sighed and shook his head. "But, in this case, I can't say that you're wrong. Even if there *was* some way around all this, I've had too much on my plate to be of much use to anyone."

"To be fair, Stan *was* once a normal guy. Well, normal as normal can be, I suppose," The Gamer pointed out, shrugging. "Maybe we're looking too far into this? Maybe it really is as simple as him being scared and looking for some familiar faces."

Xander shook his head. "No, that doesn't seem right, either. You've got a point about him being... well, *human*, but..." he scratched his jaw with the bullet casing, trying to get a hold on his thoughts before he spoke them. "Scared or not, he was always one for plans and logistics above all else. If the stories I've heard are true, he was sort of a chicken-shit even as a human—ran from home and whatnot—but it was never for nothing, you know. He wouldn't just go somewhere without some sort of plan. But then why wouldn't he just have put that plan into action from the get-go?" He sighed, "Or at the very least *tell* me about it?"

"Maybe because he decided it wasn't a good plan," The Gamer pointed out. "Maybe it had something to do with you and he changed his mind. Like, maybe he was thinking of giving The Power to you."

Xander looked over at him, "What? You're saying that *I* could *take* his power?"

"Well, not by force, dipshit! I mean, this *is* Stan we're talking about!" The Gamer laughed and shook his head, finally pulling out a notebook and flipping through the pages. After a moment of scanning the dog-eared pages, he shook his head and put it back; beginning the search anew. "If it were as simple as just having a vampire bite him or drain his psychic energy or something like that, I doubt he'd have held onto his powers for this long. If somebody tries that shit—tries to just jump him to steal his powers—they're gonna get fried. However, if he *wants* to transfer them…" he let the thought trail off and linger on that note.

Xander looked down; it *did* make sense to the situation, but could Stan really have been planning something like that? "Do you really believe that's what Stan had in mind?"

"You're asking me to be his head-shrinker now, too? Fuck! I don't know what he was thinking," the man took a long gulp from his energy drink before setting it down and investing both hands in searching the notebooks. "It's like you said, yourself: he's always been sort of a chicken, Xander. There's no way around that fact. But he's also been one to put others ahead of himself. Maybe he *started* off wanting to ditch The Power. It'd certainly get the ones that are after him *for* those powers to get off his back, and if he puts The Power into somebody like you—somebody not human, I mean—then he'd be pumping up something that was *already* stronger than any of them were before they got juiced-up."

"Do you think something like that would really work?" Xander asked, "Making a non-human even more powerful by moving The Power into them?"

The Gamer's heavy shoulders shifted in an uncomfortable shrug. "I'm not positive, Xander. I'm not an expert in this; not many are with the exception of those *like* Stan and these others. But if what you told me is true and this other guy is just going around *making* more of them, then obviously there's some sort of power lending-slash-moving process happening. So if *that* much is possible, then it stands to reason that the energy could be flat-out transferred. All energy—magical *or* natural—works on the same physics; you can move it around from container to container."

"So why wouldn't he go through with it? If it gets those guys off his back *and* puts The Power into a stronger fighter, then why wouldn't he just—"

"Because Stan's a coward, Xander, *not* an asshole!" The Gamer spun in his chair and gave Xander a look, "*Yes*, Stan would be putting himself in the clear by transferring The Powers, but he'd *also* be painting a target on your ass while doing it. Just look at me! I'm no different than he is; I'm a total chicken-shit loser! Damned proud of it too; I've gotten more high scores with my name on them than anybody within a hundred-mile radius because of it! But I'm not gonna go around squatting a fresh batch of my problems on my friends, either! If I knew that the only way to get some murderous assholes off my tail was to pass some sort of baton over to you even I'd think twice… and keep in mind that I *hate* you!"

Xander forced a sneer at The Gamer's closing quip. "Aren't you a peach; all fat and fluffy like one too." He sighed and started tossing the bullet casing from palm to palm, staring off into the distance as he thought out loud. "So this guy was after the same powers as Stan, and then he succeeds in getting them —sort of—and then decides he doesn't want to share in the glory with anybody else. So, naturally, he tracks down Stan, but he *also* knows that Stan's been using these powers for years; he's smart enough to know that he doesn't stand a chance on his own…"

The Gamer nodded, "Right… so he starts recruiting the others to help him overpower Stan; probably kept his sights on fellow crazies like him who he'd be able to keep under his thumb."

"Crazies who he knew he could control *and* eventually over-power," Xander added. "Stan figures he's planning to kill the three of them himself once everything's finished."

The Gamer nodded, "Makes sense. Hard to be the only one if you're sharing the spotlight with three others."

Xander bit his lip as something occurred to him. "So if this guy takes Stan's powers and then *reclaims* whatever he'd given to the other three, what would he become?"

A shiver rippled through The Gamer as he considered the possibilities as well. "In a word: terrifying."

"I figured. So it's probably a good thing for *everyone* if he doesn't reach that point. So the big question becomes if I'd be able to kill these guys on my own if I *did* have Stan's powers…"

"I can't guarantee that you'd win," The Gamer smirked, "but you'd certainly pose one hell of a threat. Especially to the three that were created."

Xander frowned at that, "And what about the ringleader?"

Another shrug. "I wouldn't be placing any bets one way or the other."

"Why not?" Xander frowned.

The Gamer rolled his eyes, "Because you're speaking of a hypothetical situation wherein Stan just *gives* you The Power! It *can*—from my understanding—be transferred, but Stan is a supercomputer with a virus protection software that will most likely fry you—if not kill you—if you even try to just *take* them. He has to *willingly* open up the connection for these powers to move from him to you—something that he's obviously not too keen on, or he'd have done it by now—and, even then, there's the question of whether or not you'd even be able to handle it!"

"Why wouldn't I be able to handle it?" Xander gave him a look.

The Gamer chortled at that, "You think this is all just a matter of 'here, take this monstrous dose of otherworldly magical power'? This is a sort of magic that most aren't equipped to handle; we're talking insane levels of energy. All of that takes focus and control, both of which you lack in *laughable* ways. Can the energy from one source be placed into another? Sure! But the second source needs to be *capable* of handling that energy! You try and dump a Big Gulp's worth of something into that itty-bitty bullet casing and you've got a mess on your hands. Now imagine that the contents are raw magical energy and that the bullet casing is just a thimble-sized hunk of meat..." He mimicked an explosion and made a splatter gesture with his hands, "Then you got a *bloody* mess on your hands. The difference in this situation is that you're a rather large hunk of meat and there's no guarantee there'd be hands left to get messy. Still... a vampire with that kind of magic. Wow!"

Xander sighed, "Okay. So there are *a lot* of things standing in my way of handling things *that* way. But do we really have any other options? You've already said yourself that there's not too much in the way of weapons for this sort of situation."

"No. No, there aren't many weapons for this sort of situation at all," The Gamer rubbed his eye with the pad of his thumb. "So unless you've got the know-how to invoke your very own power-granting being I'd say your best bet for solutions is Stan."

Xander dwelled on that a moment, trying to map out how a follow-up discussion with Stan on the subject would go and forced himself to stop when he felt himself getting a headache. Finally, letting out an unsatisfied sigh, he nodded to The Gamer for his input, "Right. Thanks anyway."

The Gamer chewed his lip and shrugged. "I'm sorry I can't be of more help to you, buddy. You know I'm always here when you need me, but some things are just outside of my expertise."

Xander forced a smile and nodded. "I know," he said, then, as a second thought, "As useless as they may be, though, is there any chance I can get some of that new firepower you were telling me about?"

That earned a grin from The Gamer. "Looking for The Gamer to pimp your arsenal once more?"

"Yeah," Xander rolled his eyes and smirked. "Yeah, I guess I am."

∼

THE GAMER SMIRKED to himself as he watched Xander carry the weighted duffle bags filled with new weaponry up the stairs. Though each one of the bags were easily a hundred pounds and he'd struggled to pass them on, the young vampire—still a scrawny brat in his eyes—hoisted each over his shoulders as though they were a set of Hefty bags stuffed with Twinkies. Shrugging away the moment and tossing a bean burrito into the microwave so he'd have something waiting for him when he got back, The Gamer punched in ninety seconds on the old appliance and eyed the crisp-looking blank check that Xander had just cut for him in the Trepis Clan's name before starting after his blood-sucking client.

"You be careful with those, now," he called after him, laughing. "Wouldn't want you blowing your pretty blood-red eye out of your head or anything."

A monotone "HA-HA" echoed down from Xander as he turned the corner and headed for the back door. Before stepping out, Xander set down the bags and turned towards him to offer him a moment of sincerity.

The Gamer sighed. *Those* moments were the ones he despised the most; the taunting moments of "fatass" and "scab-muncher" were safe and cozy for him, as were the more aggressive times when he'd been certain that somebody was going to be bleeding by the end of the exchange. But the calm, quiet, buddy-buddy, "I'm so glad to have you as a friend"-moments were the sort of times that he could barely stomach in the movies, and heaven help the blogging community if he ever had to sit through a cut scene in a video game that he couldn't skip with that sort of cheap, Oscar-reaching garbage oozing out at him. He always swore to himself that "the next time" somebody —didn't matter who; mythos or not—started to have one of those moments with him, he was going to prove that a fat man could throw down.

At that moment, however—the newest case of 'the next

time"—he was staring down Xander Stryker, a vampire warrior who'd washed more *real* blood out of his hair than his level 72 orc warrior did. In fact, The Gamer was pretty confident that Xander, were he to ever leap into the world of D&D, would make short work out of his orc warrior. It was for that reason that—though he'd never admit it—the still-leveling Paladin he'd created a year earlier was based entirely on the young vampire warrior's specs.

It was also for that reason that The Gamer decided that the *next* time somebody started a sincere moment with him would be *the* "next time" when he'd prove that a fat man could throw down.

"Thanks," Xander said, already bringing the moment to peak levels of discomfort, "I know I was a dick earlier, but you've really given me a lot to work with here." He sighed and shook his head, "Just been a really tough couple of months, you know?"

The Gamer forced an understanding smile and mentally counted three gentle bobs of his head—no more; no less—to keep the moment from getting any weirder. "It's no problem," he said, smirking then and trying to shift the tone of the moment, "I'm pretty sure if you *weren't* a dick to me then I'd be pretty worried."

Xander sighed, "Yeah... and that isn't right."

The Gamer frowned. *Damn it all to The Dark World's pit and back again! Make this END!*

"It's alright, Xander," he assured him. "I know it's all just part of our chemistry."

Then he felt them!

The Gamer cleared his throat, "Anyway! You should get going. I've got a video conference with some... um, other gamer-type geeks in a moment—really boring shit; least for, like, a total blood-sucking, douchebag, badass like you—and I don't want to keep them waiting just 'cause I'm too busy talking to your sentimental ass."

Xander frowned at that, "You're kicking me out in the middle of a *real* conversation so you can have an *internet* conversation with a bunch of dweebs."

They were in the house! He didn't know how or where, but there was no denying that they were who Xander had mentioned—four of them; *just* like Stan—and he knew that meant trouble. Xander had just gotten done telling him how he and his entire clan *and* Stan had *nothing* against these guys, and if he stuck around much longer—if they took him out of the fight before the fight had even begun—it'd be over for *a lot* more than just the two of them.

Game over, man, The Gamer thought to himself. *Ultimate game over...*

"Yup," The Gamer started forward to push Xander out the door, "you can hate me about it later; maybe write an angry poem about evil fat men in your little emo diary or whatever. Just *go!*"

Xander growled and pulled away from his efforts to herd him out. Shooting him a blood-stained glare, he straightened out his jacket, retrieved the bags of weapons, and nodded.

"I'll be back soon for some more synth-blood, Gamer. Make sure you pencil that in around your geeky podcasts or whatever."

The Gamer frowned at that, realizing that Xander actually seemed hurt by the dismissal.

Forgive me, my friend.

"Dwayne!" he shouted after the vampire legend, then, realizing that it meant nothing out of context, he cleared his throat and checked to be sure his psychic shields were up. He didn't need to have Xander getting suspicious and probing his mind for potentially deadly reasons to stick around. Then he offered what little sincerity he could, "My name—my real name—is Dwayne Theodore Brinkley... the third. I'm a Pisces, I'm bipolar, my sister died of diabetes when I was eleven and I've been eating myself to death ever since, and the only sex I've ever had has been paid for or over the internet under the username 'JacobsLadder' on Twilight fan forums. The only time I ever felt like I mattered was when people saw my high scores or when I was praised for my magic weapons…" He chewed his lip, looking down; the fear was beginning to take him, but he suddenly felt like he had to say one more thing, "A little over two years ago I was going to kill myself. I was convinced my life was going nowhere and that I'd never amount to anything or be remembered for anything"—he looked up, still fighting the tears, and smiled—"but then an old friend showed up with the most beautiful pair of revolvers I'd ever seen, and a gangly, newly turned vampire-punk showed up to pick them up. And I saw in that little shit's blood-stained right eye a miracle waiting to happen, and I knew that if I stuck around, I could do some really cool things for that arrogant little fucker…"

Xander narrowed his eyes and set down the bags, starting towards him. "Why are you telling me these things?" he asked, shaking his head. "This isn't… you're talking like—" His eyes widened and one of the bags jostled open as Xander's aura went to work pulling a few of the new guns to his hands, "Where are they—AHH! NO! Game—*Dwayne*, stop!"

The young vampire and the two bags hovered in the air a moment as The Gamer worked his magic. He had little time and even less hope at that point.

"Thank you, Xander Stryker," he whispered, though he knew that the vampire's auric mind would receive the message loud and clear. "It's been an honor gaming with you."

"Shit! No!" Xander struggled, and The Gamer felt his aura begin to fight against his magic. "It doesn't have to—dammit! Let me go! I can help! I can fucking heeeEEAAAAAAAAAAHH!"

Xander and the bags flew out the door. The Gamer worried —if for only a moment—that the force he'd used had been too excessive, but nevertheless knowing that Xander would survive it. If there was anything on God's green Earth that *could* kill the son of Joseph Stryker, it wasn't anything that a fat man and his magic could cook up.

But a fat man and his magic *could* keep him safe just long enough to—

The lights flickered in the house—waning between too-bright and too-dim; between bleak and blinding—before dying out completely.

And then they were there; standing in front of The Gamer as though they'd been there all along.

"You're involved with the vampire, I see," the voice was like acid eating through a newborn child; malicious and laced with tainted potential and wasted innocence. "And I imagine that means that you're involved with Stanley Ferno, as well."

"I'm also involved with your mother, bitch-boy," The Gamer shot at the blond man in the trench coat standing several paces ahead of three faceless silhouettes, "and would you tell her I left my wallet on her night sta—"

The air in The Gamer's lungs turned to steam and the wind to fuel his words fizzled to dryness.

"You protect them with vulgarity and insults, I see. A valiant —albeit stupid and pointless—effort. And besides," he stepped closer to the heaving man and stared down at him as he dropped to his knees, "I killed my mother when I was fifteen, so if you have, indeed, been bedding the fermented retch's corpse, I should thank you for finding some sort of use for her in death that she so severely lacked in life."

The black curtain of darkness that was the blond man's coat-wrapped body shifted as he raised a foot and kicked The Gamer onto his back. As the gasping man stared up at the shadow-drowned darkness of his back hall, he watched as four of the shadows writhed and grew; each forming features and limbs that came down upon him.

He clenched his eyes against what was coming, remem-

bering every powerful spell he'd unlocked and every high score
he'd earned.

Game over...

"Stupid son of a bitch!" Xander growled to himself, clutching
at the still-bleeding bullet hole in his side and leaping the chasm
between one rooftop and the next as he pushed himself to move
as quickly as he could back to The Gamer's shop. As soon as his
feet hit the surface he was back in overdrive, crossing the
distance before any potential onlookers could complete the
blink of an eye, before launching himself over yet another
chasm to yet another rooftop. His body was beginning to
scream from the demand of jumping in-and-out of overdrive so
many times. Leap, linger, land; jump into overdrive, jolt across
the laughably short distance to edge, drop out; leap, linger, land.
Over and over; again and again. "Stupid, self-sacrificing"—his
rant cut short as he jumped into overdrive yet again, then the
jump into the air and out of overdrive—"*lying* son of a bitch!"

He turned the chastising inward then, realizing that The
Gamer had sensed the four pseudo-gods in his home earlier on
in their conversation. His efforts to get Xander to leave, his
heartfelt—and uncomfortable—confession; Xander rolled his
eyes—*confessions*. He'd *known* he was about to die, and he
wanted to get Xander out of there before they made their move.

And, in doing so, he'd hurled Xander's body into the sky in a
wide arc that landed him nearly three miles away. Slamming to
the city street in the middle of a gang turf-battle was the least of
his worries then, however. With the startled, curse-spewing
gang members abandoning their mission to kill one another
and harmonizing in their combined terror of the disheveled,
snarling creature that had fallen out of the sky and *not* died.
Several of the cursing kids had tried to remedy that latter

condition by unloading a panic-fueled bullet storm on Xander; only one of which had actually found its mark by puncturing his jacket and grazing his side just below his ribs a moment before he'd snatched up his bags and vanished into overdrive.

Finally, the alley that led to the back lot of The Gamer's shop opened up and, for a fresh change in the pattern that had come to mean everything to him at that moment, beckoned for him to drop down rather than just to leap once more to the next rooftop.

Landing on top of the Hot Pocket and game-wrapper filled dumpster—the loud clatter of impact scaring off several vermin lingering under the giant metal bin—Xander stayed crouched down for a moment to assess the scene. Letting his aura snake from his chest and start a sweep of The Gamer's building, Xander surveyed the scene inside with his mind's eye.

Only The Gamer occupied it.

Though just barely.

Xander was kicking through the door before he'd even had a chance to tell himself to jump from the dumpster—his body beginning to act on instinct alone. He bit his lip as the sound of the door slamming open awakened him to his situation and he shook his head at himself; those sorts of instincts could get him killed.

Just ahead of him was the mangled and still-shaking body of The Gamer, his arms held out in front of him—unable to fall at his sides despite all evidence that they wanted to—and stammering through a mouth that was charred into a permanent, agonizing yawn. Xander was at his side before he'd even had a chance to tell himself to move from the doorway.

Stupid! he chastised the two of them.

"What the hell did they do to you?" he demanded, looking over what remained of The Gamer's body.

Every inch of him was blackened and charred; his limbs trapped in his last twisted moments by the coating of cracked carbon that covered most of his flesh. Whatever remained of his clothes and shoes had been fused to the rest of him. By some strange and terrible twist of fate, however, he wasn't dead. As Xander stared down at the poor magician, he could see the pain and desperation in his eye—the left; the one that hadn't ruptured in the assault—and he could hear the last futile pumps of his heart deep within the stone-like caverns of his petrified body. He'd been beaten, suffocated, battered, torn, and burnt into a twisted living fossil of his former glory.

Even his aura looked burnt!

He tried to speak, but his withered tongue proved useless; only dark, reeking smoke issuing from his gaping maw.

He tried to move, but only succeeded in chipping away at more of his right hand until several of his fingers began to disintegrate.

Xander stared, wanting to offer some comfort but not knowing what gesture he could possibly extend at that point. The Gamer was, for all intents and purposes, already dead; any words would fall on deaf ears and any contact would surely only tear more pieces from his tortured body.

"I'm sorry this happened to you, my friend," Xander finally said, reaching out with his own aura to numb The Gamer's pain before finally shutting down his brain from the inside. "But you have my word that you *will* be avenged."

9

MAGIC INSIDE

*H*alfway home from The Gamers, Xander had abandoned his control of his thrashing aura and, in doing so, had nearly driven the car ahead of him off the road. Though the driver of the Smart Car was convinced that it was simply a sudden and powerful wind that knocked their small vehicle about the two lanes of the highway, Xander knew otherwise.

And, awful as it was to admit it, he hadn't cared.

He'd almost *wanted* to see the small joke of a car careen into the guard rail; it certainly wasn't enough to tear through it.

In the end, however, Xander had peeled his Firebird around the swerving car ahead of him and screamed past, lest letting the speedometer drop below one-twenty until he was off the main road and tearing through the tread on his way up the hill of the mansion.

Estella, obviously sensing his arrival, was already in the lobby waiting for him, while some of the more perceptive aurics were lingering in the hopes of catching a glimpse of what they'd felt approaching for the past few miles. Aside from them, a few therions and sangsuigas had also lingered, both as company for the aurics or simply meandering the halls as they would on any other night. A few others scurried away as their subconscious instincts warned them of the approaching storm that was their leader.

Though he was finally home—finally among his mythos colleagues—his aura continued to thrash and swell with rage.

"WHERE IS STAN?" Xander roared as he slammed through the front doors of the mansion.

A number of the clan's members flinched at the suddenness and hostility of their leader's entrance. Though many knew that he had a short fuse, few had ever seen Xander truly angry— usually that privilege was reserved for the rogues who were about to face his wrath—but, at that moment, they were shown just how terrifying the spectacle could be.

"Xander?" Estella hurried towards him, keeping her voice low enough to not startle the few clan members who had not yet fled the scene; those who were either too worried about their leader or too arrogant to be seen retreating. Reaching Xander, she lay a palm against his heaving chest—her eyes widening at his racing heart—and looked up at him, concern outweighing all else on her face. "What is it?" she asked. "What do you need Stan for? Why are you... you're bleeding! What happ—"

"Just some human punks on the street. Don't worry; it's almost healed already," Xander said, hoping to stop her concern before it had a chance to rise any further. Dropping the duffle bags of weapons onto the floor, he let what little control he held on his aura work to close the door behind him. "Standard round; grazed the skin under my jacket. It's already healing."

Estella frowned at the news—never one to celebrate the sight of him with any sort of injury—but recognized it for what it was and pressed the issue no further. Looking him over once more for any other injuries and giving the bag a quick glance, she applied more pressure through her hand, and

Xander felt a current of warm and calming energies flood his system.

He stepped away from her touch. As much as she meant to him—as much as he knew that just looking into her blue eyes would help ease the storm in his mind—he didn't want to relax then; didn't want to let go of the pain of what he'd just been forced to endure. He wanted to be angry when he was face-to-face with Stan.

It was what he deserved!

"The Gamer's dead," Xander's voice was cold and flat; his eyes darting everywhere *except* Estella's face as he scanned the mansion for Stan's signature. Despite every promise he'd made to himself seconds earlier not to, he dared a look into his lover's eyes. "I had to do it, Estella. They got to him and he... he was suffering."

Xander forced his extended fangs to retract and worked to reel in his aura, giving up the battle when he accidently knocked several picture frames from the wall in the process.

Several more of the onlookers shied away, realizing that there was more to what was happening than they wanted to be involved in.

Estella stared back at him, her eyes widening with shock as the reality of his words sank in; though she'd only ever met The Gamer a few times, she knew who he was and what he'd meant to Xander; both as a supplier of weapons and synth-blood as well as a friend. Her aura strained and stretched over her head as her own anger welled. Nodding her understanding, she gestured towards the stairwell to the lower levels. "With Trepis," she whispered.

Nodding, Xander walked by, reaching out with this left hand long enough to give Estella's forearm a gentle, reassuring squeeze. He couldn't offer any more sympathies or promises—not with words, anyhow—and he hoped that the gesture would suffice for the time being.

"WHY DIDN'T you tell me the truth?"

Stan stayed kneeling over Trepis, neither seeming surprised by Xander's arrival nor by the question. For a long moment there was nothing but silence and Xander's growing suspicion that his old friend hadn't even heard him, but then, finally, "And what truth would that be?"

"Don't play that fucking game with me! You know what I'm talking about!" Xander growled at him.

Stan turned to face him then; looking over his shoulder with cold eyes, "Unless you want me to scan your mind—and we both know how much you hate that—then you're going to have to be a little more specific."

"I just visited The Gamer," Xander declared, not working to hide the accusatory tone that proved eager to carry the words.

Stan raised an eyebrow and smiled as he raised to his feet and turned to face Xander.

"Oh, The Gamer? How's he doing? I was hoping to give him a visit sometime soon."

"He's dead, Stan!"

Stan's smile vanished. "What? How?"

"How the hell do you think?" Xander growled and shook his head. "Those... those *monsters* showed up and fucking mutilated him! They goddam unloaded every torture they could think of on the man in less than two minutes, and left him alive enough to..." he looked away. "They left me no choice but to finish the job."

Stan stared for a long moment. "Xander, I... I had no idea they'd take it this far."

"I hope you'll excuse me if I refuse to believe that," Xander sighed, forcing himself to relax. "But that's hardly the point; I didn't come here to tell you about what happened to him. I came to get the truth! Before he died, he told me that you can *give* The Power to others. Is that true?"

Stan frowned at the question and turned away, shrugging his shoulder as he knelt down again and returned to petting Trepis. "It is true; I *can* do that. There isn't much that I *can't* do, to be honest, but it stops being a question of whether I *can* do something and starts becoming a question of whether I should?"

Xander sneered at that, "But was it a question you were asking yourself when you first came here?"

Stan's body tensed at that. "I don't think I need to answer that."

"Then you *did*," Xander took a step towards him.

"I didn't say that," Stan's voice was flat again.

"Then you didn't?" Xander pitched the question like a weapon, knowing that Stan would be boxing himself in no matter what the answer.

Stan sighed, "I didn't say that, either…"

"Then what are you saying, Stan? Huh?" Xander stepped around him and Trepis to glare down at his friend. "People are *dying*—people who are supposed to be your friends—and you're justifying doing *nothing* because you feel it's unethical? This could change the game; shift the entire scales on the outcome of this battle! If you put The Power in somebody who can fight them—in *me*—then they'll stop chasing you and I'll be able to—"

Stan let out a calming breath and shook his head, "Even assuming that they *would* leave me alone when I'm powerless—and, believe me, they're not the types to spare a victim just because they're helpless to protect themselves—then I'd be handing you *and* The Power over to them on a silver platter."

Xander scowled and shook his head. "That's not true! If I have it then I can fight them!"

"Xander," Stan pulled his hand from Trepis' side and rested it on his knee, "this power is more than most can handle. Sometimes it feels like more than I can handle. I don't want to imagine you trying to control it."

"That's bullshit! If you can handle it than so can I!" Xander pressed.

Stan scoffed, "Even if you could I wouldn't want to risk it! Somebody like you with this power could be more dangerous than they are!"

Xander's eyes widened at the accusation. "What are you talking about? I'm not going to—"

"I hope you'll excuse me if I refuse to believe that," Stan turned Xander's words against him. "Absolute power corrupts absolutely, and, quite frankly, I don't care how much you insist you can take on the whole world and win. You can barely get through a single fight without being ripped to shreds, and this is so much more than anything you've ever faced."

"I'm not about to say I've never had my ass handed to me," Xander admitted, "but I've always been able to handle—"

"This is *not* something you can just 'handle,'" Stan shot back.

Xander shook his head, "But you're able to handle it just fine, right? Care to explain how that works?"

Stan sighed. "Lots and *lots* of effort."

Xander frowned, "And you don't think I can do it?"

Stan looked him square in the eye and shook his head, "No, Xander. I *know* that you *can't.*"

BETWEEN HIS NERVES from delivering the mercy-kill to The Gamer—he sighed and shook his head; delivering the mercy-kill to *Dwayne*—and the lecture that felt dangerously similar to an insult, Xander couldn't take much more of the world. Heading up the stairs and back into the lobby, however, he felt a major weight lifted from himself when he saw Estella waiting for him. While she still wore the look of concern he'd left her with before, she was no less a source of strength and peace of mind for him.

And she deserved an apology.

Starting towards her, Xander worked to clear his throat, not wanting his own body to muck up what was already a difficult process for him. Though Estella was one of the few people Xander felt a genuine sense of obligation to for such things—save for his late mother—it was, nevertheless, a tolling process that he had to mentally recite each time an apology was owed. The process of accepting responsibility was never an issue, though; taking the blame had become nearly his entire adolescent life, after all. Despite this, apologies— genuine and sincere apologies—were something that he felt needed to be as much for himself as for the recipient. If he meant it, he believed that he needed to feel legitimately at fault *and*, more to the point, cared enough to offer some symbol of his regret at putting another person through whatever it was he'd done.

When Estella was involved, apologies were far more frequent and never insincere.

He'd sooner see the world and every other person and mythos occupying it burn and turn to ash at his feet.

And then he'd probably apologize for that to Estella, as well.

But *only* if he meant it.

Like he did at that moment.

Picking up the two duffle bags in his left hand, he held out his right hand to his lover and, as her sad eyes met his own, he offered her a smile.

"Come on," he ushered her, taking her hand with enough force to effectively help her to her feet without giving her any discomfort, "it's been a long, awful night, and you deserve a lot more explanation than I offered."

Estella blushed and walked beside him as they started up the stairs.

"There's a lot of weapons in that bag," she looked over at him. "Did The Gamer—"

"Dwayne," Xander felt himself blurt out before looking over to Estella and biting his lip—flinching as his left fang pierced the side of his lip—"He told me his name before they... well, before they arrived," he explained, "Dwayne Theodore Brinkley."

"Dwayne," Estella spoke the name and smiled, looking like it meant something to her to know that he'd be known as more; a sentiment that Xander most certainly shared. "Did Dwayne think those weapons would help against the ones that are after Stan?"

Xander shook his head. "No," he said flatly, "he and I were of sound mind by the end of our talk that nothing *but* Stan and his powers will help against those motherfu—" he stopped himself, reminding himself of Estella's aversion to curse words, "Those... *bad* people."

Estella blushed and looked over at him, a smile creeping at the edges of her mouth at Xander's ongoing efforts around her. "It's alright," she finally said, offering a coy smirk as she continued up the stairs with him, "I think they're motherfuckers, too. In fact, I might go so far as to say that they've proven themselves to be mother*fucking ass*holes!"

Xander stopped in his tracks and looked over at her as she took another three steps before pausing as well to look back.

"What?" she feigned innocence, "Is there some clan rule that says only you can have a potty mouth?"

Xander laughed and shook his head, "No, nothing like that— vulgarity is almost a prerequisite just to get in, actually—but I just never thought that... what I mean is..." he chuckled at his own stammering and shook his head, "You've just really surprised me—in a good way—over the past."

She smiled at that, and Xander couldn't help but feel like the sight—Estella smiling over him, beautiful and strong, and representing some sort of hopeful moment to follow—was the perfect symbol of the past few weeks.

As though she was reading his mind, she offered a casual shrug at his compliment and said, "You've been working to protect me and help me stay strong for *years*, Xander. It's only right that, in a moment of need, I offer you the same commitment. We're a team, after all."

Her words hit Xander like the shot from the gang member's gun: unexpected and stinging more than he felt it should. All of a sudden it was becoming harder for him to assume the role of strength and power that had been placed upon him and he felt his knees buckle beneath him.

Estella was beside him in an instant, supporting him and asking him what was wrong.

"I'm… I'm sorry," Xander finally let the words slip free. Looking up, he saw her eyes—those beautiful blue eyes—and was suddenly terrified that he'd somehow condemned her to some awful fate. The terror of his new role in the mythos community and his lingering self-doubt and growing self-hatred overflowed at that moment, and the sight of Estella's eyes went blurry as a flood of tears began to grow. "F-fuck. I'm… I'm so sorry, Estella. I'm sorry. I'm sorry. I'm… I'm s-so fucking sorry."

Taking a firm hold on Xander and helping him to his feet, Estella kept her surprise and concern hidden from her features —though it was practically screaming from her aura—as she helped get Xander to their room and locked the door behind her.

Xander dropped to his knees and struggled to peel out of his jacket as the foreign-yet-familiar sensation that he was burning from the inside-out spread over his body. Before being turned into a vampire, he'd suffered from the agonizing sensation whenever his rage or sadness grew too overwhelming, which had been more frequent than he liked to admit.

After his dormant auric powers were released, however, he'd found that the sensation—the binding, boiling torture that had plagued him for most of his life—was actually his own aura reacting to his thoughts and turning inward on himself. Struggling to see past his blurred vision at that moment, he could see the phenomenon occurring once again; the red, semi-transparent coils of bio-electric energy—laced with bolts of darkness that looked like black lightning crackling across their thrashing lengths—wrapping around him. As his anger intensified at the flood of memories, the heat in his skin grew more unbearable and he cried out and shook under the pain. He couldn't control his muscles enough to even shrug out of his own jacket.

Futility slammed down on him and a vision of Gerard from their battle flashed before his eyes.

Anguish washed over him in a boiling current and the vision warped and twisted into Bianca.

Thoughts of doubt and burdening reminders of his responsibilities whispered in his ear and the vision wavered and turned into Lars.

And, through it all, the burning agony throbbed from beneath his own skin—cooking him from the inside-out—and the vision shattered and became Devin.

"I'm sorry... I'm sorry..."

The words wouldn't stop pouring past his lips. His father and mother—"I'm sorry... I'm sorry..."—Depok and The Odin Clan—"I'm sorry... I'm sorry..."—Marcus and Dwayne—"I'm sorry... I'm sorry..."—even Estella; the memory of finding her those few months after she'd been turned—been lost to him—and how weak and starved she'd been. All because he hadn't been there to stop it! All because he'd *failed!*—"Oh fuck... oh fu—I'm so sorry... I'm so goddam sorry!"—The tears rolled down his face as he whimpered in agony as his own aura worked to kill him. So many countless others he'd failed; so many more that he'd yet to fail but could see with ever-growing clarity he'd be unable to save...

"I'm sorry... I'm sorry... I'm sorry... I'm sorry..."

Then, just like that, the pain was gone; the burning grip of his aura lifted. The visions and the agony they brought faded.

Only Estella remained.

There; right in front of him.

Holding him and chanting with him: "It'll be alright... it'll be alright... it'll be alright..."

Her face.

Her words.

Her touch.

Her magic.

She'd saved him again. More times in that single act than Xander felt he could boast for her over the past year.

Blinking, he reached out—his hand shaky but never before so certain—and he cupped her cheek, feeling even more of her rejuvenating magic seep through her pores and into his palm. Though there was still concern and desperation in her face, he could tell that she was able to see his body, mind, and aura returning to him, and she pulled him into a tight embrace after he finally got his stifling leather jacket to fall from his shoulders.

"H-how do you keep doing that?" he asked with a weak chuckle.

Estella let out a laugh that just as quickly finished as the remnants of a stifled sob. "I'm magic, remember?" she chided as she started to pull back again, her aura beginning to settle.

Xander, however, wasn't ready to let her go just yet, and as he pulled her against him—her lips coming to meet his own with all the speed and ferocity of their kind—he silently promised himself to explain what had been bothering him all along.

But for now, there were more pressing matters at hand to attend to.

"THE VAMPIRE'S woman has some spark in her," Lars scoffed, looking over at Devin. "We should probably kill her sooner, right?"

Devin stood his ground, not looking away from the night-bathed stone wall that still shimmered in his eyes with their reluctant brother's infernal barrier. Though to any onlookers— any who he'd allowed to see them standing there, of course—it would appear as though the four of them were gazing intently at nothing, for him and his crew it might as well have been a television projecting the inside of the Stryker-vamp's bedroom. He'd been intrigued by the vampire from the beginning, sure, but the more he witnessed the specimen the more curious he became. It had been his hopes to see the vampire—nothing more than a child, really—return to the fat wizard's petty shack of leisure and lingering intrigue, but he'd never have suspected for his return to take so little time. He was well aware of the over-glorified speeds that their kind were capable of achieving, and he was neither impressed nor intimidated by such displays; but what the vampire had shown him in his return eagerly tran-scended the realm of simple speed. It was the enthusiasm and rage that intrigued him most. While others would have slowed or lagged from fear of what they knew they were running into, the Stryker-vamp seemed more afraid of himself; seemed outright eager to face anything and everything so long as it kept him from facing himself.

So when he'd returned to the fat wizard's home and seen what they'd done to him, Devin chose to let him live. All four of them had stood not far from him as he gaped at their handi-work; the fat wizard working with his final moments to tell him that they were close enough to tear his head off if they'd wanted. His burnt-up tongue had wagged to issue a warning, while his charred hands worked to point them out, only to crumble like spent kindling in a dying flame.

It had all been for naught.

The Stryker-vamp had been unaware of their presence, and Bianca's idea to hold the dying wizard's life a moment longer paid off in spades. Though she had been the second of his makeshift legion to be inducted, she'd proven herself wise beyond measure; a fact that he was beginning to see as a potential threat. And while her potential mutiny was a waning concern, he'd been impressed with the foresight she'd used in forcing the Stryker-vamp to end his friend's life.

It had served to break him; to push him further into the void of insanity Devin had seen him perched on during their first encounter. He'd nearly killed a poor, old man on his way home —an old man that Devin had personally sent Gerard to dispatch as they soared overhead; tracking his new intrigue's path—and he'd terrified his own comrades with an enraged entrance. Then, to his amusement, he saw the rage carry down into the underground levels, where their brother's original intent was thrown into his self-righteous face as a potential solution. Laughable as the claim was, however, the accusation and rising aggression worked to their benefit; the waters of their friendship muddying as settled truths were stirred to the surface.

But that cursed blood-witch!

The four of them had unified their efforts in driving the final coffin nail to the Stryker-vamp's dwindling hold to sanity, only to have his half-blood harlot go and settle him.

Somehow…

Lars cleared his throat then. "Devin," he called over, "would you like us to kill the—UGCHH!"

Lars gripped at his still-scarred throat as Devin's aura lashed out like a serpent and cinched his windpipe shut.

"Can you not see that I'm enjoying this?" Devin snarled, not bothering to look away, though the direction of his gaze meant little with the scene playing out in each of their heads.

"Yeah, retard," Gerard chuckled. "Ain't ya never watched porn with your buds before? Only fags talk during the show!"

Lars let out a cough as Devin's hold retracted and he was finally allowed to breathe. "I... I didn't think... we were here... for *that*."

Bianca rolled her eyes and shot an irritated look over her shoulder at the two, "Not that you boys ever learned a damn thing from any of it."

Gerard scoffed at that. "Learn? You say that like I should care how whoever's being crushed beneath me should feel!"

"Good thing for you, too, since you'd be 'crushed' to know that your needle-dick would make women laugh if you weren't too busy choking them," Bianca quipped back. Still smirking at her own joke, she "looked" back at the wall, wetting her lips. "Hmm... but this vampire, on the other hand... *he* could teach you a thing or two," she mused to herself, "though I wouldn't mind being taught a lesson by him. Me-yow!"

"Bianca!" Devin finally shifted his focus, letting the vision of the Stryker-vamp's moment of passion with the blood-witch fade away. "Am I to understand that you're feeling something for that creature?"

Bianca cleared her throat at that and shook her head, "No. Nothing like that. Just, as you and the others suggested, enjoying the display. That's all."

Devin sneered at the confession and started a slow, methodical pace around the three; letting his focus move on to both Lars and Gerard. "Hear me now, my pets; *when* I so decide that such actions will benefit *me*, I will allow all of you a moment of satisfaction at their expense. And, yes, that will permit whatever satisfaction you desire. But, until that time, I'll have none of you stray from the cause, and—when that time *is* upon you—" he fixed his glare on Bianca then, "I'd like to remind you that it will be *us* teaching *them* a lesson! *Not* the other way around! Am I understood?"

Though it was clear whom the message was most directed towards all three were quick to nod their heads.

"The blood-witch, however," Devin said as he started away from the mansion and headed with his legion in tow into the woods, "will be *mine!*"

10

"... IF I DON'T."

*T*he throes of orgasmic ecstasy were, as they always were when Xander and Estella made love, drawn-out and intense; the magical and auric waves that came rolling from the two bodies scattering everything within the room that wasn't secured or magically tethered. While several of their belongings fell into the former category—framed art, books, and other knick-knacks scattered about the room—succumbed to the waves of energy and clattered to the floor, most of everything else, falling into the latter category, had been enchanted by Estella earlier on to protect against their moments of passion. Though they were forced to exert a certain degree of self-control—lest they recreate the destructive force that had leveled a stretch of forest that prior December within the clan's walls—the spells did a decent job of absorbing the "impact" of their combined climaxes without simultaneously acting as a wrecking ball enchantment.

Though Xander *had* been forced to replace over a dozen doors over the past few months...

Withdrawing from Estella and falling beside her, both still

panting from their exertion and wearing the telltale glow, he begrudgingly returned to reality.

"Sometimes I wish I could just *live* in that," he said with another sigh.

Estella looked over, her eyebrows arched, "You mean you want to *live* inside *me*?"

Xander laughed and shook his head. "No... well, no, that'd be nice too, don't get me wrong," he laughed again, "but I meant I'd like to live in that... you know, that *oblivion* that your mind becomes when you come."

"The oblivion?" Estella studied him for a moment, "When you come?" She laughed and shook her head, finally catching her breath. "You know what, Xander; I think I could fall in love all over again with the dope you become after sex."

Xander rolled his eyes and stuck out his tongue at her, "While I could fall in love with the sparkplug you become after sex."

"Fair enough," she smiled, planting another kiss on his lips. "As long as you never stop loving *me,* I think I'll be alright."

"I don't think *anything* could make me so crazy as to let the most perfect thing in my life go," Xander said.

Estella blushed.

Xander watched her for a moment, appreciating her in ways he couldn't bring himself to articulate, before remembering his promise to himself and sitting up.

"I feel like I owe you some explanation," he said, trying to focus on the negative thoughts he'd been having *before* Estella's magic and passion had made it little more than a distant memory. "About everything that's happening, I mean."

Estella frowned and shrugged, "If you really want to. I know you've been under a lot of stress, and, believe it or not, I can fit a lot of the missing pieces in on my own. If it's going to hurt you to talk about it, I'd rather go unknowing."

Xander shook his head, "No, I think it's only right that I'm honest about a few of the details that have been chipping away at me; if nothing else to get it out in the open and maybe get your thoughts on some of it. I've been a total dick lately, I know, and I don't think apologizing is enough."

Estella nodded, turning herself to face him more and giving him her attention.

He bit his lip and took in the vision of her waiting on what he had to say while she was still naked. The vision was not unlike a cryptic-yet-beautiful piece of gothic art; a topless, porcelain-white beauty with raven-black hair and the bluest eyes he'd ever seen enshrouded in a wide, rippling aura of sunrise-orange; the slight sheen of sweat that still clung to her skin catching the dim light from the lamp that had fallen to the floor and casting a stretched shadow of her form on the ceiling above him.

How could any man be expected to reflect on anything else —let alone anything so awful—while basking in such a sight?

He sighed…

He *had* promised himself.

Closing his eyes to the view, he began from the beginning.

IT WAS NEARLY an hour before Xander had finished explaining the situation in its entirety. As he let the truths of everything he'd learned about Stan and what Dwayne had told him before he'd died flow, he came to realize that the anxiety from the situations he was detailing seemed to melt away as he did.

Finally, as he finished telling her about the possibility of taking Stan's powers into himself, he let himself fall back against the headboard and, once again, move his focus up to Estella.

His lover blew out a deep breath, looking down. "I… I had no idea it had gotten so out of control."

"I just don't know what to do, anymore," Xander groaned. "Stan won't fight them, and I can't get him to give me his power so I can…"

Estella looked over at that and shrugged, "That might not be a bad thing, sweetie. That much power *could* do a lot of damage. It could even *kill* you if it wasn't—"

"Oh no…" Xander sighed and, cupping his face in his left hand, looked down, "Not you too, 'Stell!"

"What?" Estella frowned.

Xander pulled his hand away and waved it in resignation towards the door and the rest of the mansion. "Stan fed me this load of bull talking about how I'd turn into some kind of villain if he did give me his powers."

Estella moved then, shifting forward so she could rub Xander's shoulder, "I don't think you could ever become a villain…" she shrugged her own shoulder, "*But* I do believe that you wouldn't come out of something like that the same as before."

Xander closed his eyes and let a breath he'd been holding in bleed slowly past his parted lips. "Those guys are dangerous, 'Stell. Stan not fighting them has already gotten somebody close to me killed—and, damn them, I had to do it myself!—and it'll only be a matter of time before they break through the barrier. I can't just sit around and do nothing, but everywhere I go—everyone I talk to; even *you*—tells me that there's nothing that can be done!"

Estella stopped rubbing his shoulders and resigned to just draping her arms around him in a tight embrace. "I'm not saying that nothing can be done; just that there's a better way to do it than risking you—body *or* mind—to the cause. I'm sure you'll figure it out, though. You always do."

Xander nodded slowly, "I hate to imagine what will happen if I don't."

Estella offered him a tight squeeze before rolling to the edge of the bed and starting to stand. "I'm going to take a shower," she announced, making a show of letting her bare behind sway as she made her way to the bathroom; her aura swirling with intent and showing Xander that the gesture was more of a stress reliever than a tease. In either case, it worked. Then, a short moment later, "Maybe you should see if somebody's down in the dojo to spar with. I'm sure Timothy would love a lesson from his favorite mentor."

Xander gave her a face, "I'm his *only* mentor."

"That only makes it easier to keep the role, darling," Estella giggled before starting the water.

"Well what if I'm feeling dirty?" Xander called after her, getting up as well. "Maybe I want to shower, too!"

Estella poked around the corner and shook her head, "Nope. You don't meet the sweat requirements. You must be at *least* as reflective as a disco ball to enter this den of cleanliness."

"That's ridiculous!" Xander shot back. "You're not *that* reflective—no vampire is!—and who references disco balls anymore?"

"Nice," Estella sneered playfully at him, "and I got your disco 'balls' right here:" she stepped into view long enough to shake her breasts at him before turning away. "Now go to the dojo and spar with Timothy! You both will feel better for it!"

The bathroom door closed and Xander heard Estella lock it from the other side.

You know *that I could just unlock that from here, right?* he called out with his mind to her.

"NOT IF YOU KNOW WHAT'S GOOD FOR YOU, YOU WON'T!" she called out, yelling to be heard over both the running water and closed door.

Xander sighed and shook his head, starting for the closet to find his sparring gear.

Whatever! I'm gonna go spar with Timothy... he paused for a moment then added, *And NOT because you told me to!*

"WHATEVER YOU GOTTA TELL YOURSELF!" Estella's voice was already muffled and garbled by the flow of water.

Slipping into the ripped-up red tank top and black sparring pants, Xander snatched a roll of tape for his knuckles and, finally, his training gloves before starting for the door. Reaching for the doorknob, he spotted the massive crack that stretched from the center-hinge and spaced out in a giant, sideways 'V' to each of the opposite corners. Taking in the sight and sighing with the realization that he and Estella had destroyed yet *another* door, he made a mental note to get it replaced *again*.

Starting down the hall, he opened up a psychic channel to Timothy's auric signature—a direct, one-way line to his pupil that would be heard by him anywhere in the mansion—and issued the call:

Yo, Tim! Get your butt to the dojo, ASAP! I need a workout and I'm sure you're eager to beat me up.

DIANNA AND SAWYER were finishing with their own sparring session in the dojo when Xander arrived. Though Sawyer still held some animosity over their previous encounter, he offered the clan's leader a smile and a friendly nod as he began to towel off; only his thrashing, jagged aura offering any real evidence that he still harbored a lingering grudge. This, however, was a good sign for Xander, who'd held onto grudges for far less for far greater periods of time; knowing that one of his best warriors—and a warrior who trained new recruits, at that—wasn't so quick to forgive *or* to forget only reinforced his confidence that the right decision had been made. A vampire warrior who didn't know to keep their guard up around a potential adversary never lasted long. Which was probably the only reason Xander had lasted that long.

Dianna, however, was just as cheerful as ever, which only

made the air of intimidation that much more eerie, as she was also one of the deadliest humans Xander had ever met. Then again, that Dianna had secured a place within the clan at all was an outstanding testament to her abilities, just as the fact that none of the other clanmates had tried to *kill* her was a testament to her charm. Less than a year earlier, she'd been dedicated to terminating mythos with a prejudice so extreme that it had driven Richard, her brother and fellow hunter, insane. Maddened with a psychotic vendetta to avenge their hunter-parents, Richard had continued to experiment with new ways to modify his body with mythos blood. In the end, Dianna had seen who the real monster was. Renouncing everything she'd ever known, she had made the choice to side with Xander and the others against her insane brother, and, with her help, they had killed Richard and left him to rot in a watery grave that had almost been his own.

Though the decision to let Dianna live, let alone to extend an invitation into their world, had created some difficulties both with The Council as well as with those who'd suffered at the hunters' hands before her reformation, Xander's persistence —and the encouragement of Sawyer, who, despite his own losses at the hunters' hands, had taken Dianna as his lover—had not been in vain, and the unconventional decision was made into a revolutionary reality with The Council's approval in March of that year. Since then, Dianna had been working directly with Sawyer to teach new recruits how to defend against human attacks without compromising the secrecy of their kind.

After all was said and done, though, Xander was just glad to see that all those unsightly mythos "upgrades" had been reversed. Save for the magic tattoos she still wore from her previous life—tattoos that she'd since refused to use—Dianna was once more a human.

Granted, she was a tough-as-nails and take-no-crap human,

one who'd proven herself in the world of nonhumans more times than Xander could count, but still only human.

"Here to train with Timothy?" Dianna asked, catching a towel as Sawyer tossed it to her.

Xander nodded, already starting to wrap his hands in tape.

Sawyer smirked at the sight and nodded towards him, "Is all that really necessary? He *is* just a kid, after all."

Xander smirked at that, "Says the one who looks like he just got his ass handed to him by a *human*."

"Hey!" Sawyer started towards him, "Just because she's human doesn't make her weak!"

Xander looked up at that and nodded, "And just because Timothy's a kid doesn't make *him* weak."

Sawyer blinked at that for a moment, realizing that he'd just jumped head-first into Xander's trick.

"Besides," Xander finished wrapping his hands and flexed a fist around the fresh bindings to break in the edges, "if you're so confident then why not try sparring with him yourself?"

Sawyer smirked at that and shook his head, "No. I think you've made your point. After all, *you've* been training him all this time, so it's only fair to assume he'd kick my butt."

Xander nodded again, "Kicks mine all the time."

"XANDER!" Timothy's voice rang through the hall outside the dojo as his light-blue aura was bouncing with almost as much intensity as his young body as he sprang into the room.

Xander held out a hand palm-out to stop the little vampire in his tracks before pointing to his feet.

"Shoes," he reminded his student.

Timothy blushed and nodded, plopping onto his bottom and beginning to wrestle free of his Nikes and grass-stained socks, tossing them into the hall as he freed himself of each article.

The nejin Satoru wasn't far behind, stepping through the entrance a moment later. Though Xander had seen a great many things—including a great many inhuman species—in his time as a vampire, the nejin still caught him off guard each time he saw him. Though a transformed therion bore many animal-like features—not necessarily always canine as the term "werewolf" would imply—the nejin were not shapeshifters; they occupied only one form, and that one form was cat-like. Satoru, the only nejin Xander had ever met, was just over six-feet tall and bore a striking resemblance to a jaguar; as though somebody had placed the big cat's head on the toned body of an Olympic athlete and, liking the aesthetic, followed through with the tail, claws, and markings over the entire body. In the beginning, Satoru had kept himself covered in countless layers of hooded, baggy clothing—which, while hiding his features, also served to hide the nejin's many blades—but, as his confidence had grown since that time, he'd taken to wearing a simple, dark-blue pair of *hakama*, the traditional pants of the samurai. While Xander had yet to learn if Satoru's dedication to the Japanese warrior's life-style was solely his own or if it had something to do with the history of his species, he could attest that the nejin's skill with a katana—or any sort of sword or bladed weapon, for that matter —were not to be taken lightly. Though the interest to know more was, at times, overwhelming, Satoru's ongoing silence made any real hope of conversing an unrealistic fantasy. Whether this was also a trait of his kind or if he'd just taken a personal vow of silence was also a mystery. Despite all the mysteries surrounding him, Satoru was unconditionally loyal and dedicated to protecting Timothy, which, for Xander, was more than enough to trust him. The two exchanged a wordless greeting—a nod of Xander's head being met with a bow of Satoru's catlike own—before the nejin offered a similar greeting to Sawyer and Dianna and finally settled cross-legged in the corner with a book of haikus.

"Are you ready?" Timothy jumped up, brandishing his fists; his small fangs already partially extended out of excitement.

Xander raised an eyebrow at the boy, "Are you?"

Timothy frowned and looked down at his feet, making a note that he'd heeded his mentor's previous order.

Xander rolled his eyes, "Your stretches, Tim; gotta get warmed-up first. Jumping jacks, pushups, and sprints: a hundred of each." He started to turn away before looking back and raising his index finger, "And don't think that I won't be counting!"

"Only a hundred?" Timothy smirked a moment before his body shimmered into a blur as he began going about the routine in overdrive.

Sawyer watched him for a moment before looking up at Xander. "You can *count* that?"

"No," Xander admitted, shrugging as he tapped his temple, "but he can, and if he knows he cheated then it doesn't take much for me to know, too." He glanced over at his pupil once more before remembering something, "Oh, yeah? I wanted to ask about how Ruby's training is going?"

Sawyer rolled his eyes and shrugged, "It's... I mean, dammit, Xander, you realize that she has *no* history with combat or—"

"I'm aware," Xander nodded, "which is why I assigned her to train under *you*, Sawyer. You're one of our best, and if anybody can get her up to speed with everything than it's you."

Sawyer seemed only momentarily swayed by the flattery, "True as that might be, Xander, she has had *no* training in *any* sense for an entire year since she was turned. I mean, do you realize what she did for a living as a human, Xander?"

Dianna frowned at that, "I don't think that's fair, Sawyer."

The warrior frowned at his lover's insight and nodded, "I'm... I'm sorry, but it's just a lot to drop on me, you know? Especially with everything else that's going on?"

Xander raised an eyebrow, "Are you saying you *can't* do it then?"

"Now now, I didn't say *that*," Sawyer shook his head, "I'm just saying—"

"Good," Xander smirked and patted him on the back, "I knew I'd picked the right man for the job."

Dianna giggled at that. Then, collecting herself, she asked, "Speaking of which, I was thinking of taking Ruby for a 'girls' night'-thing. Is Estella upstairs then? I'd love to bring her along, too."

Xander nodded, "She was taking a shower when I left. I'm sure she'll be finishing up now if you want to catch her."

She smiled and nodded to Xander before turning to plant a kiss on Sawyer's cheek and starting out. "Bye, babes," she called, "Hope I didn't hurt you too badly."

Xander smirked and gave Sawyer a look.

Sawyer glared at him, "I *let* her win!"

Xander chuckled and gave the warrior's shoulder a pat as he stormed by, "Sure you did, champ. Don't forget to get another ice pack for your ego while you're at it."

As Sawyer's grumbles faded down the hall Xander and Satoru shot one another a knowing look and shared a chuckle.

Timothy was just starting to finish his warmups as his mentor turned towards him, and Xander could already see that the exertion in overdrive had started to have an effect on him. He'd been training the sang boy since he, Satoru, and the rest of a group of ragtag mythos had tracked Xander down after their home and, with it, their vast, unconventional family unit, including Timothy's parents, had been destroyed by Dianna and her brother. Though it had taken some time, Timothy was finally able to forgive Dianna—knowing that Richard would've just as quickly killed his own sister for disobeying him as the mythos creatures he'd been hunting—and was even beginning to form a bond for the human, who shared a love of Disney movies with him.

It was an endearing thing to see his work with the Trepis Clan actually working out. Though bringing together so many species *was* an unprecedented move on Xander's behalf—

inspired by his late father's efforts to join the vampire species under one roof—the decision to allow all species into their clan *was* changing things the world over.

Like anything else, however, Xander could only hope that the changes he was making would be for the better.

"You look dizzy," he chided his pupil, "even a little tired."

Timothy shook his head, but in doing so teetered under his own compromised balance. "Noooo," he drawled, trying to focus his swimming eyes on his mentor. "I... I'm n-not di—WHOOP!" the little vampire stumbled and caught himself before he fell over, laughing at his own folly. "I'm not dizzy at all!"

Xander smirked at the not-too-convincing display, "Or tired, huh?"

Timothy shook his head again and—again—started to teeter before widening his stance.

"Do you remember what I'd told you to do to warm up?" Xander asked.

Timothy nodded, "You said to do a-hundred jumpin' jacks an' pushups an' sprints!" He bit his lip then, seeming nervous, "Wait... was there something else?"

Xander shook his head, "Nope. There was *nothing* else. In fact, you did *more* than what I said, didn't you?"

"Huh?" Timothy furrowed his brow, confused.

Xander nodded, "You finished all that pretty quick, didn't you?"

"Yup!" Timothy beamed, "'Cause I used overdrive! Just like you taught me!"

"Like I *taught* you, huh?" Xander frowned and shook his head, "No, I don't think that sounds right, Tim. See, everything I've taught you about overdrive has been about efficiency and getting a job done faster, right?"

Timothy pouted, "But I *did* that! I got my warmups done faster, just like you taught me!"

Nodding, Xander started towards him, "That's true. You *did* get your warmups done faster, but did you come down here *just* to warm up?"

"N-no..." Timothy blushed, already seeing his folly.

"No, you didn't. You came down here to spar; to *train*," Xander stopped in front of him and smirked, "and by using all that energy *just* to be in good shape for sparring, you've given me—your opponent—the upper hand." Xander dropped down into a crouch suddenly and kicked out; his foot sweeping the little vampire's legs out from under him and sending him toppling onto the dojo floor.

"Oomph!" Timothy grunted as the wind was knocked from him.

Xander rose to his feet and held out a hand to help his pupil up. "Remember: overdrive takes up a lot of your energy. If you use it to run into a fight you won't have the energy you used in getting there to actually fight. Do you understand?"

Timothy frowned, getting to his feet. "But if it gets you there faster, isn't it better?"

"It could be," Xander shrugged, "if you weren't just getting into a fight that you're then condemning yourself to lose that much faster."

"But what if people are in trouble?" Timothy asked. "What if you have to get there faster to save the people who the bad guys could hurt?"

"What good are you to those people *sooner* if you're too weak to protect them when you've arrived?" Xander challenged.

Timothy paused to consider that. "Then," he sighed, obviously troubled by the logic, "it's alright to let people be hurt just so you won't be too weak to fight?"

"It's never 'alright' to let people get hurt," Xander corrected him, "but your duty is—"

Timothy giggled.

"Really?" he rolled his eyes, "*Anyway,* your *job* is to recognize that if you are unable to stop the ones who *are* hurting people then you've already let them get hurt. But it goes further than that, Tim, because if you lose in a fight *because* you were too exhausted to fight by the time you got there—if you get hurt too badly to continue fighting or *worse*—then do you think the bad guys are just going to *stop* hurting other people?"

Timothy shook his head, "No."

"And why is that?" Xander pressed.

"Because bad guys do what they do until they're stopped," the little vampire recited.

Xander nodded and tried to ignore how much this conversation reminded him of what had happened with The Gamer. "You got it, buddy," he said. "So the next time I tell you to warm up you're not going to waste all that energy *before* we spar, right?"

Timothy shook his head.

Xander smirked, "Besides, why do you think we get such nice cars if not to drive into a fight, right? It's certainly not to get girls."

Timothy giggled.

"You going to need some synth-blood to get your strength back before we spar?" Xander motioned towards his gym bag.

"No!" Timothy made a face, "It tastes like shit!"

Xander couldn't help but laugh as Satoru's cat-eyes shot upward and narrowed at the child-vampire's swearing.

Still laughing, Xander fought to speak, "Tim! Where'd you hear that?"

He regretted asking as soon as the words were past his lips.

"From you," Timothy beamed again. "I heard you and Mister Sawyer explaining to Mister Osehr that he was lucky for being a therion 'cause he didn't need to drink that nasty synth-blood 'cause 'it tasted like shit from an alv-whore's ass.'"

Satoru closed his book and glared at Xander.

"Whoa there, big guy," Xander held out his hands to the

nejin. "In my defense, I didn't realize the kid was there when Sawyer and I were saying those things, kay? Had *no* idea; none! Would not have talked like that if I had." Reaching out with his aura and opening a psychic connection with Timothy, he added, *I totally did sense you there, by the way; like I give a rat's ass if you hear me swear. You know better than to talk like that around other people, right?* He glanced over long enough to see Timothy stifle a giggle and nod before looking back to Satoru. "I'll work on watching my mouth around the mansion from now on, alright?" —*Like hell I will*—"I'm sure others would appreciate it, too." —*Like I give a shit.*

Timothy burst out laughing.

Satoru, realizing what was happening, peeled back his lips to display his teeth.

Xander chuckled and shrugged, "I don't suppose you'd believe I was telling him a fart-joke, would you?"

A book of haikus whistled through the air towards Xander's head.

A blur passed as Timothy jumped in front of him to intercept it. A moment later, his pupil was handing the book back to Satoru and patting him on his head.

"C'mon, Satoru, Mister Xander's just being funny. I'll be good, I promise; no swearing around anybody else, I swear it."

Satoru sighed and rolled his eyes, retrieving his book of poetry and leaned back again.

Xander smiled as his pupil returned to his side and he nodded, "Thanks for looking out for me there, buddy. Mister Satoru looked like he wanted to fuck my shit up like a total badass, huh?"

The two vampires cackled as the nejin growled up at him.

～

THOUGH SPARRING WITH TIMOTHY *HAD*, in the beginning, been a practice in restraint for Xander, his vampire pupil's progress in those past eight months had turned the boy into a fighter every bit as skilled as many of the clan's warriors. While he still lacked a great deal of the fundamental disciplines, his raw talent coupled with the skills his late father had taught him during "play" sessions were already proving their worth. It was for this reason that many of Xander's sparring lessons with him had begun working lessons in combat tactics into their sessions.

Like every other session, the two started at a slower human pace; Xander conditioning his pupil to drive with the right motions as they began to kick and punch at one another. With the attacks coming in slower, the evasions and blocks resounded with less impact—the gentle *thuds* and soft sounds of the vampires' clothes rustling as they ducked and darted—as Xander continued to quiz his pupil on their prior lessons:

"You're fighting a top-heavy sangsuiga?" Xander made a low sweep with his left arm to deflect a punch from Timothy aimed at his ribs.

Timothy leaned back to dodge Xander's counter with a right hook. "Lure them into overdrive and then focus on their legs and ankles so the fall is harder."

"Good," Xander jumped back as Timothy kicked at his right shin, tumbling back and taking a knee as he braced his arms over his head as his pupil flipped in midair to drop an aerial kick down on his mentor's head. The sound of the little vampire's superhuman attack being deflected by his mentor's well-timed guard echoed against the bamboo walls. "Getting a little fancy with that one, aren't you?" Xander smirked at him and nodded, "Alright, we'll kick it up a few notches." He lunged, "You're unarmed in a gunfight?"

Timothy ducked under a sidekick, driving an uppercut into his mentor's calf as it whistled over his head. "Use overdrive in quick bursts to see the bullets' paths, take out the closest bad guy, steal their gun, don't stop until they're all dead."

Xander grunted and stumbled, shifting into a new stance to favor his good leg as he struck out again and again and again with the injured leg; keeping his pupil busy with blocking the attacks as he worked to loosen the cramp he'd caused. "Clever little bastard," he cursed under his breath. "Give me an example of fighting dirty."

"Tri—" Timothy growled as his forearms grew noticeably sore from Xander's repeated kicks and, with the next one, he opted to roll under the kick and place himself behind Xander. "Trick question."

Xander spun with his elbow, forcing his pupil to duck away from the attack and forfeit any plans for his own. "How is it a trick question?"

Timothy jumped into overdrive and speared into Xander a split-second later, knocking his mentor over and smirking down over him. "Because any tactic used to bring the bag guys down is a fair tactic if it means getting the job done!"

Xander, panting and looking up at the boy's proud-looking face, grinned at his own handiwork. He might have been struggling with the pseudo-gods situation, but there was no denying he was one hell of a mentor.

The two didn't need words or psychic messages to simultaneously jump into overdrive, taking their sparring session to the next level. As Satoru watched the two vampires vanish from sight, he felt the energy in the dojo rise; the sensation like an electric current passing between his whiskers. Something crashed near the wall to his left—then two more at nearly the same moment in two spots on the wall across from him—before a momentary blur that could've been either Xander or Timothy flew upward towards the ceiling, leaving a mass of splintered bamboo. It was Timothy that came crashing down to the floor, but, before Satoru could get to his feet to check the little vampire for injuries, he vanished once again. A moment later Xander fell into view, tumbling across the floor, passing through the dojo entrance, and slamming into the wall on the opposite side of the hallway; the shocked gasps and whimpers of several female vampires sounding as the clan's leader nearly crashed into them. Once again, however, before any concerned onlookers could protest or check the fallen vampire for injuries, he was gone.

Again and again the dojo walls were assaulted by the unseen combatants, and Satoru was forced to roll free as a momentary blur in front of him gave warning enough before the spot he'd been seated in erupted in a mess of shattered bamboo tunnels. As the din of the vampires' super powered sparring match drove on more and more of the clan's members began to poke their heads in to try to watch the unwatchable spectacle; the sight of the dojo taking the impacts of their blows and the sonic booms that were beginning to pour out of the air as a singular, ongoing drone of thunderous kicks and punches being deflected—like the amplified sound of a hummingbird's wings assaulting the air —before, at last, a loud *BOOM* drove the onlookers back several paces and the two vampires collapsed to the floor…

Laughing.

The fight had lasted no more than ten seconds, yet in that time the two vampires had turned the dojo into a decimated warzone of splinters and craters.

Xander, tears pouring down his cheeks from his cackles, started to stand; the beginning of a black ring forming around his hazel left eye and an obvious limp in his left leg lagging him.

Timothy jumped to his feet—his cheek swollen with a bruise and a similar limp putting a drag in each step he took—still laughing as he followed Xander towards his gym bag.

"God damn, Tim," Xander let a few lingering laughs belch out of his chest as he shook his head, "You really handed my ass back to me in that second half. I mean, just *look* at all that!" he pointed towards the state the dojo was in. "I'm gonna have to have this entire room rebuilt!" He looked over towards the sound of one of the lingering onlookers, spotting the area on the wall across from the dojo's entrance, "Damn! Just look at that!" He shook his head again as he retrieved a thermos of synth-blood and took a long pull from the bottle, already feeling the rejuvenating effects healing and revitalizing his battered body.

Timothy smirked, "It's not all my fault, you know! You're not fighting as good as you usually do!"

"I'm not?" Xander raised an eyebrow down at his pupil as he held out the thermos to him.

Timothy shook his head, plopping down on the floor and accepting the proffered synth-blood and taking his own pull; flinching at the taste as he swallowed it. Once he'd regained the ability to speak—his face still twisted in disgust—he said, "You really think I could do all *that* if you weren't?"

Xander didn't answer.

"Is something wrong?" Timothy finally asked.

"No, I've just…" Xander shrugged and sat beside him, "I just have a lot on my mind lately. It's nothing you have to worry about, though."

Timothy shrugged and passed the thermos back to Xander for another swig, "I'm not worried," he confessed. "I know that, whatever it is, you'll be able to handle it; you can fix anything that goes wrong."

Xander took another long drink before handing it back, letting out another long sigh, "I wish it was that simple."

"It *is* that simple," Timothy assured him, making another face as he took another drink from the thermos.

"I'm not so sure about that, buddy," he moved to rub his left eye as the broken blood vessel that was bruising the area knit shut. In a few hours the stained skin would flake away and there'd be no sign it had ever existed. As he watched, Timothy's injuries faded; his lagged aura flaring up with renewed energy. Xander smiled and looked down at the empty thermos; silently marveling once again at how well the stuff worked, especially since it had brought him back from the edge of death many times in the past.

"It is! Watch!" Timothy jumped to his feet and lunged to attack his mentor at that moment.

Xander sighed and threw his aura out, catching the little vampire by his ankle before he had a chance to land an attack. Held back but still airborne, little Timothy's body flipped upside down—seemingly floating a few feet above the floor to all those who couldn't see the aura holding him—and dangled by his leg. Watching his pupil's harmless flailing a short distance from him, Xander began laughing again.

"Hey! No fair!" Timothy barked at him.

Xander smirked, "Oh? I thought we just went over this; there's no such thing as 'fair' or 'not fair' in a fight, remember? There's no such thing as dirty fighting if—"

"But only the bad guys use powers that can't be blocked in a fight!" Timothy spat.

Xander's smirk melted away, "Huh?"

Accepting, for the moment, that he was condemned to hang upside-down, Timothy stopped struggling and crossed his arms in front of his chest. "My mommy and daddy were *both* sang, so *I'm* sang; I can't use my aura. Your daddy *was* an auric—one of the most strongest aurics in the whole world, Mister Osehr told me!—so you *can* use your aura. How am I suppose to be able to fight you *and* your aura when the eyes my mommy and daddy gave me can't even *see* it?" Timothy pointed an accusatory finger at Xander, "You taught me that there's no such thing as dirty fighting against a bad guy because the bad guys use powers that the people they hurt can't fight against, so dirty fighting is okay 'cause they do it to others."

Xander frowned, "But if I don't fight dirty—"

"It's not fighting dirty against the bad guys *because* they're already bad!" Timothy glared at him, "But I'm *not* a bad guy, and I can't use auras like you! Fair's fair, or else you're just another bad guy, and then the good guys get to fight dirty right back!"

Xander stared at his pupil for a long moment, abashed by the wisdom in his words; wisdom that he was certain even Timothy didn't yet fully understand. Finally, forking his aura and righting the little vampire before returning him to his feet on the floor, Xander nodded.

"'just because God is stronger than the devil...'" he whispered to himself.

"Huh?" Timothy cocked his head.

Xander smiled at him and shook his head, "Nothing. Just something a friend of mine told me that you helped me understand better just now."

Timothy perked up at that, "I'm smart, huh?"

Xander smiled and nodded, ruffling his pupil's hair. "You sure are, buddy," he said as he led him out of the destroyed dojo, "Probably smarter than me, even."

11

LIKE THE WOLF

*A*s Xander started up the stairs from the dojo and onto the main corridor of the first level near the back of the mansion, he caught sight of his friend, Osehr—a therion elder who'd been the leader of the pack he'd stayed with that previous winter—as he came in through the back entrance neighboring the gardens that he maintained. Using his only hand to brush some of the excess soil from his pant legs, the aging shapeshifter seemed unaware of the clan leader's presence as he drew nearer.

When Xander began to grow nervous that he might startle his friend, however, Osehr spoke up: "I was wondering what you'd been doing with yourself, my friend."

Xander smiled at that, "Like getting you to stand still is so much simpler? You've kept yourself well-hidden. Where've you been?"

Osehr smiled—his sagging, well-aged face tightening with the broad gesture—and pointed back towards the gardens. "I've been teaching the pups how to care and tend to the flowers."

"Guess our excuses are about the same," Xander smirked. "I just got through with a sparring session with Timothy."

"Oh?" Osehr's smile broadened, if such a feat were possible. "And how is the young vampire's progression, might I ask?"

Xander scoffed and shook his head, "He's kicking my goddam ass! It'd almost be embarrassing if it weren't just proving how good I am at training him!"

Osehr barked out a laugh, "He *is* a fast learner, and you *are* a superb teacher!"

They continued on down the corridor, and though Xander couldn't be sure who was leading whom or where the leader was even headed—he certainly had no direction or destination in mind—they nevertheless ventured onward and continued their chat.

"How is Trepis?" Osehr asked.

Xander sighed, wishing the subject hadn't needed to be dragged up, "Not doing so well." He looked away for a moment to fight the flood of emotions until he was certain he wouldn't tear up, then, "I don't think it'll be much longer now."

"And this new friend of yours—this magic man—" Osehr looked over, "he can do nothing to help?"

Xander paused. "How'd you know about...?" he sighed and shook his head, realizing the answer halfway through his question

"Word *does* travel fast here," Osehr admitted, pausing to wait for him.

Xander rolled his eyes and started following again, "Apparently."

"So?" Osehr pressed.

Xander frowned, "What?"

Osehr groaned—the sound from the old shapeshifter's throat coming out like a labored growl—and he waved his only arm, "Can your magic friend help Trepis?"

Xander blushed, embarrassed to have already forgotten the subject and shrugged it off as stress. "No. At least not according to him. He says there's nothing that he can do—nothing that magic can do—to save him."

Osehr frowned at that, "I thought it was magic because anything was possible."

Xander rolled his eyes, "Well, this is the *real* world, and there are rules on how *real* magic works."

"Where is the fun in that?" Osehr growled.

"Tell me about it," Xander said with a sigh.

There was a long pause as Osehr studied Xander, his jaw jutting out as he did. "You seem troubled."

Xander scoffed. "You mean more than usual?"

Osehr didn't let the grim humor lighten the mood the way Xander wanted it to. "Yes," the therion admitted, "Very much so."

It was Xander's turn to groan then; he was growing tired with telling people who were too good at reading him about what was on his mind. "It's this whole thing with my friend— the 'magic man'..." he scratched behind his ear before shaking his head, suddenly wishing he was back in his room and alone with Estella again. "There's some bad people after him; very powerful people."

"As powerful as him?" Osehr asked.

Xander shrugged, "Basically... pretty much... not really... kind of... blah blah fucking blah!" He sighed, "Every time that issue comes up, I get a whole new bullshit story. Each one custom-built as an excuse on why he *shouldn't* fight them but insisting that nobody else *could*. I'm just going to say that they're *almost* as powerful as him and leave it at that."

Osehr let out another barking laugh, "In battle, 'almost' means the difference between life and death." He raised his stump-arm and wagged it obscenely for effect, "This is what I got for being *almost* prepared in our battle with Lenix."

Xander frowned and nodded, "Yeah, 'almost' was what got Marcus killed, too. Remember?"

Osehr looked down sadly.

Xander sighed again, "But yeah. I pretty much told him *all* of that already."

"And what did he say?" Osehr asked.

Xander sneered, "He said he's too scared to fight. All he's done is run, but he seems tired of doing that now, too."

Osehr stopped to think about that, looking down with a deep, contemplative expression, "Too scared to fight..."

Xander nodded, leaning against a nearby support beam, "I know. It doesn't make any sense to me either."

Osehr shrugged, "It makes sense to me; it's just not my nature. You and I and many others like us are predators; fighters to the end. We do not run, we fight—tooth and claw and soul—or we die trying. We are like wolves, and those like your friend are like the deer. It does not make the deer wrong to run from the wolf, because the deer don't have the teeth or the claws or soul to fight. The deer run because it is how the deer stay alive."

"You're saying my friend is a deer?" Xander frowned.

Osehr let loose another barking laugh. "No, no, my friend, I am saying that your friend is not wrong to *not* be a wolf. The life of a deer may not be the life for the wolf, but this does not mean the deer is not important. Your friend does not fight because he sees purpose in being peaceful."

"So what does that say about us?" Xander asked.

Osehr shrugged absently, "It says that there are still those out there in the world who rely on the protection of those who fight for them."

12

ABANDON HOPE

*A*fter Osehr's wisdom and Timothy's clarity—deliberate or not—Xander couldn't bring himself to head back to his room, and knowing that Dianna was probably already out with Estella made the decision that much easier. As little as he liked the idea of facing his old friend once again, Xander disliked the idea of wallowing alone in his room that much more. Like before, he found Stan with Trepis, this time sitting in the corner of the room while the ailing tiger sleep. Stopping at the doorway, Xander couldn't help but take in the scene of how tired and weak both of them looked.

Stan didn't look up or make a move to acknowledge Xander's arrival. Not letting his eyes move from the spot on the floor just in front of his shoes, he simply started talking: "Guess our chat's not over yet, huh?"

"No," Xander took the first step inside, "Not by a long shot."

Stan sighed and finally looked up, letting his eyes linger on Trepis a moment. "You know…" he let out a drawn-out sigh and smiled to himself, "I remember when your dad first brought him into this mansion." He shrugged at that, "Mind you, it was an entirely different time and place then—I've gotta commend

you for the modern edge you've given it—but it wasn't without
its charms, albeit there was still some tension floating around
the halls with the decisions your father and Depok had made"—
he let his eyes move up to Xander—"but, again, nothing that
you're not experiencing, as well. Trepis was just a cub then;
your father saved him from some sick fuck's renegade-mythos
circus," he chuckled at the idea. "Sort of a fucked-up thought,
isn't it? Some band of rogue vampires traveling around in some
mangled circus tent like a hell-born scene out of Barnum and
Bailey's worst nightmares!

"I guess the whole scene was pretty warped, even for the
likes of your father, who, bear in mind, had already seen his fair
share of sick and otherworldly shit from the bottom of the
mythos community's barrel of batshit crazies. Still..." Stan
sighed and looked back at Trepis, "You gotta wonder what sort
of monster can ever think to treat such a marvelous creature
with such disrespect. All natural reasoning set aside, it should
come as no surprise that your dad slaughtered the whole lot of
'em—I'm sure Yin and Yang were sight to behold in the center
stage while he did it, too—and it was, for the most part, the
same sort of happy ending you'd expect from your father's list
of success stories. Sadly, our fuzzy friend's mother didn't
survive the whole ordeal—something your father never forgave
himself for in the long run, I feel—and I think the guilt of not
being able to save her was what drove him to bring that
mewling bundle back here.

"Depok thought he was crazy, of course—he was always the
voice of reason and reality like that, you know—but the entire
clan was just..." Stan smirked as the memory flashed before his
eyes, "Xander, you've never seen such a little bundle mean so
much to so many. That beautiful baby tiger just... he brought all
of those vampires together. The tough, the brave, the smart, the
shy, the terrified, the confused—it didn't matter—they all forgot
how different they were and just honed in on the creature your

father had brought in; as though he'd *known* that Trepis was the icon that the entire clan needed to settle their differences.

"Anyway... your dad called me over to meet this little miracle solution to the Odin Clan's brewing civil war, and I remember him saying to me, 'Stan, do you know why I like tigers? Because they're strong; strong like you wouldn't believe; raw power and energy rolling off them like liquid lightning' he'd said; I remember that because it was the first time I'd ever heard him speak like that. He later carried that sentiment over to your mother and, eventually, his talks of you when they'd found out she was pregnant with you. But, and this was the part that really got to me, he'd said, 'but I don't like them because they're strong; that's just their charac-ter, not their soul. No, I like tigers because, even being known for their strength and power, they symbolize grace and intel-ligence.'"

Stan sighed again, "Your old man used to tell me that grace and intelligence were what made power worth having, and it was those words that kept me from going on some insanity-driven, blood-soaked, power-hungry rampage through the city on many occasions. And I think it's the fear of somehow dishonoring those words and the man that spoke them to me that's driven me to be so reluctant to use them the way you want me to."

Xander stared for a long moment, struggling to stifle one swell of emotion while a slew of others crept up behind it; memories of his late grandmother and of his battle with his misery-loving, murderous auric of a stepfather. And, more than any other, memories of the time he'd spent with Trepis. Trying to ignore the several tears that had begun to trickle down his cheek, Xander forced his face to remain stoic. "What does that have to do with anything?" he asked, his voice abandoning most of his efforts.

Rising to his feet in a single, fluid motion that defied gravity,

Stan shrugged a single shoulder, "Nothing, I suppose. So what is it that you want?"

"I want…" Xander blushed as he realized he hadn't really gone there with a clear understanding of what he wanted. "I wanna know why you won't fight back."

Stan stared at him for a moment, "Besides the elaborate and drawn-out explanation I just provided, you mean?"

Xander glared at him, "Yeah, besides that. You can't expect me to believe you're letting all this happen 'cause of my father; my father would've kicked twice as much ass for half this much pain! If you were really interested in honoring his memory, I don't think you'd do it by—"

"I'm afraid of losing myself," Stan blurted out.

Xander pulled his still-open jaw shut and stared for a moment, taking in his friend's response. Then, "Losing yourself?"

Stan nodded, "Having this power isn't all fun and games. It's a constant battle to stay in control. You can't just put this kind of power in a human being and not expect it to change them."

"But you haven't changed at all," Xander spat.

Stan shook his head, "Not since you've known me, no."

Xander looked down, beginning to understand, "So what could happen?"

"I'm not sure," Stan shrugged. "I still can't see the future—nobody can—but I'm afraid that I might end up like them; like Devin and his crew."

Xander clenched his fists and shook his head, "No! They're *insane*, Stan! Nothing—not a goddam thing—could ever make you become like that!"

Smiling at Xander's passion, Stan seemed to relax a bit, "I appreciate your faith, but it's not enough to convince me that I'm in the clear just yet. In fact…" he let his words trail off as his eyes moved to the emptiness at the door.

Xander frowned and looked back, taking in the view of the hallway. "What?" he asked, "What is it?"

"On march the banners of The King of Hell," Stan whispered.

Xander narrowed his eyes, "What? What the hell does that—"

"Stryker!"

The sudden call from the hall made Xander jump, and as he returned his gaze in the direction of Stan's own he saw a sang warrior—one of the newer recruits whose name he'd yet to memorize; his dark, copper-colored hair drenched with sweat and his pine-green eyes wide with fear—appear in the doorway.

"Stryker, m'lord," he repeated in a thick Scottish accent—Xander cringing at the "lord" title, reminding himself to enforce some sort of clan rule against it—before seeing Stan and Trepis and forcing his panicked demeanor to settle.

Xander frowned, squaring off to face the news the warrior had come to deliver, "What is it?"

"I'm sorry, but the intruders have returned," the warrior kept his voice low, his words all but inaudible if not for the natural pitch it carried, "and they've already breached the barrier!"

13

ALL HELL

*X*ander was in overdrive and heading for the upper levels, taking the steps two at a time—passing the time-frozen clan members; faces held in the grips of fear or determination—before the Scottish warrior had even had a chance to finish the panicked exhale following the news. Here-and-there, Xander spotted other sangs darting about in over-drive, as well, several of their bodies suddenly freezing in front of select doors as they dropped out of overdrive to warn the inhabitants or simply slamming a fist on each door as they ran past them; knowing that the collected impacts would issue their clanmates to answer when the sound waves finally reached their ears. Behind him, Xander felt a familiar aura approach and extended his aura to secure a psychic connection.

I want you to sit this one out, he pleaded.

I'm not letting you go into this alone, Estella shot back, appearing beside Xander in overdrive as they made their way—side-by-side—to their chambers. *Hate me later if you have to, but this is happening with or without the clan leader's consent.*

Xander scowled at that as he cast an auric tendril ahead of

him and pushed their door open to keep from bursting through the already broken polished oak.

Once inside, they both returned to normal speed, Estella heading for the reserves of synth-blood to bring them both up to full strength for what was coming while Xander tossed the duffle bags that Dwayne had given him onto the bed. Sensing a thermos spinning through the air towards the back of his head, Xander let his aura snake out of his back and snatch it before bringing it around to his waiting left hand. Unzipping the first bag, he let his aura once again emerge, forking it off again and again until he could unload the weapons and lay them out in front of him; categorizing their inventory while a few stray auric tendrils snaked across the room to retrieve his jacket, holsters, and boots.

ESTELLA WATCHED her lover work in silence, holding her nose while she downed her own thermos of synth-blood in as few gulps as possible. She, Ruby, and Dianna had just been getting out of the garage—shopping bags hanging from each of their hands like overripe fruit on the branch—when a pair of warriors had caught sight of them and told them that they'd detected four mysterious subjects lingering near the gates. Even then Estella had known that the ones who had come after Stan had returned, and it hadn't been long before she'd felt the first powerful blow on the magic barrier threaten to tear the enchantment apart.

The barrier was already down by the time she'd dropped her bags and jumped into overdrive, vanishing out of the garage before Dianna could offer a single word to the matter or Ruby could even think to follow after. Navigating back into the mansion, she'd felt Xander's energy pulsing nearer and, knowing he'd be heading towards his weapons and supplies in their room, she set herself on the same course and fell in beside him. She hadn't had a chance to get a decent scope of the power that the four beings had when they'd first come—Xander and Stan's insistence that she not involve herself keeping her far from the scene, and her own nervousness compelling her to shut her mind and senses to what had gone on that day—but the aftermath that she'd witnessed and the panic that it had instilled in Xander led her to believe that it had not been over nothing.

Oh, how she'd underestimated them...

It felt as though the very pits of the earth had gaped open and freed a biblical plague of murderous intent on their home. Everything that Xander had been concerning himself with— everything that Estella had been working so hard to calm his mind of—was every bit the nightmare he'd said it was. And it was practically at their doorstep, ready to kill them all so they could take Stan and his own powers.

Just so they could be *stronger*.

Estella shivered and finished the synth-blood—holding her nose to stifle the awful taste—before tossing the bottle to the floor and starting up behind Xander.

"Give me a gun," she demanded.

Xander growled in frustration as the guns on the bed began to float into the air and load themselves. Estella fought to ignore the awe-inspiring phenomenon, reminding herself there was an unseen appendage emanating from Xander that was doing all the work. Once again, she wished that she could see and work more closely with her own aura; at that moment more than ever before.

As the morbid mockery of Disney's *Fantasia*—Xander replacing the wizard-hat wearing Mickey as he commanded a squadron of dancing guns, knives, and ammo magazines— began to settle back onto the bed, Xander shifted his blood-stained gaze back to Estella. "I don't suppose it would do any good to ask you *again* to sit this one out?" he sighed, glancing over at her as he went about inspecting and loading a new pair of black and white pistols; the third generation of Yin and Yang.

Estella held out her hand for a weapon. "None whatsoever, and you'd look a hell of a lot smarter if you stopped acting like it would."

"Ain't that the truth?" he forced a short-lived laugh that faded as he shot her a sideways glance, "Still, you've never liked handling guns since Richard, not unless it's totally necessary."

Estella bit her lip, "I'd say this qualifies as 'totally necessary,' Xander. These guys have magic far stronger than my own. My tonfas alone aren't going to be much use against them."

"From what I've gathered, *nothing* is going to be much use against them." Xander sighed, but forced a smile for her sake, "Though you do look *really* cool when you fight with those tonfas."

Estella flexed her waiting, still-empty palm, "You think that flattering me is going to butter me up enough to let you talk me out of fighting?"

Xander looked away, "You can read minds now?"

"I don't need to read minds with you, Xander. Now stop stalling and give me a gun," she demanded.

Xander groaned and tossed her one of The Gamer's automatic pistols, "What kind of rounds?"

Estella shook her head as she grabbed the gun out of the air and tucked it into the empty holster beside her tonfa holsters. "It doesn't matter," she admitted. "None of them will do any good, anyway."

Xander paused and looked up at that, "Then why bother with the gun?"

Estella blushed and shrugged, "It makes me feel safer."

Xander studied her a moment longer before nodding and tossing her another automatic pistol and three spare magazines for each.

"Those are the new and improved exploding rounds," he explained. "They should make you feel plenty safe."

Estella looked at the topmost round in one of the magazines before she tucked them away. "What makes them 'new and improved'?" she asked.

Xander was a whirlwind of weaponry as his hands and aura worked together to secure the weapons onto his body. "Knowing The Gamer," he smirked over at her as a set of three enchanted throwing knives were strapped around his left thigh, "it's a bigger bang and a lot more death for whatever's inside that bang. That being said, I'd appreciate it if you kept yourself out of that bang."

Estella nodded and blushed, unable to offer any sort of response as she marveled at the sight of her lover as his red leather jacket floated into the air and slipped over the shoulders of its owner as if of its own free will. Then, as Xander adjusted the jacket, a new kukri with a dark enchantment swirling around its sheathed blade followed after it with a similar enchantment and was secured to his back. Though she wouldn't have believed it if she hadn't just seen them vanish under the crimson coat, Estella reminded herself that the vampire warrior in front of her—no longer the gentle, sentimental soul she knew as her lover, but the ruthless, cunning warrior that had taken the mythos community by the throat—was hiding, aside from his arsenal of *organic* weapons and the exposed kukri, six pistols loaded with enchanted rounds, a sawed-off double-barreled shotgun with similar slugs loaded within, a slew of magic-infused blades, a pouch of cherry-sized explosives (that had taken down an entire parking garage one year earlier), and, quite possibly the most deadly weapon concealed under his jacket, Xander Stryker's heart.

Finally, he turned towards her and nodded, "Ready?"

SELENE AND HELIOS—ESTELLA'S custom-made tonfas—had become every bit as much a part of her nightly patrols as the Yin and Yang variants had become for Xander. While the weapons were ideal for the peace-loving Estella—operating on blunt force alone and not incorporating any blades or bullets to incapacitate her enemies—the elongated batons with the perpendicular handles jutting out a third of the way along their length allowed Estella to wield them not just as a pair of melee weapons, but as a pair of spell-directing tools as well.

Not unlike a pair of magic wands.

Xander's lover had fashioned her weapons from the wood of a willow, explaining to him early on that it was a symbol of life and immortality; something that she felt represented her new life as a vampire. For several nights she had trekked out into the forest, each night's outing taking longer than the previous night's as she hunted down the perfect tree, which she'd given her thanks to prior to beginning the process. Estella had then shaped the tonfas by hand, meticulously carving a series of rune symbols into the wood. When she'd finished carving them, she'd taken several strands of her hair and tied them around the grips of each one; when Xander asked about this she'd told him that many witches would bind the tool to its user with their hair when constructing their wands. With this, it helped to infuse her personal energy into the weapons. After completing the two, she'd taken them to The Gamer be coated in a protective layer of enchanted alloy. As he went about the process, he'd suggested giving each tonfa its own identity—much the same way Xander's original revolvers had—and, with Estella's enthusiastic agreement, he'd worked molten metal into two hues that the two of them worked best.

Their names, much like their conception, were the perfect fit for their owner: Selene—a shimmering silver tonfa that glimmered like moonlight even in pitch blackness—was named after the moon goddess of lore and was used for Estella's defensive and protective spells; Helios—radiating with a brilliant gold sheen that mimicked the sunlight—was named after the sun god of lore and allowed Estella to direct her attack spells. Together, the two symbolized her drive to protect and heal and motivate prosperity.

Xander, on the other hand, felt they symbolized just how badass his lover was becoming.

Watching as she retrieved the pair from their elongated case under her side of the bed and securing them into the holsters at her back, Xander lifted her silver jacket with his aura and floated it into her waiting hands. Certain that she was just as ready as he wanted himself to be, he gave her one last nod before he turned and took the lead.

Sprinting through the door, he shot forward towards the ivory-white railing that overlooked the lower levels. Though the corridor fed into the staircase a short distance to his right, the stairs were already congested with so many of the clan's warriors. While impatience was certainly a factor in his brash and seemingly self-destructive act—an act which those who knew him well enough would come as no surprise—of blindly vaulting over the railing, he felt that his place was at the *front* of the battle, and he would be failing his comrades as their leader if he allowed himself to be lagged by a crowded staircase. As his body went into a freefall between the wide set of stairs on either side of him, his warriors and colleagues howled and cheered; raising their fists and issuing a chorus of praise to their leader. Behind him, Xander watched with his mind's eye as Estella showed no more reluctance to throw herself over the railing than he had; the petite, raven-haired beauty tucking herself into a head-first dive—the silver tails of her jacket slapping at her hips like a pair of angel wings.

As the two dropped past the stairs and the warriors occupying them, more and more began to follow their example; hollering their war cries as they, too, pitched themselves over the bannisters and railings and dropped like a deadly, armed storm of mythos fury.

Ready to kick some gods' asses? Xander called out to her.

In his mind's eye, he saw her thin, scarlet lips twist into a scowl, *It's the least they deserve for what they've done!*

That's the spirit, Xander pressed, watching the floor shoot up at them. *Just don't get stupid or crazy out there, okay?*

Even without looking at her, Xander could feel her aura spike at that. *Look who's talking,* she shot.

Below them, the warriors that had reached the first floor flooded through the doors—a few of the more brash warriors who knew better than to worry about the mansion's wellbeing breaking through the windows to allow greater numbers to flood out into the lawn. Casting his aura further out, Xander "spotted" the four pseudo-gods—marching side-by-side from the massive, jagged gap that they'd blown out of the side gate— letting the warriors charge them by the dozens. The torrents of magic that rolled from each of the intruders interfered with Xander's auric-fed view of their entrance, and the vision skewed and faded with every current of energy that rippled from any of the four as they drove onward.

"PITIFUL CREATURES! I CANNOT BLAME YOUR LOYALTIES," Devin's voice echoed in both the ears and minds of everyone occupying the mansion, *"AND, WERE IT ANY OTHER CIRCUMSTANCE, I COULD BRING MYSELF TO ADMIRE THE EFFORTS, AS AN ANTEATER MAY ADMIRE THE DESPERATE BITES FROM A COLONY OF ANTS. BUT YOU'RE HARBORING SOMETHING OF MINE—SOMETHING I'M NOT SOON TO GO WITHOUT—AND YOU WILL COME TO SEE YOUR DEDICATION AS THE SOURCE OF YOUR END!"*

The already unnatural and warped impact of Devin's psychic voice seemed to be weaponized; some of the warriors—especially the therions, Xander noticed—suddenly tensing under the pulsing force of the voice in their heads and dropping like ragdolls as they began to succumb to seizures. All around him, Xander could feel the auras of select warriors spike and twist erratically as they collapsed.

And Estella appeared to be among those impacted by it!

Abandoning his focus on the floor and his warriors and even his opponents, Xander corkscrewed in midair and cast his aura out. He'd learned in his battles with the hunters that previous Christmas that he could enter the minds of others and use his control to activate or deactivate specific control centers. It had been with this method that—while being held under the frigid waters of a frozen lake by the murderous, gilled psychopath— he'd killed the not-so-human hunter that had threatened him and his friends. Reaching up and into Estella's brain, however, he neither scrambled to stop a beating heart or awaken old nightmares or systematically turn off every life-function in her body, but to activate her magic and supercharge it; to force her magic to construct a barrier around her and block Devin's seizure-inducing influence from impacting her the way it was impacting countless others.

He knew he'd hate himself later for not fighting to protect all of them, as well, but he felt no shame at that moment admitting he'd let every one of them march directly into Devin's fire before he let *anything* happen to her.

Keep your defenses up, he reminded her as her aura began to right itself under his influences. *Please... I don't know what I'll do if something happens to you...*

Confident that she'd right her freefall with her mind once again her own, he twisted his body in midair once more and cast a pair of auric tendrils from his chest and gripped the railings on either side of him, using his gained momentum to propel him forward—fighting the downward pull—and drawing one of the pistols from his waist before putting three explosive rounds in the wall in front of him; the wall separating him from the four pseudo-gods.

The resulting explosion rocketed chunks of brick and debris out onto the lawn, the warriors who hadn't succumbed to the seizures scooping up those who had and jumping free as the blast began to rain down over them. Caught off guard by the unconventional entrance-cum-exit, Devin and the other three fumbled to get a grip on what they were seeing. Their delay gave Xander an opening, and the largest of the bits of debris—a slab of brick and mortar the size of Xander's body and guided by his aura—was driven directly into Gerard's chest. The hulking pseudo-god loosed a startled grunt as he was propelled backwards until he was sandwiched between it and the stone wall surrounding the mansion.

"YOU FUCKERS AREN'T INVITED!" Xander roared, baring his fangs from the makeshift perch of the hole he'd created.

MOMENTS EARLIER, the waves of magical energy that rippled through the mansion from the enemy-leader's words sent a series of pained convulsions through Estella's guts that threatened to push her into hysterics. Around her, the dimensions of the mansion seemed to fluctuate and warp; the furthest wall suddenly seeming dangerously close while the nearest railing grew progressively further. With the proportions of her surroundings growing unreliable and the color spectrum shifting with every panicked blink of her eyes, she lost track of what was happening around her.

Blink.

The floor seemed miles away; the wall so close it could've been scraping her back as she dropped; the railings of the stairway waving about like overcooked noodles.

Blink.

The floor was so close she was surprised she was still alive to see it; the walls and ceiling of the mansion so painfully far that the very world seemed to pale in comparison to the sheer scope of its size; the warriors on the other side of the railing were nothing more than a heap of chipped bones.

Blink blink blink.

Red became green; blue was suddenly blinding white; the marble floor turned acid-green and threatened to scorch her should she allow herself to—

Keep your defenses up, Xander's voice cut through the haze and distortion. *Please... I don't know what I'll do if something happens to you...*

Then, as sudden and unexpected as the madness that had preceded it, clarity!

And, with it, the realization that she had moments to act before she crashed to the floor!

Spotting the floor for where it was and what it was, Estella called upon her vampire instincts to flip in midair—putting her feet below her—and whispered a minor enchantment under her breath. A pocket of air swelled under the carpet, raising it several inches from the hard, unforgiving floor and cushioning the impact as she landed. A series of explosions went off just ahead of her—the bursts too close together to be certain how many in total; three or four from the sounds of it—and the mansion shook from the impact of whatever had caused them. Knowing that their home would suffer far worse if she let such a thing falter her, she took off in a full sprint, barely allowing her weight to force the carpet back into place before she'd taken off towards the nearest opening—a shattered window—and leaping into the chaos on the other side.

"YOU FUCKERS AREN'T INVITED!" Xander's voice bellowed from overhead, and Estella cast her gaze upward long enough to see her lover crouched like a hungry predator in a gaping hole that, she assumed, he'd been responsible for.

At least I know what all that ruckus was about, she thought to herself before shifting her gaze towards the other side of the courtyard.

Standing on either side of a tall, lanky blond man with burning blue eyes—who she assumed was the one Xander and Stan had called Devin—were a smug-looking black girl with shiny, slicked-back hair and a leering man with sandy hair wearing a long, tan coat that whipped about despite the calm air surrounding them.

Estella frowned, *But where's the four—*

The sound of stone grinding on stone pulled her away from her thoughts and she shifted her gaze further back. Near the opening that the four had created in the mansion's surrounding wall, was a massive block of what had once been a part of the mansion's walls that had been embedded into the side of the stone wall. As Estella watched, she saw the slab of mansion-debris begin to shift and twist—seemingly working to free itself from the side of the stone wall—until it finally burst into a cloud of brick dust and a large, uneven man that looked every bit as coarse and jagged as the brick he'd just erupted from.

"Now *that* wasn't very nice!" the fourth said; his growling voice, though low and bass-driven, echoing unnaturally far.

Xander's energy sparked then as he leapt from the hole and arced in the air—his silhouette cutting through the moonlight as he passed over Estella's head—and she saw her lover level a set of guns in his direction.

"SEE WHAT YOU THINK OF MY MANNERS AFTER THIS, ASSHOLE!" Xander screamed, freeing a storm of explosive rounds towards the larger of the "gods" as he began to descend upon the other three.

Estella's eyes widened and she fought her own nature to call out to him, not wanting to distract him as he dropped into the center of the three; afraid that a single word might draw his attention long enough for them to—

She couldn't finish the thought; couldn't allow herself to consider it as a possibility.

The myriad of exploding bullets began to go off at the still-intact base of the wall where the jagged "god" had been standing —*had* been standing?—and Estella felt her stomach knot as he appeared like a shimmering phantom above Xander and drove both his fists down on her lover's back. The calculated fall towards the other three became a cannonball trajectory that slammed Xander down at their feet, the resonation of his impact sending a tremor through the air that struck the still-standing warriors of the Trepis Clan more mentally than it did physically.

Ahead of her, several of the braver warriors, letting loose a series of enraged howls and snarls, charged towards the four then. Estella watched only long enough to see two of the seven warriors tear their shirts off as their bodies began to twist and inflate into their therion forms before she, too, let loose her own cry of support and jumped into overdrive to charge the four. The warriors ahead of her slowed as her perception shifted to facilitate the process—the two partially-transformed therions freezing in their current state and offering her a night-marish glimpse of the broken, malformed bodies that had yet to complete the shift from one beautiful creature to the next—as she sprinted by them, and she spotted another sang nearing the four in overdrive as well. Seeing his leader's lover charging into battle with him, the warrior offered her a nod—unable to project a psychic message like Xander—before drawing a sword from his back.

Xander had told her many times before that a sang fighter needed a blade before anything else; that Marcus had nearly tortured him into accepting this truth over all others. A sang-suiga vampire in overdrive was faster than bullets—could move faster than a bullet could travel through the barrel of a gun—so, while it was an effective means to dodge bullets, it was impractical to carry a gun that was rendered useless the moment a sang used their greatest ability on the battlefield.

"Short of cold clocking an unknowing enemy with the grip," Xander had always repeated his late-mentor's teachings, *"a gun is just dead weight."*

Seeing the other sang in overdrive with his swords echoed the already echoed lesson in Estella's head, but, while the logic of carrying a cutting or stabbing weapon at such speeds was undebatable, she didn't feel that she could bring herself to carry anything like that.

Though she'd yet to explain the reality of her aversion to guns and knives to Xander, she felt a certain endearment that he'd been so willing to accept her preference on her claim to abhorring violence as much as she did. However, while she *did* abhor violence and pain—she had, as a human, been prone to tears if she saw a dead animal on the side of the road, and even her first few months as a vampire were spent starving herself nearly to death due to her refusal to feed—she'd come to grips with the truth that, because of creatures like Lenix or the hunter Richard or these four "gods," such weapons were essential in not allowing all power to fall into the wrong hands. Despite this and her growing realization that she, too, would have to arm herself with something more lethal than Selene and Helios at *some* point, Estella could never shake the memories of the few times she had, as a human, used a spell to "spy" on Xander and seen his own pain and suffering—experienced it as though it had been her own—as he'd brought both gun barrel and razor tip to his skin in an ongoing effort to end his life. Though their friendship had faded after the tragedy that had taken his mother, Estella had never stopped caring for Xander—couldn't stop worrying about his wellbeing—and, as her magic training progressed, she'd taken to leaving her body with something she'd called "the spell of sight"—a means of directing her astral body into the mind of another which allowed her to see and feel everything that they were seeing and feeling. Though she'd only cast the spell on Xander a couple of times, the first time had been enough to feel the terror of having the cold metal of the Yin-revolver's barrel pressed against her temple while the memories of Xander's history with cutting flashed in her mind; enough to leave the haunting vision of the glistening razors jerking over his quivering arms and birthing a spurting trail of Xander's life in its wake into her mind.

And though it hurt her like nothing else to keep that truth from Xander, she couldn't bear the thought of burdening his conscience with such a confession; couldn't bear to imagine what knowing what the memory of his acts—acts he'd committed in secret and out of pain—had done to her.

Even then, with the two guns holstered at her sides, Estella felt the pain of Xander's self-destructive past ebbing at her strength.

Still, glancing down at her silver and gold tonfas as she readied a blow at the head of a god-like opponent, she couldn't help but feel that she needed something more...

As the sang warrior swung with his sword at the "god" in the long coat, Estella saw their enemy's eyes shift in their sockets to settle on the warrior. Seeing this and realizing that the warrior's target was not as helpless as they'd come to expect when in overdrive, she shifted her direction and pushed herself towards him. Though she knew there was no hope of reaching the attacking warrior in time to save him, she knew that her magic could.

The warrior's sword cut through the air...

The air cut the sword right back.

The moonbeams reflected across the length of the swinging blade, and, as Estella worked to cast a concussive spell to knock the vampire warrior away from his target, she caught sight of the moonbeams twisting and rippling as the metal of the blade fragmented. At first, she couldn't be sure of what she was seeing as the blade seemed to stop moving as a singular piece but, rather, become a series of many hovering pieces; the vampire warrior's hand still moving to strike, but his weapon doing something else entirely. Finally, as the strike was completed, there was no longer a blade attached to the hilt clutched within the warrior's hand, but a trail of tiny, razor sharp "slices" that had once been the blade. Knowing she didn't have much time, Estella swung Selene and directed the spell, watching with a relieved satisfaction as the vampire warrior was slammed in the back by the magic and pushed away from the leering "god" as he directed the hovering blade fragments back at their owner.

The warrior pitched through the air a moment as the spell carried him away from the "god's" attack, only to have his body freeze in midair as he fell out of overdrive and back into the laws of physics.

Estella's heart sank.

Contorted in midair—his body upside-down and twisted towards her—the warrior's face was a frozen mask of confusion…

And pain.

The first sliver of his blade had been buried just above his right eye, and a razor-thin trail of the other shards traveled down his face and chin, across his throat and onto the left side of his chest. Though he'd been wearing a Kevlar vest, the supernaturally driven shards of metal had still been driven through the protective, bulletproof surface and along the surface of his heart and halfway down his ribs. Despite the lively look of awe at having been swept off his feet by Estella's magic she'd been too late to save him and, whether he knew it at that moment or not, he would be dead before he hit the ground.

There…was… not-hing… you… could've done, Xander's voice chimed in Estella's head, the words drawn out and lagged as though in slow motion.

Looking at the "gods'" feet, she spotted her lover, his eyes already fixed on her as his body began to move towards her.

I... I tried, she said as Xander's psychic connection allowed her to share her thoughts.

Xander's body caught up with her own and he sprang to his feet and lunged towards her, his aura breaching his left thigh and yanking the three throwing knives strapped just below it. As he scooped her up in his arms, Estella—forcing her vision to stay in overdrive even with her feet no longer on the ground—caught sight over his shoulder as his aura flung the three blades back towards the four, whistling at unnatural speeds towards their targets before, like the warrior, they slowed and froze in midair; the enchantment that The Gamer had infused in the metal shimmering like toxic ether along the shimmering metal.

What sort of spell is on those blades? Estella asked, fighting her growing anguish at her failure for the warrior.

We probably won't find out, Xander confessed, *I tried something like this with some exploding rounds in the room they destroyed when they first showed up.*

Estella frowned at that, *What happened?*

The room was destroyed, remember?

Estella's cheeks went hot with a blush, but she wasn't sure if it showed at that speed. *So why bother with the knives?* She asked.

Because I doubt they'd think to check their feet when there's knives flying at their faces, Xander offered as he threw out his aura and knocked the other advancing warriors off their feet—stopping their advance on the "gods" without them even realizing it—before he dropped to his knees with her still in his arms, wrapping his body around hers as he fell out of overdrive with her.

Behind them, all hell broke loose.

∼

MOMENTS EARLIER, Xander knew better than to think that Estella couldn't handle herself in a fight. With every bit of skill and training he'd ever received replicated within her courtesy of her magic, he'd have to confess that he couldn't handle himself in a fight before he could pass the judgment on her.

And the entire world already knew that the son of the legendary Joseph Stryker could handle himself in a fight.

Moreover, as a human—even as a *kid*—Estella had been all about tact and grace, and though this trait had never been used for fighting at that time it had certainly come into play more recently. Though he didn't like to encourage his lover to put herself in the same danger he found himself in so often, it was more for his own peace of mind than his concern for her safety. The few months he'd been without her after she'd fled from him and the reality of what she'd been turned into had been hell for him; the incessant panic and concern that the girl he loved was out there—coupled with the occasional fits of dread that she *wasn't* still out there—without the training or dedication to her own survival had given him a new appreciation for what he'd had with her. When he'd finally found her—her vampire body beginning to consume itself out of starvation—and they'd reclaimed what they'd had before Lenix's attack, he'd sworn to himself that he'd never allow that sort of risk to befall her ever again.

An oath that, despite his acceptance of her undeniable skills as a vampire warrior, drove him to worry each and every time there was any risk looming over her head.

And though it hurt him like nothing else to keep that truth from Estella, he couldn't bear the thought of burdening her conscience with such a confession; couldn't bear to imagine what knowing what the memory of her decision to run—to run from him for letting her come to such a fate and to run from herself for feeling guilty about the life she'd awoken to—had done to him.

Gerard's cheap shot on him had been expected, and while he hadn't been thrilled at being barreled into the ground at the feet of Devin and his other cronies it had nevertheless put him where he'd needed to be. Spotting Estella a moment later, however, as she wailed like an enraged banshee and vanished into overdrive, had *not* been a part of his limited calculations. He'd rushed into overdrive as fast as he could, his vision adjusting in time to witness Estella's attempt to save the brash warrior from Lars' attack and the anguish in Estella's eyes that followed thereafter. The truth that the vampire had paid for a stupid mistake made no difference to her; she saw it as a loss for their clan and a loss that she'd allowed to happen. He'd been able to see the complex-yet-convoluted network of guilt blossom like a hideous flower within her mind just as he'd caught up to her speed.

But, at that moment, dealing with the pseudo-gods was a bigger concern.

He'd needed distance *and* a distraction, and if he could serve up a decent helping of pain for Devin and his punks in the process it would be all the better.

Retrieving the pouch of "cherry bombs"—one of Dwayne's more clever-yet-unstable inventions—and leaving them at the feet of the four intruders, Xander had made a note of slamming his palm down on the entire bag as he'd risen to carry Estella away. Just a few of the explosives had been enough to destroy an entire building, so the idea of what a dozen-or-so of the little things could do when set off between the knees of the likes of Devin was enough to give him hope that this might work.

Dropping to the ground and casting one of the largest auric shields he'd ever had to, Xander let time return to normal around him and felt a swell of pride as four god-like auras flared up in shock right as the night turned to day for an instant.

14

BREAKS LOOSE

*T*here hadn't been enough time for Stan to come to grips with the realization that Devin and the others were about to break through before Xander had vanished from the room. Though there was nothing keeping him from calling out to the vampire—nothing to keep him from moving a psychic message while he was in overdrive or even to pull him back into the room—there was the fear of what it would mean if he did. Trying to stop Xander from doing what he'd set out to do would mean trying to validate what couldn't be validated; to justify the unjustifiable. Stan had spent his entire life fleeing from his problems, and since obtaining those powers he'd spent every moment trying to hide the coward he'd been behind nothing more than over-glorified illusions. Xander, however, because of a bold act nearly two years earlier when Stan had stopped a vengeful vampire and her friends from killing him and Marcus, refused to believe that Stan wasn't the brave, all-powerful bringer of justice that he'd seen that night.

When the truth was that *none*—not Xander or Marcus or even the rogues that he'd killed while protecting his friends—had been as surprised by the event as he'd been.

Shortly thereafter, when he'd heard of Devin's escape from prison and realized that he'd be coming for him, Stan's true nature had returned. He'd ran. It was what he knew, and he was certain that he'd left the mysterious moment of heroics behind him; swearing he'd never let himself take such a risk again.

But as the realization that Xander and Estella and an entire clan dedicated to following their orders were about to throw themselves into the flames of Devin's insanity—flames that Stan had brought upon them—he could feel an unfamiliar drive rising within him.

He had to fight.

Even knowing he'd lose, he had to stop running.

He'd spent *years* shadowing Xander as a boy—keeping a watchful eye on his late-friend's son—and as the little boy grew, he'd come to be his guidance counselor and even dared to become his friend.

What sort of shadow could abandon its subject?

What sort of guidance counselor could shirk one in need of guidance?

What sort of friend could allow the people he cared about to feed themselves to a fire?

"Alright, Devin," Stan let out a sigh that had been growing in him for years, letting the rage against his enemies and the passion to keep his friends safe push him to do the unthinkable, "here I come!"

HALFWAY UP the stairs from the lower levels where Trepis was being kept, Stan felt the mansion tremble under a familiar force. Pausing on the steps long enough to analyze what he was sensing, Stan felt himself smirk.

The Gamer's magic was an unmistakable trademark; the

portly magician's work as much a creation of passion as it was an incredible skill.

"Your legacy lives on, my old, gaming friend," he whispered to himself, feeling the lingering traces of three of his late-friend's exploding rounds begin to settle on the air, "And in a thriving legacy, no less."

Knowing that Xander had been the one to fire the rounds—who else within the clan would've been brash enough use The Gamer's wares to put holes in the mansion?—Stan hurried his pace, sensing the rising tension just outside. As he hurried to join the others, he let his vision venture from his body so that he could survey the scene outside—leaping from one warrior's mind to the next to get different angles from the battlefield—before crying out in pain as his astral leaps landed him into a body that was already half-dead.

The partially faded and blurred view of a sang warrior who was watching an upside-down and grief-stricken Estella...

"What the hell is going on up—"

A flash of potential energy as many more explosives carrying the magical signature of The Gamer flared to life.

Stan rolled his eyes, "Xander, you crazy bastard..."

Xander had miscalculated...

Again!

The blast from a dozen of Dwayne's "cherry bombs" was far more immense than he'd considered in his effort to get Estella away from the pseudo-gods. In hindsight, he'd decimated an entire parking garage and spread chaos over an entire city block from the rubble with about two times that number, but they hadn't been set off all at once. If it hadn't been for the morbid irony that Lenix had redirected traffic and pedestrians to offer them a clear battlefield, the death toll would've been far larger than the single fatality; Lenix's.

That, however, had been with only a few well-placed explosives at various spots in the massive concrete structure...

Not a full dozen set off all at once a short distance from Xander, Estella, and his home!

Realizing that there was no way to stop the force of the blast from encompassing the entire mansion and everyone occupying it, Xander whispered a silent apology to his colleagues and refocused his aura to surround just Estella and himself to protect them from the blast.

Estella screamed.

The combined auric force of the warriors spiked in a sudden panic.

Xander's heart grew heavy with the realization that something irreversible was about to happen.

The four pseudo-gods, standing at ground-zero, took the full impact of the blast and disappeared from Xander's auric radar shortly after; he guessed they'd either been blown to bits or, at the very least, blown off the property; in either case, he wasn't too keen on celebrating just yet. All around him the force of the blast worked, destroying the already damaged side of the mansion's wall and half of the neighboring side into rubble, sending chunks of grass and soil into the air, and stripping the Fall-kissed trees of their dwindling load of colored leaves. But, somehow, the mansion and all of the Trepis Clan's warriors were untouched.

Feeling the blast collapse as the magic subsided and swallowed itself, Xander dared to look up for the source of whatever miracle had arrived to save his home and his colleagues.

Stan stood over him, his arms held out and casting a massive, shimmering wall of semi-transparent blackness in between the source of the blast and the mansion.

He'd saved them all!

Xander blinked, trying to absorb the reality of what had just happened.

"Stan?"

∼

ESTELLA, still trembling, forced her eyes to open at the sound of Xander's bewildered voice. Had she heard him right? Could it really be...

Looking up, she spotted their friend standing over them; his face as clean and god-like as he'd made it the night he'd arrived and draped in the same oily cloak that he'd arrived in. As he lowered his outstretched hands, a small plot of the earth opened up beneath him. As his hand—just as black and oily as the rest of his body—received the walking stick that rose up to meet it, the inky blackness spread across its length and began to bubble and grow and reshape. The air blurred around the inky mass as every facet of its being—shape, size, and apparent density—appeared to be modified within Stan's hand. Estella's eyes widened at the spectacle, feeling the energy rolling outward before suddenly pulling inward; she gasped as she realized that Stan was actually drawing energy out of the air around him—calling upon the atoms and molecules floating about from the blast—to reform the walking stick into something else.

She remembered playing with a similar spell years earlier, though on a far smaller scale and with far greater effort. It hadn't worked for her at all; the efforts to combine hydrogen and oxygen molecules to create a drop of water on a notebook page only serving to set the paper on fire and force her to get water from the bathroom's tap to extinguish it.

At that moment, however, Stan was creating something far more complex than just a drop of water...

Spinning the staff in his hand, the blackness seemed to recede—pelting from its surface like blood whipped from a blade—and Estella marveled at the beautiful sword that the walking stick had become. The massive blade was just as tall as her, and nearly just as wide; she figured that the weight couldn't have been less than two-hundred pounds from the bulk of the weapon. Despite this, however, Stan seemed no more burdened by its weight than he had the walking stick's. The length of the blade ran with an indentation that was adorned in foreign markings that Estella didn't recognize, and as Stan moved to grip the hilt in both hands the energy from his two palms seemed to spark within these; the trail of symbols lighting up with a bright blue glow at the base before traveling up to the tip of the blade. As the final symbol illuminated, the entire sword shimmered and glowed with the same radiance, cutting through the darkness ahead of them like a lantern.

Though there had been no sign of the four "gods" prior to that moment—none of their bodies visible to any of the keen eyes of the clan of nonhumans or their distinct energy traceable for those sensitive to such things—the bright blue glow from Stan's sword instantly exposed them. With the light ripping them out from their enchanted camouflage, the four shrieked in agony under the beam of light.

"Xander," Stan sneered at the sight of the four, "perhaps you'd like to do the honors."

Estella's lover, though just as awestruck as she, didn't linger as he reached behind him to retrieve the sawed-off shotgun tethered to his back. With a sharp yank, the strap snapped and the weapon was freed from his body as he leveled it towards the nearest "god"—the hulking brute that had slammed him to the ground—and fired both slugs into his chest before whipping the spent weapon towards the "god" in the coat. Leveling his gaze at the makeshift projectile, the shifty "god's" eyes narrowed, and the shotgun disassembled itself in midair before falling to the ground in pieces.

Stan let his left hand release the sword—the glowing blade

not wavering as he did—and held it in front of him; his fingers vibrating mechanically as a wave of energy passed between them. Reaching for her tonfas with a shaky hand, Estella watched as Stan's magic gathered the shotgun's components and lifted them into the air a short distance from the "god" that had dropped them there. As the "god's" eyes narrowed in skepticism at the sight of Stan's work, the first piece—the short length of the two barrels—rocketed towards him; slamming into his forehead and throwing him off his feet. Shortly after that, the rest of the pieces began shooting after him; the gun's pieces flying with the same deadly velocity as the slugs it had fired moments earlier.

A short distance away, the first "god"—clutching the tightly paired wounds in his chest and groaning like a cement mixer filled with rocks—writhed on the ground; his body shifting around the wounds as though hoping a new shape might relieve the pain.

Further back, working to fix his fractured skull and caved-in sternum, was the "god" in the long coat; several of the smaller bits of the dismantled shotgun still lodged around his body.

Estella sneered at him, remembering what he'd done to the sang, "Serves you right!"

"I'LL TEAR YOU TO FUCKING PIECES!" the "goddess" shrieked and lunged, her body seeming to rise and swell like an ocean wave as she descended upon Xander.

"NO!" Estella bared her fangs and spun Helios in her right hand, bringing the golden tonfa down on the woman's collarbone—her left arm and neck stretching away from the searing impact of her offensive enchantment—as she slammed the butt-end of her silver tonfa squarely between her opponent's breasts. "I've had ENOUGH!" Estella hissed as she watched the breath fumble out of the woman's lungs before she drew back, slamming the two tonfas together and raising the heaving "goddess" off her feet and flinging her into the air until she was nothing more than a shadow on the night sky...

Then Estella flung her back to Earth, bringing her crashing down on the jagged rubble of the destroyed rock wall ahead of her.

For the first time in Estella's life, she felt a wave of happiness at the sound of breaking bones and pained whimpers.

XANDER AND STAN gawked for a moment at Estella—her blue eyes shimmering with an electric fury behind the thick curtains of sweat-slicked black hair that hung about her heaving face—as Selene and Helios sizzled and sparked with the residual magic still coursing through them.

While he was usually reserved with his words to Estella when others were around, the heat of the moment was proving to make an exception to his own shyness in such matters.

"Alright," Xander nodded to her, "*that* was fucking awesome, and I'm going to have to do something about how good you look later. Before then, though, I've got—UUGH!"

Devin was suddenly inches from his face, the psychopathic pseudo-god's fist buried—Xander heaved and looked down; *literally* buried—inside his stomach. The ripped fabric of the turtleneck had already begun to grow darker with the blood that had begun to seep around his leering attacker's fist, which he could feel shifting about within his guts.

"XANDER!" Stan moved to swing with his monstrous sword, only to have Devin shoot him a look that encased his entire body in a shimmering, fiery pool that forced his attack to come at him in slow motion.

Devin wet his lips, smiling at the sight of Stan's desperate face as he inched towards them. Then, seeming bored with the spectacle, he looked back at Xander. "I've had quite enough of this ridiculous dance," he spat. "I'm afraid it's time for you to—"

"DON'T TOUCH HI—" Estella lunged at Devin, only to have the pseudo-god's free hand rise up—lifting her off her feet as he did—and suspend her in the air.

Devin cooed, "Oh, the blood-witch; noble and pure, yes?" He sneered, "We've seen the harlot that dwells within you, girl; nothing more than a *whore* in queen's garb. A hypocrite who shuns pain and suffering and death who wantonly slides down upon the shaft of a *vampire warrior*—a being who by his nature consumes death and brings suffering and, what's more, has sworn to a life of bringing *more* of it to his own kind—and behaves like there's justice in one but not in the other!" Devin's condescending sneer stayed locked on Estella while his eyes rolled in his skull to address Xander, "She saw fit to drop my female upon the rocks, little vampire; shall I reciprocate her gesture and do the same to her? I doubt very much she'll fair quite as well as Bianca, though."

As if to punctuate his statement, the sound of pained-and-enraged growls drew the eyes of the onlookers towards Bianca, who had begun to pull herself from the wall and reform her shattered bones. A moment later, Lars, ripping the shotgun's trigger from his jaw and letting the wound seal behind it, glared at Stan. Shortly after that, Gerard, too, rose to his feet, picking the sizzling, shimmering shotgun shells—the enchantment struggling to fight his own body's magic—from his chest before he crushed them in his fist.

"For that," Gerard growled at Xander, "I'm going to crush your skull nice and *slow!*"

Lars laughed, moseying casually around the still time-lagged Stan. "My my... how the righteous have fallen," his laugh erupted into a cackle that pitched his head back. As the roar of hysterics reached an ear-piercing crescendo, the sound turned to an enraged roar that brought his impossibly gaping mouth inches from Stan's strained expression. "IT'S TIME TO DIE, YOU OLD GOAT!"

Lars' fist was a blur as he swung—his coattails whipping up from the force of the attack—and slammed squarely across Stan's jaw. The impact resounded like a car crash, and the enchantment that had forced Stan's unnatural crawl lifted as he was thrown across the lawn as if fired from a cannon.

Gerard stomped his foot on the ground, and a tremor shot across the lawn—upturning the earth as it did—until it was beneath Stan's flailing, airborne body, where it shot upward like a mountain birthing itself from the soil to grab him out of the air. Then, with the same abruptness as its appearance, the tower of raised earth sank back again and dragged Stan down with it.

Xander whimpered at the sight, still feeling Devin's hand worm through his belly.

"Now that our brother is no longer a factor in our dealings..." the pseudo-god grinned and made a note of clenching his still-raised free hand, eliciting a pained whimper from Estella. Xander's eyes locked on his lover—her body still hanging in the air within Devin's magic grip—and he saw her fight to keep from crying out; her aura thrashing about in a blind panic around her forced composure.

She was suffering...

He was *killing* her...

And she was trying to hide it for his sake.

Stan... Xander fought to hold a connection with his friend's wavering aura, *Please! I know you're still there! You can't be taken out that easy! I know I was wrong—wrong about everything! About you, about your fear and your reasons! About your struggle to be more than them!—but I need you to give me The Power, Stan; Estella's dying! Please don't force me to watch her die, Stan... please don't let them take her from me!*

The silence—both inside and outside Xander's head—was unbearable; Devin's eager face hanging in front of his, silently beckoning for an answer to Estella's fate that Xander knew would make no difference to the decision he'd already made for her.

Devin wanted to hear him beg.

If he did, Estella would die.

If he didn't...

Please, Stan...

Then, an answer!

Be careful...

The world seemed to go calm and still then; the pain in his guts not vanishing, but simply no longer mattering enough to hurt. Darkness and fear seemed to peel back like shedding skin to reveal unfathomable truths lurking behind the stigma of mystery. Xander looked to Estella, not fearful for her fate but eager to rewrite it; her suspended magic-filled body shimmering with the same beauty and perfection as a lone ornament hanging upon a pine branch. He moved to look at Devin —the pseudo-god's face turning worrisome as he saw the fear and agony fall from Xander like the leaves of the season—and he saw within the twisted, angry features the very bits and pieces that he was made of; saw the atoms swimming about in their clusters; saw them packed and decorated about in nature's design; saw the streams of magical current that had come to drive him. The streams connected him to the other three—their bodies seeming tethered to him as though they were subconsciously aware that to stray would condemn them to the normalcy they'd long since abandoned—and he saw, riding along the threads that held them, the fear and insecurities that they shared; that compelled them to take Stan's powers. They wanted so badly to feel a sense of ownership to the world that they'd glorified that power as the only way of achieving it.

But now that power was inside Xander...

And he would show them ownership.

"I see now," Xander murmured, feeling his face twist into a smirk. "I see, and I know."

Devin curled his lip, "What's this noise, boy? What are you—"

"I'm going to make you pay," Xander whispered in Devin's face as he willed his intestines to grow rock-hard before draining the heat energy from the pseudo-god's hand.

Hissing in pain, Devin moved to yank his hand away from the sensation; the abruptness putting too much strain on the tortured cells of his hand, which had frozen to Xander's insides. Fighting to free him from the smirking vampire's stomach, Devin jumped back and cried out as the sound of something shattering echoed within the depths of Xander's body.

Estella fell to her feet, freed from Devin's magic and malicious clutches.

Devin fell to his back, eyes wide and minus his right hand.

Xander chuckled at the sight; seeing the jagged ends at the pseudo-god's wrist as he and his three artificial colleagues gaped. He started towards them, willing the skin of his belly to close and, upset at the treatment of his turtleneck, willing the fibers of the shirt to reknit, as well; the unsettling sensation of the chilled blood that had soaked into the material easily remedied as he forced every blood cell to dry and flake away with his steps.

The tortured ground of his home seemed to sing with every step, and he willed his excess of energy to sink into the earth with his advancement, allowing new, stronger grass to grow behind him. Seeing the state of his property in his free-roaming mind's eye, he casually willed the damage to reverse itself; his smirk growing into a full smile as he watched the scattered debris roll and lift within his all-encompassing aura and return to its rightful place. With the mansion and its stone walls rebuilding themselves around them, the pseudo-gods narrowed their gaze on Xander with the realization of what had happened.

Xander flexed his torso and looked down as a small auric tendril seeped from his stomach, returning something that didn't belong there. He laughed at this and held it out towards the four, his smile only growing and growing as he did.

"You dropped this," he said with a laugh as he presented Devin with his severed hand.

15

MAKING GODS SWEAT

*A*ll around Estella, the damage that the mansion and its surroundings had suffered was reversed. Ahead of her, Xander slowly walked towards the "gods," holding out the hand that he'd torn from their leader while it had been *inside* his body. Estella didn't try to make sense of any of it; most of her life had been dedicated to mastering the arts, and in the blink of an eye Xander had shifted the tides of the battle to almost laughable degrees. Somehow, Stan had gotten his power into him, and, from the looks of it, he was controlling it better than any of them.

There was no making sense of any of it now.

It was magic; pure and simple.

"Well," Xander spoke in a low, sing-song voice, waving the hand as though he might toss it towards the four, "don't you want this back?" Every step he took was met with a shaky retreat by the four, and after the fourth mirrored step away from him he sneered. "Believe me when I say you're going to want this," Xander growled, "because you won't last long without it."

The blond leader shivered—the act seeming more out of

irritation than fear at that moment—and straightened himself, flexing his right arm at his side. Moving the jagged stump of his wrist to his mouth, he kept his narrowed gaze transfixed on Xander as he chewed away the ends of the wound—where the skin looked dead; almost frostbitten—and spit the wads of meat onto the ground between them before running his tongue across the fresh, vital meat. Though the gesture urged Estella to vomit, she stifled the reflex; watching as the areas that his tongue touched seemed somehow awakened. Finishing the process, the fresh blood began to bubble as the splintered bone began to rebuild itself; the muscles and tendons following after it—wrapping and winding like a visceral ivy—and encompassed it. As the bones of his hand forked off into five digits and the muscle crept over the knuckles and along the start of his fingers, they began to wag and, as they elongated, the gesture evolved to wiggles. With the meat of his hand in place and the tips of his fingers completed, the skin at the "god's" wrist began to shimmy along the entire network, replacing the hand he'd lost.

"No need for your generosity, boy," he countered, making a note of raising his new middle finger to Xander. "You're hardly the first one to take a piece of me, and I've never asked for any of those parts back, either."

Xander seemed neither impressed nor surprised by the display, and, as his advancement on the four continued, he gave the severed hunk of meat in his hand a squeeze and Estella gasped as it erupted into flames within his hand. Hearing the sound, he looked over to her, offering her a smile and a reassuring nod, as the mass continued to burn within his grip; no sign of pain or discomfort showing as it did.

"It'll be alright," he promised her, his voice—previously as echoed and terrifying as the others'—sounding once again like his own. "It'll be over soon."

"Insolent little maggot! Our brother graces you with The

Power and you feel that you're strong enough to take on the likes of *us* within moments of it entering you?" The blond man's lip curled back as Xander said this, the moment of awe and uncertainty seeming to pass as he heeded Xander's comforting words to her as a challenge. "We have had this strength for *years*; we have honed and trained the skills in torture and torment to the point of—"

"You're lackeys are nothing more than a cast of Jerry Springer rejects dragged into a grandeur delusion by a desperate pyro with an inflated god-complex," Xander rolled his eyes. "Whatever you *think* you know about the powers inside you—inside *us* now—are the product of an excited glimpse of an iceberg from a distant ship from a stupid *human* child!" He let his fangs extend then and he made a note of piercing the meat of his hand just below his left thumb. Holding up the palm and displaying the twin trails of blood that had begun to seep across his hand, he smirked, "Let me show you how deep the iceberg goes."

With that, he whipped his hand outward, letting the droplets of blood fly across the space between them. Clenching his fist then, the blood drops began to inflate and reshape as they came down upon the four. In the short time it took to reach the "gods," each of the swelled blood drops—seven in total, Estella could see—had become large, crimson bat-like creatures with the gnarling, snapping tiger faces.

The "goddess" shrieked as two of the blood-bats fluttered around her, and she wrapped her arms around her head and sank into a quivering mass as they screeched around her.

The hulking "god" moved to drive a massive fist into the first blood-bat that came at him, only to have his fist pass through it as simply as a water balloon. The creature erupted back into blood and his hand and forearm was coated in the liquid, and, grunting in confusion, the "god" watched as the mass began to crawl and spread like a living puddle across the entire length of his arm.

Seeing two of Xander's creations coming at him and already starting towards the "goddess," the "god" in the long coat took in a deep inhale before blowing outward towards them, the resulting gust consuming the four creatures in its fury and blowing them into the night sky.

The blond "god" stepped forward to meet the three blood-bats coming at him and, with a flick of his hand, they erupted into flames—screeching out as they fizzled and left the stink of clotted blood on the lingering breeze left from the previous "god's" spell—and dropped to the ground.

"I'm already bored of your clichéd exuberance, boy!" he said through clenched teeth, "On my first day with The Power I turned my prison bars into serpents and impaled five guards in my escape on them alone! Would you like me to tell you what I did with them?"

Xander smirked and chuckled, his grin returning, "If you were a prisoner, I'd imagine you sodomized them. By the way," he cocked his head towards the hulking "god" as he started to whimper and twitch from the spreading mass of blood that had coated his entire arm, "you might want to do something about that."

Estella stared, unable to move or think as she watched the blood's hold on the "god's" hand drag him closer to the other three.

Estella...

At first, she couldn't figure out where the voice was coming from—couldn't bring herself to focus on anything but the scene before her—but as the call grew more desperate, she finally pulled herself away from Xander's battle.

"Stan?"

Please... I can't get out, the voice pleaded, growing distant; weaker. *Cant... breathe...*

"Oh gods..." Estella started to run towards where she'd seen Stan get dragged underground and stood over the sagged spot in the lawn. "What can I..." her mind raced as she tried to think of a spell that would free him. Finally, realizing that time was against her, she knelt down and pressed her palms to the ground.

The spell wouldn't be pretty, but it'd get him out.

"... you might want to do something about that," the empowered vampire winked at Devin.

Not wanting to humor the arrogance but unable to deny that there *was* something coming at them, he growled at his own resignation and turned to face Gerard as his right arm—coated in a layer of the vampire's enchanted blood—dragged him closer to him.

"Devin!" Gerard's voice was, for the first time, panicked, "I can't stop it!"

"You fool!" Devin snarled, "It's an enchantment! Fight it! Fight—"

His order was cut short as he was forced to duck under the blood-controlled right arm. Gerard grunted and cursed, working to yank his limb back into his control as it swung at the nearest ally it came across. Darting out of range, Bianca left Lars open to the possessed arm's wrath.

"What the fu—" Lars moved to back-step from an incoming uppercut, only to have it connect with his shoulder and send him corkscrewing to the ground.

"Devin! I can't stop it! Get it off of me!" Gerard pleaded as, with none of his comrades within punching distance, the arm turned on him and drove itself three times into his face—breaking his nose and jaw in the process—before wrapping its hand around his throat.

The vampire began to laugh.

Devin's body shook with rage, his hands balling into tight fists and erupting into flames.

"Lars! Bianca!" he growled under his breath, feeling the two snap to attention as their names resounded within their heads, "Rid Gerard of his burden! I need to teach this trouser-stain a lesson in respecting his superiors."

DARKNESS. Even more darkness closing in.

No air; no strength; no hope.

An all-encompassing and crushing weight pushing what little breath was left from his lungs. The pungent, acrid soil pushing past his nostrils and lips; eager to accept him as a part of it—to *make* him a part of it—and soak up all of him until nothing but his memory remained.

Stan had heard Xander's cry to him—had been forced at that moment to weigh the options; let the world fall into Devin's hands and, to christen it, take Estella, or to take a chance on the suicidal, rage-filled, young vampire he'd watched grow for eighteen years—and, with those two options before him, he chose the lesser of two evils.

If he'd allowed himself to use The Power to free himself from his soon-to-be tomb, he might've been tempted to fight the decision—to fight Devin and the others—and hold out to the futile hop that had proven pointless so many times in the past.

Maybe it was better this way...

Maybe it was better this way...

Maybe it was be—

His world—the only world he knew anymore; a world he'd come to feel safe in; a world he'd expected to die in; a world he'd been trapped in less than sixty seconds—vanished around him, swallowed in a flood of sudden moonlight and washed in a monsoon of dirt.

He'd been burdened with life!

He'd been saved!

Coughing on the flood of air and hope, he scrambled to the surface, spotting Estella—on her knees and heaving from exertion—as she partially eclipsed the left-side of the nearly full moon.

"What did you do?" the two of them said in unison to one another.

They stared for a moment, trying to come to grips with what the other meant before flinching at a loud, pained cry from Gerard and turning back to face Xander and the others.

As Stan's eyes darted across the scenery, he saw that the damage—all of it—was gone. The mansion stood just as tall and proud as it had the night he'd arrived, and the wall showed no signs of ever having suffered Devin and his goon's entrance. Even the warriors who had suffered at the hands of the four monsters were, though obviously terrified by whatever had transpired while Stan had been trapped underground, back on their feet and *not* seizing.

"*KILL HIM!*" Devin's voice rang out, and Stan instinctively moved to cast a barrier to protect the onlookers from succumbing to his impact once more.

Only to remember that he no longer had The Power.

Xander, however...

SECOND VERSE; *same as the first,* Xander thought, casting out his aura in a massive barrier to contain the seizure-inducing waves that carried on Devin's psychic roar. Folding his aura around the four, he trapped the dark spell within the pocket of his barrier and dropped it back in on them, smirking as Gerard and

Bianca both buckled under the effects; their eyes rolling back in their heads as a tremor rolled up each of their bodies. *Nothing but a carriage of destruction dragged by four one-trick ponies.*

Gerard's arm, which Lars and Bianca had worked to cut free of their comrade—Bianca pinning him in place while Lars drove his open hand through his shoulder like a blade—writhed and flexed under the enchantment a moment longer until the blood controlling it fizzled away. Gerard continued to wail over the pain of his lost limb.

Lars and Bianca, however, heeded their regained control and charged at Xander with all the fury and wrath that he remembered from their last encounter.

"Don't think I've forgotten about that cheap shot I owe you for," Lars called to Xander, leaping into the air and beginning to cast another of his illusion spells.

Xander smirked, able to watch the "code" of the spell as Lars assembled it—this time trying to create a false reality where Xander had no arms or legs and was helpless to defend himself —and he allowed the pseudo-god to finish his work before he dealt with him.

It really was too beautiful of an illusion to interrupt the creation of.

Bianca, more keen on a direct scare-and-attack routine, had already worked the illusion that she was a shambling corpse; rotted and dripping from the inside-out with all numbers of insects and creatures—many of which she'd made up specifically for that spell. While the initial sight *was* alarming for Xander, it was nothing that a new spell couldn't fix.

And, lucky for Xander, Lars—who was beginning to descend upon him—had just finished with a doozy of a replacement.

Reaching out with his aura, Xander tweaked the incoming illusion and rewrote the target.

The spell fell upon the unsuspecting Bianca, who collapsed to the ground and cried out in terror as she watched her arms and legs shrivel away before her very eyes. The scene was enough to make Xander's laughter return.

Lars could see that his spell had been redirected before his feet reached the ground, and panic at his realization that he would be forced to fight Xander without the benefit of an illusion on his side sent his aura into a panicked frenzy.

"You're right to be afraid," Xander said with a chuckle before jumping into overdrive and repositioning himself to be behind Lars when he finally landed. The pseudo-god whimpered as he fell, finding his still able-minded opponent not where he'd been expecting him. Leaning in behind him, Xander felt his ever-growing smile broaden as he whispered, "I have to appreciate your tolerance for Devin's bullshit, Lars, but you haven't *seen* crazy yet."

Lars shivered at that and looked back over his shoulder. "Wh-who in the hell are you?" he stammered.

Xander grinned at that. "Oh? For shame! You don't *recognize* me, Lars?" he chided, clucking his tongue several times. Once again, he repositioned himself—jumping into overdrive and cycling around Lars a few times to appreciate his growing expression of panic—on his right side, forcing him to spin clumsily to face him again. "I suppose it's a simple enough mistake, though"—another shift; another clumsy rotation— "You've only been hunting me for *years!*"

He vanished again, this time dropping out of overdrive over Bianca—leaving Lars to whip about in a panicked desperation to see where he was—and wiping the enchantment on her mind as though it were crumbs on a coffee table. As she came to grips with the reality of what had happened to her, her breathing steadied and her wild eyes came to settle on Xander.

"You're disgusting, girl" he chastised her. "You crash through life and view people like stepping stones to carry you one misplaced step further in your futile goals," he leaned in over her and bared his fangs, letting his own illusion that his mouth was coated and fill with the gore she expected of his kind and laughing at the feared whimper she emitted. "But people aren't stones, girl, they're bridges—the only hope you have of crossing the troubles in this world—and you've gone and burned them all! Now you're trapped with *me*, and there's no hope of escape for you!"

Bianca howled in terror as Xander found one of her most traumatic childhood memories and dragged it to the surface of her mind; creating a cycle with the event and enchanting her body to relive the events over and over and over. Her body went rigid as the hallucination took hold and she began to convulse with the same seizures Devin had cast upon the clan's warriors.

"One more word, child," Xander let his voice echo within her skull just as much as within her ears, *"and Daddy's gonna put another cigar out on you; this time in your eye, you hear?"*

"Dear god... it can't be!" she gasped, clapping her hands over her eyes. "You're not him... You're not him! You're *not* him! YOU'RE NOT HIM! YOU'RE *NOT*! YOU'RE NOT YOU'RE NOT YOU'RE NOT YOU'RE NOT YOU'RE NO—"

"Xander!" Estella called out.

Xander looked up at that, feeling a haze begin to disperse in his head at the sound of her voice.

"Estella?"

His eyes fell upon her and Stan as they approached, both of their eyes transfixed upon Bianca and her writhing fit.

Estella bit her lip, "What are you doing to her?"

Xander followed her gaze and smirked, chuckling at a trail of saliva that had rolled from Bianca's lips and started down her left cheek. "Nothing she didn't have coming," he responded.

Estella frowned down at the sight, "I suppose, but..."

"See how you like somebody fucking with your bitch, vampire!" Lars growled, running towards them and throwing another illusion spell at Estella.

"Be quiet, asshole," Xander sighed, snagging the spell out of the air with his aura and slamming it back into Lars' chest with enough force to send him careening back and into the mansion's wall, several warriors jumping free as the pseudo-god's body sailed past them as it did.

Lars' cries intensified as the illusion took hold and his own mind convinced himself that his face was melting from his skull.

Good one, boy, Xander thought to himself, *you've got this god-thing down, don't you?*

Well, Stan did *train me when I... wait, what?*

Xander blinked, staring outward yet staring at nothing. "Who...?"

"Xander?" Estella shook his arm, "Are you alright?"

Stan frowned, looking at the scene around them. "Gerard's grown his arm back," he told them. "We should get the others inside; work on getting another barrier up while Xander finishes this." He turned to Xander then, narrowing his eyes, "You *will* finish this, right? Tonight?" He shook his head, putting a hand on Xander's shoulder, "Xander, it's very important that we don't let The Power linger in you for too long."

Stanley, you old-fashioned, sentimental idiot, Xander thought, *do you have any idea who you're—Stop it! Don't think that way! He's... he's just... a lying bastard! He wanted to dump this joke of a magic-slinging barbershop quartet on us and... us? Wait... focus, Xander; focus! What did—You might want to duck, boy!*

All his life Xander had relied on his instincts to survive. When his stepfather had gone on his rampages, he trusted his instincts to find him a good hiding place, though they hardly ever kept him hidden for long. When the kids at school had picked on him, he'd known to let his instincts tell him when to run and when to fight. When the decision to either stay a miserable human retch or be inducted into the world of mythos as a vampire, he'd leapt at the chance to claim his legacy. And when his instincts told him to duck when he knew there was danger about, he'd always done so.

And he'd kept his head for it each and every time.

This time was no different.

The air streamed over his head as Xander dropped into a crouch and let Gerard's new arm past with all the force of a meteor cutting through the atmosphere.

"Squirrely little twerp!" he grumbled as the force of his failed attack dragged him several paces away.

Nearby, Stan grabbed Estella by the shoulders and pulled her free of Gerard's path as he tripped over the still-whimpering Bianca and nearly came down on them.

"**STAY AWAY FROM HER!**" Xander roared, seeing Estella's panicked aura coil as she realized how close the god had come to knocking her over. "**SHE'S MINE!**"

Before he or his instincts could decide what to do, he was upon Gerard with an uncaged fury.

"... proud to announce that our late comrade's son, Xander Stryker, has taken up the mantle as..."

Gerard's head was in his clutches and he dragged the bulbous, misshapen mass into his knee.

"... something's wrong with Trepis."

The kukri's handle was in his white-knuckle grip and he cackled as he felt the curved, enchanted blade sink into the god's left shoulder.

"... your clan, son; those mythos in there rely on you for guidance and protection..."

A leather-clad elbow was driven with enough force into a sternum built like a brick wall; the elbow won.

More laughter.

KILL THEM ALL, XANDER! KILL... THEM... ALL!

Kill... kill... kill... kill...

""What's happening to him?"

"... magic's been keeping him alive, but his age is finally keeping up with him. He won't last more than..."

... kill... kill... kill... kill...

Stop playing with your prey and ERADICATE THEM!

Bicycle kick; broken ribs and a punctured lung. Overdrive behind Gerard and triple-jab to mid-back; fractured vertebrae. Overdrive back to front and kick in the left kneecap; immobile.

Now he's MINE!

"... can't help what's..."

"... won't be able to protect her forever..."

"... you fail, we all fail."

"Let's try not to lose any more friends..."

"... going to die if..."

"... be dead by..."

"... dying..."

"... dead..."

... kill.... kill... kill... kill...

16

DUST IN THE WIND

*E*stella stared as Xander's body became a blur of ferocity and precision. The once intimidating "god" that she'd seen as an immovable, towering beast—her mind unable to fathom that such a creature had ever been a normal man at any time—becoming nothing more than a massive plaything for the red-and-black blur that was her lover to knock about like a cheap toy.

"What's happening to him?" she whispered, leaning towards Stan.

Stan stared, shaking his head slowly, and drew in a ragged breath, "The Power… it can tell I'm not its host anymore; it's trying to bend him to its will."

Estella frowned at that, pulling her focus from Xander. "Bend him to its… why did it never do that to you?" she demanded.

"It did. Every single day," Stan said in a low tone, still unable to look away, "I just knew how to keep it under control. Every day it got stronger and more persuasive, so I had to get stronger and more resistant along with it. Now that it's in Xander, he's facing day-one in his struggle for control, but it's had over twenty-five years' worth of training on me to drive off of..."

Aren't you glad you've got me now?

"I DON'T EVEN KNOW WHO THE FUCK YOU ARE!" Xander clutched his head and screamed into the sky.

"Xander! XANDER! What's wrong? What's happening? Please," Estella rushed towards him, her eyes flooded with tears. Her tiny hand fell upon his jacket and he saw a vision of his hands buried between her breasts and tearing through her ribcage in a hungry search for her heart.

"NO!" he pushed her back, feeling his entire world shatter at the thought of hurting her. "Don't... I'm fine. I'm..."

She'll never understand you; she's seen what you can do! Just look at Gerard! The god's a TANK and you've turned him into a crying, sniveling wreck! You could kill him now, you know; could kill them all! You could kill every single one of them... starting with **her!** his eyes moved to Estella on their own.

Her? he blinked, not understanding his own thoughts. *But she's not... she's—*

Estella bit her lip, her hand still reaching out to him, though growing more unsteady by the moment. "X-Xander?" her voice was so meek; so scared.

He laughed... and then wondered why.

She's no different than anybody else here. Look around you; the structure—two arms, two legs, one head with an inferior mind buried under carbon and proteins and water and—

She IS different! She's—

HOW is she different? What makes her different from him or any of them or her over there. They're all just specs of organic matter clinging to a ball of rock hurtling through the small void of nothingness. You can't get more insignificant than—

Why am I thinking these—

Oh my, my dear boy, did you still think that your mind was so much better than Devin's? He has the right idea; he just doesn't think BIG enough! You can take it all! Kill the girl, kill the old goat, tear this entire legacy they've forced on you to the ground—burn it all and everyone in it—and TAKE... IT... ALL!

Who are you?

I'm you, Xander. Now you tell me, who the fuck are YOU?

Xander shivered and looked down at Gerard. The god—he frowned; had he always thought of them like that?—was barely able to cry out in pain through his broken jaw; the gaps where several of his teeth that had been knocked down his throat whistled with the forced exhales that labored around the punctured lung.

Kill him. Kill him! KILL HIM!

"GET AWAY FROM HIM!" Lars—finally having freed himself of the enchantment—tackled Xander at the waist and knocked him to the ground, beginning a barrage of high-speed punches to Xander's face.

"Oh?" Xander willed the bones in his face to reform just as quickly as Lars broke them, "Are you done with your little trip?"

"You know, the others thought I was crazy for being so eager to track you down," Lars told him, accentuating the last three words with a solid punch to his face for each one. "But right now—at this moment, you punker piece of shit—I can't *stand* the idea of any of the others getting the pleasure of taking you out!"

Xander erupted in another bout of laughter, "Oh my! I'm touched! Do you want to kiss me, too? To what do I owe the honor, exactly? Will Devin give you a bigger piece of pie for killing me?" Xander's aura shot from his chest and threw the heaving god off of him, giving him an opening to jump to his feet. With Lars still coming down from the force, Xander grabbed his flailing wrist and dragged him down with enough force to drive him into the ground. "I don't know, tough guy, I think that having me *and* The Power—you know, what he's been working so hard to make his own—"

Lars yanked himself free of the ground and took another swing at Xander, "*Our* own!"

Xander caught his fist and cackled, "I know what I said, sport. Now, where was I? God, I *hate* being interrupted; remind me to show you how annoying your wagging tongue is after I've taken it out of your head. It was something to do with... oh, that's right! Your boss!" Xander smirked, twisting Lars' hand suddenly, breaking his wrist, "So what *is* Devin going to think when—in this fantasy-world of yours where you kill me, I mean —you destroy what's had you and your inbred 'siblings' following him from continent-to-continent for the past few years?"

Fighting past the pain of the broken wrist, Lars kicked Xander away from him and healed the injury before advancing on him, "You're insinuating that I'm afraid of Devin?"

Xander doubled over with laughter and Lars, seeing an opening to land a hit, moved to grab him.

Xander jumped into overdrive and reappeared beside him, driving a sidekick into his crotch. Still laughing, he said, "Insinuating? I didn't know it was supposed to be a secret! I mean, just look at you! *All* of you"—he motioned to the broken Gerard and the sobbing Bianca—"You're a lot of total messes from beginning-to-end; nothing more than a waste of life *and* power; you see it even now, and the reality of just how expendable you are..." He smirked, "And it *terrifies* you *almost* as much as Devin does!"

Lars' eyes widened, the fear and desperation in his aura rolling in thick bundles. "What are you talking about?"

Xander wagged his finger at him, "Oh don't be coy, Lars; Now..." he jumped into overdrive again, this time not to reposition himself around the startled god but to take him. Reaching out, he sank his thumbs into the time-frozen god's eyes and, when he was certain he had a good hold on his body *and* mind, he dropped out of overdrive and relished in the sound of Lars' shrieks, "... let's go on a trip down memory lane, shall we?"

∼

~One year, eleven months, two weeks, three days, and seventeen hours earlier~

THE SHIT WAS SO *pure it might as well have just come out of the ground!*

The bitch... not so much; put that skank in the ground!

Pulling the needle from his tear duct and blinking against the lingering sting, Lars let the shit swim around his head—nothing like a direct shot to the brain, motherfucker!—before he looked over to see how the low-rate hoe was liking her cut of the shit.

He rolled his eyes, shivering as his still-tender left eye flexed the duct and reminded him of where his high had come from.

Still...

Bitch was passed out beside him.

Sighing, he moved to see if she'd used all the shit he gave her and, brushing one of the more daring cockroaches that had taken up residence in his mattress from her left tit, he reached over her and plucked the needle from her right arm.

"Jeez! Ya stupid cow, you couldn't even find a vein, huh? Guess this really was your first ride!" he laughed and, when she didn't wake up to laugh with him, he punched her in the back of the head. "STUPID BITCH! DON'T'CHA HEAR SO—" The sweet high started to spiral

down the shitter as he realized that she wasn't bitching at him or pulling no switch out of her taped-up shag-bag for hitting her.

She wasn't doing a damn thing.

Just lying there like...

No. Couldn't be.

Just faking for a free place to sleep!

"Yo, bitch! Wake your doped-ass up and get the fuck outta my pad! If you ain't gonna be suckin' my dick then I got no use for you up in my shi—" he moved to shake her and, as he did, her body rolled onto her back—her jacked, back-alley boob-job sliding across her chest like moldy meatloaf—and he saw that her eyes weren't closed. "Oh no..." he felt his already jazzed heart kick up another few notches, "No, bitch! No! You ain't dyin' up in my shit, you hear me, bitch? YOU HEAR ME?" He rolled to his knees and started slapping her, "Wake up, skank! Go die in the fuckin' gutters if ya gotta, but not in here! Get up out my pad and fuck up somebody else's high, you cheap waste of—"

He stopped and whimpered.

She wasn't moving; wasn't even fucking breathing!

"Oh shit! Oh fuck! Fuck... FUCK! Fuck me, man... fuck me side-ways! What the fuck am I going to—"

FLY AWAY, LARS. FLY FAR, FAR AWAY. JUST GIVE YOURSELF TO THE WIND AND FLY SO FAR AWAY THAT NOT EVEN THE MEMORIES WILL FIND YOU!

Lars cried out and, grabbing his piece from beside his bong and tipping the green work of art as he did. Ignoring the stink of old bong-water as it splashed across the floor, he jumped to his feet. The sudden movement sent his head swimming and he staggered, stepping into an old plate of Velveeta and slipping; falling against the window and shattering it. Startled by the sound of breaking glass, he looked over his shoulder and saw the mid-day ghetto below; the sounds of angry drivers and angrier pedestrians bleeding into his studio apartment.

"Shit, son!" he drew in a deep breath of chilled fall air and looked back—driven by equal parts of vertigo and rage at whatever punk had

decided to break into his pad—"I doesn't know who you think you is, comin' in here all unannounced an' shit, but I'm gonna put a few rounds in yo' knee, then I'm'a call up some my top-choice niggas to fuck yo' shit up!"

YOUR MOUTH IS AN AFFRONT TO MY GLORY, LARS! TAKE MY INVITATION TO GLORY... OR DIE!

Lars frowned, thumbing back the hammer only to have the piece go off in his hand.

The bullet punched through the hoe's skull, a quick spurt of blood and brains splashing out across his mattress before it slowed to a trickle.

"SHIT! Oh god... oh god... oh god... motherfucker, you have chosen a REAL bad time for—"

AN ANSWER, LARS! YES... OR NO?

Lars shivered, "C'mon, man... I don't even know who you is."

I'M THE VOICE OF YOUR SALVATION, LARS? WHO WOULD YOU LIKE IT TO BE? GOD? THE DEVIL? I CAN BE ALL OF THEM, LARS. ANY OF THEM, OR ANYTHING ELSE YOU WANT. BUT I NEED... YOUR... ANSWER!

"Wh... what do I need to do?"

JUST FLY, LARS. JUST FLY AWAY FROM IT ALL.

Lars heard something then—like when a bird flew into his window a few nights ago; breaking glass and a sharp impact following a loud flutter—and he turned to see that the already broken window had vanished, leaving a wide space leading out into the city...

Eleven stories down.

"C'mon, man..." *Lars whimpered,* "There gotta be anotha way..."

WHAT IS IT THEY SAY, LARS? *the voice pressed on, and he felt the pressure urge him closer to the biggest leap of his life,* **IT'S MY WAY OR THE HIGHWAY.**

Lars gulped, looking over the edge at the bustling city below him.

"Aw, what the hell," *he sighed, tossing the gun to the floor,* "I was coming down, anyway..."

~

"NO! NOOOOOO!" Lars thrashed and pulled against Xander's grip on his ocular cavities as they shared the memory of his rebirth. "THAT AIN'T ME! THAT AIN'T ME! LET MY ASS GO, YOU SHIT; YOU FUCKIN' LYIN' SHIT! THAT AIN'T ME!"

"Oh it's you, Lars," Xander laughed, finally tearing his hands free and kicking the blinded god to the ground.

Estella gasped and let out a whimper a short distance away and Xander felt a pull in his head as a haze started to lift.

Lars' whimpers dragged him back.

"That… that ain't me. It ain't; it can't be…"

Xander started towards him, "It looks like Devin gave you a much broader vocabulary along with The Power." He stopped, standing over the sniveling god—watching as his previous life flooded back into his memory and showed him who he truly was—and he shook his head. "It's time to die, Lars," he whispered.

"I ain't gonna stop ya," Lars resigned, falling back against the weight of his epiphany. "This shit's been a long time comin'."

"Yes," Xander grinned as he slammed his foot down on Lars' head. Then again. Then once more just to be sure. "Yes it has."

Gerard cried out, drawing Xander's attention away from the dead god at his feet. Though he'd been severely broken prior to Lars' interference, Xander saw that he'd taken the time his late comrade had earned him to begin rebuilding his body.

Though there was still much work to be done before he could even stand.

"You… you *killed* him!" Gerard murmured, seeming more stunned by the achievement than the loss.

Xander looked at him, seeing that there was no remorse—no sadness or pain or even regret in the god's aura; he sincerely felt nothing for Lars' death short of the implication that he, too, could be killed—and he shrugged. Turning to face the still-grounded god, he paused to shake some of the lingering bits from his boot, addressing Gerard as he did, "Yes, it would appear I did. Must just tie your guts into all sorts of knots to know that you won't be far behind, I imagine; especially when Devin promised you immortality." He narrowed his eyes at him and began to chuckle, "Would you like me to show you just how vulnerable you really are?"

"D-Daddy?" Bianca's voice chimed a few paces away from Lars' body as the hallucination started to lift.

"Oh," Xander frowned, turning towards her and cocking his head. "You brought yourself back, huh? All on your own, no less." Another bout of unstoppable laughter drew forth and he started towards her, preparing to finish the job.

"Oh my…" Estella couldn't bring herself to look away.

Stan stared in awe; his eyes transfixed to Lars. "I… I can't believe it," he whispered to himself. "Like he was nothing; he destroyed him as though he were nothing. So long…" he shook his head, "Just like he was nothing."

Estella looked at him, watching his eyes waver in disbelief as they cycled between the headless body of the one Xander had called Lars to the broken behemoth and then, finally, to the black woman who's dream-like state seemed to be lifting; her own eyes, which had been so wide and unblinking a moment earlier that it hurt Estella's own eyes to look, growing heavy-lidded and burdened by whatever they'd been forced to witness.

"Is… it's not really Xander doing these things, is it?" she asked, her insides churning at the possible answers that awaited her.

Stan didn't answer for a long moment; his eyes just

continued to work the cycle between the three "gods" that Xander had brought down with such little effort.

"Stan…" Estella began to reach out to him.

"Huh…?"

Estella bit her lip, "I asked—"

"I heard," Stan stopped her, his voice tense with the threat of having to hear Estella's words again.

She frowned, realizing that he was no happier with the question than she.

Still…

"Well?" she pushed for an answer.

Stan sighed, "It *is* Xander"—he nodded towards him as he loomed ever-nearer to the "goddess"—"but it's not a part of Xander that he shows; not often and not like this, at least."

"I…" Estella felt her throat knot up, "I don't understand."

"Yes you do," Stan nodded. "You just don't want to. It's the part of us—the part of *everyone*; the part of you and me, even— that we don't want the world to see or even know about. It's the part that we collectively understand isn't right; the primal drive to take every step in life for nobody else, and to take down as many as possible to ensure success and strength. *That's* the part of the mind that The Power thrives on the most, Estella, because without that sense of entitlement and ownership it has no reason to be called upon. Magic exists to create a desired outcome, you know that; without any desire for any sort of outcome we have no reason to push for anything. It's what got our ancestors out of the trees and put tools in their hands; it's what made shelters into homes and homes into cities and cities into…" Stan sighed, "It's in all of us, Estella; the drive to achieve and gain more. It's what makes us human or vampire or *whatever*; and The Power knows to target that part of the mind it occupies. *That*"—he pointed to Xander again—"is Xander Stryker"—he let his arm drop and shook his head—"but not as you or I know him. That's the

Xander that's driven entirely by his personal needs; his personal goals."

Estella bit her lip, "But... but at least he's killing them, right? He's killing those awful people—awful as the acts might be—so that we'll be safe, right?"

Stan shook his head, "No, Estella, he's killing them for the same reason Devin—their leader—was after *me*: to prove that he's better than them. And he *is*; he's most certainly better," Stan brushed a fallen bang from his vision and looked at Estella, his eyes—for the first time in all the time she'd known him—showing with uncertainty and weakness. Looking back at Xander, he took in an audible, shaky breath before letting it out slow, "But once he's killed them all—possibly even Devin—then what? I've been there, Estella; I've faced the reality of knowing that I was so powerful I could do *anything*, and it took more time and patience and control than I believe he has. It's a lonely, tolling, and guilt-ridden realization. And *that's* the part I'm most afraid of for him..."

Estella stifled a sob in her throat, "Wh-why?"

Stan wiped his eye, "What did Xander do the last time he felt lonely and tolled and guilt-ridden?"

Estella's eyes widened—visions of Yin's barrel pressed to Xander's temple and razors dragging across his forearm flashing in her memory—and she turned towards Xander.

"Oh gods... no!"

"XANDER! STOP IT!"

Turning towards the source of the sound, Xander spotted Estella coming towards him

Then, spotting her, the haze began to lift once again; a clarity breaking through as he felt his lips drag into a smile at the sight of her.

But she was crying…

He took a step towards her, "Estella?"

"Xander, you can't do this! You have to stop! You have to stop all of this!" her eyes darted about the lawn, beckoning Xander to follow her gaze.

He saw Gerard, unable to stand.

He saw Bianca, quaking in utter terror.

He saw Lars…

"Did… did I do this?" he asked, looking up at Estella. "'Stell, what'd I do?"

Estella stifled a sob as she started towards him, "Xander—baby—you gotta get rid of that power. It's—"

"**I'LL GET RID OF YOU AND THIS ENTIRE PLANET BEFORE I**—No! That's not right! I can't let this—**KNOW WHAT YOU ARE AND DO WHAT YOU MUST! THE POWER DESERVES MORE THAN A WEAK**—AAAHHHHHHH!"

A great wind picked up as Xander's aura cycloned about him, lifting the sniveling Lars, the whimpering Gerard, and the seizing Bianca—*but where, oh where, was that dastardly Devin?*—and hurled them into the sky, ridding the mansion and everyone there of their presence. A sweep of the grounds and every level and room of the mansion told Xander that Devin was nowhere on the property and he worked to replace and strengthen the barrier Stan had put into place.

Something wasn't right—that much was obvious—and he wasn't about to endanger Estella and Stan and the others in his effort to figure it out.

"It'll end tonight," Xander grinned to Stan, his feet beginning to rise from the ground with the laughter already starting to spew past his lips once again.

"XANDER! NO!" Estella rushed towards him, "THIS ISN'T YOU!"

"**Then what *is* me, 'Stell?**" he asked, a single tear beginning to roll down his cheek before it evaporated. "I... I *love* you. Please don't **forget that...**"

Then, with the barrier finally in place, Xander felt its magic take hold of him—his own aura added to the energy sources that it would keep out—and he was cast away from his home.

17

HOME-SWEET-HOME

*T*he magic of the mansion's new barrier threw Xander with enough force to let him see the curvature of the Earth, and, for a brief moment, he felt that he might break free of the atmosphere and get to escape into the void of space.

A chance to conquer other worlds and...

No, he thought to himself, forcing himself to appreciate the beauty and peacefulness of the moment rather than turn it into another mission to kill or control. While he'd indulged in his share of complexes and power trips, he really just wanted to see an end to this nightmare and find peace with Estella. He just wanted to—

*I'm not thinking big enough! I could do better than her! Hell, I'm Xander-fucking-Stryker! I could have **ten** Estellas if I—*

What am I... ten? Why would I—no! This doesn't make sense; this isn't me...

But it is! How 'bout you stop with all this—

How 'bout I just sleep, Xander thought, closing his eyes; it could've been the thinness of the air at that altitude—or maybe the exertion of taking out Lars and beating Gerard and casting so much on Bianca—but, whatever the reason, he suddenly felt tired.

So very, very...

"WHAT ARE you going to do with your life, Xander? I see the potential, but..."

Stan?

"Grace is what makes power worth having, Xander."

Grandma?

"I need you to promise me that you won't die."

Estella?

"... you'd better watch that temper..."

Depok?

"Hey, son..."

XANDER'S EYES SNAPPED OPEN.

"Dad?"

For the second time that week, Xander crashed to the ground from a magic-induced flight. This time, however, the magical force was stronger, the drop was harder, and Xander was imbued with the power to punish the concrete more than it could ever hope to punish him.

The sound of the deep, hollow, and—thankfully—vacant mining plot taking the force of Xander's fall was like thunder birthed from the pits of Hell. Somehow, while he'd been unconscious—could he *really* have just fallen asleep in a freefall like that?—his mind had known enough to wrap his aura around him in a shield, and, as he watched the widened crater of the rock quarry, he noted with more than just a little celebration that he hadn't suffered a single injury in the process. He moved to take a step and heard the slosh of water at his boots. Looking towards the source, he saw that the pit—made all the deeper by the cataclysmic force of his magic-fueled fall from the sky—was beginning to fill with water. Frowning at this, he moved to the edge of the chasm and worked to pull himself up, eager to see where he was.

The site, though clear of all workers, was still littered with mining equipment and fresh tire tracks several yards from the opening; a small trailer with **LOVECRAFT COAL & STEEL** emblazoned across the side and a small, handwritten scrap that read "management" taped crookedly to the door still squeaking on its rusted suspension from the force of Xander's fall. Further out and raised on a pair of bent rods for any passersby to see was a large sign declaring **LAND AVAILABLE FOR RENT**, though the word "land" had been spray-painted over and replaced by "YOUR MOTHER" above it; several smaller tags of "HA HA" or "FUCK YOU" decorating the space around it. Though he was certain a human's vision would only allow for a vast and seemingly empty wasteland of nothingness, Xander's superhuman senses could pick up the hints of the city a few miles ahead—the faint, artificial lights and sounds of the night life refusing to be totally lost in the distance—while the smell and sounds of water hinted towards the source of the now-flooding quarry.

Glancing back, Xander spotted the inky-black and rolling surface of the night-bathed lake—the same lake that he'd nearly drowned in last winter—and saw the narrow fissure that had opened up between the quarry and the shore; feeding each new wave into the depths of the crater.

They're still out there, he thought to himself, glancing back into the sky and considering how Bianca and Gerard might have fared in their expulsion from the mansion. Devin, wherever he was, had been smart enough to sneak off when he had; even then thinking his name made Xander's blood boil and swirling the dust and sand at his feet. Both Bianca and Gerard had been injured though—Bianca's mind still fractured by whatever Xander had done to her and Gerard's body...

Xander sighed and shook his head.

What in the hell did I do back there?

Something badass!

Xander stopped and took a deep breath. The thoughts *were* his own—he'd come to learn the difference between an outside voice in his head and his own thoughts even before being turned into a vampire—but something in them felt...

You wanted the power, you have The Power. Why are you letting this get to you?

Feeling like his own mind was an unsafe place to think, Xander rubbed his temples and took another deep breath, starting to walk towards the city.

"It's alright, Xander," he mumbled to himself, "just a side-effect of the—**I'm not sure I like how you downplay what I am to you.**" Xander stopped in mid-step and shook his head, "H-hello? Who... what are you?"

Xander's body pitched and he began to laugh, shaking his head. "**Identity crisis. Broken mirrors. Ripples in the reflecting pool. Face inside; right beneath the skin. Inner demons. Any of this getting through to you?**"

"No... no, you can't be," Xander clutched his head and clenched his eyes. "This isn't right! I've got to get..." he pulled his hands away and blinked against the wave of blinding lights all around him. "What the fu—where am I?"

He cackled at his own question and shook his head, "**Fast lane of the east-bound thruway, sport. Bold, I admit, but not very safe.**"

Xander gasped, hearing the zipping sounds of traffic around him and blaring of car horns and the cursing of angry drivers—their calls of "crazy asshole" or "get out of the road, moron" growing louder and then immediately further as they careened past him—and he looked up to see the cars whipping around him. "East-bound thru—How?"

Despite the confusion and growing terror of the possibility of being hit by a truck, the laughter started up again as he was bathed in the blinding glare of a pair of semi-truck headlights; the crippling roar of its horn echoing in his ears and causing him to flinch in mid-cackle. The sound of the horn shifted with a sudden flash of movement and Xander felt his feet dangle in the air before he opened his eyes and watched as the toes of his boots had begun to drag over the surface of the truck's cargo bed.

Though the laughter—like a broken faucet—continued to spill from his mouth, his bewildered whimpers began to shift and throw the pitch of the sound; ranging them between choked giggles and airy cackles. He was neither rising nor falling like he should have if he'd merely jumped over the truck, and this dawning realization brought the laughter forth twice as hard. "I... I'm flying? H-how...?"

He bobbed in the air a moment—as if to further prove to himself what he already knew—before he was suddenly standing in the middle of a crowded sidewalk; none of the pedestrians seeming to notice his appearance amongst them. **"Magic, child; the answer to all things. Energy defines it all. You tell the power what you want, The Power makes it happen!"**

Xander, finally able to take a full breath without all the laughter, did so and stuffed his hands into his jacket pockets and started to walk with the flow of the pedestrians' traffic. "What I want..." he repeated to himself.

Beside him, the aura of a woman toting an overstuffed paper bag filled with empty cans spiked with concern as her eyes shifted towards him.

He giggled under the worried look and shrugged, **"The Power; magic makes it happen. You got it!"**

The woman's eyes widened further, and she moved to duck away from the crazy kid who was talking to himself. Not needing any unwanted attention, he reached out with his aura and struck the memory of him from her mind; her tense body and hurried pace suddenly relaxing as she fell back into a regular pace and continued on her way.

"**Aw! You're no fun!**" he chastised himself, starting to laugh again.

More people looked.

Xander's aura snaked out again and again, wiping more minds.

It's better than having a bunch of humans running around talking about us... he rolled his eyes and shook his head at himself. *Running around talking about* me*! It's risky to draw so much attention!*

"**Risky for *who*? You're a *god* now!**"—a man looked over his shoulder and sneered at him before starting towards the cross-walk; another auric tendril, another tweaked mind—"**Stop that! These people should know who's going to be in control around here! It's *better* that they know! Not like they can—**"

"That's not our... not *my* choice to make!" Xander growled to himself, rubbing his eyes with the pointer finger and thumb of his right hand. "God, I just want to go—"

As his hand moved away from his eyes he stopped in mid-step and gawked as he realized he was standing in front of his old house. Looking around, he felt a moment of anxiety at the unexpected shift in setting; no more streetlights, no more cars, and no more freaked-out, glaring pedestrians.

Just his childhood home...

"No... give me the city and all the pissed off humans you like, but not *this!*"

He laughed at himself.

Memories rushed back at him.

Memories of laughing and roaring back-and-forth with his

mom when he was four years old while they acted out the destruction of a building-block city with a Godzilla figure she'd bought for him earlier that day.

"Oh no!" his mother's voice echoed in his mind with the shrill cries of the make-believe citizens, *"It's Godzilla! Run for your lives! Aahhh!"*

Then they'd laughed...

Just as he was laughing then.

He felt his hands clutch around something and he looked down to discover the Godzilla toy from his childhood clutched in his grip.

"H-how did—"

"The Power makes it happen," he laughed harder as the toy suddenly belched a stream of bright-blue fire before turning to dust in his hands and vanishing.

More memories...

Memories of walking home with Estella as a kid and telling her, once again, that she couldn't come in, explaining that his mother wasn't feeling well. Though the memory of Estella's disappointed face was still painful, it was better than the face he'd see if he'd brought her in during one of Kyle's rage-driven fits. If she'd seen him getting hit by his stepfather, she might not want—

"AH!" he cried out as a sharp sting throbbed at his lower back and he reached beneath his jacket and drew back...

"Blood? But h-ho-heh heh HA! **Hopeless, aren't you? You *think* it hard enough, The Power makes it happen! That Kyle had the right idea; he wanted it, he took it."**

Xander frowned, shaking his head and wiping the blood off his hand with his pant leg. "He was a fucking bastard; a *monster!* And if that's the sort of person you want me to be then—"

"You're already like him! Didn't you see what you did to Lars? Didn't you see the fear and pain in Gerard and Bianca?

Even your woman was fucking *terrified* of what you did back there! How is *that* any different than—"

Xander cried out as the belt that his stepfather had used to beat him appeared in his hands. Again and again he reminded himself that it wasn't the same length of bloodstained leather— that it was just a replica birthed by the memory in his mind— but no matter how many times he repeated it to himself he couldn't bring himself to believe it. Unable to look away from his late-stepfather's favorite implement of pain, he watched as his hands acted on their own to fold the leather over once, then again before snapping it against its coils.

The sound drew a sob from him, and he fell to his knees, laughing uncontrollably before he'd even landed.

"Oh my, but you're a self-destructive one, aren't you? You have the power to create *anything*—to make anything in your mind a reality—and you're dredging up pain and misery! Is that why you came here?"

"I… I didn't want to come here! You said that it made what I *want* happen!"

"Then I guess you don't know what you want, do you?" he giggled and shook his head at himself.

"I know that I don't want to be *here*! Why would I want this?"

"You've been thinking of going home ever since you left that vampire nest."

"I didn't mean I wanted to come…"

"Doesn't matter what you *think* you want; it acts on what you—the you *behind* you--wants! And, because of what *you* wanted, we're here now!"

Xander blinked at that, still shaking his head before he realized that he was already inside. Flinching at the totally alien interior—the foreign décor and strange pictures and new paint; the *wrong* paint—he felt his breath hold in his lungs. He blinked, and the paint was back to the light, sky-like blue that he'd remembered from his childhood.

Or had it been darker?

Another blink, another hue adorned the walls.

He felt a wave of peaceful nostalgia and dared to smile.

No! It's not real! This isn't your house! This isn't—

"Sure looks like your house, boy-o."

Xander sighed, growing tired of arguing with himself, and looked behind him—doubt beginning to crown his happy delusion—to confirm his suspicions. The door had been ripped from the hinges and was in pieces beneath his feet.

"If this is my house," he felt his heart sink, "then why did I have to break in?"

"Oh, that? Just a pesky formality; barely a blip on the radar."

The door under his feet vanished, dropping him an inch with its sudden absence. As his boots hit the floor—resounding with an eerie, threatening *thud*—he heard a child begin to cry and a low, reassuring voice rising to meet it.

Xander grimaced with realization before he'd even turned, but let his eyes follow the source of the noise towards the living room entrance to his left, where he spotted a woman and a little girl huddled on the couch facing him and, a short distance from them, holding his hands up in a peaceful gesture, a man.

Squinting at the man, Xander realized that, though his mouth was moving in an obvious effort to negotiate with him, an intruder, he couldn't hear a single word he was saying. Looking past him and towards the woman and child on the couch, Xander saw that, like the man, their mouths were moving—the woman's mouth opening and closing in wide, gaping bursts as though she was screaming and the little girl's mouth hanging open in an ongoing wail of fear—but no sound was being made.

As realization dawned on him, he nodded to himself. "Because I don't *want* to hear them, right?" he asked himself.

"You got it."

Once again spotting the child as she tried to tuck her face into her mother's chest to hide the reality of the scary man from her vision, Xander remembered his own moments of terror in the house—in that very room—and how he'd looked up at Kyle in the same way. His mind clouded as more memories flooded, and he saw the world from the little girl's perspective—seeing him staring back at her and wanting nothing more than for him to be gone; to have the peace and normalcy of every other night—just as he, himself, had cried. For him, though, terror and crying *was* normalcy; each and every night representing a new reason to cry. The scene was like a shadow of his past.

Only now, a little girl was staring at him with the same terror and fright that he'd once worn on his face every time he stared at his stepfather.

Kyle…

He shook his head. "Doesn't make any sense. Why would I come here?"

All at once the muted family's cries erupted:

"What did you do, you son of a bitch? What did you do to my—"

"My baby… my baby… my baby…"

Xander jumped back, startled by the sudden flood of noise. Blinking against the panic and rage, he moved his eyes between the man and woman before realizing that the source of their words had something to do with the little girl. Already panicking about what the magic could've interpreted from his racing thoughts, he shifted his wide, worried gaze to the little girl…

He gasped, realizing that he was looking at himself.

An exact copy of his childhood self now occupied the spot on the couch where the little girl had once been sitting.

"How in the…"

"The magic makes it—"

"No!" Xander hissed under his breath, "This isn't what I want! THIS ISN'T WHAT I WANT?"

"Then what *do* you want, you crazy freak-show," the man clenched his fists, huddled around his wife and child. "Just take it and *go!*"

"My baby... my baby... my baby..."

"What do I do?" Xander asked, "How do I make this right?"

The man rose and started towards him, "That's what I'm asking you, you sick bastard!"

Xander saw the man advancing on him, fists clenched and ready to attack him, and he began to cackle again.

"You crazy son of a bitch!" the man seethed, "Come into my house, terrorize my family... what the hell did you do to my dau—"

Xander's laughter intensified as the man broke into a sprint towards him, raising his fists. Once again, his hands moved on their own, his left catching the attack before his right hand flicked from left-to-right and the man was hurled off in the direction of the motion; whipping across the room and slamming into a bookshelf. As he fell to the ground, bits of splintered wood and the contents of the broken shelves fell on top of him.

The woman let out a cry and pulled the child-Xander copy to her, protecting him like it was still her own daughter. "No! Don't hurt us! Please don't hurt us!" she pleaded.

She cared for her child so much; it didn't matter that it didn't even look like her anymore...

Xander blinked, the woman's selfless love for her child reminding him of his own mother—remembering the night she'd died and how she'd thrown herself to Kyle and his sadistic, rape-happy friends to keep him out of their clutches—and he sobbed as he saw his mother before him, holding little-him against her chest.

"M-Mom...?" he took a step towards the two before dropping to his knees. "N-no... please, I can't take this. Not all over again. Don't show me *her* like this..."

The little girl—still wearing his adolescent self's body and face—looked up at the strange turn of the conversation and, seeing her mother's shifted form, ripped free of her mother's grip and threw herself back to the end of the couch. "Who are you?" she demanded, "Where's my mom?"

Xander growled, watching the chaos that the magic was unfolding on this poor, unsuspecting family, and clutched at his temples, shaking his head.

"No! No, this isn't right! Turn them back! Turn them—" he giggled and slapped himself, "**Still don't listen so good, do you?**"

Xander blinked against the sting of his own slap and looked up to see that both the woman and little girl had returned to normal.

Though their couch's pattern *had* been changed to the one he remembered from his childhood...

"I don't... **Stupid! The magic! The magic, the magic, the—**"

The little girl screamed and, seeing that her mother had magically returned, leapt back to the safety of her breasts, "What's wrong with him, Mommy?"

Xander glared at her and jumped to his feet, "**What's wrong with... THIS IS *MY* HOME!**" The mother and daughter quaked with terror under his enraged claim and, seeing their fear, he pulled himself back. "No... No! This *isn't* me! Who the hell are yo—" a fresh bout of laughter interrupted him. Then, "**See for yourself.**"

∽

It hadn't been a full minute after Xander had been thrown from the mansion's gates by the new barrier he'd put up before Estella had dragged Stan to the garage and taken the closest car, a silver Mercedes-Benz with a bold, chrome "AMG" tag on the back, to track him down. Though she couldn't figure out why he'd added his own energy signature to the restricted energies on the new barrier—effectively locking him out of his own clan's mansion—her first concern was making sure that he hadn't been hurt in the fall.

Something that Stan assured her over and over again was impossible.

That assurance, however, was quickly squelched by a new set of concerns.

"Oh gods… What if we can't find him? What if those… those *monsters* get to him before us?" Estella chanted to herself, itemizing all the things that could go wrong.

Stan shook his head, looking out the window, "I'd be more worried *for* them if they did, Estella. It's not them that we should be worried about."

Estella didn't dare to take her eyes off the road—more out of fear of abandoning her search than missing something in her driving—"What do you mean?"

She felt Stan's worrisome gaze move towards her as he sighed. "It's like I already said, Estella; Xander is… well, he's always been troubled. You know that as much as I do, possibly even more. He's got a dark, painful history that's led to a self-destructive personality and a great deal of rage. Add on top of that the pressures of his new life as a clan leader *and* everything that's happening to Trepis and… I mean, Estella, he was at risk of losing his mind *before* I showed up; *before* I gave him The Power." He shook his head again and looked back out the window, "The Power is just going to use all of the shit that's happening to him. It'll use it and dredge up everything it can— and with Xander that's *a lot* of ammunition, I assure you—to break him so it can assume full control." Another sigh and another headshake, "I can't imagine how long he'll be able to avoid just giving in to all of it."

Estella fought the urge to cry. "But... but Xander's always been a fighter; *always!*" she pointed out, "He'll fight this too! He has to!"

"Xander is a fantastic fighter, Estella, there's no doubt about that," Stan agreed. "But this is what I've been trying to tell him; it's not about fighting *outside* enemies! You saw what he did to Lars! The others will be lucky if there's any pieces left of them when Xander's done with them, but his greatest struggle in this case is *him*. He's always been in an ongoing battle with the darkness inside him, Estella, and I just gave that darkness a whole hell of a lot of firepower."

Estella bit her lip at that, then, finally, looked away from the road and squarely at Stan. "What about their leader?" she asked, "What about Devin? You mentioned his crew *and* you brought up Xander's inner struggle, but why'd you leave *him* out?"

Stan wormed his fingers through his hair and clutched it tightly, "Devin's a madman, Estella. And madmen can always see their own when they get close enough. If Xander can survive his own insanity long enough to actually encounter him, then Devin's going to see the struggle that's happening inside him and he's going to use that to tilt the scales in his favor." Yanking his hand from his dirty-blond hair and leaving it in a ruffled, feathery mess, he audibly dropped his arm back into his lap. "I honestly don't know if Xander can survive himself in this state, but I *can* tell you there's no way he'll be able to handle—"

"I get it!" Estella hissed through clenched teeth, unable to handle another syllable of Stan's reality. "I... I don't want to hear anymore. I just... I won't let that happen then!"

"Good," Stan nodded, though Estella could hear the doubt in his voice. "Now, do you have any ideas where he could be?"

Estella started to shake her head but thought better of it. "I... I can feel *something* that might be him. It's like when I first tried to track him after he'd become a vampire; it *feels* like him, but too much is different to know for sure, and it's... it should be so easy to pinpoint, too. I mean, he used to *live* around—" Her eyes widened and she slammed on the brakes, cutting the wheel hard to the left and throwing the Mercedes into a sharp spin to face the other way before peeling off once again, "I know where he is!"

Xander faltered, flinching under the blinding fluorescent flood and minty stink of...toothpaste?

His eyes started to adjust and, when he looked up, he saw his own reflection staring back at him from the upstairs bathroom of his house. He shook his head and forced himself to redefine the reality in his mind: the upstairs bathroom of the house he *used* to live in.

Looking back at the reflection in the mirror, he narrowed his gaze; feeling like something was off with the sight. His hair —an overgrown and tangled black mass—was in need of some attention, but it was hardly anything new for him. His lip was trembling with the anxiety of the night, and his shifting jawline could use a shave...

He shook his head and leaned closer to the mirror, moving his gaze about the messy-yet-familiar view of his own reflection and narrowing his mismatched eyes to pinpoint the—

His reflection birthed a grin as he saw that *its* right eye was hazel, while his *left* wore the blood-stained orb with the piercing black pupil dilating at its center.

Xander had been forced to come to grips with the reality that the bloody stain that clung to what had once been the whites and hazel-iris of his right eye was a permanent disfigurement. There was no question for him that, every time he looked in the mirror, it would be there—on *his* right-hand side; hanging in the reflection's left—but, staring at himself in the mirror, he saw the mirror-opposite of what *should* have been.

"What... what's going on?" he stammered at his haunting, mirror-born doppelganger.

He felt his mouth twist into a vicious sneer as his reflection did the same, "**You didn't think that I wouldn't want my own blood-stained *right* eye?**"

"But... you're supposed to be me," Xander shook his head, glaring at himself. "Why would *I* need to copy—"

"**The magic *makes* it happen, Xander!**" the reflection glared right back, "**You don't *want* to be me, which means *I* don't want to be you? Get it? Your desire to remain separate is creating me!**" the reflection moved nearer to him, though Xander hadn't felt his body move to create the reflected act.

Oh no... Xander tried to shut his eyes to the madness in front of him, *I really am losing my mind!*

"**Not yet,**" his reflection reached out—his own hands remaining fixed on the sink in front of him—and passed through the mirror as though it were nothing more than an open window. The hands flexed and the fingers wriggled, seemingly celebrating their freedom from their reflective prison, and took hold of Xander by either side of his jacket's collar. "**But you *are* starting to piss me off! You don't like this any more than I do; this fractured psychosis you're forcing on yourself; forcing on *me*! The Power's not supposed to be used to *break* the mind, *boy*; it's supposed to free it so you can break everything else!**"

"I've never been too good at following rules," Xander bared his fangs—the leering reflection reaching through the wooden frame doing the same—as he ripped free of the grip and backed away; the reflection forced to do the same and returning into the mirror. "Sorry to disappoint you."

"**YOU'RE ONLY DISAPPOINTING YOURSELF!**" the reflection roared at him.

Xander sighed and shook his head, "Why am I here? Why did you..." he shook his head and scoffed at himself, "No...

you're me, right? Just a fractured part of me..." he looked up at the reflection, "Why did *we* take *us* here? What is it that we're hoping to find here?"

His reflection seemed to calm down at that, "**You tell the magic—**"

"No. No! I *know* that much; I've heard you, I know! The magic took me here because I somehow *wanted* this, I get that! But if you're supposed to be a part of me—some part that knows more than I know about myself—then you tell me what that reason is; tell me *why* we wanted to be here!"

The reflection stared for an unbearable moment, and Xander smirked at that; he'd forced the malicious part of himself into a corner where it couldn't wag the unknown in front of him like bait. Now he had to be honest with himself:

"**You were feeling hopelessly fearful *and* like you were a terrible monster,**" his arms lifted off the sink and spread out to illustrate what was around him. "**So you took us to the version of home where those two co-existed. You took us *home*!**"

Xander shook his head, reclaiming his arms and moving towards the faucet to turn on the tap so he could splash some cold water on his face. "But I'm not afraid anymore!" he reminded himself, "I... I *killed* Kyle! The monster's dead! The monster's—"

From behind the cover of his palms and the soothing chill of the water against his flushed skin, Xander heard his voice echo back to him. "**Is it? Is the monster *really* dead?**" he heard it say.

Dropping his hands from his face, Xander came face-to-face with his *new* reflection; Kyle's reflection. Everything he remembered of his abusive stepfather's face was suddenly a mockery of his own features. It was his own hair, his own eyes—it *was* him! —but the structure and expression was unmistakably Kyle's.

"No... no this is just another trick. You're just trying to break me! That's not who I am; I'll never be like—Y-you... you're just trying to break me!"

The Xander-Kyle reflection began to cackle once again, "**And it's working, *son*!**"

THE MERCEDES ROARED down a quiet residential street, squealing like a monster every time Estella yanked the wheel to turn onto a new street; each time bringing them that much closer to *the* street; Xander's old street. She'd walked the path before—knew it well enough from her childhood to navigate it now; even at over eighty miles-per-hour—when she was a little girl. She must've walked the path to Xander's house dozens of times, if not a hundred.

Though he'd never once invited her in, in fact he'd even gone so far as to *deny* her the few times she'd been bold enough to ask.

In hindsight, however—now that she knew of the nightmare that was his abusive stepfather; a misery-hungry auric vampire who did everything he could to generate the emotions he craved in his victims—she could see why.

In some ways, she almost resented Xander all the more for it. For whatever reason, her own safety or his fear of being judged or something else entirely, he'd kept her away from the reality that was hurting him; kept her away from the possibility of helping. She bit her lip at the thought—taking another turn at breakneck speeds and pitching the speedometer all over again—and realized that any other reality, any path that *hadn't* been the tragedy that *had* happened, could've been that much worse. She'd seen firsthand as a warrior what lengths a desperate rogue vampire would take when faced with the threat of capture, and if anybody had tried to pull Kyle away from his meal ticket it could've been far worse.

"HOLY SHI—Dammit! Will you slow down! You're gonna *kill* us with this—"

"The only one between us who could be killed by something as simple as a car crash right now is *you*," Estella snapped, shooting Stan a glare. "And considering the fact that you practically signed your name all over Xander's death warrant, I'm not sure I'm too concerned with your safety!"

"He was *begging* me for The Power, Estella!" Stan glared back at her, "He said you were dying and *begged* for me to give him the means to save you! I was buried deep enough underground for at least *three* bodies and looking at near-certain death if I didn't climb out and *certain* death if I did! Then my friend—the *son* of my *best friend*, I might add—starts telling me that another friend—a beautiful, innocent girl who I'd watch grow up for *years*—is about to die and that he can't bear the thought of losing her!" he shook his head and looked away, sighing, "What was I supposed to do?"

Estella frowned, "He... he said all that? He told you to give him The Power... for me?"

Stan nodded, "From the sound of it, you wouldn't have lasted much longer without it. I can't say I'm glad that all of *this* happened, but I'm not about to apologize when you're still breathing 'cause of what I did." He sighed again and looked out the window, shaking his head. "Damn... it's been so long since I've been out this way; I can barely remember which street it is."

Estella shrugged, "I guess it's a good thing I'm driving then."

Stan frowned at that, "Maybe you should go on ahead. Fast as you're going, you can be there in a flash if you use overdrive."

Estella shook her head, "And then I'd be there on my own and trying to handle Xander with a power that I know *nothing* about. Believe me, I *want* to be there *now*, but if I'd be doing more harm than good on my own then I'd rather take my time and get there with you." She cursed as she zipped by the street she'd needed and cranked the wheel at the next street to loop around, nearly taking out a mailbox as the Mercedes fishtailed on her, "So there's really nothing left of that power in you, is there?"

"No, nothing," Stan shrugged. "I'm no stronger than any other human."

"What about your magic?" Estella asked, "Your own magic, I mean; the magic you had *before* all this."

Stan chuckled, "Yeah, I guess *that's* still there. But it's nothing compared to what I had."

Estella took another right and brought herself back on course. "Then can't you conjure whatever gifted it and have them do it again?" she asked, "Or maybe *they* can stop Devin and the others; give us Xander back the way he was!"

Stan shook his head, "They're not a charity, Estella; they're barely even sentient... not in the way we'd consider, at least. They—well, *It; Them*... whatever—will answer if you call out to them the right way. They'll poke in to see what's up if some-body's able to actually reach over to their side, and if you know how to finagle whatever pokes through you *might* get lucky enough to get some insight or even a gift like I did. But they're not..." he sighed and pinched the bridge of his nose, "Damn... it's hard to explain. *It* isn't interested in interactions beyond whatever little exchanges occur in those instances. In their eyes —if they actually *had* eyes, I mean—we're nothing more than pretty little auras inside rotting meat sacks. It's the auras they appreciate, they're *made* of them, after all, but the rest of us— our brief lives, our qualms, our troubles, our regrets; any of that mundane randomness that we drag along with us—means nothing to them, and they don't care if it kills us or not. In the end, when we finally reach the end of our limited journey and we 'finish' here, our auras pass over to join with the rest of them; *that's* their concern in what goes down on this realm. It's not happiness or sorrow, peace or war, or even the threat of all of *this*. What happens here in our world means *nothing* to them. And if we were all to suddenly die tomorrow—all of us; I'm talking the entire goddam world, Estella—then they'd have all of those new auras come to them at once. It'd be a pleasant little payoff to an irrelevant set of circumstances in a realm they *do not* care about. In many ways, they'd *want* it that way! So if they decided to help *anybody*, it wouldn't be us; it'd be the likes of Devin who want nothing more than to hand them all those auras on a goddam silver platter."

Estella shivered, "My god..."

"That's one way to look at it, I suppose," Stan shrugged and looked up as the car came to an abrupt stop in front of Xander's house. As the two of them stepped out of the car, they marveled at the sight as though it were some sort of haunted attraction. "So he's in there, huh?"

Estella nodded, "Yeah. *And* others; a family, I'm guessing."

"Must be the current owners. Can't imagine they're too happy about all this..." Stan sighed.

"Pardon my French, Stan, but I don't give a damn how they feel about this!" Estella was already starting towards the house, "I need to make sure Xander's alright!"

Rushing through the still open door—they stopped for a moment when they realized that the open entrance was totally missing the door; the hinges arched at an angle with the screws hung limply in their slots—they started to look around for any sign of Xander. Hearing a voice, they poked their heads around and saw a bruised and flustered man ranting into a cordless phone. Behind him were a woman and a little girl, both shivering in post-traumatic fear.

"—don't know if he's on drugs or... I just don't know!" the man continued on the phone, "He broke through our door and then he... he assaulted us! He's—" He stopped in mid-sentence when he spotted Estella and Stan and took a cautionary step away from them. Holding up his free hand out of fear, he stammered, "Oh god... t-tell me you're not with—"

Estella started towards him, "He's not a—"

Stan grabbed her shoulder then and pulled her back, "We're sorry for the intrusion, sir. I'm Sheriff Crowley and this is Deputy LaVey. Your neighbors called for us; said they heard a commotion in your home. We were off duty but were the closest to the location and were told to check things out. Where is the attacker?"

The man blinked for a moment and then looked down at the phone in his hand, blushing. "Oh! That... that was fast. Uh... just hold on a second," he held up his free index finger to them as he spoke into the phone once again. "I... uh, I guess the neighbors made the call for us. Somebody's already here. Thank you." Letting out a relieved sigh as he hung up, the man moved to rub his shoulder, "He's... Well, I guess he went upstairs. I mean, we *think* he did."

Stan quirked a brow, "You think?"

The man nodded and shrugged with the shoulder he wasn't rubbing, "Well, none of us actually *saw* him go up there; didn't see him go anywhere at all, actually? One minute he was in front of us—raving like a lunatic and...and, well, just scaring us out of our wits, you know?—and the next thing we know he's gone! *Poof!* Just like that! Guy's tripped out of his mind—I was a hippie in my day, so I know a bad trip when I see one—but he must be some kinda David Blaine-doper; he was creating all these weird illusions and such—terrified my wife and daughter —and, somehow, he even switched out our damn couch before he vanished."

Estella frowned, "Your couch?"

Stan shook his head at her, "You said that you *think* he went upstairs?"

The man nodded, "Well, I thought he'd gone back out through the door—like, maybe we'd just missed him bolting out the door in all the chaos, right?—but then we hear his weird laughing-crying rant start up upstairs and... well, that's when you showed up. How'd you get here so fast, anyway?"

Stan shrugged, angling himself near the stairwell to listen for Xander, "Right place; right time. You said he assaulted you, is everybody alright?"

"I... I guess," the man looked back towards his family, "He threw me, I think; seems impossible now that I'm thinking back on it, but he did. Must've been pretty hard, too, because I went through the bookshelf over there"—he pointed to the other side of the room where a pile of books and DVDs lay in a clutter around some shattered shelves—"and banged up my shoulder pretty bad. Then he... he..." the man shook his head, "Look, it was a really tense moment; we were all really scared. We... we thought we saw things—impossible things—but we feel like we all saw the *same* things, and... and that's just not possible... is it?"

Stan shrugged, "Can't say, sir, that's why they gave me a badge and not a head-shrinking certificate. Just for my report, though, what is it that you and your family *think* you saw?"

The man blushed and rubbed his shoulder some more, "I... we're really not sure. He was staring at our daughter, and when we looked to see if there was something, he was staring at in particular it... it was like... like she wasn't our daughter anymore. She looked different; like a little boy. I went to hit him then—that's when he threw me—but my daughter insists that when she looked up at my wife it *wasn't* her! Now my wife and I *both* agree that our daughter looked different—even agree on every detail of what we saw—and, while I can't say that I witnessed what my daughter saw, I have to imagine that she isn't lying considering what had happened to her! The whole thing shook her up pretty bad."

Frowning, Estella pushed past Stan, "Do you remember what the little boy looked like? The one that you and your wife saw in place of your daughter?"

The man narrowed his eyes at the question, "I... he—well, *she*; it *was* still my daughter, I mean—suddenly had this mess of short black hair and her blue eyes had turned brown... no, green?" he looked over his shoulder, "Honey, what was the color you said her eyes were? Hazel or something, right?"

"Y-yes! H-hazel!" the woman howled, sobbing at the mention, "That... that *monster* turned my baby's beautiful blue eyes *hazel*! It wasn't her! That *was not* my daughter! Oh god... what did he do to us?"

Estella frowned at that and looked back at Stan. "Black hair and hazel eyes?" she repeated, "Xander turned her into *himself* as a child? Why would—"

Stan was already nodding, "Came to his old house, started seeing things the way he remembered. Little girl was reshaped to look like him; I'm willing to guess that the mother was probably reshaped to look like his own mother. If they were returned to normal it means that Xander got a grip enough to see what he was doing before he went upstairs."

"Then why would he go upstairs?" Estella asked, "Why not just leave? That doesn't make sense!"

The man followed the exchange between them before frowning at Estella, "You look a little young to be a deputy, Miss... uh, what was it again?"

Estella frowned, looking over at him, "Crowley... no! LaVey, I'm deputy LaVe—"

"Crowley and LaVey?" his eyes widened, "Like the Sata—just what is this? Who are you people? What are you doing in my—"

Before the man's demands could stretch on any further, the contents of the house began to rattle as something crashed through the ceiling upstairs.

Stan cursed and started to sprint up the stairs, "Dammit! Xander! Stop!"

The man moved to chase Stan but, when Estella moved to block him, he glared down at her, "Did he just call that kid Xander? You two *know* that freaky little punk? What's going on he—"

Estella glared at him, "Enough of that!"

Chanting a spell under her breath, Estella watched as the enraged man's eyes began to roll back before he passed out. Behind him, the woman cried out and moved to get up before she and their daughter slumped back against their new-old couch, as well. As Estella finished chanting, she nodded to herself, confident that the family would wake up without any recollection of what had happened that night. Then, turning towards the stairs and following after Stan, the two went to work checking all the closed doors until they finally came across the bathroom.

Inside, the mirror was broken—the majority of the glass shards occupying the sink—with the words "I'M NOT HIM" spelled out in the bits of cracked mirror that still remained in the frame. Above them, the ceiling—now a gaping hole—gave the two of them a perfect view of the starless sky.

18

MUDSLIDE

X ander whipped and writhed through the night sky, his newfound ability to fly suspending him—like his mind —in an agonizing pitch between too-high and too-low. In an instant he felt himself grow weightless with his altitude, the sky opening up into an infinite and inky cosmos that beckoned to him, then, mere moments later, he was skimming the streets— the leather of his jacket skidding across the concrete as he flew at speeds that forced him to shift to overdrive to follow—as his cries and cackles merged into a single cohesive shriek of insanity. Car horns wailed, people cried, trees split and toppled, and wildlife shrieked as he tore through the air and all the environments existing between where he was and wherever his body was taking him.

Somewhere safe…

He had to get somewhere safe!

Somewhere secluded; somewhere he knew and trusted to be…

He slammed into the dusty ground of the quarry for the second time that night; his body bouncing from the momentum before he rolled several meters further and fell into the watery crater. The world went black and cloudy as water enveloped him, the searing heat of his own rage bringing the icy pit to a boil in an instant. Crying out as he felt his skin begin to blister against the magically charged searing waters, he leapt from the depths and scrambled up the sidewall of the chasm before yanking himself free and falling to his back on the dusty flat of barren landscape.

He wanted so badly just to rest; just to get his thoughts and wits about him…

But the resonating footsteps that shook the ground he was resting on proved that wasn't about to happen anytime soon. Opening his eyes and staring up through the screen of dust that he'd kicked up in his crash landing, he felt another laughing fit start in his chest and creep up his throat.

He did nothing to stop it.

"I'll give you this much, kid," Gerard's voice thundered as it drew nearer to him, "I'd never have thought you'd give us quite this much trouble." His sneering, misshapen head came to occupy Xander's view, "I guess you're not a total loss, huh?"

"**No, fuck-face; not all of me, at least,**" Xander laughed, making no effort to stand or move. "**I guess you're here to avenge that humiliating ass-kicking I gave you earlier, right? Or does this have something to do with me wasting Lars? 'Cause if you're going to avenge him, you probably owe me for that second *and* third asshole I blew through his neck the other day too.**"

"Lars was a tool," Gerard shrugged, "and having two assholes in his throat made sense, since he talked a lot of shit that he couldn't back up anyway." He shook his head and lunged to grab Xander then, only to have him vanish from the ground and appear a short distance away; back on his feet and bone-dry despite his time in the murky water. Gerard growled and shook his head, starting towards him. "You're as fast as he was, though," he shrugged, "smarter, but just as fast. I hope you don't mind me pretending you're him while I smear you all over this rock."

"**What is it with you and rocks anyway, Gerard,**" Xander asked, cocking his head and smirking, "**I'm noting a bit of a theme with you lackeys, and I can't help but wonder what that's all about.**"

"How would I know that?" Gerard spat, shaking his head. "I ain't here to philosophimate."

Xander's laughter started up again. "**Oh, I don't think there's much risk of** *that* **happening, don't you—**"

Gerard vanished.

Xander's shoulders sagged, "**Oh shit...**"

Anticipating the attack, Xander spun around and readied a right-hook on the emptiness behind him.

Gerard's energy swelled into being *beside* him.

Xander rolled his eyes and dropped his raised fist, "**Well fuck...**"

"Not as dumb as you thought, huh?" Gerard scoffed before driving a cinderblock fist into the side of Xander's head and sending him sprawling back into the crater; back into the murky water.

Without his burning rage to maintain its boil, the temperature of the lake water that had been flooding the chasm since his first fall was sickly warm while still reminding Xander that it was too cold to be swimming. Spitting the dank liquid from his mouth and trying to work it free of his nostrils, he looked up and spotted Gerard staring back down at him from the top of the crater.

He made no move to follow.

Xander chuckled, "**WHAT'S WRONG, SHIT-FOR-BRAINS? TELL ME YOU'RE NOT AFRAID OF A LITTLE WATE**—oh shit..."

"'oh shit' is oh-so-right, darling," Bianca's voice sloshed behind him and Xander turned to face the source. Though there was only about three-to-four feet worth of water—though that was steadily rising with each new wave from the lake feeding into it—in the crater with them, somehow the twisted goddess had kept herself hidden it its depths. As Xander watched, the shimmering black water seemed to stretch ever-upward; growing and taking shape as the equally black and just as shimmering Bianca emerged, pursing her lips and narrowing her eyes to angry slits. "I have to say, handsome," her voice was like the husky pull of melted ice dragging across a rocky chasm, "I don't like being casted on, and you did it *twice* in one night."

"Hold still long enough and I'll make it three, bitch!" Xander hissed, baring his fangs.

Bianca cooed and clenched her fists at her side—Xander felt the water seem to grow denser at his ankles—"Ooh! Don't tempt me; I've already got plans for you without you going and getting me all hot and bothered."

Xander raised an eyebrow at that, **"The fuck...?"**

Bianca threw her clenched fists into the air and the watery hold on Xander's ankles tore him upward. Though the hold around his ankles was like ice, the water that slammed past his body—blinding him and pelting at his skin—was, once again, boiling hot and searing into his face. As he was rocketed out of the crater, a giant hand punched through the blinding wall of water and grabbed Xander by the face, tearing him from the hellish fountain and hurling him through the air and into the side of the trailer. As cheap aluminum siding and poor support took the full force of one god pitching the other into it, the trailer folded around the force of Xander's impact as it teetered off of its tires, hanging for a moment as gravity tried to decide whether to drop it back on into place or take the more destructive option and collapse onto its side.

"Come on, Universe; we all know where this is going..."

Gravity's decision came as no surprise to Xander.

Once again Xander was thrown into a laughing fit as he and

the tortured metal box slammed back; the poorly made wooden staircase to the door shattering under the management's front door and the few laughable windows breaking as its contents banged and clattered within it.

"What the hell is wrong with him?" Gerard's voice grew nearer.

"Everyone goes a little crazy their first time," Bianca answered. "Remember how you got?"

Gerard chuckled, "Village never stood a chance."

"No, dear," Bianca sighed, "they didn't."

"You know," Gerard laughed, "I'd always heard that you get hungry again after eating Chinese, but I never believed it much until I tried it for myself; damn, those kids were tasty, though."

"Quiet," Bianca told him.

"What?" Gerard almost sounded hurt, "Don't tell me you're suddenly getting squeamish on me! It ain't like *you* haven't eaten—"

"I said QUIET!" Bianca hissed at him. A moment of silence passed, then, "I thought I heard—"

"No, I hear it too!" Gerard said.

"Think it; magic makes it happen. Think it; magic makes it happen. Think it; magic makes it happen," Xander chanted to himself, fighting to keep the laughing fit and snide inner commentary stifled within his chest, "Come on. Come on. Come on. Come o**H JUST LET ME DO IT!**"

Gerard laughed, "Kid's a fucking lunaAAHH SHIT!"

The air went alive with energy as the trailer began to lift off the ground, the metal squealing and shrieking as it folded and dented under an invisible force until, in less than three seconds, it had been restructured into a giant, bullet-shaped mass. As Xander's cackles once again rose over the sound of everything else, he enchanted the massive metal projectile and slapped it on the end, sending it rocketing through the air towards the two.

Bianca dove out of the way, rolling across the dusty flat and skidding to a kneeling position.

Gerard, roaring, drove a fist into the projectile.

Xander laughed, "Bad move, Wreck-It Ralph!"

A wave of energy billowed from the center of the twisted hunk of metal as a familiar enchantment was activated and the quarry was lit up as the giant makeshift explosive round went off...

Right in Gerard's face.

19

BLOOD FROM A STONE

~One year, eight months, thirteen days, and three hours earlier~

*A*s the life seeped from the Chinaman's eyes Gerard could almost see himself in the shimmering, terror-filled orbs, and he resisted the urge to release his opponent's scrawny yellow neck to indulge his trademarked 'Buddha-be-praised' head rub. *Though it pissed the little bastards off every time he did it—some nation-wide ingrown ass hair about sacrilege or some shit like that; not like he was taking a dump on a crucifix or anything (though he'd done that during a fight, too)—he hadn't done a single show in Hong Kong without the display. While he'd initially hated the idea—the whole scene of him obscenely rubbing his shiny, bald head with both hands while chanting, "Buddha! Buddha! Buddha!" and pelvic thrusting about the stage at the audience—his manager, if Andy could be called such a thing, had come up with it as a way to really rile up the locals whenever he did a show in China.*

And god-fucking-damn if the wiry little Jewish bastard hadn't been one-hundred-and-fifty-percent right!

Finally, the Chinaman's desperate slaps against his forearms went limp and, soon thereafter, totally still; the tiny digits slipping from his oiled muscles and slapping at their dead owner's sides. Confident that it was the right time to do so, he flung the body into the audience— letting Praying Mantis or whatever the little bastard's stage name had been go free among his people—and let his tongue hang from his open mouth as he began slapping his head and thrusting at all the booing, howling members of the audience.

"*Fuck you! And fuck you! And a very big and special 'fuck you' to that hot little yellow piece of tail in the back! Be sure to visit my dressing room so I can split you down the middle like firewood, darling; I'll love you long time! Yeah? And FUCK YOU too!*"

With that, Gerard hopped the turnbuckle and, delivering a nose-splitting punch to a raving audience member in the face for getting too close, started for the shitty dressing room Andy had settled with in his contract with the rice-spitters.

"*Fucking hate this country!*" *he ranted to nobody, slamming the door—not even bothering to look when he heard something break behind him—and started towards his complimentary bottle of Hardy Perfection cognac.* "*Christ on a cum-stained, syphilitic whore!*" *he growled, knocking a nearby bucket of ice to the floor and snatching up the bottle on its own,* "*Don't these stupid savages know anything about brandy? Jeez... give me fucking ice? Why don't they just drop their needle dicks in the bottle and piss in it while they're at it?*"

Dropping down onto the overstuffed couch they'd crammed in the room for him at the last minute, he reached over to the stack of hundred dollar bills and went to flip through them before smiling at the amount and began fanning himself with it while he took a long pull straight from the bottle.

"*Now,*" *he mused,* "*where can a guy find some yellow tail in this dump?*"

THEY'RE COMING FOR YOU, GERARD.

"*WHO IN THE FUCKING HELL...?*" *Gerard jumped to his feet and looked around the room, brandishing the cognac bottle like a club.*

Seeing nobody, he curled his lip, "Whoever's fucking with me better step up before I turn their skull into a brandy sifter!"

WHILE YOUR OFFER SOUNDS MOST ENTICING, MY PERFECTLY PEDIGREED KILLER, I THINK I HAVE A FAR MORE LUCRATIVE COUNTER-OFFER TO BRING TO YOUR ATTENTION. EITHER YOU JOIN ME AND ENJOY UNTOLD STRENGTH AND GLORY—AND, YES, EVEN MORE KILLING—OR YOU CAN LET *THEM* HAVE THEIR WAY WITH YOU.

Gerard suddenly heard a growing crowd of rioters approaching his door.

"What the fuck? WHO THE HELL IS THAT?" when no response —no friendly one, anyway—was returned, he rushed to secure the latch on the door, frowning when he saw that the sound from earlier had been the latch chain getting slammed in the door. Prying the door open to retrieve the wedged end of the chain, he saw the enraged crowd of Chinese men coming towards the door with knives and crowbars, howling in rage.

He only understood his name within the garble of Cantonese.

"Oh shit!" he gasped, slamming the door shut and bracing it with his shoulder as he worked the bent chain into place on the door. "What the fuck do those chinks want?"

I'M NOT SURE THEY LIKE BEING CALLED THAT, GERARD, AND THAT *MIGHT* HAVE SOMETHING TO DO WITH YOUR CURRENT PREDICIMENT. UNFORTUNATELY, THERE SEEMS TO BE VERY LITTLE TIME FOR YOU TO CONSIDER MY PROPOSAL, SO I'LL BE NEEDING AN ANSWER BEFORE THEY BEAT YOU TO DEATH.

Gerard had barely taken in the full scope of what the mystery voice had said before the mangled chain separating the enraged mob from him snapped and they flooded the room. Though he got a few hits in on the first men to leap at him, the sheer numbers quickly over-whelmed him, and he was buried in a flood of howling Chinese *protestors. All at once his body was subjected to untold agony as any number of blunt weapons were brought down upon him with bone-splitting fury while he was cut and stabbed repeatedly.*

THAT DECISION *IS* STILL PENDING, GERARD. I CAN HARDEN YOU TO THEIR ATTACKS? DO YOU ACCEPT?

"YES! YES, GOD DAMMIT! I AGREE! JUST GET THESE FUCKERS OFFA ME!"

XANDER SHOOK his head as he dropped out of overdrive over Gerard, who had been blown clear across the quarry and onto a ledge just within the inner rim of the crater. As he came to—head still reeling from the explosion and trying to come to grips with his returning memory from his prior life—Xander clucked his tongue and waved down to him.

"Now *that* looked like it hurt, and I'm not talking about that big boom back there, either," Xander laughed and jumped down after Gerard and landed squarely on his chest; the force of his fall shifting Gerard's body and causing him to skid further down into the pit. As Xander casually "surfed" down the crater on Gerard's chest—stabilizing himself with his aura and vampire-enhanced balance—he tucked his hands into his pockets. "Do you know what the riot of all this is?" he asked. When no answer came, he scowled and drove a heavy foot down on the god's chest and glared, "YOU'RE ABOUT TO FUCKING DIE, GERARD! IT'D DO YOU SOME GOOD TO PRACTICE SOME HUMILITY!"

Gerard groaned, his eyes still swimming in his head as he skidded down the side of the chasm and headed towards the water. "C-can't... can't swim," he announced.

"Would you believe that doesn't surprise me, Gerard? Not one tiny bit. Anyway, as I was saying:"—Xander mused as Gerard's body slipped into the water and his eyes flashed open in panic—"it occurs to me that I've now killed *two* of the four of you shitheads—and, please, don't be driven to argue with me just because you're still thinking; contrary to popular belief, that *does not* mean that you *are* still alive—and I haven't had to use my guns *once* to do it! Isn't that a hell of a thing?"

"I... I ca... I c-can't... can't swim!" Gerard gurgled as he felt himself begin to drown.

"Yes, like a pebble in the ocean, I'm sure, but—please, Gerard, don't interrupt me, it's rude; didn't Devin teach you any manners—I still can't get past how *great* it feels to be able to accomplish something for myself. Mind you, I *do* love my guns—not just for the sentimental value, but also for keeping me looking cool as I do; and don't you try to deny it, either— but there's a certain sense of freedom when you realize that you're not defined by your tools, do you know what I mean, Gerard?" Xander smirked and looked over when no answer came. The bottom half of Gerard's body—a portion of his lower-belly and his legs and one of his arms—were perched against the side-walls of the crater, but the upper half—the half that Xander was still standing on—was only partially visible within the dark, murky water. "Like I said," Xander mused, letting his boots lift off from the dead god's chest as he floated into the air—water trickling from his feet and distorting the already hazy image of Gerard's panicked face in the ripples— and started back towards the surface, "quite rude. I can only hope that Bianca isn't quite as brash when others are talking."

Estella could barely feel her feet as she and Stan walked out of Xander's old house; the weight of her worry for her lover growing almost too unbearable to stand under. As they started back towards the car—their gazes repeatedly shifting up towards the sky—Stan suddenly seized up and began to teeter on his feet.

Estella moved to catch Stan as he started to topple and helped to hold him up while he overcame the dizzy spell that clouded his eyes.

"What was that? What happened?" she demanded.

Stan cupped his forehead in his left hand, "Xander's killed another one of them already... Gerard."

"The big one," Estella nodded, biting her lip. "But that's good, right? At least he didn't kill Xander!"

"The killing isn't the point; it's what happens to that energy when they die!" he shook his head and started for the car with a renewed purpose, but, still dizzy, nearly collapsed again. And, again, Estella was forced to catch him. Sighing, he nodded towards the car, though Estella was already in the process of walking them towards it, "Those three are simply extensions of Devin. When one of them dies, the power that they had returns back to the source. It's probably why he left when he did back at the mansion; he figured he'd just leave Xander to kill all of them and let all of his powers come back to him before he faced him."

"So Devin's getting stronger?" Estella frowned.

Stan nodded, "I wouldn't be surprised if he was *glad* Xander was dispatching them like this. Saves him the trouble."

"But Xander—"

"Xander's only going to lose more and more of his mind if he keeps letting The Power consume him!" Stan pressed on, leaning against the hood of the Mercedes when they were close enough. "It's not meant to be used like this!"

Estella nodded, "Which is why we have to get him back before that happens! So we can get him back!"

Stan looked up at her, "And what if he's too far gone by the time we reach him?"

Estella glared at him, "He won't be."

Seeing that her resolve hadn't waned any, Stan's jaw tightened, and he looked away, shaking his head of the dizziness as Estella started towards the driver's-side door.

Stan sighed, "Estella, wait"—she did—"I'm sorry about that. I know I've been a shit ever since I got back—"

Estella turned so quickly that she didn't think Stan had even seen the motion, "You can say that again!"

Stan, catching his breath, nodded, "Alright, I will: 'I've been a shit'; a major one. I already told Xander this, but I have a feeling he spared you the details, especially with how mad you've been at me lately."

"Xander's told me a lot," Estella frowned, "But I'd be lying if I said I'm not curious if there's more."

Stan sighed, "The leader, Devin... he was a prisoner when I first met him."

Estella frowned and nodded, "I'd heard? But what was he in prison for?"

Stan shrugged, turning to rest against the car as he continued to rub his head, "Everything, I guess. Murder, rape, theft, arson—arson being his 'favorite'; his calling card; everything else was always "icing"—and pretty much anything else you can think of. He never even tried to deny it; outright celebrated most of his accomplishments, in fact."

Estella sneered, "Why would you involve yourself with somebody so awful?"

Stan let out a long sigh that trailed off in a groan, "I... I guess it started when I'd learned that a friend of mine from my hometown had killed himself. Our old priest... he was a bad man—made the same mistakes as a lot of other bad men in his line of work—and I found out about all of it pretty early on. But..." he looked away, shame distorting his saddened features, "like so many others, I neglected to tell anyone. Instead, I ran; I ran away from town. I ran from my childhood—my parents, my friends, my dreams—and I ran away from my faith. And I kept right on running until I landed myself in this very city and came face-to-face with a therion who wanted to give me my first welcome and my final farewell all in one."

Estella frowned, leaning against the car as well, "What'd you do?"

"*I* didn't do anything," he confessed. "Joseph Stryker did."

"So that's how you met Xander's father?" Estella felt the threat of a smile at the corners of her mouth.

Stan laughed and shook his head, "Xander never told you this story, did he?"

Estella shook her head, "With the exception of the other night, Xander hasn't talked too much about the past. Plus, he's never been one to air out others' dirty laundry."

Stan smirked at that. "Well, that's nice of him, I guess," he frowned and pulled a pack of cigarettes from his pocket.

Estella frowned, "When did you start smoking?"

Stan shrugged as he pulled one of the cylinders from the pack with his teeth, "Never really quit. I just never smoked too often before, and now that I don't have The Power to stave off the nicotine monkey he's tearing at my shoulder with a vengeance." He held out the pack to Estella, who shook her head at the offer. Shrugging, Stan tucked the pack away before focusing his limited magic on the tip, smirking with satisfaction as it lighted and he took a long drag. Then, taking the cigarette between his index and middle finger and blowing out the cloud of smoke, he nodded to Estella, picking up where he'd left off, "So yeah, I was saved by the mythos legend himself. *The* Joseph Stryker stepped out of the shadows and into my life as a shining beacon of strength and integrity and confidence—everything I'd lost the moment I'd left home—and, against almost every law that exists in yours and Xander's world, he let me keep my memories of him; let me dig deeper into that world." He took another drag and rolled his free hand, "I was invited into the Odin Clan, I got to meet Depok, and I used the library there to learn about amazing things; things that I later used to call upon the forces that gave me The Power." He smirked, returning the cigarette to his lips and shaking his head, "Joseph Stryker, it would appear, had a way of picking seemingly ordinary human beings to change their lives in incredible ways..."

"I don't understand," Estella shook her head. "What does this have to do with Devin?"

Stan nodded and sighed out another long cloud of smoke, "Right... *him*." He flicked some ash off the end of his cigarette before pursing it between his lips, "Well, it's like I said: I didn't tell anybody about what my priest was doing. And, like I also said: I'd left my friends behind. Well, I was just a young man then, and about fifteen years later—while I imagine you and Xander were still friends in grade school—I received a call that one of my old classmates had been found in his apartment a few days after he'd hung himself. He'd already been living a pretty solitary life; everyone told me that he'd become a loner. During college he'd apparently gotten into some trouble with drinking —some DWIs and a few counts of public drunkenness—and, after he'd done some jail time and a great deal of community service, he'd started with AA and, eventually, started counseling there, as well. Right before his death, I guess he'd started talking more and more about what the priest had done to him as a kid —I guess he'd been at it longer than I'd thought," he frowned at that and took a longer drag, shaking his head again, "I'd say that I'm glad I dodged that bullet, but I have a hard time stomaching that logic—and it finally drove him to kill himself."

Estella whimpered, "Oh my... Stan, I'm so sorry! I—"

Stan held up his hand, "Don't pity me. Not yet. Not until you've heard the rest." Another drag; another sigh; another headshake, "I can't say that I felt bad about what happened to Bruce—that was his name; Bruce—" Stan's body seemed to tense around the name, "but I *did* feel responsible; like, if I'd only *said* something when I had the chance, then maybe that priest would've faced some actual justice instead of just dying a dirty old man. It wouldn't have been in time to stop his attacks on Bruce—that was already long behind us—but maybe he wouldn't have felt so ostracized; maybe his entire life would've been different." He looked over at Estella, "So I didn't feel bad *for* Bruce, not really, I guess, but I did a *really* good job convincing myself that I cared so that I had an excuse to feel guilty. I wanted to bring him back; to use The Power that I'd acquired out of randomness and selfishness and have it *mean* something for Bruce... or for me. I've never been able to decide. But, as you probably already know, magic doesn't work that way, and I found myself feeling more and more guilty. A moment of desperation drove me to call to the other side—to *beg* for Bruce's life to be returned—and it told me what I already knew: it couldn't be done; not with natural magic. Then it told me of Devin—already in prison at that time on multiple life sentences—because some clever attorneys said he was too crazy to warrant to the death penalty—and that he was doing things with magic that were making the cosmos nervous. I thought it was giving me another answer for my quest to absolve my guilt, but I can see now they were trying to warn me of a danger that they saw in him."

Estella frowned, "Even the things that gave you The Power were afraid of Devin?"

Stan gave a slow nod, "It would certainly appear that way. And it makes sense, too; an aura might not *remember* who it was in its human life—might not carry that identity over with it to the other side—but they most certainly retain the essence of what sort of a person they were in life. Somebody like Devin— somebody who thrives off of destruction and pain and malice— well, an aura like that crosses over and it can prove to be a disruptive force; something like that *might*—if it gets to be bad enough—cross over to *this* side, as well." Stan scoffed and shook his head, "I was such a fool to think they were telling me to *ask* him for help with my problem when, in fact, they were probably asking *me* to help *them* with their own potential problem; hell, maybe *that's* why they really gave me The Power in the first place. Universe is funny like that."

Estella frowned, "So what did you do?"

Stan waited a long moment to answer, staring after a trail of smoke as it snaked through the air. "I went to him," he finally answered. "I went to him and I asked him what he knew, and then he went and asked me the same thing. And I made the mistake of telling him the truth. I told him what I'd turned myself into; practically drew him a road map of how to become even more powerful." He jammed the cigarette into his mouth and inhaled until it had burned down to the filter. Then, holding the smoke inside his lungs long enough to make Estella's chest hurt, he tossed the remains to the street and finally let out the smoke. "I learned later—*after* he'd escaped from prison and started his morbid crusade a short time before Xander's eighteenth birthday and all the things that happened with it— that he didn't just get the other side's attention and humbly ask it for power... he went after them, dragged something back, and *ravaged* it. And when you take your power like that—when you force the other side—things don't work out quite right." Rubbing his head one last time he spit on the street—casting the wad of phlegm away with the same irate glare as he had the cigarette butt—and started around to get into the car. "So there you have it, Estella; my guilt forced me to make mistakes that multiplied my sins too many times over to ever forget, and when I heard that Devin had escaped—burning the prison to the ground and ending the lives of inmates and prison guards in the process—I knew that he'd come for me, so I ran. I lied to myself again, of course—I'm good at that, I guess—and told myself that I was running from Devin for Xander's sake; so that he wouldn't have to come home from his vengeful mission and step right into *that* world."

Estella looked after him for a moment, "Devin is what he is… because of *you?*"

Stan paused at the passenger door and shrugged, "Like I said, Estella: don't pity me. All of this is my fault; *all* of it! And I've been a shit—just like you said—because I've been *feeling* like shit for what I did ever since then. And now Xander's burdened with the strength I've trained myself to shoulder for years, and I can't figure out how I feel about it…"

Estella blinked, suddenly feeling numb, "How you feel…?"

Stan nodded, "The guilt is overwhelming, and I'll understand if you want to beat the crap out of me with those pretty magic sticks of yours when I'm done—believe me, I'll feel better if you do—but I feel this overwhelming excitement that whatever The Power is turning Xander into will be enough to end this for good. I just can't be sure that he'll survive it if he does, and, if he does, I worry about what sort of fresh hell he'll choose to bring upon the world if he can't bring himself to get rid of it."

Estella narrowed her eyes at that, and she felt her hand move to her back to draw her silver tonfa, Selene, from the sheathe hidden under her jacket. She was in overdrive an instant later, coming around the Mercedes and dropping out still in mid-sprint so that Stan would see her coming. Swinging the tonfa around by its handle, the longer end came to rest against Stan's face—Estella pulling back the force at the last minute to just make contact rather than break his jaw—and she glared at him, shaking her head.

"I don't blame you for the creature that monster turned himself into, and you shouldn't be so quick to take that credit for yourself. Just because you were the first one to show a madman a knife doesn't mean you made them a killer, and you're hardly the first person to inappropriately deal with guilt —you've been dragging up the reminder of Xander's five-year ritual all night, after all—but if you make the mistake of convincing yourself that Xander's strength is *anything* but his

own, or if you allow yourself one single *moment* of credit or
peace of mind for the outcome of this night, then I will not stop
hitting you with this 'pretty magic stick' until I can put my
pinky through one of your ears and watch it pop out the other!
Do you understand me, Stanley?"

Stan stared—dumbfounded by Estella's hostility—and slowly
nodded.

Estella stepped back, spinning Selene in her grip as she did
and tucking the tonfa away at her back.

"Now get in the car! Whether he knows it or not, he'll need
us once he's finished cleaning up your mess."

20

A DROP IN THE BUCKET

*B*ianca had been patient enough—if patience in matters of life and death could truly be called such a thing; something even the two warring sides within Xander's head "agreed" upon—while he'd birthed himself from the gaping chasm that he and Gerard had vanished into; his lonely arrival evidence enough for Bianca to plug in the rest.

"It's done then?" she'd asked, though the nod accompanying the question was enough to tell Xander he didn't need to answer.

Instead, he'd smirked—the residual giggles from his ongoing laughing fit causing his lips to part into a wicked grin—and finally drawn his hands from his jacket pocket to shrug innocently. "**Was there ever any doubt?**" he'd asked back; exchanging one unneeded question with another.

Bianca had shrugged and taken a single step back as Xander floated to the dusty ground. "Can't say I'm sorry to see him go," she confessed, "he was a racist—at least he *was* when Devin first found him; he was kind enough to rid us of some of our lesser qualities from our prior lives—and I never felt right being around him knowing what was lingering in there."

Xander scoffed and shook his head, "**Yeah, wouldn't want anybody to judge you on the color of your skin while you're killing them and destroying their homes, right? Even worse when the possible judgment's being cast by a fellow murdering arsonist.**"

Bianca offered a bow at that, "Glad to see you understand."

"**So you say that Devin was 'kind enough' to tweak you all from the fuckups you were before he made you all... like this?**" Xander said as he'd cocked his head and chuckled, "**So what sort of a fuckup were you? Or don't you remember, either?**"

"Can't say," Bianca shrugged, "But whatever you did back at that fancy mansion of yours definitely proved I've got some daddy-issues. I imagine I'm better off not knowing."

Laughing at that, Xander had shaken his head, "**Better off or not, Bi, I'm going to show you *exactly* who you were before I kill you. You can call it a courtesy if you like, but—in reality; or as real as all *this* is—I'm just really, *really* fucking curious.**"

"Naturally," she'd sighed.

Xander had taken a step towards her then, pointing behind him towards the crater with his thumb. "**Maybe you can shed some light on something for me; our rock-headed friend was totally dense,**" he chuckled at his own wordplay.

"I'll do what I can, I suppose," Bianca had said with a shrug.

"**Well, it's like this,**" Xander started, "**I've noticed something of a trend with you and the others of Devin's design. Lars was a total airhead, Gerard was dumb as a bag of rocks, and you're a total wash-up; and I'm just dying to know what's going on with that trend.**"

Bianca glared at him, "You're asking me why we're all idiots, is that it?"

Xander cackled and shook his head, "**No, no—I mean, those are your words, not mine; totally accurate, though—but what I'm *really* asking is the whole *elements* theme, you** know; Lars with the air and wind and whatnot, Gerard with the whole rock and earth routine, and your constant water theme. What's the deal with all that?"

"Devin prefers fire," Bianca stated flatly, staring at Xander like the answer had meant something to him.

Xander raised an eyebrow at her.

She'd sighed and rolled her eyes, "Cute *and* stupid, perfect." She'd started a slow pace in a wide angle then, though Xander made no effort to keep her in front of him or even in his sights at all. "In magic, all things are broken into five elements: fire, air, water, earth, and spirit."

Xander chuckled, shaking his head, "**That a fact?**"

Bianca's glare had burned into his back, "Hey! You asked!" There had been a moment of silence as she'd taken a few more steps around him—maintaining her distance as she did—before continuing, "I'm sure I don't need to tell you that Devin likes to work with fire; he prefers it," she'd repeated, "so when he was creating us, he decided to sacrifice the bulk of his control over the other elements—'cept for spirit; none of us much got what that meant—so he didn't have to lose any of his control over his preferred element."

"**So what's that all mean for you dipshits? You all seem to have the same abilities to me,**" Xander had finally turned to face her.

"I'm sure it all translates into similar outcomes," she'd nodded, "but the process of getting those outcomes is different. I can't speak for them, but I always feel my own magic passing through me like a current; feels like I'm floating in a pool of total control, and all I have to do is 'splash' to make something happen. And if I let myself sink into it, I can change myself and the world around me to be whatever I want"—Xander had frowned at that, remembering the few times she'd changed her appearance—"So I guess the big question now is, what's it like for *you* to have all of Stan's magic; to have *all* the elements in one place?"

"It feels like I'm going crazy," Xander felt the confession slip free of his lips before he had the chance to stop it.

Bianca had perked up at the response, "Oh? Crazy, you say?"

The laughter had returned then, and, with it, the malice, **"Yeah, I'd imagine a psycho-bitch like you might know the feeling, right?"**

Bianca, finishing her cycle then, had stopped and frowned at him, "You know, it doesn't have to be this way."

Already starting to chuckle, Xander had tilted his head towards her with an **"Oh?"** to push the issue.

Shaking her head, she'd smiled at him, "Pardon me for saying so—I know you've got that little witch-bitch back home and such —but I feel like *we* could have something, you and I; that we could take out Devin and rule on high as king and queen of the world!"

Xander's stifled laughing fit had come out at full force then, folding him over and causing his knees to shake.

A long moment passed with his cackles rolling over the dusty flats of the quarry and echoing within the crater beside him. **"Are... are you fucking kidding me? You're joking, right? *Please* tell me you're joking! I am *literally* a moment from ripping you apart and..."** he shook his head and let more chuckles slip free, **"and you're coming on to me? Do you throw that pussy at *everybody* that can kill you?"**

"Not at all," her calm composure had thrown Xander into more hysterics as she'd calmly gone on, "just the ones I want inside me."

Xander's laughter had trailed off then with a dribbling of giggles, his head shaking and distorting the sounds with each oscillating pass of his head. **"Well, I'm sorry, sister, but you're just not my type."**

Bianca had growled at that—the first sign of emotion she'd

shown during the entire exchange; behind Xander, the sound of the lake's waves rolling heavier than before grew more noticeable—"And just what *is* your type, *vampire?*"

Jumping into overdrive then, Xander had closed the distance between them before she'd finished the last syllable of "vampire," and appeared with one of his pistols already drawn and pressed against her head.

His eyes were cold and vicious then, burning like hellfire a few inches from Bianca's as he growled, "*LIVING!*" and then pulled the trigger.

Unsurprisingly, the bullet had found only empty air and a dusty ground to bite into; birthing another—much smaller— crater in its wake.

Xander and Bianca's battle kicked up a sizable cloud of dust in the area surrounding the quarry in only a few short seconds. As the battlefield grew hazier, Xander broke free— popping out of the stifling cloud and floating over the lake's now-angry surface—and turned his gaze back towards the void of suspended dirt to try to get a read on Bianca's location.

"**Come on... where are you, you little bi—**"

Bianca rocketed up from the center of the lake right below Xander, screaming in rage and sending a streamline of frigid lake water as she shot towards him like a bullet. Twisting in midair, Xander brought his left foot around in a whistling kick that connected with Bianca's right shoulder. Though he earned a cry of pain from her in the process, the kick was too little and too late to stop her from slamming into him and snaking her thin, wiry fingers around his throat.

"When you get where you're going after this, pretty boy," she growled in his face, "Don't you dare go telling whoever's waiting for you that I didn't give you the option to be so much more." Xander gurgled around another bout of laughter, which only served to stoke Bianca's fury that much more. "STOP

LAUGHING AT ME, YOU LEECH! YOU'VE GOT NOTHING
TO BE LAUGHING ABOUT ANYW—"

An ear-splitting shriek cut past her enraged words as a pair
of foot-long bone-barbs erupted from around Xander's neck—
piercing through both of Bianca's wrists—as he willed his
collarbones to grow some new extensions.

"**I'd say I got *plenty* to laugh about, bitch!**" Xander giggled
as he lunged forward and slammed his forehead—momentarily
reinforced with an increased bone density for the attack—into
her face. Bianca's body pitched back, only to have her still-
pierced wrists keep her tethered to him. "**Like, for example,
how hilarious it is that one of Devin's little half-assed
lackeys thinks she's going to one-up the source of her power
—see, that's fucking comedy *gold* to me!**" he said between
stifled chuckles. Then reaching up to his left shoulder and snapping the bone-barb free of his body, he repeated the action with
the right side and, still holding Bianca by her perforated forearms, drew back both of his feet and drove them into her chest.

Her right arm jumped from her shoulder's socket as her
body went one way and Xander pulled her arms the other; her
left arm, however, was ripped free of her body.

The goddess's cries pitched and spiraled as the body did the
same. Xander watched for a moment—enjoying the spectacle of
the flailing limbs and tortured shrieks of Bianca's silhouette
against the refracted moonlight on the thrashing water's surface
below him—before eyeing the left arm that he still held in his
grip.

"**Tonight has been a fun night for me, Bi; I want you to
know that before you... well, you know.**"

～

*THIS ISN'T ME! These monsters need to be stopped—yes!—but this is...
this is indulgence, not justice!*

The two have been one in the same with me in the past before. Why should tonight be any different?

It is different, and you're not me!

I'm not sure you know who you are anymore.

I know who I'm **not**! *And this isn't... this is* exactly *what they do;* exactly *how they fight! How can I believe this is me!*

Maybe you just don't want to admit how much like them you always were. You've seen two of their pasts—guilt, regret, outcasts, degenerates, sinners—

What does sin have to do with this?

You talk of justice; of paying for crimes against humanity, right? You've hurt people. You've let people get hurt. You still do. What makes you so different?

Because I know it's wrong!

No you don't! You're just inventing excuses to not **be like them; that doesn't make you a saint, Xander; it makes you an egomaniac!**

Then why bother stopping them?

Because you're better than them, that's why. The one true law —the only justice—in the universe is strength; the stronger conquer the weaker. Stronger gravity drags the weaker on their path; stronger suns swallow weaker ones on their cycles about the cosmos; the larger meteors travel farther. Did you expect the very law of all things to change simply because you decided to birth a consciousness? Do you think it's just to defend the weak just so they can feel secure enough to remain weak? You got The Power because you knew that your weakness would lead to the girl's death. You didn't expect anybody else to do it for **you; you demanded The Power and you—**

I... I demanded it...?

What? Suddenly you weren't there? Suddenly that's **in question now, too?**

No... but I... I didn't earn it...

So what?

Something Stan said...

He's an old fool who wasted The Power!

Is that who you are?

I'm you!

No...

YES!

Stan said that that Devin took the power—he did it wrong!—*and that's what made him who he is... could I be—*NO! SHUT THE FUCK UP, XANDER! THIS IS JUSTICE!—*could all of this be* —ENOUGH OF THIS! YOU GOT WHAT YOU WANTED, NOW USE IT!—*I'm turning into something... something just like Devin because I didn't...*

You don't remember who you are, Xander?

I... I don't?

I see the potential.

Stan, my power.

Grace is what makes power worth having.

Grandma, my wisdom.

Promise me that you won't die.

Estella, my strength.

Better watch that temper.

Depok, my salvation.

"Hey, son."

Dad?

"Same shit, different day, huh? What sort of fresh hell you dropped yourself into now?"

I... I don't know, Dad. I feel... I feel like I'm losing touch with who I am. Like I'm not me, or... or like I'm not who I'm supposed to be; like somebody else is in control.

"Well that's pretty weird, huh? Taking Stanley's power like that must be messing with your head. So is this the time you just give up then? I've been watching you fight your entire life, so it seems like sort of a waste to see it all amount to nothing now just becau—

SHUT THE FUCK UP, OLD MAN! NOBODY NEEDS A DEAD AURIC'S—

"I might be dead, son, but you talk to me like that again and I'm going to whoop your ass."

That... that was me?

"Well it certainly wasn't me, Xander, and who else is in here?"

I just thought...

"No, you didn't think at all, son. You're a Stryker, and a Stryker puts their mind before their madness, got it? You're creating all sorts of hell up in here just because you can't admit that maybe you're a bit of a jerk; that maybe you are a little bit insane! And it's turning that part of you into its own personality! You want to do this right? You gotta stop giving the reigns over to somebody that you're creating! Remember: everyone's psychotic, son; its only when a psyche doesn't fit in with others that it's seen as different, and this Devin-creep is cray-zay with a capital 'C.' Own up to your troubles, accept that we're all a little bit crazy sometimes, and show them what that craziness in the right hands can mean! And then get back to that groovy clan and that pretty girl of yours, and don't worry so much about our striped friend, kay? Trepis has had a long and happy life and I'm sure it's just breaking his fuzzy balls to see you resenting all these great changes in your life just because it's his time to cross over.

"Thanks, Dad."

"It's what I'm here for, bud. Now go kick some ass!"

"**WHAT THE HELL? What just happened? What was all tha—** enough!" Xander took a deep breath and let it out slow as he focused on unifying his thoughts. "I *wanted* this. Not just The Power, but an excuse to vent the fear and anger I've been feeling. I wanted to be as crazy and violent and vengeful as Devin and the others, and that means that all of that *was* me—all of *this*"—he looked down at Bianca's severed arm—"*is* me—and... and that's okay; so long as it's them—so long as I stop this madness tonight—it's okay..."

What are you saying?

Xander smirked, "I'm saying you *are* me—at least until I get The Power out of me and stop talking to myself—and that we're allowed to be batshit crazy for tonight."

*Well... we never **did** **get to celebrate our birthday properly.***

"No," Xander laughed. "No, we did not."

"YOU FUCKER!" Bianca shrieked up at him, stabilizing herself in midair and starting to fly back up at him, "You skinny, pasty, leather-loving joke of a gothic soap opera!"

Xander smirked at that, zipping to one side as Bianca tried to kick at him. "That's pretty funny," he said.

Bianca paused, suddenly nervous by the calmness in her opponent's voice; her aura writhing with confusion and suspicion. "Then why aren't you laughing," she demanded.

"Not in a laughing mood," Xander offered the only explanation he could.

"The... The Power, it's not—"

"Oh it's still in here," Xander nodded, dropping Bianca's arm and reaching under his jacket, "I've just decided that I'd sooner be behind the driver's seat than let it drive the entire time."

Bianca's eyes widened as she followed her lost limb's fall before it vanished into the blackness of the lake's waters with a small splash.

"Relax, princess," Xander rolled his eyes, drawing one of Dwayne's pistols from its holster, "I've seen enough of you grow lost bits and pieces back to know that your sentiment over *that* is unnecessary. Unless there was a ring or something on one of those fingers," he shrugged, "not that it'll matter in a minute."

He leveled the gun on her.

She sneered at him.

"Haven't you learned anything?" she shook her head, "We can't be killed by bullets!"

Xander let himself laugh at that, "Haven't you learned anything from *me*, yet? I never try the same thing twice!"

Pulling the trigger, Xander began to let his perception jump into overdrive—watching the bullet creep from the barrel as he did—before letting the transition finish and, flying beside the time-frozen explosive round and beginning to rewrite some of Dwayne's enchantment on it. Though the explosive rounds had always served him well in battle before, he'd learned that—these pseudo-gods not being typical mythos, after all—expecting the same outcome had been a mistake from the start.

Finishing the new and improved spell, he flew forward again —still in overdrive—and perched himself behind Bianca's time-frozen body; her eyes already beginning to trace after him as she raced to follow his movements.

You were right, you know, Xander spoke into her mind as he gradually let his body slip from overdrive, watching as the bullet began to creep towards her once again. *You'd said that a normal bullet—even one enchanted to kill my kind and others like me— wouldn't work against the likes of you... well,* us *now. So it got me to thinking about what you'd said earlier, about your magic and how you felt like you were in a pool and such. So then I got this crazy idea— crazy being a theme right now, you see—about what would happen if I took you—a happy little swimmer in a big, beautiful pool—and I made the pool-water... well,* not *agree with its swimmer.* Xander chuckled and shook his head, *It's a silly metaphor, I know, but I couldn't help but work off of what you'd told me, so I figure all there is left to do is watch, right?*

Bianca's eyes were already widening with fear as Xander, dropping out of overdrive, pushed her forward and into the bullet.

A pained grunt shot past her lips as the bullet punctured her belly and the magic was released.

The initial force of Dwayne's original enchantment was neutralized almost instantly as it found no mythos blood to incinerate. With its primary goal nullified by its target, the bullet was left with only the simple explosive programming that it had been built for, but this too was extinguished by Bianca's body; her own magic-driven defense mechanism absorbing the explosive spell and assimilating it with the rest of her body.

Xander smiled as he watched all of this happen; as he saw the bluish energy of Bianca's body break down The Gamer's greenish enchantment and "swallow" it up, turning everything back to her own, singular blue.

She turned towards him, already shaking her head. "I told you, pretty boy, you can't kill us that wa—"

Bianca stopped, seeing Xander's still-smiling face a moment before she lurched forward and clutched her gut. As Xander watched, the solid blue energy of her body began to ripple and shift; the magic that her entire body had just absorbed beginning to turn red and black. As the magic in her body succumbed to the new spell it was a part of, it began to reject her as the wrong owner.

"Wh-what the hell did you do to me?" she asked, her own voice gurgling as water began to pour out of her mouth.

Xander shrugged, "I guess you can say I pissed in your pool."

~One year, ten months, one day, and four hours earlier~

"Come on, girl," *Tyrone called out from his truck as he struggled to keep it beside Bianca's slow-moving pace on the side of the bridge.* "I'm not playin' any of these games wit'you! I tol' your ass already, that skank was up in* my *business when you walked in! I don't know what you* think *you saw, but you bettah believe we're gonna talk 'bout it in this truck! NOW GET IN THE MOTHA-FUCKIN' TRUCK!"*

"You can eat a dick, Ty! In fact, you can go ahead and eat an entire bag of dicks!" *Bianca whipped around to face the rusty Ford and the* cheating, parole-dodging, jobless dirtbag steering it. The suspension squealed like her sister's baby as Tyrone hit the brakes to keep her framed in the busted passenger-side window. "You was jus' mindin' yo' own business, right? Bitch came and just plopped her fat ass right on your honest, monogamy-loving cock, am I right? That about sum it all up, Ty? BULLSHIT!"

"Bitch, I ain't for bringing hand down on a girl when it can be helped, but if you don't stop screaming in the streets like a crazy skank I'm'a hafta show a bitch her place!" Tyrone narrowed his dark eyes at her.

Bianca laughed at him, "Motherfucker, please! You already showed one bitch her place today and, judging from that skank-ass bitch, I'm bettin' yo' 'place' bettah be put on quarantine 'fore that jungle-fever dick o' yours causes a bigger fuckin' wave of disease than that little rat-monkey from 'Outbreak!'"

Tyrone growled and threw his truck in park before working to get his door open; his sweaty mitts slipping on the handle a few times in his hurry to get out.

"Fuckin' bitch! Show your ass some motherfuckin' jungle-ass fever! Shit's clean as a fuckin' whistle—make yo' bitch-ass blow on it to be sho'!" he slammed the truck door, only to have the rusted hinges snap under the force. The door gave a weak rattle as it tried to stay secure but slipped from the truck and groaned as it fell; hanging from the top half of the door at a funny angle. "Are you fuckin' kiddin' my ass right—"

Bianca fell back with laughter, leaning against the guardrail of the bridge as Tyrone started cursing over his broken door. "Motherfucker, you shoulda been more worried 'bout putting some fresh strips of duct tape on yo' broke-ass truck then worrying where yo' next taste o' pussy was coming from!"

Tyrone slammed his fist on the hood of his truck and glared at her, "Keep yo' skank-mouth shut! If your bitch ass was back on your corner in Lyell sellin' some of that loose-as-fuck pussy then maybe I could afford to keep this hunk of shit runnin'!"

Bianca's blood boiled at that, *"I AIN'T BEEN SELLIN' ON LYELL IN YEARS, YOU LIMP-DICK ASSHOLE!"*

"What the fuck did I just tell yo' ass 'bout screamin' at me in public, bitch?" Tyrone stormed around the truck and jumped up onto the sidewalk, coming towards Bianca, "Yo' jack-off daddy shoulda taught his little shit-whore of a daughter to watch her fucki—"

"THAT MOTHERFUCKER WAS JUST AS WORTHLESS A PIECE OF SHIT AS YOU!" Bianca cried at him before the first back-hand cracked across the side of her jaw. Hitting the ground, Bianca glared up at him—spitting a wad of blood from her mouth as she wiped her busted lip on the back of her hand—and forced herself to laugh, "Daddy could at least hit a girl right. My sister was right 'bout you, Tyrone; she tol' me I'd regret dating a loser white-boy!"

"That a crack about my dick, bitch?" Tyrone fumed down at her.

She laughed again—that time with sincerity—and shook her head, "It wasn't, but now that you mention it—"

Tyrone kicked her in the side.

"M-mother-fucker!" she clutched at her side and dragged her knees up to her stomach to protect against another attack.

"I tol' your ass, bitch!" he spat—literally—down on her, "I tol' your ass I'd teach you some fuckin' manners!"

"Got yo' manners right here, cheating motherfucker!" she pulled the folding knife that her sister had given her from between her tits and flipped the blade. Tyrone's eyes widened at the sight of the weapon, moving to back away, but Bianca was faster.

"Stick it in 'til it won't go no further, then twist it."

She whispered the instructions to herself as she followed the steps.

Twenty-seven times.

Stab, twist, repeat.

Stab, twist, repeat.

Ankle, calf, back of the knee, thigh, hip, then she went to town on the cheating, abusive asshole's dick; over and over and over. Stab, twist, repeat. Nothing left to stab; nothing left to twist. Stomach, side— stick that pig in the fucking ribs!—and ever-upward. Two more holes

were in the side of his neck before she went for his heart like he'd gone
for hers. It took a few tries, but one of them was bound to get the point
where it mattered. As he collapsed to the ground, Bianca kicked him;
aiming her sister's hand-me-down stilettos for the bastard's face until
his teeth were on the sidewalk and his own momma wouldn't recognize
him.

"YOU WANNA BE MAH DADDY, ASSHOLE! THEN YOU GET
WHAT HE HAD COMING! YOU GET WHAT HE HAD COMING!
YOU FUCKING GET WHAT HE HAD COMING!"

All around her, people had begun popping up to watch. Lights from
cell phones shone as her neighbors and friends and random strangers
started filming and snapping pictures of her.

Somewhere in the distance, the sirens started coming in.

Bianca didn't give a shit.

She couldn't stop herself.

Not now.

"FUCKIN' COME AND LAY HAND ON ME AND MY SISSIE!
SICK FUCKING BASTARD! SICK, DISGUSTING, PERVERTED
DIRTBAG MOTHERFUCKER! YOU GET WHAT HE HAD
COMING! YOU GET IT, THEN I LET THE FUCKIN' PIGS TAKE
ME IN SO I CAN GIVE HIM WHAT HE HAS COMING, TOO!
GET WHAT YOU FUCKIN' GET!"

The sidewalk was already running red with blood and fury when
the pigs' lights arrived and added to it. Most of the onlookers had
already booked it—eager to upload their videos to YouTube and Face-
book rather than turn their phones over to the pigs as evidence—and
the ones that remained were already booing before the cop cars had
even stopped.

Then Bianca heard two of the most beautiful sounds she'd ever
heard in her life:

The first thing was water.

Though she'd crossed that bridge plenty of times before, Bianca had
never had a chance to appreciate the sound of the manmade river that
fed the power plant on the other side of town. Whether it was because

she'd had her earbuds in or because she'd been shooting the shit with her home-girls or even arguing with Tyrone in his broke-ass truck, there had never been a moment for her to genuinely listen to the sound of the current that passed below the bridge.

Either way, the water called to her...

The enraged demands of the pigs turned to desperate pleading as Bianca turned and climbed the railing, one of two things—the other being the hundred-foot drop—that separated her from the water.

The other sound, she wasn't positive even was a sound, was a voice.

And the voice, like the first sound, beckoned her to continue.

THAT'S RIGHT, BIANCA; GO TO THE WATER. THE WORLD HAS FAILED YOU—DIRTIED YOU—AND THE WATER WILL MAKE YOU CLEAN ONCE AGAIN. THEN, BIANCA, YOU CAN JOIN ME IN GETTING YOUR COMEUPPANCE AGAINST THE WORLD!

Feeling like, for the first time in her life, she could trust a man's promises, Bianca jumped...

XANDER WATCHED with a sense of growing empathy for the girl that Bianca had been before Devin had turned her into one of his lackeys. Ahead of him, the goddess could barely keep herself held together—could barely keep herself floating in the air—as the water molecules in her body began to seep through her pores and orifices. Though it looked like she was crying, Xander had to repeatedly remind himself that it was just the fluid in her body seeping from her eyes, just as with her ears and nose and mouth; her entire body taking on a damp sheen that almost glowed in the moonlight.

Dipping her head forward to drain her mouth and throat of liquid that was flooding both, she looked up at Xander with increasingly dead-looking eyes.

"P-puh-plea-ease..." she gurgled around a fresh mouthful

that almost instantly replaced what she'd expelled. Again she dipped, and again she repeated: "Please... kill him; ki-kill Devin!"

Xander let out a deep breath, putting his pistol back in the holster under his jacket—taking a moment to inspect the blood from Bianca's severed arm and fight against his instincts to lick it from his palms; unsure of what ingesting her blood might mean for his already magic-driven madness—and finally looked up at her, nodding. Her aura, which had been receding and shriveling in the same way as her body, was almost non-existent then, and as the pain and sadness behind her eyes faded her body dropped out of the sky, plummeting like a shriveled husk into the belly of the lake.

"Had every intention of it," he whispered after her before turning and starting back towards the city.

21

BURNING DESIRE

*D*O *YOU TRULY BELIEVE THAT YOU'RE GOING TO STAND A CHANCE AGAINST ME, CHILD?* Devin's psychic call rang in Xander's head with enough force to send him toppling in mid-flight. As he fought to control his body—to reclaim the air currents and the energy surrounding him that allowed him to fly—he felt his head go light and his vision faded as he began to fall towards an apartment complex. Something groaned with a metallic strain and Xander felt a gash open on his face. Slamming against what he guessed was the surface of the roof, Xander knocked his head—his vision returning as he did—and cried out as he rolled over the edge of the roof and crashed into a billboard. His vision cut out again as Devin's enraged psychic waves continued to ripple across the city, and, while no words carried on the current, he could feel the sheer force scrambling his mind as it did.

Falling...

Xander couldn't see to know what waited below him, and the thought of being impaled on an antenna caused him to scramble to cast out his aura; to call upon his mind's eye to see for him.

Devin's psychic waves, however, wouldn't allow his aura to breach his body, keeping his only means of navigation locked away within him.

OH NO, LITTLE VAMPIRE! I'M NOT GOING TO LET YOU DIE; NOT YET. NOT UNTIL YOU'VE HAD A CHANCE TO SEE THE DEPTHS OF YOUR FOLLY; THE RIDICULOUSNESS OF YOUR ADOPTED CAMPAIGN AGAINST ME!

The wind was knocked out of Xander's lungs as he slammed back-first against something that rattled under his weight. To his left, somebody cried out; the sound of footsteps running, growing distant shortly after. A small dog's sparked yapping drew nearer, accompanied by the sound of small paws scrambling. Slowly, Xander's vision returned, and he caught sight of the starless night sky—the hang of the moon telling him the night was only half over—and, letting his gaze follow the pattering sound, he spotted a small, panting terrier leaving clouds against the window of an apartment, it's yapping growing more eager with Xander's movement. Sitting up with a groan, Xander looked around, seeing an old Spanish soap opera playing on the television in the corner of the room while a TV tray with a half-eaten muffin and a steaming mug of tea rested in front of an empty couch.

"Shit..."

Xander rubbed a sore spot on his side where he'd landed on one of the pistols. As he straightened up on the fire escape platform he'd crashed down on, he noticed that his right arm had been dislocated when he'd caught it on the railing coming down. Rolling his eyes and reaching under his jacket with his left arm to get a firm grip on his shoulder, he clenched his teeth and yanked it back into place.

A MERE SAMPLE OF THE AGONY YOU'RE IN STORE FOR!

Hope you've got more than that in your bag of tricks; I've been beat up worse than that by people claiming a lot less power than you. And for the record, you're hardly the first self-certain psychopath to roar threats in my head, asshole! Xander shot back, rolling his neck and shoulders until he'd worked most of the kinks out, *And my luck at dodging your kind guarantees you won't be the last eit—*

THERE ARE NO OTHERS LIKE ME! AND I PROMISE YOU THAT I WILL BE THE LAST ONE YOU EVER—

You're going to be very *disappointed with the situation you've worked yourself into if you think you're the only one like you in the world, Devin. I've dealt with any number of assholes with your superiority complex—everything from fellow mythos to humans; hell, even a housecat claims the same god-complex you do!—and I've fought and killed more power-raving lunatics than I have seconds in this day. So you're a power-wielding, psychopathic, asshole? Guess what? So am I now! I've got the same power—only better—I'm just as goddam crazy —but without a narrow-minded vendetta to dilute it—and, what's more, I'm coming out the gate with more power than you ever had while your cellmate was playing bumper pool in your butt! So I suggest you start considering your threats better, 'cause when I come for you— and believe me, Devin, I'm coming for you!—I'm going to show you just how* crazy *crazy can get!*

Silence; inside and out.

Xander let out a deep breath and nodded. "That's what I thought!" he scoffed, looking over the edge of the fire escape to get a better idea of where he'd landed. "Now... which way to—"

Xander would've cried out under the bottomless well of sheer, fiery agony he'd been dragged into, but he discovered immediately after the first blistering jolt of pain that there was no longer any air in his lungs...

∼

No! No, I don't want to see! I don't want to seeEEEEEEEEEAAAAAAHHH!!

But see, you will, Xander! You've so eagerly watched my disciples' pasts! Now choke on mine!

Body—not his own—lanky, gaunt, tall; sullied; blond bangs swaying over his unwavering eyes as he swayed melodically at his own court hearing. He stared—he was forced to stare—at the judge, a sneering wide man behind a black robe, a polished gavel, and an overly waxed mustache.

The courthouse was unnaturally quiet—the hushed murmurs all condemning Devin for his crimes; more and more confessions of his past acts coming to light through the gossip; and Xander was forced to feel the growing pride as Devin mentally acknowledged each sick, twisted, and horrendous claim as being totally true—and the only sound that cut through the thin film of fearful whispers was Devin's right ring finger as it repeatedly clicked within a grooved pocket in his thumbnail.

CLICK... two... three... four... CLICK... two... three... four... CLICK...

He'd finally been caught—or, rather, it was the first time he'd decided to go so far as to let his actions be seen; what they saw as "catching" him he saw as putting on a show—when he'd decided to take his love of pain and misery and death and, of course, fire culminate into a glorious singularity. His cousin, Nancy, a pretty little redhead who fancied herself a witch (of all things) was one of the few in town who hadn't already shunned him on suspicion alone—a shame for her!—and she was never against letting him come over to watch movies or read her newest library books on the occult with her. On that most faithful days, after perfectly executing his plans, neighbors and police found Devin standing proudly on his cousin's front lawn; her virginity still staining his jeans and her home burning to the ground. Though she'd survived the ordeal—unhappily—she'd be confined to a wheelchair for the rest of her life with only one leg left—they never had found the other one; you sick fucker!; I'm not done yet, vampire!—and there was little chance that reconstructive surgery could do a thing to reverse the damages to her face and torso.

What Devin hadn't told the courts—what even Nancy, or at least her interpreters, hadn't told the courts—was that Nancy had put forth a rather passionate and magical effort to protect herself. At that moment, after Devin had set fire to her bedroom drapes and let the lighter fluid and gasoline he'd taken over do its work, he'd moved to descend upon her for the fifth time that night, she'd drawn a jagged circle out of a Sharpie and, by some strange twist of her nearly severed tongue, conjured a barrier between himself and her. For a long while the strange, nearly invisible shield held him back, and as he pounded and hollered about how she wouldn't be able to retrieve the parts of her he'd taken off from inside her barrier he'd made a note to himself to look more into this magic thing.

When the blaze had gotten to be too great, however, he'd been forced to sacrifice his efforts and flee for the safety of the front yard, eager to see his handiwork from the outside and equally as eager to see how quickly Nancy could crawl without a leg and most of her fingers.

It was for that faithful night that he was seated in the courthouse that day, and it was this day that he'd chosen as the anchor to set Xander's forced witnessing of his life.

The judge cleared his throat and moved nearer to his microphone, locking eyes with Devin—Xander feeling the growing urge to cackle well in his own chest despite the anguish all around him— "Unless there is some reason my sentence should not now be pronounced I ask that Devin Antonius Raston now rise for sentencing. Mister Raston, this is the sentence of the court that your custody be committed to the department of corrections for confinement in the Massachusetts state prisons without the possibility of parole for the remainder of your life. Your rights will appeal with respect to the disposition of your case, and your attorney will appeal them with you—"

"Your honor, with all due respect I must request at this time that the court relinquish me from any further contact with Mister Raston."

"The court acknowledges your request, Mister Sullivan, and asks you to remain seated for the remainder of the sentencing."

"Why, Mister Sullivan, I'm hurt? Is this about that salad fork reference?"

"Bailiff, can you please put Mister Raston in cuffs and escort his attorney, Mister Sullivan, from the courthouse?"

"Yes, your honor."

The sound of ratcheting metal echoes within the trapped confines of his head and he feels the tight pinch of the cuffs at his wrists and ankles.

"Ow! Bailiff, that's too tight!"

"Ask me if I give a shit!"

"Bailiff!"

"I'm sorry, your honor."

"Excused! Now please escort Mister Sullivan and yourself from the courtroom."

"Yes, your honor."

"Thank you, your honor."

"As you can see, Mister Raston, the extents and depths of your depravity have already made this courthouse and this judge's life quite tiresome and burdensome. I have several testimonies from multiple professionals—doctors, therapists, and law enforcement officials alike—who feel it would be wrong of me to not take into account the obvious psychosis that is at work here; to address you and sentence you as I might any other man or woman who might come in here on similar charges. But I'd like to offer a personal rebuttal—and please let it be recognized that this does not reflect the views of this courthouse or my associates—that in all my many years as an attorney and following years as a judge upon this bench, I've yet to see even a fraction of this sort of grisly aftermath

enter past those doors. Now I can't stress this... this horror quite enough, not to you or to anybody with us today; I have never in my life experienced anything that could come close to the limits of cruelty"—he was forced to watch a memory of bringing his father's hacksaw to the back shed where Devin kept a litter of puppies he'd stolen from the farmer's sister—*"of* **malice**"—another memory of tricking the retarded neighbor-girl to masturbate with a broken beer bottle he'd found behind the movie theater—*"of* **human indecency**"— Xander was forced to watch as a childhood memory of Devin beating a boy half to death with an aluminum baseball bat on the playground for wetting his pants—*"and of* **blind and utter brutality**"—a horrific slideshow of fragmented memories; beatings, bullying; escalating into torturing and murdering and raping; all with such vivid detail and sensation that Xander felt as though he were the one perpetrating the acts—*"as the cases I have spread before me, Mister Raston. I would tell you that this case and my dealings with it will serve to haunt my dreams for every night henceforth, but I've come to know you— resentfully so—enough to know that you would celebrate that small victory in your cell while you live out your life sentence. My only true regret, Mister Raston, is that you will, at some day, come to pass, and on that day your soul will be free once again to carry out your heinous acts, and on that day, Mister Raston, I fear that Hell may receive a new devil. Do you have any final words for this court at this time?"*

"Don't you have a daughter, Judge?"

You didn't!

Oh yes, I did!

"GET HIM OUT OF HERE!"

"I'll be looking her up when I get out, Judge. Tell her not to worry—but do be sure to tell her—that I won't be in there long!"

"Get him out! Get that sick bastard out of my courthouse NOW!"

Oh god... no! You didn't! Not after—

The first person I visited after I got out, actually. Even carved a little message to the judge after I was done so he'd know I hadn't lied. I always keep my promises, vampire.

REMEMBER THAT!

Segmented; twisted.

Cell mate found decapitated with the toilet seat, his own penis forcefully buried in the neck stump. When found, he was reciting Stephen Crane poetry to the decapitated head, which was perched on his left knee and being "bounced" for good measure.

He was forced into isolation.

When they came to move him, he was put into traction for pulling a guard's eye out with his teeth.

And there he sat, huddled in his corner and exploring the vast reaches of his limitless—terrible!—mind. Day-in and day-out he explored, finding that he could travel from his body and take others' bodies while he slept. Most of the time he used this ability to take more victims—forcing small-time thugs to carve up their fellow inmates or possessing a volunteering priest and raping one of the kitchen staff; men or women, he wasn't picky—while, other times, when he found himself blessed with more patience, he'd venture out of the walls of the prison in the body of the guards or a visitor. On those occasions, as he excitedly eyed the outside world with the same hungry potential as a child in a candy store or a pedophile in a preschool, he'd eagerly searched out more knowledge of the world of the occult that his cousin—his favorite victim; his crown jewel; his bridging moment to the vastness of magic's destructive potential—had inadvertently introduced him to.

Libraries.

Book stores.

Specialists.

Séances.

And the glorious internet; a place of nearly as much sadist-driven horror and hatred as his own mind!

And—OH!—the things he'd learned.

Then, satisfied with his outing's educational fruits, he'd bring his borrowed body to the top of whatever great building he could scale and, as the wind whistled by his host's ears, he'd slip free and return to his prison... and the jailhouse that held it.

Over time he'd come to jump into bodies and then practice the spells and incantations he'd learned over the fresh corpses of new victims or with whatever resources he'd needed; learning to reshape matter by possessing the kitchen staff or bend reality as a prison guard during the lunch hour.

It all became so easy, and so boring!

Up until the day he showed up.

Stanley Lucas Ferno; the man who showed him he could be God.

And a new horizon began to breach in Devin's dark mind...

And the rest, as they say, is history.

BY THE TIME Xander was secure back in his own mind—back in his own body and his own reality—he realized that he'd already thrown up all over the fire escape. He'd remembered Estella explaining once about the spell of sight that she'd used to see the world through his eyes, and how she'd felt and seen everything the way he'd felt and seen them. With his wits returning to him, he realized that Devin had just forced him into his mind to reenact every hideous crime he'd ever committed and returning Xander to his body feeling like every bit the sadistic, murderous, rape-happy arsonist he'd been forced to piggyback within.

"I'm going to make you pay for that," Xander grimaced as he stood on shaky feet, spitting out the lingering taste of vomit; unable to get rid of the vivid tastes from his forced memories.

WE'LL SEE, BOY! Devin laughed in his head, *WE'LL SEE!*

Roaring in agony and rage at what he'd just been forced to endure, Xander shot from the fire escape with enough force to tear the metal from the brick and send the crumpled structure falling down the side of the building. Flying into the sky, he clutched at his temples and fighting to put up enough of an auric barrier to block out everything he'd just experienced.

But no such barrier existed…

22

A FRIENDLY REMINDER

The urge to succumb to the madness swelled as Xander told himself again and again that he wasn't like Devin, the urge to distance himself as far as possible from any association with such a creature and such acts turning everything else—the laws of physics and his role within them—into nothing but a luxury that he couldn't indulge.

Several blocks over, a public fountain's water began to rise from the three angels spewing the fluid back into the basin below them; drying the spectacle and leaving only the mass of metal that had once been the contributed wishing coins of passersby, but had somehow fused into a single metallic slab.

On the other side of the city, the Jameson's brand new 72-inch HD TV turned inside out; the nest of exposed wiring masking the late-night infomercials and causing Mister Jameson—finally home after a late night at the office—to dribble the leftover soup in his mouth all over the new Armani suit he hadn't had a chance to get changed out of yet.

Directly below Xander and starting up the steps to his apartment building, Tony, just getting off his cab-driving shift and *still* grousing about the strange fare he'd taken from the airport to the high school in the middle of the night. Grumbling about "Houdini tricksters," he started down the hall, rolling his eyes as he overheard Missus Rodriguez spouting to the superintendent about the demon-child who'd just died on her fire escape before vanishing off to Hell again. Sharing a look with the super, he turned to his own apartment door and worked the troublesome lock before finally getting the door open.

Though Missus Rodriguez was terrified and insistent that they get a priest to bless the building immediately, she was quick to pause her rants as Tony, the nice cabby who'd taken her husband to the hospital after his stroke at no charge, passed out in the hall outside his apartment. As she and the superintendent rushed to see what the matter was, they caught sight of the inside of his apartment and all of the furniture that was, by some strange miracle, suspended on the ceiling.

Superintendent Chuck decided to go back to medical school.

Xander could see all of them—every person and place his wayward magic was touching—but he couldn't find a way to turn off the chaos in his head as Devin's history plagued every corner of his mind.

He simply rose; higher and higher and higher.

But no height could free him from any of it.

Though he'd lost track of when the urge to fly upward had become the drive to plummet back to the ground, Xander was able to steer himself towards the park in the distance—the water of the manmade pond shimmering a short distance from a familiar gazebo—and drop to his knees; uprooting several yards of grass and soil as he did.

"Sick son of a bitch," Xander heaved and shook his head. "You're going to wish you hadn't shown me all of that…"

Looking around, he spotted a set of park benches in the distance that overlooked the running trail and the pond. Eager to sit and rest his feet and mind, he dragged himself to his feet and started for them. As he approached them—the toes of his boots dragging along the ground as he shuffled; still not physically tired but growing emotionally weaker by the second—he let his mind wander to Estella and his clan and even Trepis, realizing that he already missed them.

Especially Estella…

Stepping around the bench he'd subconsciously aimed himself towards, Xander stopped short when he saw a young boy, no older than thirteen, lying on top of it and bundled under a beat-up jacket and trying to sleep. Sighing at being robbed the chance to even *sit* with ease, Xander frowned and turned away, starting towards the next bench a short distance away.

Behind him, the boy's aura shifted as he woke up and drew back from the sight of Xander walking away from him, "I… I'm sorry. Is this your bench?"

Xander paused and looked over his shoulder at him, "What? No. Why would it be my bench?"

Shrugging and sitting up, the boy rubbed his arms for warmth. "I don't know," he admitted, "Some kids at school said that I didn't belong anywhere, and that when I ended up on the streets, I'd have to… do things just to have a place to sleep. I figured if I avoided taking any claimed benches then I'd—"

Xander sneered at the implications and held up a hand to stop the explanation, dropping the hand soon after when the boy's eyes widened at the blood on them. "Well, it's not my bench, so you don't need to worry about any of that," he assured him before frowning and taking a step towards him. "Do you mind if I sit down a moment, though? It's been one hell of a night and I just need to take a load off."

The boy shrugged and shifted over on the bench, "I guess not." As Xander moved to sit he caught sight of the boy looking at his blood-stained right eye out of the corner of his vision. Then, without missing a beat: "What's wrong with your eye?"

Xander scoffed, "You saw the blood on my hands but it's the eye you ask about?" He shrugged and looked ahead of him, enjoying a moment of peace, "Though, to answer your question: nothing's wrong with my eye. I mean, not really; it still works like an eye should, I guess. I just... I fucked it up a few years back and..." he frowned, finding himself in his Estella-self-censoring mode around the minor and looked over, "Sorry."

The boy laughed at that, "Sorry? For what? Saying 'fuck?' I just told you that my classmates told me I'd have to *do things*—like, *sex*-things—just to be homeless! I have other kids telling me that I'm such a loser that, even at rock bottom, I'd have to suck hobo-dick and let them *fuck* my ass, and here you are—some creepy dude with bloody hands and a fucked-up eye—and *you're* apologizing for telling me that you fucked up your fucked-up-looking eye? Excuse me for saying so, man, but that's fucked up!"

Xander stared at him, blinking for a moment. "Yeah," he nodded, "When you say it like that it sounds pretty stupid, doesn't it?"

The boy nodded, "Yeah. Like, *really* fucking stupid."

"So why are you out here anyway? Don't you have a home?" Xander asked.

The boy's aura swelled with embarrassment and he looked down. "I do... I-I mean, I *did*," he admitted. "But I ran away."

"You ran away from a home to sleep on a park bench?" Xander gave him a sidelong glance, "You wanna talk about shit that sounds 'really fucking stupid?'"

"Yeah yeah, I get it!" the boy groaned, "But some kids started telling me how I should kill myself, so I stood up for myself and told them that assholes who say shit like that always get what's coming to them. A teacher overheard me say that and reported me for threatening to kill them. Then they dragged me into the principal's office, made a big deal about me being a psycho and scared the hell out of me about how I was going to end up in prison. By the time my father showed up to pick me up, I was already holding all that in. He was already pissed off about being called off of work to come pick his 'troubled' son up, so when he saw that I was about to start crying he told me that if I was going to be a 'troublemaking faggot' then I might as well leave his house tonight." He dragged the arm of his sleeve under his nose to mask a sniffle and looked away while he wiped his eye, "So, when we reached the next stoplight, I jumped out of the car and ran."

Taking in the boy's story, Xander gave a slow nod and looked away while he wiped his tears away; not wanting to embarrass him any further. "That was pretty brave, you know," he said with a shrug. "I know that's not exactly what you want to hear—trust me, I'm not a counselor—but you fought back against those kids, you held out against the injustice at your school, and then you refused to let your father's cruelty and misunderstanding become a shackle for you. I can't say that you did the right thing in choosing homelessness, but you showed true courage against all of that. And, just so you know, I recently got a *really* unwanted crash course in sick crazy bastards and all the shit they do and... well, let's just say that you don't fit the bill, so—big surprise coming—your school's got you pegged all wrong."

The boy stared at him for a long moment, "Really? You think I was brave?"

Xander smiled and nodded, "Yeah, I really do. And, while I can't go into too much detail, I'd like to think that I know a few things about being brave."

The boy bit his lip, his eyes once again drifting to Xander's bloodstained hands, "Have you killed anyone?"

Xander's eyes widened and he looked over, "What?"

The boy shrugged and nodded towards Xander's hands, "The kids said that the badass hobos have killed people." He looked down then, "And that I'd be like a training dog for them."

"These classmates of yours sound like the sort of twisted youths that might benefit from a kick in the balls," Xander sneered and shook his head. "But I'm sorry to tell you that I'm not a hobo."

"Oh... right, sorry." The boy sighed and looked down, his aura rolling with a heavy guilt, "I just figured that, you know, you being out here in the middle of the night and all."

Xander looked over and shrugged after a moment, "Well, I'm not a hobo. I *have* killed before," he admitted, figuring he'd be wiping the kid's mind by the end of the conversation anyway. "Actually, I've killed a whole bunch of times," he chuckled and shook his head, "but I'm not homeless."

"Wait? What? You *have* killed before? Like, to protect yourself or something?"

Xander shrugged and nodded, "Sometimes. Other times to protect others."

The boy's eyes lit up with excitement, "Holy shit! Really? So, are you like some kind of spy or assassin or something? Like, is that *terrorist* blood on your hands?"

Xander frowned and looked down at his hands for a long moment, "I... uh, I guess. I mean, not like how you mean, but— in that they used terror to get their way—yeah, I guess you could say that." He laid his hands palms-down on his knees to hide the bulk of the dried blood, but realized then that it showed past his fingers and the sides of his hands. Sighing, he looked up at the sky, "I'm actually in charge of leading an entire group of others like me—we call ourselves 'warriors,' though, not 'spies' or 'assassins'; we're kinda old fashioned and cheesy that way—and I'm in the middle of some craziness right now."

The boy's eyes remained locked on Xander's hands, "So... that's from somebody you've killed *tonight*?"

Xander nodded, "Yes. One of a few, actually; one I drowned and the other I stomped to death, but I'm pretty sure most of him washed off when *this* one"—he held up his hands to illustrate Bianca—"tried to drown me in a whirlpool."

The boy gaped, "Oh shit!"

Xander nodded, "Yup. And I'm actually planning to kill one more before the night's over, too."

The boy smirked, his aura giving away his youthful excitement at what Xander was telling him. "So cool! So, are they, like, bad people or something?"

Xander nodded, "Really bad. In fact... do you know about that fire that burned down the apartment building downtown?"

The boy bit his lip and gave a slow nod, "Yeah... one of my friends lived there, actually."

Xander frowned and looked away, not expecting for him to have such a personal connection to the event. "I'm... I'm sorry," he said, realizing he was empathizing with this boy with each new detail that emerged. "Well, the ones I'm out to kill are the ones that set the fire, and they're out to set a lot more if they get the chance."

The boy smiled at that and turned more in the bench to face him, "And you're out to kill them? Wow! You really are brave!"

Xander sighed and shrugged "Well, that's the thing. In order to be strong enough to fight them, I had to do something that might turn me into something like them—drive me crazy just like them—and I'm starting to wonder if I'm already too late."

The boy frowned at that, "Well, do you want to set fires and hurt innocent people now?"

Xander bit his lip and looked down, "Sometimes, yeah; more frequently since I took this job."

The boy stared at him for a moment, "But you haven't yet?"

Xander shook his head, "I've scared some innocent people— not that I meant to, but I'm not sure that matters much to them —but I haven't hurt anybody yet, no."

The boy smiled and shrugged, "I think that makes you braver than them."

Xander looked up at that, startled by his words, "What do you mean?"

"Well, in all my favorite movies and video games, the best

good guys are the ones that *could* be bad, you know?" the boy said, "Like, it's cool that they go around beating the shit out of the bad guys and monsters, but I always believed it was so simple for the *goody-goody* good guys to be good. It's like, how hard is it to be a good guy when you never show your crazy side, right; and everybody's got a crazy side, so the *goody-goody* assholes just don't seem real! But you, you're real! So what if you want to do bad things sometimes? *Everybody* wants to do bad things sometimes, but when somebody has all of that badness in their heads and they *still* fight past it *and* beat the shit out of the ones who are fucking everything up, then it's, like, *twice* the insult to the bad guys, 'cause they're not only getting beat up and killed, but they also look like totally lazy assholes with no self-control." He smiled and nodded to himself, looking proud of his analysis, "*Those* are my favorite kind of characters, so if that's the sort of warrior you are then I know that you're brave."

Xander smirked, "Then I guess I *do* know a thing about bravery, huh? Guess that means you gotta take my word for it now, right?"

The boy nodded, "Hells yeah! I mean, if you think I'm doing something right then I must be!"

Xander started to smile and nod but stopped suddenly when he felt a looming presence in the distance, and he looked over his shoulder towards the source. Though there was nothing visibly there, there was no denying that something *was* coming. Sighing, Xander looked back at the boy; his aura starting to snake out of his chest so he could wipe the memory of their conversation from his mind. Then, stopping the red-and-black tendril of bioenergy when it was only halfway across the bench, he sighed and pulled it back into his chest.

"You should probably get back home," Xander avoided eye contact, feeling guilty for deciding to let the boy keep his memories, but somehow knowing he'd feel even more guilty if he did take them. "Your dad was a dick, but sometimes people are dicks when they don't mean to be. Just keep on doing what you do and don't let the bullies turn you into one of them, alright?"

The boy frowned, looking in the direction that Xander had looked and—unable to see anything with his human eyes—frowned at the night-bathed void. "One of them is coming, aren't they?"

Xander nodded.

The boy nodded and got up, stepping away from the bench before looking back, "Thank you..." he frowned, "I... I probably shouldn't bother to ask your name, should I?"

"It's Xander," he grimaced, the truth slipping free with the same dangerous freedom that the decision not to sweep his memory had been made. "Xander Stryker." He sighed and shrugged, "It's not like the name will mean anything to anybody."

The boy frowned at that; seemingly insulted, "Why not?"

Xander smirked, "Because Xander Stryker is a ghost around here."

The boy laughed, "That's a funny thing to say, especially since you look more like a vampire."

Xander couldn't help but laugh at that, "So I've been told." He took another glance back, gauging the distance and looking back towards the kid, "So, while we're on the subject of names, what's yours?"

"I'm Joey," the boy smiled and then shrugged, "well, that's what everyone calls me, at least. But I've always preferred Joseph."

Xander smiled at that and nodded, "You know, I prefer 'Joseph,' too; it's a much more powerful name. Oh, and about those bullies..."

The boy, Joseph, looked over, blushing, "Yeah?"

Xander stood and rolled his neck, letting some of the

tension crack free, "Don't give them an inch... ever. They're the *real* vampires—they thrive off of sucking the happiness and life out of you just so they can feel alive—and they *hate* it when you don't let their efforts destroy you." He smirked and shrugged, "And if not letting them bring you down doesn't work, you hit hard, you hit fast, and you make it the hit that you want to be remembered for."

"Not too many people encourage kids to hit their bullies," Joseph pointed out.

Xander shrugged, "It's not always the right way, and it's definitely not the easy way... but sometimes the best way is to prove to the world that you refuse to be a victim."

Joseph blushed, "You sound like you know from experience, Xander."

Xander shrugged, "I've had my own bullies to deal with, but none have been as bad as I am to myself."

"Then you should follow your own advice and remind yourself you won't be a victim... even if it is to yourself," Joseph said.

Xander smiled and nodded, "Good advice."

Xander flinched then as he felt Devin's energy and heard the force of him landing a few yards behind him. Glancing over his shoulder, he spotted the psychopathic pseudo-god—his long blond hair wet and swirling about his head as though in an undersea cyclone—in a nearly iridescent-white, button-up shirt. As he started towards him it appeared as though Devin was nothing more than a floating torso and a malice-filled expression, but as he stepped into the light of a nearby lamppost Xander saw that, like Stan's full-body "coat," Devin wore a pair of inky-black pants that seemed as much a part of him as his own skin.

"Go now," Xander called to Joseph, refusing to take his eyes off of Devin.

As Joseph's aura began to hurry away, Xander let out a long breath and took his first step towards the end.

23

INTO THE FIRE

"*Y*ou won't last much longer," Xander called out to the blond pseudo-god as he approached him.

Though Devin smirked and wet his lips at his words, the response came inside his head, *Perhaps not. But what of yourself?*

Stopping in mid-step, Xander narrowed his eyes at Devin, trying to pierce his psychic barrier to see what the psychopath was getting at, but finding his mind unreadable.

Devin laughed aloud as his psychic words rolled on, *You don't even see what you're becoming, do you?* (laughs again) *Soon you'll be nothing more than a dying storm; no emotion, no memories. Just a mass of dwindling power.*

Xander growled, baring his fangs and hissing in an instinctual challenge. "SO WHAT MAKES YOU SO DIFFERENT?" he demanded.

Devin laughed again—the same out-of-control, insanity driven laughter that had plagued Xander all night—and shook his head, spreading his arms in a perverse mockery of a crucifixion pose. "Look upon me, boy! Take it all in; bask in it! And, as you do, consider what you know of those who you've come to encounter like *us*—those with The Power!—Lars and Gerard and Bianca knew *nothing* of their former lives—a brain-dead druggie turned eager chatterbox; a prized underground entertainer filled with hatred and bigotry reduced to nothing more than a laughable hunk of clay eager to crush anything I aimed him at; a fading survivor with no hopes or dreams turned into a malice-driven wildcat—and that new reality became so engrained in their reality that just revisiting those lives broke them. Lars was begging for death, Gerard didn't put up a struggle as he drowned, and Bianca..." he smirked and shook his head, "she actually thought that you had a chance against me; never considering for a moment that everything they were was *lent* to them by me! Each one of their deaths has marked a return on my investment—all of their power *plus* the strength and conditioning they've added in nearly two years—has returned to me, boy, and I've *never* been stronger. You, on the other hand..." he chortled and shrugged, "You're a fading light, and soon you'll let whatever's lurking beneath the surface—we both know what I mean—take you and remold you, and when it does you'll remember nothing of who you were, who you loved or hated, or any of this legacy business I keep seeing bubble in your brain."

Xander seethed and took another step towards him. "So what makes you so different?" he repeated through clenched teeth.

Devin *tsk*ed him and shook his head, "No patience; no good. I'm getting to it, *vampire*; I'm getting to it!"

JOSEPH GAPED from behind the tree he'd hidden behind to watch Xander and the strange man fight. After hearing Xander's words—building a possible reality around the bizarre-yet-awesome guy with the bloody eye and death-covered hands—he was a little disappointed to see the two simply standing there and talking, but, as he focused on their dialogue, he found the content anything but dull.

Powers?

Memory loss?

Vampires?

Could all of that really be real?

Could he really have been sitting there, talking and sharing his thoughts with a real-life vampire?

He struggled to contain his excitement as he continued to watch.

"YOU'VE WITNESSED MY PAST, vampire; you've experienced my experiences and shared in what I have to share. You *know* who I was before I even *knew* of The Power, and while those pathetic cattle wearing people-masks waved their judgments like gavels and their gavels like hammers in an effort to contain me, I flourished. My story, before my power, was already everything that The Power represents; I was made for it and it was made for me! That old fool Stanley told me that the process was arduous and nearly impossible, and that I'd have to *ask*—to actually implore *anything* for what I was rightfully owed!—for The Power that he'd shown me when he came to me looking for a secret to resurrection."

Xander frowned, "Stan... came to you?"

Devin cackled, "Oh yes, my naïve little cousin, he did. He worked his magic and clouded the minds of the prison guards and the powers that be just to visit me in solitary—something they swore up-and-down would never happen; I was a madman, remember? A danger to any who even tried to occupy the same space as me—but he was something different. Given, I *did* try to kill him when he first arrived—put forth a stunning display, too; I might add—but Stan neutralized everything I threw as though waving off a horde of flies. Imagine my shock. Imagine my rage. But, before you do, imagine my *intrigue!*" he shivered with excitement at his own memory, "Here was a man —or so he appeared—who made *everything* I'd come to *know* appear to be nothing more than the mere tip of some far greater mass of potential massacre. I had to have what he had!" He shook his head and sneered, "But *ask* for it? Never! When I was ready, I crossed over, tracked down the strongest power source I could find, and I brought it back with me. And then, with the squirming mass of... well, with *It* writhing in my otherwise lonely little cell in solitary, I *did not* ask, I *did not* plea or beg or implore; I fucking raped and tortured it, vampire. I punched through glowing green flesh and felt organs I couldn't even name burst under my grip. I pulled bones that have never been studied by any on this realm from that body and I carved and beat it with everything I pulled out. Do you understand me, *boy?* I didn't get The Power by asking—by allowing it to wash over me in some splendid miracle as sent by on high or whatever biblical diarrhea Stan's been regurgitating all this time—I got it by *taking* it; I tormented that which Stan would have had me grovel to and it was only when I'd eaten half its fleshy husk that it gave me everything I demanded and vanished back to its realm where it didn't have a body I could ravage. You ask what makes *me* different? You ask why my memories are still my own and why I control The Power rather than letting it control me?"

He took another step, his long, blond hair once again sweeping up as his feet lifted off of the ground.

"*IT'S BECAUSE WE ARE ONE IN THE SAME, YOU WITLESS CURR! AND WE HAVE NO REASON TO TAKE FROM ONE ANOTHER WHILE THERE IS SO MUCH OUT HERE FOR US TO FUCK UP!*"

Xander had seen enough of Devin's outbursts to know to put up an auric shield as his booming voice resounded within his head just as much as in his ears. As his aura wrapped around him, however, he caught a glimmer of an energy signature in the distance behind him. A weak one. A frail one. A *human* one.

Xander grimaced with realization and cursed as he jumped into overdrive.

Joseph! You stupid kid! Tell me you didn't...

But the sight of the teenaged boy already collapsed to the ground—in the time-frozen throes of his own seizure—confirmed his suspicions. The boy had stuck around to see Xander fight. He'd gone far enough to create the illusion that he'd left the park, and then he'd ducked behind the tree he was shadowed under and watched. Though Xander couldn't be sure if Devin knew that they'd had a witness to their exchange—if the seizure-inducing waves had been meant for him rather than a weak effort to catch Xander off guard—he knew that it didn't matter; Joseph was officially a victim of Devin's madness.

Whether or not he knew that human boy had been there before, he was certain to know after that. Xander had vanished into overdrive, and the reason wouldn't be long hidden; Devin would see his eagerness to save the boy, and he'd use that against him.

"Just because God is stronger than the devil doesn't mean that the devil isn't more powerful."

Shit! Xander thought to himself.

Stan had been right!

So long as Xander was compelled to save Joseph—so long as Joseph represented a boundary that he wouldn't cross—Devin had strength over him.

And that strength could only multiply.

But he couldn't let him die!

Dropping to his knees—gouging up grass and dirt as he skidded to a momentous stop beside Joseph—Xander kept his perspective in overdrive while his body grew just as time-frozen in his eyes as the rest of the world. He needed time, and while overdrive was about speed, the shift in how he saw the world could offer him the illusion of time.

But if that night had taught him nothing else, it was that a strong enough illusion *was* real.

Reaching out with his aura, Xander entered Joseph's mind, shielding himself against the waves of seizure-inducing madness rippling through his brain, and began to toggle the control centers.

Stabilize, regulate, deactivate, supercharge...

Xander cycled through, resetting Joseph's brain to send new orders to the body to combat the impact of Devin's enchantment. Searching out the dormant sections of Joseph's brain, he began to activate and empower his innate control on magic; toggling and tweaking the nerves to awaken with enough sense to protect themselves.

Basic psychic control: activated.

Defenses: supercharged.

You're going to feel and know a great deal more about a power within you than you did a second ago, Joseph, and I want you to use that knowledge. The moment you can hear these words, you tell your body to follow its instincts—instincts I've awakened within you—and you fight this! You shield yourself from what's attacking you and you fight this! And then you get your ass home!

MY, OH MY! DO WE HAVE A LITTLE EAVESDROPPER IN OUR MIDSTS? AN ITTY-BITTY BIT OF BUSINESS THAT I SHOULD DO AWAY WITH BEFORE WE GET DOWN TO THE REAL BUSINESS AT HAND? Devin's voice cooed in Xander's mind.

You won't hurt him, Xander shot back; *I can't say much with confidence, but I will say—as a promise, even—that you won't so much as touch him!*

OH, I'D SAY I'M GOING TO DO A LOT MORE THAN JUST TOUCH HIM, VAMPIRE!

The wave of laughter in Xander's head made him shiver and

nearly slip from overdrive completely as he finished the process. He knew not to dwell on the implications; there was no doubt to the lengths Devin would go to do what he had planned.

I'm ready to prove you wrong, Xander assured him.

Dropping out of overdrive completely, Xander kept his eyes trained on Devin's approach as his mind's eye "saw" Joseph seize a moment longer before his psychic message reached him. His aura swelled with a new drive as the awakened powers within him sparked and gained momentum like new machinery turning on for the first time; the lurches of his body shifting to sporadic twitches of his muscles learning to work all over again. Then, as his distending aura swelled and grew denser, it solidified into a sheen surface of bio-electric energy and expelled all of Devin's magic while blocking out all of the new waves attempting to get in.

Devin sneered, "What did you do?"

"I woke him up," Xander glared, reaching under his jacket and pulling out one of his pistols, "So I could prove to you that you're not the craziest motherfucker on the block!"

... INSTINCTS I'VE AWAKENED *within you—and you fight this! You shield yourself from what's attacking you and you fight this! And then you get your ass home!* Xander Stryker's words echoed in Joseph's head as he came to, feeling his own mind whirring like an engine as he... he was using magic! The crazy blond man was coming up on them, and Xander faced him, his fangs—holy shit! He really *was* a vampire!—showing past his parted lips, as he pulled a gun from under his jacket.

"... prove to you that you're not the craziest motherfucker on the block!" Xander finished before leveling the gun in Joseph's face.

His eyes widened as he tried to scurry away, "X-Xander, wait! No! Please don't! I didn't mean to…"

Shut up, kid! I've fucked up a lot in dealing with you so far, and I've gone and fucked up even more by waking up these powers in you! I should've wiped your memory; I didn't. I shouldn't have told you my name; I did. I should've kept a better eye out on making sure you were gone and not able to see all of this and learn what I am; I didn't. For all of this I could be executed by my kind several times over, so I'm doing what I've gotta do!

"You don't have it in you, vampire," the blond smirked, shaking his head. "You're not strong enough!"

"Eat shit, blondie," Xander hissed at him. "You haven't seen how strong I am!"

Then Xander pulled the trigger.

"XANDER, NO! PLEASE DO—"

BLAM!

Devin stared in disbelief as the glaring vampire fired the gun —his red-and-hazel gaze never wavering from his own—and the boy's head exploded in a gore-filled mist all around him.

"I… you didn't," Devin shook his head. "But that's…"

"Crazy?" the vampire stood and leveled the smoking gun in his direction. "I'd fucking say so too! Now let's dance, devil-man!"

XANDER KEPT HIS EYES NARROWED, his gun leveled…

And his fingers crossed.

Don't talk, don't move, don't even fucking breathe, kid! Not 'til I've got this fucking psycho far from here!

The flash illusion Xander had conjured had, for the moment,

worked on Devin, who must have seen a quite a show judging from his stunned reaction.

Good!

That's what Xander needed!

Remove Joseph from the equation—prove to Devin that he *wouldn't* be able to hurt him; take that glory away; disarm him—and, in doing so, get Devin scared; scared of what Xander was capable of and the lengths he was willing to go.

So long as Joseph didn't do anything to break the illusion he'd created.

JOSEPH FELT like he was going to hyperventilate. The gun had gone off right in his ear—the ringing was still so intense!—and the world had flashed with the threat of death just as Xander's words echoed in his head:

Don't talk, don't move, don't even fucking breathe, kid! Not 'til I've got this fucking psycho far *from here!*

The blond man stared right at him, but not with the menacing sneer he'd worn before. His jaw hung slack and his eyes were wide with shock and… something else.

Anger? Sadness?

Humiliation!

He believes that Xander killed me, he realized. *He really thinks I'm dead!*

Joseph held perfectly still; not willing to take any more chances.

Xander had risked his life in telling him what he had? He'd done it again in giving his name? And then again in saving his life… *twice?*

Xander Stryker *was* a hero!

There was no way he was a bad guy; no way he ever could be!

And he's going to win! Joseph thought to himself.

I appreciate the vote of confidence, kid, Xander's voice echoed in his mind again. *Don't make me regret giving you those powers, by the way.*

DEVIN STARED in Joseph's direction a bit longer, and Xander held the pistol steady as he silently prayed that nothing had caused the illusion to slip.

Finally, Devin scoffed and shook his head, "Makes no difference. So you gave the boy a quick death; so you saved him from what I could've done? There's still nothing you can do to save yourself!" He smirked, his feet once again lifting from the ground, "Come along then, little vampire! You won't last much longer, and I'd hate to miss the chance to see you suffer as yourself before the madness takes over!"

"It's not going to be that way," Xander glared at him, his feet also beginning to lift from the ground.

Devin shrugged and chuckled, "Either you'll die trying to stop me, or your confidence will prove accurate and you'll condemn yourself to becoming my predecessor. So which will it be, *boy*; die trying to kill the 'psychopathic pseudo-god'... or succeed in becoming one yourself?"

"IT'S NOT GOING TO BE THAT WAY!" Xander roared, flying at him and beginning to shoot at him.

24

UNANIMOUS

"What in the..." Stan looked off into the distance and Estella, knuckles white around the steering wheel, looked over at him, "Did... did you feel that? Just now? Over there," he pointed towards the park.

Estella nodded, steering the Mercedes onto the next street and screaming through a red light as she started towards the all-too-familiar park. Only a few short weeks prior to this mess, she'd gone out for her first patrol on her own and wound up experiencing a night of chaos that had pitted Xander against the homicidal auric vampire who called herself the "Night Striker," a title that had caused a great deal of trouble and confusion for Xander in regards to his last name. A radical-and-insane vigilante, the Night Striker that had once worked for The Council but been placed on the top of their execution list for enforcing her overly strict and impossible-to-obey set of laws. When her night out had crossed her path with that of her new friend, Ruby's—a young vampire who credited Xander and his late mentor, Marcus, for saving her life almost a year earlier—in that very park, beside the pond and under a gazebo, the Night Striker had set her sights on both of them.

As he had a habit of doing, Xander had saved the two of them that night, killing the Night Striker and issuing a formal invitation to the homeless runaway Ruby. The moment, however, had been tarnished shortly after when they'd received the call that Trepis was dying.

Watching the street signs for the park begin to point the way, Estella felt another shiver at the memory. Though she and Ruby had become quick friends, the lingering terror and threat from that night still weighed heavy on her.

Bringing the Mercedes to a loud and sudden stop on the grass that marked the start of the park, Estella jumped from the car with Stan and started towards the source of the fading energy. As they left the bustling, nighttime city behind them and started into the otherwise empty park, they were startled to see a young man panting as he sprinted towards them.

"Holy shit... HOLY SHIT! He's a total badass!" the boy ranted to himself, seeming to not even notice Estella or Stan as he started to make his way out of the park. "He... I have to write this; nobody will believe it's true, but I have to write about Xander! I have to—"

"Excuse me," Estella called out to the boy—startling him from his excitement in the process—and motioned for him to come over, "did you say something about Xander?'"

The boy blushed and looked suddenly nervous, taking a step away from the two, "Y-yeah...? Why? Do you know him or something?"

Estella looked back towards Stan, who shook his head. Rolling her eyes, she decided to play it coy, "The name sounds familiar. What do you know about him?"

"Only that he's the coolest guy I've ever met!" the boy smirked, "He's back there kicking the shit out some creepy fucker that looks like Omega Red!"

Estella frowned at that, "Omega Red?"

Stan rolled his eyes, "From Marvel comics, Estella! Really? I thought you were a reader!"

Estella sighed and shook her head, "I read *books*! Not comics!"

"What's wrong with comics?" the boy and Stan said in unison, two pairs of eyes narrowing at her.

"I didn't say... *really?*" Estella shook her head, "Come on! Nothing's wrong with comics, okay? Hell, I'll pick up a stack after all this is over and get right on it! But there's more important..." she trailed off and turned back to the boy, "So you saw Xander fighting in there? Did he seem alright?"

The boy nodded, "Better than alright! He's fucking incredible! I mean, he's not human—that much is for sure—but that makes him even cooler! He's like a superhero or something; like Blade or Hellboy or something!"

Estella blushed at the excitement the boy showed over her lover and she couldn't help but smile and nod, "I never thought about it that way, but I guess he kinda is pretty awesome, isn't he?"

He nodded, "It's funny that you know him, though, y'know."

"Why do you say that?" Estella asked.

The boy shrugged, "He said that Xander Stryker is a ghost-name and that nobody would remember him."

Estella smirked and shook her head, "Oh no, nothing like that. Quite the opposite, in fact. He's actually *famous*, but he doesn't like to admit it."

The boy gaped at that, "Whoa... I met somebody famous?"

"Yup, sure did," Estella nodded, "And now we gotta go make sure he doesn't tear the park apart, and I'm sure you've got someplace to go, right? I probably don't need to tell you about how dangerous being around Xander when he's 'working' can be, do I?"

"Lady, you don't know the half of it!" he shook his head and smiled, "When he's done kicking ass and taking names, can you tell him I want to turn him into a comic book? I won't try to tell people what I really saw—nobody would believe me, anyway—but I want to write about him. Can you tell him that?"

Estella smirked at that and looked back at Stan, "A comic book about Xander? Now *that's* a comic I can get into!" Turning back to the boy, she gave him a nod, "Yeah, I'll be sure to tell him. But only if you go home now and stay safe, okay?"

The boy nodded and started to walk past them before stopping and looking back at Estella; as they stared one another down, they shared a knowing moment between them—the two gently nodding to one another—before he finally broke the connection and hurried off.

Stan turned to watch the boy run off before looking quizzically at Estella. "What was that all about?" he mocked.

Estella smirked and looked over her shoulder as she started into the park again, "Just a moment between two people who fully realize how awesome Xander is."

Stan groaned behind her, "I *never* said—" he sighed, "Nevermind. Not the time. Still... shouldn't we have wiped that kid's memory or something? Isn't having him running around knowing who and what Xander is kind of dangerous?"

Estella shrugged, "What was it you said about Xander's father? Something about how he had a way of picking seemingly ordinary human beings to share his secret with and change their lives, right?"

"Yeah," Stan's voice sounded suddenly proud as he followed after her, "I did say something like that, didn't I?"

Estella smiled and nodded, "That boy looked empowered, Stan; something that Xander said or did truly changed him for the better. I don't think it would be right to rob him of this moment."

The two fell into silence as they spotted some upturned earth and signs of struggle. Examining the ground, Estella moved to touch the exposed soil only to recoil with a pained hiss as her fingertips were burned by several portions of what had been cooked into chunks of clay and glass-encrusted rock where the bits of sand had been superheated.

"Ow!" she moved to suck on her finger to relieve the burn before looking back, "Whatever happened here, it happened recently. We must have just missed them."

Stan frowned, looking out into the distance where the towering buildings of the business district glowed like an artificial horizon.

"I think I know where they're headed…"

Sawyer frowned, shaking his head as Osehr *and* Dianna *and* Ruby all ganged up on him and forced him into the Trepis Clan's garage. Little Timothy, spotting the group and overhearing their plans, was eager to jump on the bandwagon to force the clan's head vampire warrior to go out after their wayward leader, but, thankfully, the ever-silent nejin was quick to take the little vampire's hand and drag him off. Though he'd been thankful to his comrade for freeing him of at least one potential nagger, Sawyer's guard was shattered when the nejin's catlike eyes narrowed at him.

Even without being able to speak he'd made his message clear; his side was with the others'.

Damn…

"Xander could be in trouble!" Ruby's eyes were filled with panic at the thought, "We can't just leave him out there to die!"

Dianna nodded, putting a reassuring arm around the redheaded vampire's shoulders, "She's right, baby; he's done so much for us—saving us and protecting us and giving us a home —and it wouldn't be right for us to just leave him to whatever's going on!"

"Let's not forget that he's far too brash and stubborn to get through something of this magnitude on his own," Osehr added.

Sawyer held up his arms, pleading for them to listen as they continued to herd him backwards and into the garage. "Ladies... gentle... er, therion?" he shook his head as Osehr's eyes narrowed at that, "Please! Xander's told me enough about these guys for me to know that we don't stand a chance out there! I know, I *wanted* just as badly to get involved, but when Xander —*the* Xander Stryker; the bravest, brashest, most absurd-yet-brilliant combatant I've ever known—tells me that going up against those things is a suicide mission, I believe him!"

Osehr grunted, "All the more reason to not leave him to handle it alone."

The two ladies nodded.

Sawyer stared at the therion elder in stunned silence for a long moment.

He remembered when Xander had helped him to avenge the loss of his previous clan. He remembered how Xander had fought; the passion and fury and dedication—throwing his entire self into a battle—that echoed so powerfully in those around him that they felt driven to fight that much harder.

Sawyer thought of Xander Stryker, his new leader.

He nodded.

"We've gotta help him," he agreed with a sigh of resignation, turning towards the cars and stopping suddenly, his eyes darting about the rows. "Where the hell is my new Mercedes?"

25

FIREFIGHT

Xander and Devin's aerial combat had them spiraling and cutting through the sky as punches and kicks sent each one rocketing off mere moments before they clashed together again and again. The night sky grew darker as the energy that rolled from the two dragged in storm clouds—the rumbling of thunder and the flashes of young lightning mirroring the deafening roars and flashes of their landed blows —and as the rain began to fall it sizzled and evaporated against the two combatants'. Steam and fury rolled off of Xander's leather-clad shoulders as he shot towards Devin, taking the cackling pseudo-god by the throat and dragging him into the same hellish nightmare that Devin had dragged him into on their first battle.

Up over the rain clouds, where the moon's glow spotlighted the two as they cut through the heavens like a meteor.

Down into the streets, where they darted inches from time-frozen car tires and crashed through the hanging rainwater that was spit from under the treads; their collective speed making each drop feel like a pebble against their skin.

Back up—spinning in a dizzying corkscrew—and whistling

past the reflective windows of an office building; the glass rippling in their wake and, in several cases, bursting under the force.

Faster and faster still; several still pockets of energy birthing in their wake, waiting to become sonic booms and wreak their havoc as soon as they were given the chance.

Devin's face never lost its glimmer of lunacy; his grin widening as he saw Xander's rage and desperation grow.

How does it feel, cousin? he pressed.

Xander glared, *Wasn't Stan your 'brother?' What earned me the downgrade?*

Give it a moment, Devin assured him, **that time is coming. But first...**

He grabbed Xander then, stopping so suddenly that all of the blood in his body rushed to his brain and freeing the time-frozen waves of destruction. As the sonic booms that had been left littered about the city echoed, the thunderstorm seemed to be reborn all around them. Glass bits and stone and metal blew out in all directions, and the artificial lights caught the spectacle as the destruction glittered and pelted down on the rain-slicked streets. All below them, the cries and yells of people echoed.

"Ah," Devin inhaled sharply, "music to my ears!"

"You monst—OOPH!" Xander's anger was cut short as Devin's hand came to rest gently on his chest a moment earlier, only to pump a sudden wave of raw energy directly into his chest and send him sailing backwards and into the building behind him.

The scene became a blur as Xander crashed—again and again and again—through each level's ceiling; feeling like he was being dragged by an invisible force that wouldn't be stayed by any barricade. Ceilings became gaping holes in floors as he passed through, slamming through boardroom desks and cubicles as though they were playing cards. Finally, nearing the top of the building, the momentum slowed and lagged.

He burst through the top of the building, sailing another few yards from the rooftop and sensing Devin already waiting there. The blond pseudo-god's body appeared to be enveloped in flames. Xander tried to move to block, but found his own movements creeping in comparison to his enemy's.

Devin had cast the same slow-motion enchantment on him as he had on Stan back at the mansion...

"I liked your blood-bats trick, kid," Devin sneered, grabbing Xander out of the air and slamming him face-first onto the rooftop. "Thought I'd show you my version!"

Devin flew back into the air as Xander rolled onto his back in time to see his mouth drop open as though he were trying to vomit on him. Flinching at the sight, Xander was startled when a single, fiery bug fluttered from Devin's gaping maw; then three more after it. Frowning, Xander's tension faded as he moved to stand.

"I...   said...

WAAAAAAAAAAAAAAAAAAAAAAAAATTCCCHHHHHHHHHH!"

Xander cried out as a roaring black cloud of flies erupted from Devin's ever-widening mouth, each and every one suddenly exploding and raining down on him as a fiery swarm that crashed into his chest and scattered across his body.

The fire-coated flies tried to crawl into his eyes; he clenched them.

They tried to fly into his mouth and nose; he spit out the burning, buzzing bugs and clapped his hands over both—robbing himself of the ability to breathe.

PRETTY COOL, HUH? THANKS FOR THE IDEA, KID!

The burning, stifling, itching sensation of the millions upon millions of burning bug legs scuttling over his body drew a series of convulsions as he thrashed in an effort to rid himself of the swarm, but to no avail. Finally, eager to rid himself of the disgusting, painful burden, he cast his aura out in a massive orb that caught all but a few of the bugs and extinguished their flames and, with them, their existence. Free of the blinding effects, Xander gasped for air and opened his eyes—catching sight of a few straggling bugs buzzing about him as Devin dropped down upon him. A fiery leg rocketed upward, rising over Xander and hanging for a brief moment as Devin directed more of the burning energy into the limb. Then, smirking, he brought down his leg in with a guillotine force—the heat energy searing through Xander's jacket and sending the stink of burnt leather and cooked flesh into the air—and propelled him back down into the building, where he smashed through the rooftop only a short distance from the hole he'd just emerged from.

And the hellish journey through the many levels started once more.

Computer monitors exploded in Xander's face; wires reaching and snagging at his throat.

A light bulb burst in his eye as he slammed through it, blinding him for a moment before his body healed itself in time for him to watch Devin rocket through the window nearest him and punch him out of his prior trajectory. Xander bounced off the floor, tumbled through a row of office cubicles, and burst through a water cooler and the wall behind it.

He was on his feet before the momentum had stopped dragging him back, roaring in a rage as his broken, torn body repaired itself in moments.

Then, rebuilt and ready for more, he flew back at Devin once again.

Reaching out with his aura, he snagged every bit of broken office equipment and wiring he could gather and sent the mass in a horde of artificial minions through the holes he'd created. Devin cursed and snarled as the mass of broken inanimate objects came down upon him, encasing him in a shell of plastic and wood and metal. Blind to Xander's approach, the super-powered vampire was free to move; casting out his aura and ripping an opening in front of him that exposed Devin's face just as his fist passed through and smashed through Devin's jaw.

The imprisoning mass was thrown back by the force, as was Devin's jaw.

A loud, wet tear mingled with the pained grunt from the pseudo-god as the lower half of his face was torn across his left cheek; his jaw dropping and hanging in a bloody mess from the right side of his face. As his tongue lolled—working in vain to hurl his furious words back at Xander—Devin's garbled voice rose into an enraged roar that shook the building and sent more broken glass raining onto the streets. A great fire erupted around him and the mass that held him, and in an instant the makeshift prison was turned to ash—along with much of the surroundings—and, as the fire died down to a dull, body-encompassing mock-aura, Xander saw that his jaw had been repaired.

"*WE COULD BE AT THIS FOR YEARS, VAMPIRE!*" Devin roared at him, "*IS THAT WHAT YOU WANT; TO SIMPLY BEAT THE FUCKING HELL OUT OF ONE ANOTHER WHILE ANYBODY AROUND US SUFFERS THE DESTRUCTION WE LEAVE BEHIND? BECAUSE LET ME TELL YOU, COUSIN, THAT'D BE JUST FINE WITH ME!*"

Xander shook with rage, his fangs so extended in their bony sheaths in his skull that his gums ached. All around them the fire was beginning to spread, but the only heat he could feel was the one *under* his skin—the rage and fury that he'd known his entire life cooking him from the inside-out—and there was no spell to counter it.

"**WHAT SORT OF A WORLD WILL THERE BE LEFT FOR YOU TO RULE OVER THEN?**" Xander roared back, the madness-driven laughter he'd been fighting since his fight with Bianca rising up again.

"Didn't you hear the judge in my memory?" Devin asked, stomping across the floor towards him, "At some point I have to

die, and then I get to rule Hell." He held out his arms and appre-
ciated the growing inferno around them, "So why not make my
own Hell-on-Earth before I get there?"

Xander scoffed and shook his head, "**You've seen what waits
beyond this world, Devin; there's no Hell waiting for you.
Just a very pissed off hive-mind that probably has it in for
you for the stunt you pulled in—what was it you called it?
—*raping* it of The Power?**"

Devin froze at that, staring back at him as the realization
that he spoke the truth set in.

"No…"

THERE WAS no questioning the source of the energy waves
anymore; no denying that the sirens and the screams were for
anything *but* the battle between Xander and Devin. Estella navigated the Mercedes with all the precision and speed she'd come
to master as a vampire, weaving between crashed cars and
screaming humans and debris without ever letting the needle
drop below eighty. Beside her, Stan held tight to his seat,
keeping his eyes locked at the city skyline and watching the
rows of damaged buildings reveal themselves with each block
they drove. Estella jerked the wheel, narrowly dodging a
screaming ambulance as it tore through a red light and
screeched to a stop as it collided with a screaming man who'd
darted out into the street.

"It's like the goddam apocalypse out here!" Stan shook his
head. "By the time we even track them down there's not even
going to be a city worth saving!"

"I guess it's a good thing I'm not doing all this for the city!"
Estella hissed through clenched teeth as she shot down the road,
dodging another pod of panicking pedestrians before jumping
the curb and using the sidewalk to clear a multiple-car pileup

that had blocked off the street and then cutting across the courthouse entrance to emerge onto the next street over. "As bad as this may seem, if Xander loses control to that thing inside of him, *this* won't be a fraction of what he's capable of."

"You know him well," Stan nodded, biting his lip. "But what happens if he loses to Devin?"

Estella shook her head and threw the Mercedes into a drift to get in behind a line of wailing police cars to piggyback the clearing that opened up for them. "Like you said, I know him well," she looked over with a stern look in her eye. "He won't lose! Not to Devin, at least!"

SAWYER FROWNED as he noticed how congested all the streets heading out of the city were.

Heading *into* the city, however…

"Holy shit…" he whistled, looking over at the others. "You ever seen anything like that?"

"I've not been in a position to ride in an automobile before," Osehr said, leaning his head out of the window to get a better view.

Dianna and Ruby stared out at the miles-upon-miles of honking cars in the opposite lane—drivers honking and cursing in a futile effort—and shook their heads in unison.

"Do you think all of *this* could be because of what's happening with Xander?" Dianna asked, looking over at Sawyer.

Sighing, Sawyer nodded, "I can't think of anything else it could be. I mean, just look at that! It's like Godzilla just took out half the damn city!"

All of the others leaned forward to get a better view of the city ahead of them; the skyline red and furious with the sudden lightning storm—each flash of lightning catching the fat drops of rain and making it look like the sky was crying over the chaos—and creating a haunting backdrop for the skeletal-looking buildings. One of the taller buildings had been turned into a towering inferno that glowed like a honing beacon among the others, which had almost all lost power and shimmered with the borrowed illumination.

"Jee-zus!" Sawyer gaped at the scene, "What's going on out there?"

"I *WILL* BE THE RULER OF HELL!" Devin's voice sent the flames on either side of him splaying away from him as he ran at Xander, willing the fire to follow him as he did.

"You'll be no different than you are here, Devin: a whiny shit with a god-complex. Just another among many!" Xander laughed and stomped his feet on the weakening roof, splitting a chasm beneath him and forcing Devin to sacrifice his sprint for flight.

As soon as his enemy had gotten his bearings and continued his course towards him, Xander raised his arms, directing his magic grip on the ceiling above him and tearing it downward, dropping the entire upper level onto Devin as he burned a hole above him and flew towards the upper levels. The building shook around him, and Xander looked back—spotting the lower levels beginning to collapse under the weight of what he'd just dropped on Devin—and he hurried to free himself from the hellhole.

"**NO!**" Devin's voice rattled up the blazing chasm as his energy spiked and Xander sensed him soaring up behind him.

Flipping back, Xander caught sight of Devin as he shot by—his enraged eyes burning at Xander's evasion—and, gaining momentum in his flip, he kicked out at the pseudo-god.

Devin cried out and cursed relentlessly as the injury of his thwarted attack was topped with the insult of Xander using it to his benefit. Every bit of momentum and force Devin had anticipated in using against Xander was redirected under the force of Xander's kick, and Devin—burning body and all—shot through the wall and careened across the city. As Xander flew after him, shielding his eyes against the blaze, he swore that the shrieking pseudo-god looked like a shooting star against the blood-red skyline. Following after his enemy, Xander watched as he began to drop down on one of the private office buildings near the outskirts of the town, one of the few that didn't seem to have suffered any damage...

Yet.

∾

DIANNA FROWNED, pointing ahead of them as something burning bright flew in a wide arc over the city. "There—right there!—is that him? Is that Xander?" she asked.

Ruby gasped and covered her mouth, "Oh no..."

Sawyer frowned, "I certainly hope not. Whoever *that* is looks like they're hurting pretty bad..."

"It's not Xander," Osehr announced—beckoning the others to glance at him—as he smirked. "He's not that bright."

Three sets of eyes stared at him.

"Is he..." Ruby whimpered, "Are you joking?"

Sawyer shook his head, "There's no way you can be serious about that, therion!"

Osehr chuckled and shrugged, "It helps that I'm the only one in the car who can sense auric energy, too."

They all rolled their eyes and slumped back as Sawyer continued to work on navigating the mayhem of the city.

"Swear to GOD"—Sawyer growled to none of them in particular—"when I find out who stole my Mercedes there's going to be hell to pay!"

~

"DAMMIT, XANDER!" Estella hissed, jerking the wheel of the Mercedes as the energy source rocketed away from the tower of flames and started north-east, growing evermore distant with every second. "CAN'T YOU EVER MAKE ANYTHING EASY?"

"And here we go again…" Stan groaned, once again securing himself in his seat.

~

You've got him! You've got him exactly where you need him! Perforate the fucker and light him up! Do it. Do it! DO IT!

Xander didn't fight the madness as it took him, rather enjoying the suggestion that it offered. As the fire under his skin dispersed and Xander's cackles began to follow his flight in much the same way Devin's fiery trail followed his, he reached under his mutilated leather jacket and drew two of the pistols Dwayne had given him before he'd died.

"This one's for The Gamer!"

Explosive rounds cut through the air as Xander pulled the triggers over and over again. Ahead of him, Devin's body jostled and shook as round after round punched through his back; the explosive magic being instantly absorbed by the pseudo-god's body, but the holes gaping in his beaten body nevertheless. When both of the pistols *click*ed empty, Xander tossed them both—letting them fall in either direction back towards the city —before pulling the solitary Yang-revolver from its special holster under his left arm and emptying the cylinder of all eight shots into Devin's body as well. Then, re-holstering the revolver, he pushed his body to fly faster, closing the distance between him and his enemy.

For you, Dwayne, Xander thought as he pulled two of the remaining four pistols in each hand and then, immediately after, drawing the other two and all of the spare ammunition magazines with his aura, Xander began to replicate the heating process that Devin had used before. The pistols in his hands soaked in the magic-born heat from his palms as those in his aura were given the same treatment. As he caught up to Devin—his eyes fluttering in his head from the savage beating he'd received—Xander began wedging the ever-unstable handguns and ammo magazines into the fist-sized holes adorning the pseudo-god's body.

Devin hissed in pain Xander forced the burning-hot munitions into his body as he simultaneously willed his injuries to heal around the unnatural insertions. Then, finishing with the last one, Xander grabbed Devin by his long, blond hair—pausing long enough to drive his fist into the pseudo-god's face a few times for good measure—and hurled his body down towards the lonely, pitch-black building below them.

"**You wanna see Hell, asshole?**" Xander sneered, bringing back his hands and drawing upon the molecules in the air—condensing and compacting them into a small, shimmering orb of concentrated oxygen—and hurling it after him. "**All you had to do was *ask!***"

Devin hit the building and burst through the ceiling, his aura writhing in pain as it vanished inside. A moment later, screaming through the air and shimmering like a lost spirit, the condensed oxygen followed him in; the flammable, hungry ball of gas slamming into Devin's back as the unstable explosive rounds in his body went off.

The building never stood a chance.

26

FINDING ONESELF

"Oh my…" Ruby sobbed as the four Trepis Clan members watched the building Xander's battle had moved towards explode.

"Shit… HEADS DOWN! NOW!" Sawyer ordered.

Everyone heeded his call as all four ducked down—Sawyer hiding his face against the steering wheel and wrapping his arms over the top of his head while Dianna dipped below the dash in the front-passenger seat; behind them, Ruby and Osehr huddled their heads behind the seats in front of them—as the shockwave passed over them and cracked the windshield. A moment later, some of the smaller debris began pelting the car and, finishing what the shockwave had begun, the glass shattered and the four huddled further as the interior was exposed to the aftermath.

"I hate to say 'I told you so,'" Sawyer groaned under the onslaught, "but—"

"You say it," Dianna hissed over at him, "and I'm going to make an exception to my 'no more vampire-killing'-rule!"

〜

Estella watched the burning remains of the building they were pulling up to begin to settle; very little of the actual structure still standing, but the few portions that *had* remained upright were too concealed in thick, billowing flames that trying to see anything from there was impossible.

"Is there any way they could've survived this?" she whispered to Stan as she put the car in park.

Stan stared for a long moment, "Which one of them?"

"Either," Estella let the word come out with every drop of guilt it made her feel to say it.

"I... I can't be sure," Stan admitted. "This... this wasn't a natural event, Estella; you felt it just driving towards it!" He motioned to the fractured windshield that the two of them *together* had just barely been able to keep intact with a spell moments earlier. "We're in territory that I've never been bold enough to venture into. I honestly don't know what to expect from this point..."

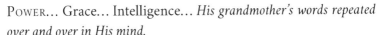

Power... Grace... Intelligence... *His grandmother's words repeated over and over in His mind.*

Xander groaned and looked up, seeing a fiery world all around Him; fading in and out, twisting and warping into visions of alternate times in alternate places.

Fire, the smell of smoke; suddenly Estella's room and the sweet aroma of freshly lit incense.

Xander moved to see if Estella was in her closet, picking out the clothes for that day—making sure not to alert her parents that somebody else was upstairs—and paused, blinking.

Aren't Estella's parents dead?

Back in the fire; the choking plumes of smoke stopped the breath in His lungs.

Suffocating...?

He was back under the lake with Richard.

Hell of a way to spend Kriss-mas! He thought to Himself, ***Drowned to death by a crazy bastard with gills!***

Crazy?

Crazy...

Xander heard groans a short distance from Him and He turned to face it, seeing a wave of faces all at once—Lenix, Richard, the Night Striker, a magic murderer, a cannibalistic vampire killer, the morphing faces of countless lunatics...

Devin.

The face settled on Devin's.

That's right... I'm killing this ***motherfucker now,*** Xander blinked and moved to stand.

Had He blacked out?

Seemed possible, though not very likely; what possible reason did a god have to pass out? A god like *Him* couldn't be exhausted, couldn't be bogged or burdened with such trivial matters like rest or nourishment. A god like *Him* had no more use for sleep than He had for useless emotions like love and fear; the memories of Estella and His near-death moments were nothing more than bad dreams—lingering stains on His frontal lobe—and He laughed at Himself for ever having been concerned about them.

Not when the very cosmos and every limitless atom in existence were His playthings.

Standing, He promised himself that, when all this was over, He would kill Estella and drain the lake; that'd put an end to such trivial reflections.

Yes. That would do just fine.

He chortled and shook His head, turning towards Lenix—no, Kyle? Richard?

"Who the fuck are you?" He narrowed His eyes down at the shifting, warping target—the setting surrounding them changing just as sporadically: Maine estate, parking garage, frozen lake, business district, loading dock, construction site, falling from a skyscraper—and blinked a few times, "**And where the fuck are we?**"

Devin. It was Devin!

The face stuck—for a moment—as he looked up and laughed. His long, blond hair was stained in blood—his blood—and he was missing most of his lower half.

"**You ain't got no legs, Lieutenant Dan!**" Xander slurred before cackling at His own joke.

"S-stupid vampire…" Richard chuckled and choked up some blood.

No… not Richard…

Kyle?

Xander blinked.

"**What was that?**" He demanded.

Kyle groaned, his weakened aura uselessly darting back-and-forth for energy that Xander refused to give. As He looked into the hate-filled glare of His old stepfather, He reached out with an auric tendril and brought Yang to His hand.

"Wh-what are you going… to do with *that*, vampire? You used up all your bullets on me, remember?"

"**WHO'S THERE?**" Xander spun, aiming Yang anywhere and everywhere—seeing only fire and smoke wherever He looked—before pausing. Frowning, He shook His head.

No, He thought to Himself, *there's no fire… not yet.*

He turned back to face Kyle and leveled His revolver.

Seeing what was coming, Kyle sneered. "So what happens after you kill me?" his voice strained and croaked around his torn throat, "I've looked into your head, and you and I both know that you've got nothing more to live for!" He laughed and spat out a mouthful of blood, "You've got no clan. No family. NOTHING!" He grinned, glaring up at Him, "So... you going to go back to trying to kill yourself?"

Clan? Family? DEATH? What use does a god have for such things?

He blinked, smelling smoke but not knowing why; He smirked to Himself then, inspired, and made a mental note to break the gas line and blow up the house when He was done with Kyle.

Xander frowned and fought the rage that Kyle wanted so desperately to well within Him, knowing that if He let the auric vampire into His head he'd feed once more and grow stronger. Finally getting control of His emotions, He reached into His coat pocket and pulled out the bullet He had been saving and...

Xander frowned. Where was the bullet? He was certain He'd put it in His jacket pocket and—He growled, realizing that He wasn't wearing *His* jacket!

"**What the fuck?**" He growled, peeling off the melted, destroyed monstrosity and throwing it into a nearby pile of burning rubble—burning? Since when was there a... looking again He saw Kyle's destroyed TV set and rolled His eyes at Himself.

Get a grip, Xander, He said to Himself. **You're losing it!**

YOU HAVE NO IDEA, VAMPIRE!

Xander blinked; had the wind just talked to Him?

Where was He?

Oh, right! Bullet!

So make one, stupid, He chastised Himself. **You ARE a god, after all!**

Xander smirked, starting to cackle at the realization; He *was* a god! Holding out His hand, He called upon the air around Him. Drawing in all the bits and pieces—all the atoms and molecules that His mind assured Him He'd need to create the *perfect* bullet—and watched with laughter as a shimmering, black and red bullet formed in His hand.

A crimson-shadow bullet, He mused over it a moment. *How apropos!*

Slipping the bullet into one of Yang's chambers, He gave the barrel a spin before slapping it shut like He had so many times with Yin. As the raging inferno inside Him shrunk down and disappeared, Xander pressed the barrel of the ivory revolver to Kyle's head and smiled, confident that this time the hammer would find the right chamber.

"If there's anything you've taught me"—He spoke slowly and deliberately—*"it's that there is always one more thing to live for."*

"You... you don't even see yourself anymore? Do you, vampire? You're gone; you've already lost yourself!" the voice echoed somewhere in the distance, and Xander fought to ignore it—though something in its words echoed some significance to Him—so that He could finish what He'd gone all that way to do!

Kill Kyle!

Kill the murderous, psychopathic bastard!

"Do it! Shoot me! Claim my legacy! At least one of us will be a god!"

With that, He pulled the trigger and put an end to his nightmares.

Stupid, vampire. You're already gone...

THE FLAMES around them were stifling, the heat alone forcing Estella to leave her jacket with the car as she and Stan fought the enchanted flames to find Xander. All around them was the essence of Xander; his energy literally clinging to every corner, rolling off of every flame, and shriveling with every burnt-up bit of debris. All around her were bits of Xander that were struggling to survive, thriving with exuberance, or already dead. Unable to fight the conflicting sensations surrounding her, she tried to block out the energies entirely and continued to scan her surroundings with tear-blurred eyes.

"Come on, Xander…" she pleaded into the crackling depths, "Just give me a sign! Give me *something*!"

From deep within the blaze Estella heard the gunshot and, before Stan could suggest they do anything else, she jumped into overdrive. Even time-frozen, the heat from the flames was searing and intense. As Estella navigated towards the source of the gunshot she felt her skin blister and char, but she refused to stop—refused to turn away or even try to fight the flames with her own magic; it would be like slapping a mile-long gasoline fire with a damp rag—and pushed herself.

For Xander! she reminded herself again and again, *For Xander! For Xander! For Xan—*

And then he was there!

Estella choked on a sob as she dropped out of overdrive and dropped down beside him, throwing her arms around him and crying; confessing how worried she'd been for him.

"I knew you could do it, baby! I knew it! I never lost faith… in… you?" Estella looked up, blinking away her evaporating tears as the cold, alien eyes in Xander's face leered over her.

"**I promised myself I'd kill you when I was done with Kyle,**" he told her, his smile broadening and bursting open with laughter as he rose to his feet.

"I… you don't… what are you saying? Don't you… aren't you happy to…" Estella narrowed her eyes at him, pulling herself to her feet and drawing her tonfas. "You're not Xander."

"**Then who in the hell am I?**" Xander laughed, floating from his kneeled position until there was enough room for him to straighten his legs and stand. Pivoting on the toe of his boot, he started towards her. "**Enlighten me, *witch*! Show me who I *really* am!**"

Estella nodded, taking a stance against Xander…

Exactly like he'd showed her how.

∾

"THERE! IT'S THERE!" Dianna pointed towards the turnoff for the ex-building's parking lot. "Oh my... is that—"

"My Mercedes?" Sawyer gasped, slamming on the brakes and putting the car in park before leaping out the door and vanishing into overdrive and reappearing beside the silver sports car.

Dianna sighed and shook her head, "What is it with men and cars?"

Osehr grunted, "Beats me. I think they look ridiculous!"

Dianna looked over, "Really? Even sports cars? Because I kinda like—"

The rear-passenger door opened and shut as Ruby stepped out, vanishing into overdrive, as well, only to fade in-and-out for a moment before stumbling to her knees in the middle of the parking lot.

"Poor girl," Dianna sighed and climbed out—Osehr not far behind—and started for Ruby, helping her up. "Come on, girl. You know better than to push yourself like that. It's like Sawyer's been telling you: *focus.*"

Ruby whimpered, "But... Xander could be in trouble!"

Dianna chewed her lip and nodded, admiring the inexperienced vampire for her dedication. Ruby had told her during their outing with Estella that Xander and his old mentor had executed the vampire that had lured her from the streets and, promising her eternal life and love, turned her. Though the crime of illegally siring new vampires was expressly forbidden by The Council—even more than openly feeding from humans —the laws *also* deemed new vampires sired illegally as warranting the death penalty as well; condemning them to death before they'd ever had a chance to awaken and plea their innocence. Despite the law, however, Xander had convinced his mentor to use their influence and track-record for excellence to demand a different fate for Ruby—effectively changing The

Council's views on the situation—and, in her case, saving her life.

When life in the clan she'd been assigned to hadn't worked out for her, Ruby had fled in search of the two vampires who'd saved her. Though Xander's mentor had been killed, she'd succeeded in tracking him down and, after befriending Estella and expressing a life-debt to their clan leader, Xander had taken her in.

It came as no surprise to Dianna that Ruby was eager to push her own boundaries to be certain that the vampire who had saved her life was still alive and safe, but, with the situation as catastrophic as it was, she couldn't allow the fragile-though-fanged redhead to bolt into a blaze so carelessly.

"We're here now," Dianna soothed her, "but it will do you no good to get yourself killed just trying to *find* Xander. Besides," she looked over towards the Mercedes and her vampire-lover's growing hysterics to the scratched body, cracked windows, and stripped tires, "it looks like Estella's already with him."

"I DON'T WANT to hurt you, Xander," Estella called out to him, bracing Selene and Helios against her forearms, "but that doesn't mean I won't. Not if it means getting through that thick skull and reminding you who you are!"

"Would you care to guess what I'm going to do with those shiny sticks after I've ripped them *and* your arms from your body?" Xander pitched back and laughed.

"I've got some guesses, baby," Estella bit her lip, holding back the flood of empathy; somewhere inside of *that* was Xander —*her* Xander!—and she knew that those words were hurting him worse than they were hurting her. "But you gotta get them from me first."

"Gladly!"

"Estella!" Stan arrived, sweating and blistered from the flames, "Get away from him! He's already gone!"

"And I'm getting him back!" Estella hissed.

Xander cackled and shook his head, "**Moment of truth, baby!**"

He vanished into overdrive.

Estella, predicting he would, was already shifting attention when he'd shimmered out of focus.

She never lost sight of him, though.

Xander's feet lifted from the ground as he shot at her like a bullet, reaching out with his hands and directing the time-frozen flames that surrounded him towards her like small, sweltering missiles. Estella sprinted towards him, spinning Selene in her left hand and redirecting the trajectory of three fireballs away from her as she commandeered a fourth with Helios and, spinning the golden tonfa in her grip and watching the fireball mirror the movement, she hurled it back at Xander.

I'm sorry, baby.

The flame went off in Xander's face, and his flight faltered and pitched him towards the floor as he was blinded. Seeing an opening in Xander's fall, Estella dropped into a slide that carried her under Xander's teetering, airborne body. As she passed beneath him, she spun the tonfas in her hands—holding the ends and letting the shorter handles catch behind Xander's neck—and yanked downward, forcing his head to slam into the ground. As the two of them rolled out of overdrive, Estella regained her footing and turned to face Xander as he rolled across the floor, groaning in pain.

"**Gonna teach the little witch-bitch a lesson in manners she won't soon**—No! We don't talk about her that way! We don't *ever* talk about her that—**You don't tell a GOD how to talk, you insolent**—I *am* you; you've worked so hard to convince me of that! And I'm telling you, as just as much the god here, that this... ends... **NO! IT ENDS WHEN I SAY IT**—"

"No!" Estella hissed, stomping towards him, "It ends when *I* say it ends, and I say it ends *NOW!*" she aimed Selene at Xander and slammed the silver tonfa downward, pinning him to the floor as she jumped into overdrive once more and, appearing over him and chanting a spell, brought Helios across the side of his head.

～

XANDER BLINKED against the dizzying haze in His...

Xander's eyes clenched against the blaring reality of His...

Xander sighed, his eyelids fluttering open and spotting Estella looking down at him.

"Is... is it over?" he asked, "Is Devin..."

"I'll say it's goddam over," Stan scoffed, shaking his head a short distance away. "Looks like you blew the crazy asshole straight to Hell! I don't know what you did, Crimson Shadow, but it worked!"

"D-don't call me that," Xander chuckled and, as the vibrations of his laughter stung in his mind, he clutched his temples. "Oh, ow... fuck!" he groaned, leaning back again, "It's official! I'm never laughing again!"

"Spoken like a true emo punk," Sawyer's voice rose a short distance away and Xander looked over, blushing.

Dianna smacked him, "Sawyer, hush!"

"Y-you?" Xander's eyes drifted about, beginning to catch sight of the others.

"Quite a few of us, actually," Osehr's voice sounded. "That was... well, I believe you'd call it a clusterfuck, Stryker. That was a clusterfuck."

"Are... are you okay now?" Ruby's small, still-nervous voice called out from Xander's right.

Xander sighed, liking the idea of lying on the ground in front of so many of his colleagues less and less by the second.

Letting out another heavy sigh, he forced himself to sit up and, with a great deal of cursing, eventually stand.

"I… I think so," Xander speculated, looking down at himself. "But I don't feel…"

"The Power?" Stan stepped up to him, once again clad in his inky-black, full-body jacket. "No, I imagine you wouldn't. Not after you decided to go all *Exorcist* on us back there. Still… you did it; you actually goddam did it!" he smiled, nodding. "I told you that you were something special."

"I…" Xander groaned and dropped his face into his palms as the memories flooded back to him, "Oh god…"

"So you seemed convinced," Estella smirked, nudging him.

"Yeah, until your woman reminded you who wags the stick at who!" Sawyer laughed.

"Whom, darling," Dianna nudged Sawyer, "and I'd like to remind *you* who 'wags the stick' in this relationship, too."

"This is why I never took a mate," Osehr scoffed and shook his head.

"*Not* just because you can only fondle one tit at a time?" Xander smirked, nodding towards Osehr's stump-arm.

Estella's eyes widened, "Xander! Did you just make a dirty joke in front of me?"

Xander bit his lip and looked down, remembering his typical reservations against such things. "I… I guess I forgot…" he stammered.

"Aaaand back to being a pussy," Sawyer chuckled.

Osehr and Dianna laughed while Estella blushed and nudged Xander again.

"It's okay," she whispered to him, "to tell the truth, hunting and tracking you all night and then… well, being dominant sort of 'reminded' me of some things Ruby was suggesting we could try?" she blushed.

Xander's eyes widened and he looked over at Ruby, who shrugged a shoulder and smirked. Though he couldn't begin to fathom what sort of suggestions she'd have had for Estella, he knew that Ruby had spent some time as a human forced to walk the streets as a prostitute and, with that fact alone, he was certain that there was an abundance of wisdom in that subject.

"After all of this," Xander sighed, nodding, "I think that's *just* what I need."

27

RETURNING

*A*s the others helped Xander out of the rubble and towards the cars, the clan leader paused, startled to see that *everything*—the fires, the buildings, the entire city!—had somehow been repaired. Staring at what had been a warzone of biblical proportions as the new morning's sun cracked over the horizon in the distance, Xander gaped.

"B-but… how? It was all… there's no way…"

"You really think I was gonna let you show me up with your little stunt back at the mansion?" Stan asked, patting his shoulder and chuckling. "Granted, all that *did* take me a bit of time to work out—you and that crazy asshole really did a number on the city, you know—but it's all where it belongs, with the exception of a few bits and pieces that had been thrown too far from its point of origin to find its way back," he shrugged. "In either case, it was the least I could do. I'm sure calling for a cleanup crew for something like *that* would've compelled The Council to execute you on principle alone! I couldn't save *all* of the people, I'm afraid, but at least they're families will have more pleasant memories of their passing—as pleasant as such things *can* be, at least—than that of… well, last night."

"And the rest?" Xander asked.

Stan shrugged, "Probably waking up from one *hell* of a nightmare right about now."

Xander stared at Stan, dumbfounded, before smiling and shaking his head. "Truly a devil on Earth," he taunted.

Stan blushed at that and shook his head, "I think I'd much prefer 'Stan.'"

"Speaking of a 'devil on Earth,'" Sawyer growled and turned towards Stan. "There's the little matter about you stealing and dinging up my beautiful Mercedes!"

Estella raised an eyebrow, "Actually, Sawyer, *I* took your beautiful Mercedes. It handled like a dream and I thank you immensely for the opportunity and the privilege of lending it to me for the night."

Xander shifted his gaze towards Sawyer, silently daring him to take the same tone with Estella that he'd tried plugging on Stan. Instead, the vampire warrior nodded slowly and offered a sincere bow to her.

"Anytime," he offered.

"Besides," Stan shrugged, walking by, "I don't see anything wrong with the car, do you?"

Sawyer frowned and turned to wave at all the damage that Estella had apparently inflicted on his prized 2014 silver Mercedes-Benz AMG, only to see that the car was in pristine condition where it had been last seen.

"But I… it was…" he sighed and nodded, "I should've seen that coming."

"That's what she said," Ruby giggled as she walked by.

~

SAWYER DROVE the Mercedes back to the mansion with Xander and Estella in the back seat—Xander passed out from exhaustion and snoring lightly in Estella's lap—while he quizzed Ruby, who'd practically begged to ride in the same car as Xander, on some of their lessons in the passenger-side seat. Ruby, only half-listening to her vampire-mentor, glanced back at Estella with her vanity mirror several times to ask for more stories about her and Xander before Sawyer would drag her back to her lessons.

Behind them in the second car, Osehr and Stan rode with Dianna, who Sawyer was sure was having a much more peaceful, quiet drive than himself.

They were finally nearing the top of the hill when Sawyer's cell phone rang and, as he directed the call to the car's Bluetooth and the voice of one of their colleagues boomed from the speakers, Xander was jostled awake.

"Sorry to bother you, sir," the voice said when Xander announced that he was with Sawyer, "but... well, they're telling me that it's almost time."

XANDER AND ESTELLA arrived at the door to Trepis' room hand-in-hand, Stan taking up the rear behind them. As the three entered, Xander gave a nod to the others, who'd wanted to escort their leader to offer the tiger his final farewells, before they left them alone.

Trepis' breathing was shallower than it had been the past few days, but, as Xander knelt down and rested his hand on the great beast's side, he was happy to see that it was also more peaceful. The tiger's eyes opened partway at the contact, a soft sound issuing from his throat as he spotted Xander, and his tail offered a single, happy twitch. Estella, already sniffling, knelt down beside Xander and placed her own hand on Trepis' side, while Stan slowly stepped around to the other side and took a knee as well.

"I'm sorry about how I've been, buddy," Xander whispered to the tiger. "But I want you to know that what you've done for me —who you've been to me—will never be forgotten. You were never a pet to me, Trep; you were a friend... and you were a symbol—and symbols never die. I just want to know that you're not hurting, and I don't want you to hold on anymore just for my sake." Xander let out a slow breath, several teardrops already rolling from his right eye as he shifted his head to look at Estella and, seeing her beautiful blue eyes stare back at him, he nodded. "I'm... I'm gonna be okay," he smiled at the sound of that and looked back to Trepis, rubbing his ear. "My father, The Odin Clan, and I would never have been who we are without you," he smiled and felt a knot grow in his throat, "and I'm beginning to realize that the sadness I've been feeling is just all the more proof of what you've meant to me." Letting his right hand slide down onto the great cat's head and spreading his fingers across the surface and said, "I love you, Trepis; now go on in peace."

The tiger closed its eyes then, seeming to understand, and a heavy breath issued from his nostrils as his aura began to fade.

"Xander," Stan whispered to him so as to not upset Trepis' final moments, "may I?"

Xander blushed, unsure of what his old friend meant but, knowing he could trust him, he nodded.

Xander and Estella watched as Stan moved his left hand onto the dying tiger's mane and his right onto Xander's right forearm, keeping the clan leader's palm pressed against Trepis' head. Then, lowering his head and taking a deep breath in, Stan began to work his magic.

Xander felt a rush of energy—strong and graceful and free— coursing into his arm where Stan touched him, and, as he looked down at Trepis as he let out the last of his final breath, he saw the tiger's body begin to swirl into a beautiful vortex of black and silver before it began to condense and be absorbed into Stan's left hand—the energy glowing the same magnificent black and silver as it traveled up his hand and past his wrist and into his arm—before it was transferred through his right hand and into Xander's forearm. Grimacing at a sudden burning sensation that traveled a strange pattern along his arm, Xander clenched his eyes and teeth against the sensation—Estella squeezing his free hand as he did—until it faded a short time later.

When he opened his eyes the body of Trepis was gone, and as Stan moved his right hand away from Xander's forearm, he saw a beautiful, shimmering tattoo of a tiger—as proud and majestic as Trepis had been the first day he'd seen him—etched where Stan had touched him.

Stan wiped a tear from his own eye and shrugged, "A little trick I learned from a tribe of people called the taroe. You know, so the big lug can always be with you now..."

Xander gasped and let out a stifled sob. "I... I can feel him," he stammered, looking between Stan and Estella; his smile widening so much it hurt his cheeks, "I can feel his energy—his *life*—inside of me. Like... It's like he's still here; right here..." he traced his fingers over the tattoo.

At that moment, admiring his new homage to one of his greatest friends that had been bestowed upon him by another, Xander Stryker—leader to the Trepis Clan—finally let himself cry.

"I HOPE I didn't hurt you too badly back there, baby," Estella repeated for probably the fifth time in just as many minutes, once again checking Xander's head for any sign of injury. "I mean, I hit you pretty hard."

Xander smiled and pulled her down onto the bed beside

him, shaking his head, "Believe me, please, when I say that I've never, *ever* felt better, Estella." He looked up into her eyes, "I mean, you... you stood up against that... *thing* that was taking over my head like it was nothing!"

Estella blushed, "Well, *not* like it was nothing."

"No!" Xander shook his head, tickling her ribs and throwing her into a laughing fit, "You're *not* allowed to be all humble and passive about this now; you're *not*!" He spun around to continue his onslaught as she fought to crawl back and away from his reach; bringing himself over her to pin her down and continue. "That dude was *scary*—real bad news all around—and you, my wonderful"—he kissed her collarbone—"enchanting"—he moved up to her neck—"and totally, recklessly badass babe"—he kissed her on the lips once; then two more times just to remind himself how good it felt to kiss her—"*you* spanked that little shit like a disobedient child and brought me back! I mean"—he rose up and slapped his palms across his chest—"*I* was terrified; totally and utterly terrified that I'd never get to see you again!" he looked down at her—taking in the enchanting sight of her— and shook his head, "And—dammit, Estella—I can't ever allow myself to feel that way again; I can't keep being afraid of seeing you go as though it might mean I'd never see you again. I'm tired of being afraid of losing you, 'cause I've finally seen what it means to see you go *knowing* that when I see you come back I'm going to get to fall in love with you all over again."

Estella blushed, "Xander, I—"

Xander lowered himself again, bringing his lips to hers and stopping any interjections. "I know about the secret you've been keeping from me—about why you *really* don't carry guns and blades—and I want you to know that my fear of letting you go was rooted in the *same* sort of fear; the fear of being without you from when you vanished." He smiled reassuringly, "But you showed me that I have no reason to be afraid, and I... I want to promise you that you don't have any reason to be afraid, either."

"What do you mean?" Estella blushed.

Xander kissed her again, "Estella, I mean that I'm promising you that tonight has shown me all the reasons I want to live. I swear to you that you'll never have to look at another gun or blade and associate it with my self-destructive past, because I'm dedicating my life to constructing a future for us"—he smirked —"and for the rest of our kind."

Estella smiled, "Really?"

Xander shrugged, "Yeah, I guess you could say that this 'clan leader' thing is giving me a bit of a god complex." He winked.

She giggled and looked lovingly up at him, nodding. "You have no idea what that means to me, Xander," she said.

Xander nodded, "I've got a pretty good idea. Which is why I need to ask you something."

Estella sat up as he shifted himself to kneel beside her, tears already welling into her eyes.

At that moment, Xander Stryker and Estella Edash's lives— while not perfect by any stretch of the imagination—held an infinite potential for growth and happiness.

An infinite potential for vast, untold magic.

EPILOGUE
THE FUTURE IS NOW

~One Week Later~

"*J*oey, you've got a package waiting for you downstairs?"

"A package? For me? From who?"

"I don't know. Just open it, silly. I gotta get going anyway, it's your father's first day at anger management; just don't tell him I told you that. You know how embarrassed he is about his temper."

"Embarrassed enough to buy me the PlayStation4 after he chased me out of his truck."

"Oh God in Heaven above, Joey, don't you go reminding me about that dreadful night! You had us *both* worried sick—your father must have combed the entire city in his truck until it was too dark to see, and then he spent the rest of the night keeping the police on their toes with calls every five minutes! I swear... I love that man, but he needs to learn to express himself better..."

but still! That was no excuse for you to up-and-run off like that! Never again, you hear me?"

"I know, I know. I just needed to clear my head; it won't happen again… Hey, Mom?"

"Yeah? What is it, Joey?"

"Do you think you and Dad could call me 'Joseph' from now on?"

"Yeah, sure, Joe—er, Joseph. Hmm… Yeah, I think I like that a lot better, too. More mature. Anyway, we should get going. I left money for pizza on the fridge."

Joseph saw his parents off and, when he finally had the house to himself, he scampered off to his room, unable to drag his eyes from the return address on the package; a PO box with the initials X&E on the return address.

Though he wasn't sure who the "E" could be, he was fairly certain what the "X" signified.

Tearing through the plain, brown paper wrapping, he found a neatly folded red leather jacket and a letter. Admiring the jacket for a long moment, remembering how the vampire-hero Xander Stryker had looked in his own, Joseph finally slipped into the gift and opened the letter:

Joseph,

I want to start off by saying 'thank you' for our chat in the park. While I've been told that it meant a lot to you and helped you find your way, I think it's important to mention that it did the same for me. You have a strength and outlook that's going to take you far, but I wanted to start you off right. I got my first jacket from a badass who taught me a lot of what I know now, and I'm excited to extend to you the same symbol. Don't worry if it doesn't fit quite right; my first jacket didn't fit me perfectly, either.

Anyway, the girl you met in the park is my fiancé and she's probably an even bigger badass than even me. (I actually just popped the big question last week and she said "yes" ~ go figure, right? Probably had something to do with the big rock I put on her finger). She told me that you wanted to write about me, and, though I'm flattered by the idea, I'm sure you'll understand that putting out any sort of stories about me could be dangerous. If my enemies found out you knew about me and my kind, then they'd be as much your problem as they are mine.

So I want to make you a little deal, Joseph. I want to see you write about yourself with this red jacket and having the same sort of adventures you saw me having (sticking around like that was really, REALLY stupid by the way). Now that there's magic awakened in you, I'm sure you can think of all sorts of cool things to do with a character based on you. So I want you to write about yourself, and then I want you to use those stories to remind yourself what a true badass you are, too. Obviously it takes a little startup to get a badass comic put out, so you'll find a few money orders totaling five-thousand dollars in the jacket pocket. Use it to get your stories in the hands of the world and help spread the message of being badass and staying strong.

I'll send more when I see issue #1 in the PO box on the return address for this package.

CREATE HOPE AND BE BRUTAL.
    Your 'ghostly' friend,
    X

. . .

PS – How you ever got my girl to finally get into comics is beyond me, but she hasn't stopped reading them ever since the night we met.

Xander sighed, eyeing his desk, once again, with animosity and an already growing sense of boredom.

"Alright, desk," he paced in front of it and all the business contained on top of it, "I don't like you, and I'm willing to bet you don't like me—suffice to say I'm sure you'd be happier sitting in front of a snooty accountant the same way I'd be happier sitting behind the windshield of a new motorcycle—but now, at this moment, Estella and Osehr are *both* on my ass to actually sit down with you and do this whole *'business thing'*"— he spoke the last two words with a nasally, winy voice—"and dealing with *them* is a lot more of a pain than being bored behind you! So here's what's going to happen; I'm going to sit behind you and do… you know, clan leader business stuff, and you're going to try *real* hard to zoom around and purr like a brand new motorcycle, okay?"

The desk, being a desk, offered no reply.

"Okay then!" Xander moved to sit in the office chair and forced himself to relax after an awkward moment, "Okay… so far so goo—what the hell?" he spotted a flashing light on his telephone telling him he had a voicemail. "God dammit, desk! You had one job; *one* job!"

Eyeing the flashing notification on the too-complex landline as though the appliance might suddenly grow fangs and bite him, Xander mustered the courage to play back the message.

BEEP!

"Hi, Xander… or do you prefer 'Mister Stryker'? I guess I should've considered that first… anyway, my name is Zoey Hartnett, and I am calling in regards to a recent passing of a close friend and associate of

mine, Dwayne Brinkley, though you might know him better as 'The Gamer'—most people do. God! I really hate leaving voicemails—with the informality of them and everything—but I feel that this is sort of important, so I hope you won't think ill of me given the circumstances." There was a prolonged pause, followed by a heavy sigh and then a stifled "Will you give me a minute, please? I'm TRYING to leave an important voicemail!" followed by another heavy sigh. "Anyway," the message went on, "I know of The Gamer's connection with you and your clan, Xander—congratulations, by the way!—and I'm sending this message as a means of branching out to reach out to you, as I'm sure you've found yourself in a bit of a bind without his services. The Gamer and I had actually been working together for quite some time" —the voice paused to chuckle—"we even formed a bit of a rivalry, though I'm sure you were well acquainted with his affinity for compe- tition. Anyway, with our history and my own resources, I'd like to offer any supplies you might need in the wake of his passing. As a co- creator of the substance, I can even offer a constant supply of the synth-blood he'd been supplying your clan with; if your facilities can handle the process, I'd even be more than happy to share the means to synthesize your own. At the moment, I am on a Council-ordered mission away from my clan, and, though I'm not exactly sure when I'll be getting back, you can contact the Vailean Clan and let them know that Zoey told you to contact them for supplies. Uh... just a quick warning, though: if you happen to reach Serena Vailean—the clan's leader—you should probably watch yourself. She's kind of a fan of yours—though I think it's more of a crush, to be honest—and... well, I probably shouldn't mention her husband, Zane"—her voice dropped to a whisper to say "he's got a bit of a temper" before she chuckled again. "Anyway, I'm sure I've used up enough of your time, so I'll be letting you go. I will contact you once I'm back home, but I do hope you'll take me up on the offer to help keep you and your clan in supply of any materials you may need. Good luck and thank you for everything you've done for the mythos community. If even half the stories Dwayne has told me are true—and I never knew him to be a liar;

eccentric, yes, but never dishonest—then I know we all owe you a great debt of gratitude. So long for now!" then, a ruffled moment followed by a faint, "Really, you guys? Were you raised in a—" click!

XANDER STARED down at the phone for a moment, surprised that, for once, it hadn't been bad news.

Rubbing his hands across the top of the desk he smiled, making a note about the Vailean clan and Zoey Hartnett—including a warning beside the name Serena and a skull and crossbones symbol beside the name Zane—before giving the desk one last pat.

"That'll do, desk; that'll do."

ABOUT THE AUTHOR

Nathan Squiers, along with his loving wife & fellow author, Megan J. Parker, two incredibly demanding demons wearing cat-suits, and a pair of "fur baby" huskies, is a resident of Upstate New York. When he isn't dividing his time between writing or "nerding out" over comics, anime, or movie marathons, he's chasing dreams of amateur body building. If he can't be found in a movie theater, comic shop, or gym, chances are "the itch" has driven him into the chair at a piercing/tattoo shop… or he's been "kidnapped" by loving family or friends and forced to engage in an alien task called "fun."

Learn more about Nathan's work at
www.nathansquiersbooks.com

THE LONGEST NIGHT (BOOK 5) PREVIEW

Read on for a thrilling excerpt from
the fifth novel in Nathan Squiers' thrilling action-horror
Crimson Shadow series,

"CRIMSON SHADOW: THE LONGEST NIGHT"

THE LONGEST NIGHT PREVIEW

Sweetly Serene in the Soft
Glowing Light

"WELCOME TO THIS DAY OF CELEBRATION! It is a great honor and a personal privilege to be here and bear witness the union of **Estella** and **Xander** as husband and wife. Together with the blessings and support of friends and loved ones, we now share in the joys of their wedding and share in the power of the love that binds them as well as the outward celebration of this occasion.

"**Estella** and **Xander**, you two have the opportunity to build an amazing life together. You are blessed to share this experience with the loved ones gathered here to support you as you embark on this journey together.

"At this time I would like…"

My god, she's so beautiful, Xander watched as Estella's aura danced around her like a sunrise. Because he wasn't one for sentimental moments or lingering sightseeing sessions, and since any contact with the sun, no matter how brief, was more painful than it was inspiring, he never had much appreciation for sunrises, but, at that moment, he thought he might learn to find some. Even then, though, he couldn't believe that they could ever compare to—

"... **Xander and Estella**," Xander's wandering mind was dragged back to the minister's speech, and he pulled his gaze away from his lover's to take in the old sangsuiga, hoping that his expression wasn't too befuddled. "Take a moment to sense the tremendous amount of energy radiating between the two of you."

Again Xander looked back at Estella and her radiating beauty. The previous night, the two of them had shared a motorcycle ride into the city, where they'd raced to the top of the tallest building—he'd let Estella win, or so he was still convincing himself—and spent several hours gazing out at the sights, talked of anything and everything, and let their feet dangle over the edge. They'd both spent countless hours out there, patrolling the streets and tracking whatever threat or mystery had earned their attention, but the city and its sights, without a looming threat to deal with, seemed every bit as romantic and mysterious as a starlit sky. Estella had joked that it was a fair compromise, since the city lights were responsible for drowning out a clear view of the stars. Hearing this, Xander had cast his hazel-and-blood-red gaze skyward and took in the vast curtain of darkness.

"You're all the starlight I need right now," he'd confessed with a shrug, looking back towards her.

Blushing at the compliment, Estella, not the least bit nervous about falling from their precarious height, had scooched closer to him and laid her head on his shoulder. "And when did you get so poetic?" she'd whispered into the collar of his jacket.

Feeling his own face redden, Xander shrugged with his opposite shoulder—not wanting to disturb her comfort—and glanced down at her. "I can't take all the credit," he admitted. "Dianna's the genius who knows about the meaning of names and such," he gave another single-shoulder shrug and sighed. "She was the one that pretty much gave me that 'starlight' line."

Estella had giggled at his admission and leaned up to kiss his cheek. "A lot of geniuses quote others' poetry, sweetheart, it doesn't make them any less of a genius and it doesn't make their sentiment any less meaningful," she gave him another kiss then, using a hooked finger and a craned neck to meet his lips.

Take a moment to sense the tremendous amount of love and energy between the two of you.

As he reminisced about their experience that night—the fireworks that their auras had become over their heads, turning the starless sky into their own private celebration of what was to come—his appreciation for their energy felt limitless.

After everything they'd been through...

"Xander and Estella," the minister went on, "I now invite you to publicly speak your commitment to your partner." He cast a smile at Xander, who caught a glimpse of the edges of a fang past his parted lips, before gesturing with an upturned palm. "Xander, would you like to begin?"

"Oh... uh, yeah—I mean 'yes,'" there was a soft round of chuckles from the audience as Xander shivered under the weight of the attention; his shaking hands fought to pull out the numbered index cards that wore his scribbled handwriting. Getting his trembling fingers under control, he took a moment to draw in a steady breath and gaze into Estella's beaming blue eyes. His nerves calmed and he felt a smile spread across his face. "God damn, you're so beautiful—sorry," he glanced at the minister long enough to get a passive wave for forgiveness. "There are a lot of words that come to mind about marriage, and when you're a man, those words are sometimes..." he smirked, "*inappropriate* for a ceremony."

There was a soft rise of laughter from the audience.

"I'm not *that* sort of man," Xander continued, "but I *do* find that the words that come to my mind are still inappropriate—

words like 'shame' and 'failure' and 'disappointment.' But these are words of worry that bounce around in my head already, and I wanted to catch the word that best described this moment. And now, before friends and colleagues, I can say with certainty that the word is 'strength.'" He paused a moment, taking in another breath and calming his tensing nerves, "I know that many of you were thinking that I was going to say 'love,' and while we're certainly in love I think there's more to this moment. This is about taking pride in the strength we've shown so far and preparing ourselves for the strength we'll need..." He caught the shimmering beginnings of a tear in Estella's left eye and he felt his own throat knot. Swallowing the tightening sensation, he pushed on, carefully slipping the topmost index card to the back of the pile to continue reading. "Strength to grow. Strength to stand together. Strength to overcome what-ever dumb bastards might stand in our way." He paused then, enjoying the moment of laughter he'd been waiting for and feeling his pride flourish that much more when even Estella gave a chuckle. "We've been to hell and back more times than I can count, but each time we've come back that much stronger and that much more in love. And while we're on the topic of words, I'll admit that I could probably never ever bring myself to weave the words to properly explain how much I love you, but to you, Estella—the witch whose special brand of magic has allowed me to overcome words like 'shame' and 'failure' and 'disappointment'—I'm sure that I'll have the strength to continue to *show* you how much I love you from this day forth as your husband."

The minster's smile broadened and he gave Xander another nod before turning to Estella and motioning for her with his other hand.

Estella's hold on Xander's hands tightened as her aura's dance quickened. "I like to begin all journeys with the guidance of those wiser than me, so I decided I'd start my vows with a quote from one of my favorite philosophers, Aristotle: 'Love is composed of a single soul inhabiting two bodies.' No greater sentiment can be said about my love for you or your love for me. Throughout these years, you have been everything for me— the strong arms to catch me when I fall, the shoulder to cry on for everything from stubbing my toe to watching my entire world getting ripped apart... but, most importantly, you have been a reliable savior to me—well, to everyone, actually..."

There was a momentary hum of agreement around the crowd then.

"No matter the circumstances," Estella continued, "you make things better. Throughout all the good, the bad, and the ugly— and we all know there were *a lot* of ugly moments in the beginning—you stood strong beside me. I thank you for making every day special for me. I thank you for going out of your way day-in and day-out, risking your life in ways you pretend I'll never know so that I'd be safe, and I thank you for going out of your way in ways you think I don't notice just to make me smile. I thank you for not trying to become my confidence, but working with me to help build and mold my own. There's not a day that goes by that I don't realize just how lucky I am to have you in my life. I truly found my soul mate with you and I look forward to spending many more years growing with you and even creating a family together. I love you, Xander Stryker."

They'd suffered countless nightmares and threats and challenges, but there they were, standing above it all and before an immense crowd of mythos. The truth was that, with the exception of those he directly worked with in his clan, Xander wouldn't be able to name even a fraction of those in attendance. On any other day, being the center of attention in front of *that* many would've made for a miserable day. But it wasn't just any other day. It was *their* day! Mentally shrugging off the rising tension of the thousands of sets of eyes locked on him, he set his sights on what mattered most and began losing himself in Estella's radiance all over again. He let the moment play out around him as they shared in their "I do"s and, when the moment finally came, he captured her lips with his own with all the ferocity and fervor of their kind. Some of those in attendance—many voices and auras Xander recognized as those from the Trepis Clan—cheered at this, and he "watched" as Estella's aura danced about in a confusing ballet of embarrassment and exhilaration at being caught off guard.

For all the times you've made me blush in public, he psychically teased.

A moment later her arms were around his neck, causing the cheers to double until nearly all in attendance were on their feet, and Xander felt his own face redden as his new wife's fangs grazed his lower lip. As they parted, he caught sight of Estella's bewitching and coy smirk.

"You mean like that?" she whispered, her smirk spreading like a wildfire into a massive, toothy grin as she added, "My dearest husband."

The minster grinned at the exchange and held out his arms as he let his voice carry out across the auditorium: "LADIES AND GENTLEMEN! IT GIVES ME GREAT PLEASURE TO BE THE FIRST TO INTRODUCE YOU ALL TO MISTER AND MISSUS XANDER AND ESTELLA STRYKER!"

THE LONGEST NIGHT LINK

Read more in The Longest Night

Made in the USA
Middletown, DE
09 February 2023

24404320R00234